All Roads Lead Me Back to You

KENNEDY FOSTER

POCKET BOOKS
New York   London   Toronto   Sydney

Pocket Books
A Division of Simon & Schuster, Inc.
1230 Avenue of the Americas
New York, NY 10020

First Pocket Books trade paperback edition August 2009

POCKET and colophon are registered trademarks of Simon & Schuster, Inc.

For information about special discounts for bulk purchases, please contact Simon & Schuster Special Sales at 1-800-456-6798 or business@simonandschuster.com

The Simon & Schuster Speakers Bureau can bring authors to your live event. For more information or to book an event contact the Simon & Schuster Speakers Bureau at 1-866-248-3049 or visit our website at www.simonspeakers.com

Designed by Renata Di Biase

Manufactured in the United States of America

10   9   8   7   6   5   4   3   2   1

Library of Congress Cataloging-in-Publication Data

Foster, Kennedy.
   All roads lead me back to you / Kennedy Foster. — 1st Pocket Books trade pbk. ed.
      p.   cm.
   1. Women ranchers—Fiction. 2. Illegal aliens—Fiction. I. Title.
   PS3606.O76A79 2009
   813'.6—dc22   2008051413

ISBN 978-1-4391-0204-6
ISBN 978-1-4391-6411-2 (ebook)

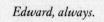
Edward, always.

ACKNOWLEDGMENTS

My thanks to Craig Lesley, who first suggested that this story might see the light of day; to Abby Zidle for her superfine editorial touch; to my old friend Gene Thompson for the lines from his limerick "If You're British;" to my colleagues Jeff Adams and Victor Chacon who schooled me in the letter and spirit of Spanish; and to Janet Reid, pearl among agents and a doggone good hand.

All Roads Lead Me Back to You

Chapter One

It was dark, though white all around. He moved slowly, afoot because—ah. Because his horse was lame. The feeder steers traveled with them, he thought, sometimes. Their cloudy forms at the corner of his eye: ruddy Herefords and Limousins, white-face Angus crossbreds, pale Charolais. Hijos de puta, always tromping in where not wanted.

His thoughts formed and dissolved behind his eyes like mist. Lazy bastards, those others. Warming their butts in the break hut. They would lose everything. Though he too had— No, not everything. Not his best horse, his roping rig. Wallet and papers zipped in the pocket of his parka.

He wanted to touch the pocket. This did not happen. Nonetheless, they were there. Receipts; money, a little. People said the Foulks Brothers paid well, when they paid. He had been paid twelve times. Pressed his luck: stupid.

His weighted feet moved grudgingly, more slowly, stopped. That was all. Nothing hurt. He knelt, settled back. He wished to clear his left eye. This did not happen. Tug at his right hand. Slither. The rein slid away like a snake. A vague shape moved past, out of sight. Lost. Socorro. Socorro.

At eight thirty Alice Andison logged out of her spreadsheet program with a nervous shudder, went into the kitchen, and filled a Baggie with oat-and-molasses horse cookies. January's numbers looked good, which worried her more than if they had looked bad. Bad numbers at least gave you an idea where you stood with the gods, but good ones left you wondering when the lightning would strike. Was I born a pessimist? she thought. No, just a clear realist. The old joke about the rancher who won the lottery ("What will you do with the money?" "Keep on ranching till it's gone") barely scratched a smile out of her; it was just too near the bone. She pulled on her thermal coveralls.

The collie Bel lay against the kitchen door, whining. She wanted to stay inside, and Alice wanted to keep her in because she was old and stiff and felt the cold, but Bel couldn't stand it. Collies lived outside, she knew. The other two were out there, in the kennel in the carport. Suddenly she struggled up, and Alice heard the other dogs barrel out past the pickup, claws scratching the cement. A volley of barks, and something went creaking past the front of the house, paused, and then the whole circus moved on down the slope toward the shed yard. Bel cried and scraped at the door.

"What in hell?" muttered Alice, a Moon Boot half on. She hopped across the house, knelt on the window seat, and made a tunnel of her hands on the frost-knit window. Nothing. Immaculate snow, ice-chip stars, frowsy locust twigs hanging still. She could hear the dogs, but they weren't shrieking like they did for a bobcat or a porcupine. She pocketed her horse treats, stood for a moment with her thumb on her lip, and went and got a big flashlight from the utility closet. Its batteries wouldn't last in this cold, but it was long and heavy, weaponlike.

She went out; Bel shot away downhill toward the barns. No question about where the party was. The high-drifted snow of the front yard had been tossed by the skirmishing dogs and by—what? Powder snow, too cold and fine to keep a sharp imprint. She tramped slowly down the slope toward the diminishing noises, shining her flashlight from side to side, its beam turning yellow, then orange. No sound now but the squeak of her boots in the powder.

On her left were long pens going down to the creek, the shadowy shapes of horses drifting uphill, sensing some entertainment. On her right the three hay sheds, with the flatbed wagon standing loaded and ready for the morning. Nothing and nobody inside, and anyway the collies weren't there. Ah, there—Sweep ran out the door of the foaling barn, caught sight of her, and ducked back in.

Gripping her flashlight right-handed, Alice slipped into the shed and flicked on the overheads. The big fluorescents flickered on, revealing the three dogs grinning in a circle around a horse that had just cleaned up a flake of grass hay left loose in the wheelbarrow. As she watched, the animal abandoned the barrow and limped urgently onward toward the stacked bales. Automatically, Alice registered breed, sex, and color: quarter-horse mare, spang-in-your-eye red chestnut. Carrying a roping saddle in good condition. And hopping lame, though not bleeding anywhere that Alice could see.

The bosal bridle on her head had no bit to get in the way of her eating. Not that anything less than a muzzle would have, it looked like. The collies looked from Alice to the mare and back, delighted with their prize. A bay colt, three years old, kept inside while a wire cut on his pastern healed, pointed an ear at Alice but kept his starting eyes on the foreign horse; even the cat Ike, high up in the bale stack with his paws tucked in, ogled her. But the mare spared nobody an ounce of attention, just went on jerking one starving mouthful after another out of the handiest bale of mixed grass.

Alice stood uncertain. Where had she come from? No saddlebags, no slicker or bedroll tied behind the cantle, so probably not a runaway from a pack string or hunting outfit—anyway, what lunatic would go hunting or camping in such weather? Forest Service horse? Same objection; furthermore, the rimfire roping rig with its two cinches, lariat neatly coiled and tied? That heavy Mexican bosal?

Her hands ached distractingly.

The rider: if not here, where?

"Anybody up there with you, Ike?"

"Mip," he replied, and licked his nose.

She walked out, thoughtful, and made her evening round of the pens, counted and observed the horses, checked that they had hay, dispensed cookies. Looked, for good measure and by the browning ray of her flashlight, into the machine shed and the covered arena. Nobody there, but anyway she was coming around to the belief that the chestnut mare's lameness and solitary state meant that she had had a fall somewhere up in the hills and parted from her rider there. Probably some time ago. Those ribs were pretty well covered, but her belly was drawn up from lack of water. (Though sprung in a suggestive way behind the cinch.) Could she have been lost for as much as three days, since before the blizzard and the deep freeze? Alice found herself calculating the rider's chance of survival, her own obligations.

She would have to try. Wouldn't she? Though it might mean miles, hours. And the rider might be, probably was, dead already. Or she might reasonably wait for morning and call the state police. Or call her sister in Waitsburg for advice. No, she couldn't; Janet would try to drive up, get stuck on the way, and freeze in a ditch. Pa, she thought longingly, as she deep-bedded the red mare in the second foaling box, untacked and blanketed her, supplied her with water and three flake—on second thought, four flake of grass hay. Pa, what should I do? But Allan was dead. And anyway, she knew what was right.

Come on, Alice. Cowboy up.

Catching up and saddling her mystified but biddable gray gelding, she led him up to the house and tied him to the porch while she went in to take her cell phone off the jack, stow it in a zipper pocket, and change her boots. Mounted, she looked down at the barns, debating with herself about the bolt-action twenty-two in the tack room. Decided against it.

"Glen: kennel. Bel: kennel. You, Glen! Kennel." The puppy crept dismally in with Bel. Alice cast across the yard a couple of times until she found the stray horse's back trail, a trench of plowed-up snow with a ribbonlike mark parallel where the mare had carried her head aside to keep from stepping on the trailing reins. Checked her watch: nine forty-five. She would give it two hours, she decided. In such cold and in knee-deep snow, that would be as much as she and her horse were worth.

The back trail led eastward from the house, into the gap through which, when not frozen solid, Dorothy Creek ran down off the high ground where the Standfast cows spent their summers. Tricky, the narrow trail along the creek. Again and again Alice brushed down drifts of powder off overhanging fir branches, so she guessed the mare must have been riderless when she passed through there. Slowly on up the gap, the gray horse Tom Fool puffing smoke, out of the gulch and onto the flat after a hard-slogging hour, and Sweep suddenly raced forward. Alice's stomach lurched. There he was, dead sure enough, and she had forgotten to bring a tarp to skid him in on. Damn. She wished she had not come.

It was a good flat piece of pasture, a long dogleg, in the middle of it the frozen rider upright as a dolmen in a waste of reflected starlight. Wanting none of this to be happening, Alice pressed forward. Sweep scurried up, crouched in front of the dark thing as if to drive it, leapt to one side. Came back and faced it, tail waving. Barked and pawed at it, dashed back to Alice.

"I'm coming. Leave it alone, Sweep." She could see the body clearly now, kneeling in the snow, arms clamped across itself and the long fur fringe of the parka's hood hiding its face. She halted her horse, dreading to look. Whereupon she realized that the rag of white vapor that passed at intervals across the front of the hood came not from the collie, but from the corpse.

At seven fifteen in the morning as usual, Alice got a call from her sister on the cell phone, the landlines being down. Janet Weston generally called twice a day, catering to her guilt about living comfortably in Waitsburg, leaving Alice alone at Standfast after their father's death. Janet called it a security measure, both of them knowing full well that between her daily calls lay time in abundance for awful things to happen to Alice: falls, tractor rolls, tramplings. Better than nothing, though. Also, the regular contact helped Janet judge her general mental and physical state. Janet harbored a belief that Alice would work herself into a breakdown if not carefully monitored. Alice harbored the same belief about Janet who spent more hours than not teaching at the local community college.

"Hey, Yan."

"Hey, Roan, what's up? You warm enough?"

"So far. You back at school yet?"

"Nope. At least another day, they're saying. Young'uns are going nuts; it's really too cold to be fun outdoors. They took the basketball out, but it sounded like they were bouncing a brick. Stock okay?"

"Yeah. But if it doesn't warm up in a couple of days, I'm getting them inside."

"Do it on Sunday, we'll come up and help. If I can get to the highway. Philip took the four-by-four to Portland," Janet's husband, a lawyer and labor arbitrator.

"Didn't get home, I take it?" Beautiful, that two-hundred-mile highway along the Gorge of the Columbia, but treacherous, a skate park in winter.

"Nope, stuck in Hood River, typing up his notes on the laptop and drinking up his fee. How are you fixed for supplies?"

"O-okay, I think."

Janet interpreted the stammer. "What's up?"

Drat! Alice thought. How to explain without launching Janet and kids onto these wicked roads— "Well, I have a—a visitor."

"!"

"This stray horse came in to the place last night, and I had to go back and dig the rider out."

"?!"

"Yeah, alive, just barely, and I don't know yet—he may be badly hurt. So far he hasn't unfolded enough to tell."

Alice had had no idea how to get him onto Tom Fool, but it turned out to be fairly easy. For one thing, he was small and light, and for another, after she hassled him to his feet and positioned the gray gelding beside him, some kind of reflex took over: in infinitely slow motion, he got himself into the saddle. Once up, he stayed there, hugging himself, with a deep unconscious balance.

She also didn't quite remember how they got into the house—slowly, mobbed by collies, herself nearly at the end of her strength by then, and with her horse still to dry out and put away (and two more flake of hay to the chestnut mare). When she got back inside, the frozen man hadn't shifted a hair from where she'd left him in the wing chair, cradling his left elbow in a way that made her suspect it, or the arm or wrist, was damaged.

Clamped mouth, closed eye, marble hump of cheekbone: he looked dead though sitting up, and did not seem to breathe. To correct a superstitious tremor in herself, Alice stoked up the fire in the woodstove, poured herself two fingers of good highland malt, and settled into the sofa to await developments. To keep a vigil, she told herself grimly, or hold a wake.

Around midnight something happened. A buzz, chattering of teeth so rapid and refined it seemed electric. The same thing at three or so, and again at a little before six when dawn was paling the windows. Nothing else. Alice went out to her chores, came back, made coffee, ate oatmeal. No change. And then Janet's call.

"What do you mean, unfolded?"

"I mean he hasn't moved or opened his eyes since I sat him down in the big chair last night. For a while I thought he was dead."

"Are you sure he's not?"

Alice snorted, daylight having dispelled the illusion. "Well, he walked in here under his own steam, so . . . and his teeth chatter every once in a while. But he holds himself like he's hurt, and the horse is lame, I think shoulder lame."

"Like they fell?"

"Yeah."

"Oh, boy." Alice heard that sharp determined sigh. "Roan, do you want me to come up? Nick and Nan and I together can probably—"

"No, don't you dare think about it. If I thought I could get the pickup out, I would. But they haven't even plowed Highway 12, so imagine the county road. By the way"—this just occurring to her—"he might be one of your students."

Janet made a complicated sound. "You mean, like, what, is he La-
tino?"

"Yeah. Or maybe Indian. No, must be Mexican; I think he said
something in Spanish."

"He did? What?"

"Well, I'm so bad at it—something like 'zorro' or 'scorro'?"

"Socorro?"

"Yeah, okay. Which means, like, help or rescue?"

"Well, succor."

"Well, that would figure, wouldn't it? I wonder—you know, you
never see a saddle tramp anymore. But he's got a sure 'nough wrangler's rig on that mare, and, I dunno—he looks like a cowboy."

A snort of derision: "Stetson, belt buckle, spurs?"

"Not a rodeo-team cowboy. Well, yeah, spurs. I dunno. Maybe it's
the horse. There's a good Cactus rope on the saddle, I'll say that." Alice
didn't know what cues she was picking up, but she felt pretty sure of
her ground. Janet thought of other possibilities: small-time cattle thief,
drug mule, serial killer.

"What are you going to do? Be careful, darlin'."

"Yeah. Just watch him, I guess. Don't you worry, though; he's small,
and not in the most robust condition. I think I'm okay."

"Keep the dogs with you," said Janet, not much reassured. "You
know, if he's really . . . if it looks like he might need medical attention,
the staters have that helicopter."

"That's a thought."

"They've been taking people up out of the river resorts and ski
lodges in the Blues, the TV said."

"That's an idea. Kinda hate to bother the cops, though, unless . . ."

"Well, true." Another plosive sigh. "Okay, take care. Talk to you
later." She knew Janet would have a think; would have other suggestions when she called back.

Alice checked: still no change. As she stood hesitating in the
kitchen in her stockinged feet, a cow on the triangle pasture moaned

and moaned again. This decided her, and she dragged on her out-door clothes. Her team had to be caught up and harnessed to the hay wagon, the cows on the Triangle fed, hay dragged out to the rough pastures where the racehorses were letting down, the wagon reloaded with bales for tomorrow's feeds. The bay colt's pastern dressed. Trough warmers checked, grain doled out to the working horses, the iced-up drinking holes in the creek chopped out. The collies and barn cats fed. By the kitchen door the thermometer read seven degrees Fahrenheit, the barometer 29.96. She tapped it with her fingernail and it creaked up a tenth. Lawsy, she thought, pulling on her ski gloves, let it be a sign.

She peered at the kid again: not a quiver. She went out.

For a time before his eye opened, he thought he was dead. Because of the music. It was faint and slow and harplike, and although he only heard it at intervals when the machinery stopped, he began to believe it went on all the while. Sometimes, though, music and machinery and everything faded away. Then when he came back everything was there again, stronger. Everything: the music and the machinery and the pain. So he concluded he must be alive. Death did not come and go, he believed, nor heaven and hell intermingle. Light swam in, finally, revealing a greenish room, fire, a white man in shirtsleeves who whispered. There was something terrible about the man, a pattern on his face. Beard? No. It mottled the whole face and head, hideous. The man came close and crooned. Nausea, panic rose. A red maw swallowed him.

"Well," warned Janet on the phone, "even if he doesn't die, he's going to swell up." The question being, should Alice pull off the frozen stranger's boots and gloves?

"I know," she agreed. "But it seems kinda . . . personal."

"Well, yeah. But anyway, you don't want his dang boots on your rug. And if you don't take his gloves off now, some medic will probably have to cut them off later. Have you got Bag Balm?"

"A big new tin. So what do you think? Hot water bottles, heating pad?"

"Oh jeez. Call Vera Jane. She's smarter about that stuff than my Red Cross manual."

"Okay, I will. Philip not back yet, I take it?"

"He got as far as Walla Walla, stayed over at the Pony Soldier. He's betting they'll plow us out tomorrow."

Alice called her neighbor Robey Whyte and asked her question, which Robey incuriously relayed to his wife Vera Jane, who did not cotton to the cell phone.

"She says no, leave him lay under a quilt for another day, just keep the room warm," Robey repeated, "and give him warm—say what?— warm broth, and warm coffee with sugar. She says, who the hell is it, and where the hell did he come from?" Nothing incurious about Vera Jane. By the time Alice clicked off the phone, the Mexican boy's one visible eye was open.

"Hey, kiddo. Feel like facing the public? Prob'ly not just yet." Lights are on, she thought, but nobody's home. She found herself treating him like a damaged horse: no bright lights, quick movements, or loud sounds. And food. If the mare was any clue, food first.

Standing behind him, she held a napkin under his chin and a cup of noodle soup under his nose. For a while, nothing happened. Then a kind of jar went through the whole thin frame. A hard, hard swallow, and the split and blackened lips parted. After that, things went forward smoothly: a little soup, a little cleanup, a little more soup. Gradual, that's the best way back to life, thought Alice.

The hood of the parka, when she examined it, proved to be stuck to his face with blood, the watch cap under it as well. Soaked off, they revealed a great raw abrasion from temple to jawbone, blood dried in the channels of his ear, clotted in his hair. The left eye swollen shut. Yes. A bad fall, on the ice of the creek probably, among the rocks, and what this meant for the rest of him she was afraid to think. Separated shoulder, broken elbow, ribs askew; all far beyond the therapeutic scope of noodle soup and Bag Balm. However, except for the scrape on his face, she found no blood. She fed him a little more soup, which seemed to go down gratefully, then knelt to unbuckle his spurs, and carefully worked his boots off.

She was his best horse ever, that chestnut. A true Music Mount. It was partly fear of losing her that made him run. Partly his luck in spotting the bus as it emerged from the gap in the snow-veined rimrock where the ranch road came through. An olive-green Immigration Service bus. Thanks to God for his good eyes.

And for the white vapor rising off the mass of steers on the feedlot: good cover.

And for the lever of the outgate to the railroad siding, right beside him where he sat his horse at the high end of the muddy, teeming lot. He had lain against the red mare's shoulder, pulled the lever over, eased her sideways through the gate. Closed the gate to keep steers from following, perverse sons of whores, to draw attention to him.

He had to pass four more gates. Two of them stood open. One of the others gave a ghost wail as it swung, but by this time the racket from the other side covered it: bawled orders, raw yells, cursing in English and Spanish as the Migra-men turned out the break hut. Avoiding the loading chutes, still flat along the horse's shoulder, he passed through the last gate and turned right along the tracks. Within ten strides they were below the edge of the bluff. Out of sight of the law. He sat up and sent the horse scrambling down the slope toward the river.

But there was nowhere to go. No road on this side of the Snake. No town in either direction, in any direction, for thirty miles. Only Tumac, almost a ghost town, no kind of a place for a man to hide himself in, much less a valuable stock horse.

If he could have gone back, if he had had any warning. If he had taken his pay and quit on Friday, he would have been somewhere else in his aged Silverado pickup, pulling the red mare and his new young gray in the bald-tired trailer. Maybe closer to his girl in Yakima, Wapato, wherever that was. On the move anyway, safe, more or less, from the immigration police. But no, he had pushed his luck, always a bad thing.

So, with nowhere to go on the Idaho side, he had to turn the horse back up the embankment and chance the railroad bridge, hoping for a road or a ranch or a town close to the river in Washington. Hoping for no train.

The mare was afraid. She touched the first cross tie with her toe. She could see the river down below; between each pair of timbers, open air. One foot misplaced—he didn't urge her, didn't touch her with the spurs. He too was afraid. But she had an eagle's heart. She stepped. Stepped again.

Perhaps he should not have run. But he had assumed that he could return. It was only as they passed the middle span of the bridge that he had known he could not. That if they did not die on the bridge, he must never so abuse his luck again. And that was while they still had a quarter mile to go, treading from tie to tie, with the Snake coiling like cold oil below. So when lathered and trembling she finally sidestepped down off the steep ramp on the Washington side, he did not even wait for his heart to return to its customary place, but turned her down the gully by the tracks, looking for a way out.

And then came the snow-squall, and then the freeze, and more and still more snow. And the fall on the iced-up creek.

The ching of spur rowels roused him to despair. Here it came, the tugging at his feet, at his hands, swift fingers rifling his clothes; all would be taken, all lost. He would be naked to the cold, alone, finished. It was a relief, almost a relief, giving up. If these pains will let me, he thought, I can die.

Unfortunately, the reverse happened. The pains increased, a skewer of fire in every joint, his fingers like bunches of salchichas, feet like campfire rocks. His stomach ached and gnawed. When he was fed, the napkin snagged on his bearded chin. He knew himself bloody and filthy, stinking. Finally, appallingly, he realized he needed the baño, pronto.

⌒

His third day on the place, Alice came in at noon to find him sitting at the dinette table.

"¿Usted tiene hambre?" she asked, proud of her español.

"Sí, patrón." It came out hoarsely, but politely. A mannerly croak. Alice hid a grin, standing on the bootjack by the front door, peeling off her thermal gear. Hungry as a wolverine, he was, pretty clearly, and looking like hell on a plate. But would he eat a radish in this house without being offered it? Not on his tintype.

She was starting to worry about her supplies, though. She made egg sandwiches since she had eggs, and tomato soup with canned milk, being out of fresh, making it a little sharp with pico de gallo. She cut the sandwiches in fours and piled them on a plate to encourage the boy to fill up. And she set the table. She had inherited high domestic standards. "I hold by the blood of my clan," her mother used to say when opposed in questions of propriety, taking her father, the real Scot, aback.

She bade the kid eat, and they ate. Afterward, she induced him to let her apply Bag Balm to his hands and feet and Neosporin to his face. That was it for him; he fell asleep in the big chair by the woodstove, so she got out her notepad and went through her stores. Tea, milk, spuds. Lettuce, carrots. A chicken. Toothpaste, an ink cartridge for the printer, chocolate grahams, kibble for the cats. Today would have been a good day to replenish, but six inches of new snow had fallen during the night, so the state highway through Waitsburg was blocked again. Iwalu village? She might have made it on horseback, but the likelihood was great that the little store there would be as bare as Mother Hubbard's cupboard. No mail, no newspaper. Luckily, the electricity had never gone out, and the phone lines were up again.

But Janet and her kids had not been able to make it up to Standfast from their home in Waitsburg, even with the Jeep. Alice and the three collies would have to spend the afternoon wrangling thirty-seven pregnant cows up off the pasture and into the covered arena, where they'd be out of the wind and easily fed, watered, and watched. The calves would start to come in about ten days, give or take.

Sitting on the stepladder, her pad and pen in her lap, she suddenly felt swept away by the sinking exhaustion that for a single-hand stock raiser was the essence of calving. It seemed to Alice that she had barely, just barely survived last spring's bearing season. And here she was, a year older and tireder, facing it on her own again. She rested her forehead on her knees, suppressing a groan. Worse still, this year she had an extra horse to look after, and this kid—unless he moved on. Which he certainly did not seem fit to do yet, any more than his horse. Though the mare's lameness was easing.

Alice sat up. It occurred to her that the boy might not realize about the horse.

He knew after the first day that the man was not scarred but freckled, his hair close-curled and grizzled. He knew his own hurts were being tended, his things not stolen. Yet confusion persisted. The man spoke absurd Spanish, quite fluent but hilariously wrong—was he doing it on purpose? If so, why? Then, too, since he had been able to feed himself, the man had required him to admit hunger—very crude. Yet the food came anyway, without stint. Again, the food, though odd, was tasty, and served with a kind of flourish. And the man himself was the cook and cleaner-up. As well as working, when outside (one could not be mistaken about this) with cattle and horses. A young dog that sometimes slipped into the house with the man—the smell of his coat confirmed this. And now this dazzling, gratuitous, totally unexpected stroke of good luck! It was true, then, the proverb: to one born to eat tamal, the corn shucks fall from the sky.

The red mare pressed into the Mexican boy, chuckling and snuffing, pushed her nose inside his coat, into his hair. He held her long face against his belly, risking a nip, and stroked her neck and tugged her ears. Bent his head to take in her breath, let her take in his. A regular old fairy-tale reunion, Alice thought, a little bit choked up. The boy threw back the blanket, touched and pressed the thickened shoulder muscles, following the swelling down the leg. He turned to her, still unsteady on his pins, and said in Spanish, gravely ceremonious, *"Sir, I am entirely obliged to you."*

"Que no mencionar," responded Alice, charmed. *"In any case, whatever obligation exists is to your steed, for she preserved your existence, certainly."*

"Truly? She carried me here?"

"She came here lonely, making loud, brave tracks in the snow. These we read backwards in order to effect a rescue."

It hurt to smile, and anyway was impolite. *"You, sir, and other people?"*

"I and my horse and my dog. This large clever dog, Sweep." The collie came into the stall and sat on her foot, laughing. Alice thought of something. "She got a baby in there?"

"?"

"¿Está embarazada?" making a big-belly motion.

The boy nodded soberly. "She keep it, you think?" his first words in English, and Alice did not know whether he meant, "Will she resorb the fetus because of the trauma of her journey?" or, "Will she carry the fetus to term?" In any case his teeth were chattering like a keyboard now, so she made him go indoors. But he pursued the question while she made a lunch of cheese toast (last of the cheese), beans, and tomato salad (last of the tomatoes).

"Patrón, you think she gonna carry the baby?" the question coming oddly tender from that scabbed, bearded, slit-eyed face.

"Well," she said, putting things on plates, "I doubt she's lost it yet." More slowly, "I don't believe she has lost the baby yet, but I am not a veterinarian. When is she due to drop it? ¿Cuándo va a dar a luz?" Pleased at having the idiom handy.

Though it was the wrong idiom. But the boy figured it out: "Abril."

"Well, she won't resorb it at this stage." She might abort, however; time would tell. "Are you ready? Get it while it's hot." Then when his mouth was full and his sausage-like fingers awkwardly occupied, "You must have used her very hard, up in the hills."

⌒

Used her hard, holy God. He had done his best to kill her with cold and snow and icy going and no shelter and no food and no water. And still she had saved his life. He felt honored to own her. She had more cow sense than any horse or even any man he had ever known. Once she was bred, he had bought the second horse to spare her. But still she had put in her six or seven hours on the sale lots and pens every day. And her eagle courage on the railroad bridge! He could not have expressed this in English, maybe not even in Spanish.

And then the güero asked him a deeply insulting question, as if he were a skill-less, horseless man, as if he might have stolen her: "Does that horse belong to you, or to somebody you work for?"

"Belong?" he muttered, actually tangled up in "to somebody you."

"¿La yegua le pertenece a usted?"

He stood up a little too quickly for politeness, got the bill of sale out of his wallet, and dropped it on the table without a word. The white man, as if unaware of any offense, studied the paper for a long time, both the sale side and the bloodline side. Indeed, there was a great deal of information in the document. He began to fear that he had allowed his pride to stampede him into trouble. It would have been better merely to have answered, "Mine," and let the insult pass. If it was an insult; the whites often said foul things out of ignorance. He wished the paper back in his pocket.

Eventually it was handed back. "Royally bred on the dam side," incomprehensibly. And then, "Would you drink coffee if I made some?"

See! There again, that coarseness.

Alice beat Janet to the punch, calling her on the cell phone from the tack room at four fifteen. She had left the Mexican kid asleep on the couch, but she guessed he slept light, given the pain he was in, and that his English comprehension was pretty good. She had a few items for Janet's ears only, and it would have been rude to discuss him in his hearing. Janet, in her office at school, searched her memory, which was extensive, and came up blank. "Guys!" hailing her officemates, "Have we ever had a student named Juan Roque or Domingo Roque or Juan Domingo Roque? R-O-Q-U-E?" They thought not. She would check the files, but didn't expect to find anything. It was not that common a surname; somebody would have remembered.

"I'm pretty sure it's on the level because it was on the bill of sale for the horse."

"So it's his horse?"

"Think so. He got a tad porky when I asked, and showed me the paper. Bought her in Idaho five years ago, dang cheap. Her sire's nothing special, but her dam side's right royal, Poco and Vandy lines, and Music Mount, far back."

"My stars."

"Yes indeedy. Plus, she's in foal, due in April if she doesn't abort."

"To who? Why would she?"

"Dunno, some Idaho horse, I would guess. I think they must have had a pretty bad time back in the hills during the storm and the freeze. Seems like they were lost up there for three or four days. You know how lovely it isn't, back in there, at the best of times. He's real worried about her."

"Is she less lame, though?"

"Yeah, she is. Looks worse, of course, 'cause the edema is going south, but she's moving better. Her eyes are bright; her coat's good. You should have seen them, when he went down there to the barn today. It was a real old mother-and-child reunion."

"No kidding? Aww. How'd he get down there, though?"

"In Dad's Moon Boots and Nick's gloves. It wasn't the least bit good for him. However, nothing's broken, looks like. He looks horrid and he smells high. But I guess I can stand that for another week or so."

"But Roan, how are your supplies?"

"Running low. But Robey said he'd get the Ski-Doo out tomorrow and try to get in to Iwalu. If the store's even open. If the Ski-Doo will even run. If I had a sledge, I'd try it with the Clydes."

"Oh, well, not to worry," said Janet blithely, "it's going to thaw. Chinook tonight." And she was right.

⌒

Robey Whyte called Alice in the neighborly way to ask, supposing that the snow machine got him as far as the crossroads store, what could he bring her? Alice gave him a five-item list. She thought he would do better on horseback but didn't say so. Robey loved his cranky machine. She comforted herself that the old crate probably wouldn't start up in the dead cold. She also thought that Robey should not go alone, tough old root though he was, but she could imagine the short sharp discussion that would follow her mentioning this or offering to ride along. Anyway, the fact was that if the cold kept its clamp on the hills, and if the Ski-Doo started, and if Robey actually got as far as the Iwalu store and back, it would be all Alice could do to cover on horseback the seven miles by road or four miles across country over the ridges to the Whytes' place to pick up whatever he might bring her.

Robey wondered on the phone how the folks up at the Hashknife place were doing. Alice didn't know, she said, aware when she hung up that she had been commissioned to find out. She tried, mentally, to fend this off. The Hashknife was closer to Standfast than to the Whytes at Robey Grade, but only in terms of time, not of effort. Besides, Alice disapproved of those people, whose lousy farming allowed yellow star thistle and vetch to invade other folks' pastures and hay ground, whose stupid hunting endangered other folks' livestock, and whose flagrant dope-selling brought a lot of short-stop traffic to the neighborhood as well as smearing the fame of the proud old Texas trail-driving outfit whose name they had appropriated. In terms of marijuana production, the nickname was apt, but that didn't any more endear them to Alice; secretly, she thought it good that they freeze and starve themselves out of the county, if only they would. However, there were children and animals up there who were innocent, who might also be freezing and starving even as she stoked her woodstove and reheated her leftover cornbread for lunch.

A couple of hours' hard traveling later, she sat her steaming horse at the top of a shale slide and peered down into the little valley where the Hashknife house nestled among junk cars and broken-backed sheds.

Exponential increase in trash on the place since she had last ridden by, she noted, the house hedged round by a range of little snow-covered alps made of something that bled red into the surrounding snow. Antifreeze containers? Were they winterizing all those old junkers? A waste of time and money. Better to raise chickens in them.

She was happy to see smoke creeping from both chimneys and pale lamplight shining from at least one window. Blue evening already, down there. A pack of mutts came barreling up the hill toward her but ran out of gumption at the bottom of the slide, sat down and barked and bayed like the consciously bold, secretly cowardly brutes they knew themselves to be. Sweep and Glen ignored them. Alice checked them out, though, squinting under her hand, and thought that their bones were well upholstered. Well, folks, you've got heat, you've got light, and if you get real hungry, she thought, you can eat the dogs.

Chapter Two

THE FIRST BIG SOFT BUFFET OF A CHINOOK WIND ROCKED THE STANDFAST house as the moon was setting. Domingo on the sofa woke up and pushed the red point-blanket off his face. Outside, the temperature rose forty degrees in fifteen minutes. At four in the morning, the whole snow-pack slid off the roof in a cataract.

Everything trickled and gurgled; the landscape seemed to be chuckling under its breath. Alice told herself a joke in her sleep, and woke laughing. Going down to chore, she believed she could smell the grass and mud of her pastures surfacing through the defeated snow. The wind blew steady and warm, the creeks chortled, the dogs chased each other goofily like puppies. In a couple of days, she thought, the girls can go back on the Triangle. One last good browse before the babies come. "And I," she sang to Sweep, half-addled with cabin fever, "am going to town!"

They ate the last of the eggs for breakfast; she made the leftover Spam into sandwiches with the last of the kosher dills.

"These are for lunch. You know how to use the microwave? 'Cause I gotta go to town." Giddy at the prospect; Spanish thrown to the winds. "Do you want anything from the Safeway?"

"No, thanks. Yes, a—" miming shaving, hair-combing.

Alice stood still, shocked. All this time, he could have been . . . the fact that a person comes to you dirty and smelly doesn't mean that's necessarily his preferred state. God, Alice, what a way to treat the kid!

"Discúlpeme, por favor, por ser tan mal anfitrión, a bad host." She rummaged the bathroom for towels, a plastic razor, the free toothbrush from her last dental checkup, feeling shamefully remiss. "Please make yourself at home."

"*A thousand thanks. The obligation is altogether mine.*" So graceful a phrase, thought Alice; so villainous a face. But she set off for Walla Walla in the pickup in high good cheer anyway, taking Bel and Glen. She felt pretty easy about leaving the kid alone on the place. Steal what? Take it where? For one thing, he was unfit for travel; for another, so was his horse. And for a third, as she told Janet later, he seemed well brought up. Most Mexicans do, Janet warned. Most cowboys do, Alice countered, and are.

Left alone in the house, Domingo sat wrapped in the red blanket for half an hour, listening to the liquid sounds outside and considering what had happened to him. It seemed he was meant to live. He was on the mend. It was possible to think consecutively, not just huddle in the dark like a sick wolf, fending off pain minute by minute. He felt, if not exactly welcome in the house, at least that he did not give much trouble. He believed the red mare was going to recover. She was receiving such excellent care; he could not have tended her better himself. Could hardly have tended her at all in the state he was in.

And now here he was, left in solitary possession for—how long? Until the afternoon, certainly. Left with the means, the invitation, the admonition almost, to make himself at home. With his whole heart he yearned for a shower, a shave, clean clothes. He stood up and made his tottery way to the table.

Something about the luxurious fluffiness of the towels acted as a warning. He froze, instantly seeing the whole plot bare: el güero was off to fetch the immigration men. He had admired the mare's lineage, yes! He, Domingo, would be scooped up, jailed, and shunted below the Border, his chestnut mare and her princely foal the new and unquestioned property of this crafty gringo bastard! He felt sick, stupid, but lucky; having spied out the trap early, he had time to thwart it. His eyes shot this way and that, located parka and boots. Sitting to pull them on, he remembered the Baggie of sandwiches in the refrigerator; that would do for food on the way. Abruptly he realized that his boots were useless, his feet still swollen and screamingly tender. The others, the big insulated boots he had borrowed to walk down to the barns, where were they? But they would not fit in a stirrup.

And now he thought of the mare herself. Another march like the one that brought them here would ruin her; certainly she would slip her foal. They would be captured, and she would be good for nothing but the canner. Better to leave her and take another horse; the white guy would take good care of her. But that was the point, that was the point! He could not bring himself to part with her. Besides that, he had no idea where to go, which direction. Wapato, Abuela Fidencia had said; near Yakima. But what was this place, here? He could not have told where he was within a hundred miles.

Panting, he sat down, willed his thoughts to stop reeling from fright to fright. The fact was, he was stuck. If it was a trap, then he was caught. If it was a trap.

It probably was a trap. To put oneself in the power of the whites was to invite entrapment. If el güero were anything like the Foulkses, owing him wages, it would certainly be a trap. But this man owed him nothing. However, the mare—she was a powerful temptation.

Wait. The other truck, the big flatbed for delivering hay, why had he not thought of it before? He had seen it in the machine shed. Where was the key? In it, probably, or on the hook by the kitchen door. Would it pull a horse trailer? Yes, if it had a ball hitch; he couldn't remember. He had never stolen anything in his life, but now, he told himself, was the right time to start: la ocasión hace el ladrón. He had the Moon Boots on and was making for the back door when the red point blanket caught his eye.

It meant something, that blanket. He knew it well, its loft, warmth, its smell of woodsmoke. The saturated scarlet of it flared at him like a pulse, one formal broad point-stripe showing. It occurred to Domingo not to leave it flung over the back of the sofa, but to fold it properly.

But when he thought of this and acted on the thought, the knot of panic in his mind loosened and refused to reknit. The blanket, this house had received him warmly, generously; not just his valuable live-stock but his dirty, destitute, barely breathing self. At last, with a shaky sigh, his hands in the heavy red folds, he yielded himself to the luxury of trust.

A shower, a dabbing shave to avoid the hideous scabs on the left side of his face, and an hour standing nervously bare-shanked in his parka by the throbbing washer/dryer made him new, stronger, calmer. Self-respecting. Eating his sandwiches, he decided to walk down to the shed yard, visit his mare, and take a closer look at some horses he thought he had seen at a distance in one of the pens, the biggest ani-mals on the planet if he could trust his eyes.

Instead, he fell asleep, waking with a horrid shock to the sound of not one but two vehicles creeping up the lane to the house.

Fifteen minutes later he was sitting at the dinette table, supplies having been brought in, collies ejected, the electric thrill of panic dying away. "My sister Janet Weston. This is Domingo Roque."

"Pleased to meet you. My sister told me we had a guest. Welcome to this house. Your injuries are mending, I hope."

"Yes, all thanks to the master's care. Please accept my th— Your sister?!"

"My sister, the boss, Alice Andison." Seeing his mortified confusion, *"Did you mistake her for a man? Not surprising. Please don't apologize; she hasn't taken offense."*

Domingo felt duped. There was nothing about Alice Andison's shape that suggested femininity. Though the smallness of her hands was thus explained, and her readiness to cook. But not her strength, or her solitary condition. Women did not ranch on their own, in his experience.

"I believe the young man has taken you for a fella, Roan, all this time," Janet said.

"Not surprising," Alice chuckled, putting things in cupboards. "Being as I'm sort of a . . ."

"A mule."

"A mule, a roan mule." The sisters grinned at each other. Janet feared for her, though; she had worked herself thin on the place. Hollow-cheeked, no bosom; her behind had all the womanly roundness of a pair of ham hocks. No wonder the lad made a mistake. Though Alice felt that she worked only as hard as the place required. As it happened, the place required all of her, body and soul, heart and mind. She did not regret this.

Domingo noticed that while la patrona spoke Spanish carefully, with many comical errors and Castilianisms, la hermana conversed in fast slangy Mexican with a northern lilt. She sat down at the table across from him and kindly but frankly took stock of him.

"Can you see," she asked, "from that eye?"

"Little more, every day." In truth Janet had never seen anything quite so awful looking, the lid dark and swollen, the visible part of the eye wildly bloodshot. But open. According to Alice, that was new, hopeful.

Alice handed around coffee and store-bought gingersnaps. Domingo could see a family resemblance now, the hair of both women brown like the tarnish on copper, narrow gray eyes, long noses, thin lips. The sister had no freckles, no curls, a little gray in her hair, and a nice figure when she took off her down jacket, voluptuous almost. She was the elder of the two, and the taller. He still could hardly think of the other one as "she."

"*Not to be rude, but where are you from?*" the sister inquired.

"*From Zacatecas, ma'am, from Rancho Lomas Chatas.*"

"*A small place?*"

"*A very big place, with a large population of horses and cows. But the nearest town is Santo Tomás Apostol del Oriente.*"

"*Ah, the shoemaking town?*"

"*Exactly.*" Impressive local knowledge; although any town in that part of Mexico might well answer to the same description. "*How do you know about that place?*"

"*Bunches of Mexican students at my college.*"

"From Santo Tomás?" This was unexpected, exciting!

"From Zacatecas. But, if you don't mind telling, where did you come from when you came here?"

Domingo recoiled inwardly from the probe. He would have liked very much to know where "here" was. But in fact there seemed no reason, nor any way, to lie. *"From Idaho."*

"So you crossed the Snake? By truck, or—?"

"No, lady; by horse."

The sisters glanced at each other. "That's about a hundred miles from here, closest bridge, by road," Alice murmured, and took another cookie. They seemed disposed not to believe him, those two pairs of pale eyes rather coldly assessing. Well, let them not, what cared he? Then he thought of his horse, her bravery, and felt indignant on her behalf.

"I was working for the Foulkses, at their feedlot along the river there," he explained, suppressing heat.

"Hm. Roan, do you know of a stock finisher called Folks? I may not have heard the name right. Folks, did you say, brother?"

"Yah, Foulks. Is near to Tumac."

"Sure," confirmed Alice. "Foulks Brothers; they've got a cow out-fit and a commercial feeder operation along the Snake somewhere, though I've never been . . . Wait. *Is it possible to know in what lumber— what manner your horse traversed the river?"*

"Patron-na? For the bridge." What did they suppose, that she flew?

"Pero," objected Janet, *"no hay puente ahí. Quizás en Lewiston . . ."*

"Pues, sí, lo hay. El puente del ferrocarril."

Janet's mouth fell open. Alice said, "Did I get that right? He rode over the railroad bridge? Over the Snake River on the railroad bridge!?"

"But, man, what if a train had come?"

Domingo shrugged. Then he would be dead, instead of sitting in the warm, drinking coffee and telling them improbable tales about the valor of his mare. Why ask such a question?

"A dam of lances," Janet said finally.

"She's all that," said Alice, "and a bag of chips."

The next day, instead of putting her cows back outdoors, Alice thanked her luck that they were inside. The chinook blew warm until midnight, but heavy wet snow fell in its wake and froze, and fell and froze, and fell and froze, thawing a bit in daylight and crusting over with ice at night, for four days. Everything was in such a welter of slush, mud, snow, and ice that Alice doubted that either the Clydesdales or the big tractor could have taken hay down onto the Triangle and brought the wagon back up again.

Feeding the expectant cows in the covered arena was comparatively easy; she could drive the flatbed up parallel with the open side, and heave the hay in flakes over the fence as the Clydes pulled steadily along from one end to the other. She could muck out one end of the place with the little front loader while the three dogs held the cows at the other end. She could check their water by eyeballing the two big stock tanks at the ends instead of having to take a hatchet down to the creek.

The only disadvantage to this arrangement was that the cows themselves disliked close quarters. They preferred to be out, and they tried to get out, bending the fence panels and forcing the gates out of true, and groaning complaint, day and night. But they might as well stay in there now, Alice thought, until the calves came.

This thought darkened her mind and weighed down her spirits. She thought she might be forced to ask her niece Nan Weston to help her. Two weeks out of her last semester would hardly hurt her, Alice felt. According to Nan's mother, the high school had precious little to offer students in the senior year anyway, especially in mathematics and science. And Nan was good help, strong, skillful, and if not exactly sweet-tempered, willing for all the work going.

The problems in this arrangement were three, however. First, Alice could not tell with exactitude when calving would start. Second, with the wild winter they were having, she could not be sure, if Nan were not already up at Standfast, that she would be able to get from Waitsburg to Iwalu, much less twelve miles further up in the Palouse hills to the ranch and the cows, when the time came. Third, if Nan came, Nick would also insist on being released from the torments of school—Nick, the difficult, class-skipping, rule-flouting younger brother, between whom and his parents Alice wished to inject no cause for discord.

She had shuffled the Mexican kid down into the tiny apartment at the end of the foaling barn. Since his recovery, Alice had not much wanted him in the house; though to tell the truth she had been loath to share even before that. She had absorbed the house in stages: when their mother died in their teens; when Janet married Philip and left home; when their father died; when to her gibbering relief their nasty quasi-partner Jerry Graeme had taken himself apparently permanently off to the land of twenty-four-hour neon, keno for breakfast, and easy slots. In taking on more and more of the work of the place, she had gradually extended her solitude into all parts of the house too, until she filled it like a turtle its shell. So as soon as Domingo could manage the walk, she moved him out.

He was glad to go. The snug room in the foaling barn represented a degree of comfort and privacy that he had not enjoyed since leaving his mother's house at Lomas Chatas, long ago. Also the little place, originally a bunkroom, was attached to the barn in which his horse was convalescing, so he could look after her himself. Besides, he did not feel entirely easy on the place. Welcome, yes, in a formal sense, but not at home. This being so, he preferred to be out from underfoot. Also, he felt shy of la güera. When she was a man—when he had believed her to be a man—he had known how to comport himself, even helpless as he was. Now he wasn't sure.

He grew stronger daily. But his sore hands had lost their cunning, and the cold still struck through him like a blade. He made himself as useful as he could, but when he would start to shiver and drop things, Alice ordered him indoors and he had to obey. No point in standing on his dignity when his teeth chattered so hard he couldn't speak to object. Half an hour, forty-five minutes finished him, and she would say, "Son, go inside," in the same tone as "Bel: kennel." And he had to go.

It shamed him as a man, or it would have if she had been a real woman. Instead of a mule. What did it mean to her, that word? he wondered. The obviously affectionate use of it between Alice and the sister—that confused him. It wasn't a reproach. (And that unfraught reference to her blotched face: roan, which he first heard as ron, *rum,* but then translated: ruana, like a speckled horse.) The whole situation gave him chicken skin. On the other hand, he was well fed, warm bedded, happy in the red mare's recovery. Also, he felt that the little bits of work he did were done in a way that met with la ruana's approval.

One morning, sent into the house racked with chills, he retaliated by cooking. The result was gratifying. Alice blew in on a gust of arctic air, stopped, and snuffed like a fox.

"You made a hot lunch?"

"Of course," off-hand.

"Well, well. A fella who cooks might be worth his keep." She stepped into the kitchen to look. "What is it?"

"Quesadilla, pintos. Grin salsa."

"Grin?"

"Uh-huh. How you say?"

"Gree-een."

"Uh-huh, grin. You like it?"

"Son, I like anything that somebody else cooks."

It was good though. "How come you know how to cook?" as she cleaned up afterward. "Isn't cooking women's work, in Mexico?"

He could hardly repress a sharp answer. So ignorant, these Americans! They knew one word: machismo, and they thought it explained everything. Whereas it did not even explain machismo.

"Lot of time," he returned mildly, "guy like me, we don't cook, we don't eat."

"Guys like you? Meaning what, bachelors?"

Domingo felt searched. He stood up and got ready to go out. Then reflecting that he had been living on her bounty, at her very table, for more than two weeks, and that she was alone with him, even though a mule, and thus perhaps had a right to know a thing or two about him, he set himself to explain. *"When we men of Mexico travel for work, with no women with us to help us, then we learn to do for ourselves those things that our womenkind like to do for us at home."* It came out rather stiffly, more lessonlike than was quite polite, and he could not prevent himself from adding, almost as a challenge, *"Otherwise we would live like beasts."*

Alice said nothing. She noticed his didactic tone but pretended not to, her hands in warm water and a sleepy look on her face. Her question had been rude, possibly. And she thought of the boys, the young men, illegals up here in the Valley for the fieldwork season, who camped along the farm roads and slept under sheets of cardboard, worked their long days in the onion fields and orchards, and sent their wages home to Mexico by giro. They had no women to help them, for sure. Always half on the run, half in hiding from the immigration police. And they did sure enough live like beasts, she had no doubt. But her notion about this boy, Domingo—that he was not quite like those poor driven mesteños—strengthened.

This time Alice called the Whytes. They generally kept half a calf in their freezer from Christmas onward, but even so their other supplies might be low. The roads were much worse now than before the chinook; if she had to, though, she thought she could get down to them with Tom Fool and a packhorse, stay the night, and come back to Standfast next day in the same amount of time, uphill but unloaded. As an added incentive, she had brought them raisins and dates on the day of the big thaw, and she suspected that Vera Jane had been baking. So she was almost disappointed to find that they had no crying need. Robey was heavy with news, however, having taken the Ski-Doo into the Hashknife place to see how they were doing.

"Stinks, Alice. Like they're raising cats in all them ole beaters up on blocks. Stinks like cats. You know that fella Bick?"

"Guy with Old Testament hair? Yeah I do. He still there?" Bick, the prophet and founder of the cult-commune or whatever it was. Unless Alice was much mistaken, the focus of that group had undergone a radical shift hash-ward in the last few years, though the religious code words still flew fast and free, she noted, whenever she had anything to do with those folks.

"Yeah, and—but, you know, Alice, I feel like he wanted to run us off the place. Them goddam dogs was loose and he never—"

"Who's 'us' though? Did VJ go?"

"Yeah, you know, she worries about them kids in there. She wanted to see—but you know, I think he had a firearm in his coat, that Bick."

"Wouldn't surprise me. Everybody on that place is as wicked as a pet coon, Robey, even the kids. Why do you take any notice of them anyway?"

"Well," reprovingly, "I wouldn't have a neighbor want for help, if I could help."

"Well, true." As far as it went. Alice waited.

"Besides," she could hear him change the phone to his better ear. In a lower tone, "You know, Alice, you or us oughtta have that place. I just want to be the first to know if they ever decide to sell."

Ah. Alice held the phone against her chest and directed a significant leer at the refrigerator. Robey was supposed to be cutting back his ranching operation, was in fact a good deal less active now than formerly. But he could no more give up the sport of trying to buy up his neighbors' land than he could wear pink Levis. Like every other farmer she knew, he had his ear to the grapevine all the time for a death, a divorce, a breakup of some kind, an opportunity; she herself was no better. Where she would get the money for such a purchase was a puzzle. But a girl could dream. Just to keep her skills sharp, as it were, she tried a little diversion: "What would you want with it? It's way too steep for cropping, and too far off the road—"

"Not all of it ain't. There's a couple good flat benches high up, prob'ly thirty-five acre, south facing. Timothy'd go good up there, I betcha."

"But, dear heart, what do you want with that kind of trouble? For sure, there's nothing been done to it for ten years. You'd be paying taxes on it for ages before you'd get anything to grow."

"Yeah. Well. I s'pose." Robey recognized a dodge when he heard one. Nothing so useful to a rancher, taxwise, as owning land that for good and sufficient reasons could not be put into cultivation. "Anyways, I just wanted to kinda warn you about that Bick fella."

"'Preciate it. Hi to Vera Jane." Alice hung up.

Timothy. It wasn't hard to raise except for the one year in six when it got rained out. Excellent horse hay, for which there was a swelling market in the Valley. And of course, Robey knew all about it; Vera Jane had been assistant auditor for Columbia County for the best part of the previous decade, and she probably knew quarter acre by quarter acre where the Hashknife property lay and what it was good for. So, timothy, maybe.

However, the departure of the commune had been confidently predicted every year for the last nine, and there they still were. Also, if memory served, all the Hashknife ground was part and parcel of the old Graeme place. Did Jerry Graeme still own it, or own shares in it like he did part of Standfast? If so, Vera Jane would know that too; so was Robey really suggesting that Alice get any further involved in land ownership with Jerry Graeme than she already had the misfortune to be? Couldn't be: Robey and Vera Jane were her oldest friends, and Jerry Graeme was her oldest, just about her only enemy.

VJ, Alice said to herself, we gotta talk.

The Standfast calves started to come at the end of February. Nan Weston came up and stayed for ten days, and Nick came and stretched a weekend through Wednesday. Domingo Roque grew daily stronger and more useful. Alice gave him her own second horse, a stout little bay called Falcon, as his first mount, and Nan's paint horse Skookum as his second after Janet came up and dragged her daughter back to high school. Altogether it was the least-awful calving Alice had experienced, she told Janet, since their father died. The least bad in a decade, in part because of Jerry Graeme.

The year before had been horrendous because Jerry had not come back from Las Vegas at all, but Alice had expected him and not laid on any other help. Janet had come up, of course, after her classes every day, but had not brought the kids because she refused to allow either of them, especially Nan, to come in contact with Jerry, and they were expecting Jerry to waltz in at any moment. That was his usual way, late and breezy. And so Alice and Janet had it to themselves, and the effort, four and a half weeks of no sleep, food on the run, nonstop work in fierce weather, caused them to rue the day they were born. Caused injuries: Alice strained her back pulling a calf, and Janet got stepped on and had a broken toe, her feet numb, she didn't even know it; and they lost a cow too, so torn up inside it bled out before the vet could come.

But as Janet said to Alice, the only thing worse than Jerry's absence was his presence. In years past, when he *had* managed to tear himself away from the fleshpots of Nevada and Wyoming, they were reminded of what a handless, heedless, obnoxious bastard he was. Though ranch-raised, he had no more sense than a dude, would smoke in the hay sheds, for God's sake, and throw his horses all sweaty and steaming out into the pens at the end of work. He was foul-mouthed and foul-minded, weird about women, especially about Alice, and acted like the place belonged to him. After Allan died, Jerry had simply taken over the big bedroom at the house as if by right. Since then, though he seldom showed his face at Standfast (okay with Alice), he left his stuff in there, his dibs on it, damn well not okay with her but she couldn't do anything about it. He insisted that he had a legal right to lodge there, and Alice feared that this might be partially, slightly true.

Janet denied it. She loathed the man with every fiber of her being. She believed that when Allan and Jean had bought the hayfields along Koosh Creek from Old Man Graeme, the contract that specified a life interest for Jerry in the property meant a share of the profits, if any, but no right of occupancy. She nagged Philip about it. Philip pointed out, first, that property law was extremely complex and litigation expensive; second, that sheltering Jerry Graeme's girlie-magazine collection and sharkskin suits was a bargain compared to dealing with him in the real; and third, that the life Jerry appeared to be leading and the company he seemed to be keeping bid fair to kill him off in jigtime, and they should therefore not distract him from it.

Janet had said a particularly coarse and savage thing to Alice three years before when Alice bitched the air blue about the man's gold-bricking and general cack-handedness: "Well, you fucking well had your chance." This referred to a time when Alice had prevented Jerry from starting up the tractor with a disk harrow attached not to its tow bar but lower down, at axle height. The drag of the harrow plus the torque of the rear wheels would have forced the big John Deere over backward, crushing the driver. Alice had once seen such an accident, and wanted never to see anything like it again; besides, there was the tractor to consider. But Janet ever afterward spoke of it as an opportunity missed.

The calving this year was a project in logistics on account of the weather. Angus cows object to dropping their calves under one another's noses; misunderstandings develop, and calves are sometimes injured. The Triangle pasture between the house and the county road, where they could have spread out and given birth in peace and relative privacy, stayed shoulder deep in glazed and jagged drifts, no place for newborns. But since the population of the covered arena was about to double, accommodation had to be arranged.

"With the Noble panels, we can make room for ten in the machine shed," decided Alice, "and we'll clear out the foaling stalls and put two in each one. Your horse is okay to live outside now, Domingo, don't you guess? We can put her in with the Clydes; they'll be nice to a newcomer."

Once the movable fence panels were up, the trick was to distribute the cows to the cows' satisfaction. Though they didn't care to calve in a crowd, they nonetheless resisted separation. Pepped up with prenatal hormones, they defied the dogs, and those individuals who had formed special friendships made life difficult even for the horsemen. A great deal of bawling and groaning accompanied the cutting-out, which took place in a fog of steam in the dusk of the covered arena where the horses pressed brisket-deep through the mass of blocky black bodies. From time to time a swirl in the current indicated the invisible presence of Sweep, Glen for his own good left tied up outside, crying aloud at the injustice.

A good system evolved with Nick, who did not ride, working the Powder River chute at the gate end and Nan outside roping and leading away the cows to their new quarters. Nan turned from her pre-SAT calculus and chemistry workbooks to ranchwork with a ready hand and a smile. Her skill with the rope was better than fair, she rode like a centaur and had a tactful touch with all kinds of livestock. And between Nan and the collie Bel trembled a fine thread of communication, so the bestowal of singles and buddy pairs of cows went smoothly.

Alice enjoyed this part. In fact, everybody seemed to be enjoying himself, nobody more than Domingo Roque who, in spite of the cold and a scathing wind, brushed off suggestions that he go indoors by pretending not to understand them. Nick, up on the chute for hours at a stretch, had for some reason fallen into a habit of addressing the cows in third-year German, with obscene insertions for emphasis. "Nein, du gehst nicht mal zurück, dickhead," he would say, "es tut mir fuckin leid. Achtung, Nannie: Lebensgefahr!" Alice's face felt stretched with laughing.

So the first couple of days went well, and though they ate like tigers, at least the cupboards were full. Then Janet came up and took Nick away, and the full weight of feeding, mucking out, and keeping round-the-clock watch settled on the others as the first calves appeared. Thereafter, in staggered shifts they kept an eye on the progress of labors, clipped identification tags to the ears of newborns over the vigorous objections of their mothers, injected with oxytocin those cows that did not cleanse of the placenta after bearing, made sure the little ones stood and sucked and that the mothers showed proper maternal manners; hurried away and disposed of stillbirths, blessedly few. The cold gradually eased, which they noticed only as a change from ice to mud, and weariness gradually accumulated to exhaustion.

Of thirty-seven cows, thirty calved safely, four with twins; of the remaining seven, three were probably barren. The other four did not seem to Alice to be in any trouble, just taking their own sweet time as was their right. Of thirty-four calves on the ground, two were still-born, and the rest all stood and nursed. So far no cows had died. They had only had to pull three calves. One of these Alice had managed on her own by finely timing the cow's contractions so that she could free the baby's doubled-up foreleg. If the calf had been much farther advanced into the birth canal, she would not have had the strength, or if the cow had been a primipara. But Alice knew her cows and knew— something—that made her get right in there without delay, and sure enough, all the way inside, she felt the one waxy little hoof, then the soft muzzle, then on the next surge the hard round knuckle of the other foreleg: wrong, bent back, and needing to be unfolded in the intervals between pushes, with no room to maneuver, while the mother's inner workings resisted with all their power.

Alice fell away, gasping with effort and shaking her battered arm, and Domingo helped her up and handed her a towel. Instantly the little diver shot halfway into the world, hung upside down under the cow's tail, and plopped glistening and steaming onto the straw in its transparent sac. The cow lowed; the humans cheered. It was not clear to Domingo that help had been needed; still, the promptness of the birth after Alice's intervention answered all questions. He would have been impressed if lack of sleep hadn't flattened out every feeling except hunger and the desire to be warm and horizontal. Similarly, he would have felt insulted if he could have felt anything when, the next two times, she wouldn't let him do the trick but used the calf jack instead. He disapproved of the device, thinking it hard on calves and cows alike. Alice didn't like it either. In her father's time it had never been used, for Allan Andison possessed both strength of arm and expert knowledge of the internal topography of cows. Alice had the same knowledge; she was strong too, at thirty-seven stronger and more skillful than ever in her life before. But she knew very well the limits of her strength. And about Domingo she knew too little to take the risk. "Your hands are raw, and the inside of a cow is septic." That was her excuse, but he knew she didn't trust him. Wait, he thought, sulky. Wait, woman; you will find out.

Nan Weston went home with her dirty clothes in a duffel bag, a disgusting present for her mother. The wind dropped, a good thick insulating layer of cloud crept over the hills, and the snow began to come off. A few at a time, the herd went back out to pasture. Night watches ended. With two left to calve out, Alice sat down on a bale of alfalfa one morning at sunrise, leaned back against the stack, and woke up around ten when Domingo came in to ask her whether she knew that one of the barren cows had dropped a live heifer calf in the open overnight? Golden joy flooded her. Bonanza! Realist though she was, she did not see how things could go very wrong now. This year had been by far the . . . well, not easiest, but least godawful bearing season since their father's death. Though pretty used up, Alice wasn't prostrate, not injured, not staring disaster in the eye. She stood up and tottered out into the gray forenoon. Good hands make all the difference, she thought, stretching extravagantly.

She said as much to Janet, who drove up the next day for a report and to bring a sustaining casserole of sausages, peppers, and cornmeal.

"Those kids of yours are goddarn good, Yan. You rizz them right. They know what they're doing and they work like field hands."

"Music to my ears," Janet sighed, "though it's no surprise about Nan."

"Nicky too, though. You sure don't have to tell him twice."

"Isn't he a darling?" frank about her fondness. "If only we could tape his mouth shut. Isn't that Skookum? He's turning into some kind of a wrangler, isn't he!"

"That Domingo—that's another thing. Talk about your good help." Skookum, though handy enough, had never much wanted to face the music as a cow horse, Alice felt. But short of horses as they were, she had had to put Domingo on him for cutting out, and the pony's confidence surprised her. Now, as the sisters knelt side by side on the love seat looking downhill through the locust grove, Domingo and the collies were moving the whole bunch of cows and new calves from the Triangle onto the higher and more sheltered adjacent field. A narrow gate, deep pocked mud on either side, vulnerable babies: potentially a wreck. No rush, though, no impatience, no harm. Deftly done.

"What are you going to do about him?" Janet turned back to the coffee mugs.

"Hire him, if I can."

"Damn. I've been afraid of that very thing."

"Why damn? He's been a godsend," fervently, "and he isn't even fully sound yet."

"Damn. You feel like you need him, do you?"

"I sure as hell need somebody. I don't know whether, even with the kids . . . God, peach, remember last year? It nearly killed us."

"I know, I know. I would have taken the winter quarter off from teaching—"

"You can't be doing that. Your wages are part of the equation, part of the budget—"

"—if I'd known that skunk Jerry wasn't going to show up at all . . ."

"Even with the open winter last year, it was christawful." She wasn't going to mention hurting her back—it would only make Janet feel guilty—but the phantom pain of it took her right back to that horrible season. They had done badly in calves too; there just had not been enough of her to attend to everything. This year was, in spite of truly lousy weather, so much more profitable, so much better in every way. She reviewed it almost warmly, almost with pleasure. Partly due to the kids' good work, but chiefly because of that steady, experienced, extra pair of hands, damaged though they still were. "I gotta say, well, you saw this: the guy got right down and laid into the collar as soon as he could get his boots on. He's been a real servant, and we've never paid him a dime."

"Damn!"

"Dammit, woman, why do you keep damning?"

"Because, Alice, think!"—blowing air straight up so that her bangs ruffled—"what would possess a man to ride a horse across a railroad trestle?"

Alice leaned back and thought, leaned forward and put her mug down, said, "Damn!" Janet put up her palms on either side of her face and opened her eyes very wide.

"He's illegal?"

"Got it in one."

"He's illegal as hell."

"It's like pregnant, darlin', either you is or you ain't. Illegal or wanted by the law, take your pick. Not that it makes any difference." Silence fell, in which the twangling of a harpsichord sounded from the CD player in the kitchen. Janet went over and turned it off. "Refill?" holding up the carafe.

"It does make a difference, as a matter of fact," said Alice slowly.

"Uh-uh, Roan. Either way, you're—we're harboring a fugitive."

"Look, I wouldn't hire a felon, you know. But if he's merely illegal . . ."

A very bad decision hovered in the offing, Janet feared. Her sister had always been nearest and dearest to her. They were close in age, and their mother had died young. Janet loved Standfast itself, but loved it even more for Alice's sake, and she worried that running the place alone might be beyond even Alice. In the watches of the winter nights, lying beside her husband in their snug bungalow in Waitsburg, she accepted that it was well more than any one person could do, and swore to give up her students and devote herself to the place. By daylight, though, the budget reasserted itself. Besides, she knew herself well, knew that she wanted to teach with all her might, the way Alice wanted to ranch and Philip wanted to practice law. She couldn't make herself embrace self-sacrifice. But she clearly saw in the choice now facing Alice a threat to all three, Standfast, her job, Philip's work.

"No merely about it. Of course, if he's a bad guy, he won't tell you. You'd never know till he stole something, or carved you up with a hoof knife. But if you employ an illegal alien, and you get found out . . ." She came back with her full mug and sat down, clamping her hands between her knees.

"Are you thinking about your job, Yanny?"

"Yeah, and I'm thinking about Philip."

"But you . . . at school, lots of your students are—"

"But I don't employ them. And as far as possible, I don't know their green-card status."

"But up here? I mean, nobody would know."

"If someone found out, then Phil would pay an awful price."

"Well, but would he, though? I mean, it's done all the time, isn't it? In quantity. All the onions and asparagus around here, lots of those people in the fields are illegal, aren't they? And all the soft fruits over west of the Columbia . . . Yakima would be a ghost town without the migrants. What about those strawberry pickers of Robey's? Don't you guess they're . . . whatchacallit?"

"Sin papeles. I bet they are. But the migrants are different. There's an old, old unwritten rule about them, since Bracero Program times. They're mostly left alone during the picking season. But you're talking about a full-time, year-round employee. Just like those Colombian babysitters that keep getting the politicians in trouble."

Alice got up and fiddled with the draft of the woodstove. Janet's alarm infected her. To jeopardize Janet's situation at the community college: no small thing, not just on account of her no-longer-weensy paycheck, but because her soul was in that work. As for Philip . . . Alice's shoulders curved toward her ears. The prospect of injuring her brother-in-law in his professional life gave her the horrors. Her admiration for Philip Weston dated from their college days, increasing almost to awe. If one could be in awe of a teddy bear. But a bear of very large brain, with an unbending spine of principle.

And yet . . . and yet. The ache in her back told her she needed someone, if not Domingo Roque, then somebody else. The place was too much for one person; she'd proven it to herself. Too much even for their father, that natural stockman. The years of Alice's marriage and absence from Standfast had run Allan ragged.

Janet's mind was moving in the same channel. "You really need him, don't you, Roan?"

"I do, yeah," turning around, consciously not massaging her back. "I need somebody, and this guy seems purpose-built. If he isn't an axe murderer or something. And you know, the way he just showed up out of nowhere, just at the right time—"

"Oh, what? The Lord provides, for Pete's sake?"

"No, but . . . You know, kid, I've always been lucky." Janet coughed to hide her amazement. Totting up the score on her sister's life, she asked herself, Lucky how? She marveled. There seemed to be a subterranean stream of sunshine in Alice, always had been.

"Shit-oh-dear," she sighed. "Well, I have no suggestion to make, except to look before you jump, chickie, will you?" They turned back toward the window, in which Domingo Roque now appeared, made Skookum swing fat haunches from side to side as if dancing a merengue, and with a horrible scabby grin swept off his bill cap in a charro salute.

Maggie the Clydesdale mare stood her ground. Mose trotted off, rounding his heavy crest as Domingo came down the pen toward them, but the mare stood still, her ears poised in polite inquiry: May I help you?

"Good morning, Maggie. Would you mind helping us with the flatbed wagon today? Looky here, good stuff." His field carrots proved acceptable. He tossed the lead rope's end over her withers, half a foot above him, and still crunching and slobbering she lowered her great head for the halter. Mose, all big talk, followed them docilely up to the gate.

Alice came down the hill from the house, quick-march, hands in her coverall pockets and her shoulders hunched against the wind. While he was getting Mose's halter on, Domingo looked at her covertly. In what way a woman? he thought. Even now, wised up, he couldn't see it. She wasn't old, though; it was her pale eyebrows and her habit of quiet that had fooled him. But the shape of her: thin, but also . . . Could a person be skinny and stout at the same time? A look of compact strength, like an underfed but essentially well-bred pony. She wasn't tall: a good thing. Frankly, he was fed up to his back teeth with towering Americans who took their altitude for a badge of God-given superiority. Nor was she anybody's idea of a beauty queen; handsome, he would rather have said, as the gabachos counted handsome, had she been male. And stern, though her expression today was amiable enough.

Alice spotted him and lifted her chin in greeting, changing course for the hay shed as he brought the two Clydesdales up to be groomed and have their pulling tack put on. She took over the big gelding, who had not yet learned patience. "Stand still, you monkey," in an undertone. She had to stand on a bucket to brush his croup. "Don't you move, Sweetpea. Listen here, now." She fetched the collar and harness, the fifteen-foot reins looped up. Mose stood easy, turning his head to watch.

Standing on a bucket in turn, Domingo heard her say, "We'll take a day off today, I guess, and replace the shingles on the house roof. This wind will find a hole and blow itself out pretty soon." He said nothing, translating to himself. She said, "If you're agreeable."

"Oh, yes," not knowing what he had agreed to, but unworried. Her decisions about work always took that form: "we'll" or "let's." It was strange, but he was getting used to it. She walked around behind the team to check that he had put on the breeching properly. He did not resent this; probably if she checked again tomorrow, he would, though maybe not. You could always learn something from another horseman, was his opinion. Maybe if she had been pretty or sexy, if he had felt the least attraction. But as things stood, no.

Not that he was much of an authority, anymore, on the attractiveness of women. Not since Graciela, the all-time standard. Though he craved the act of darkness as much as ever, that rising sweet tide, suspense, sway into oblivion. Only that, for the best part of ten years, directing that yearning to any actual and particular woman caused the feeling to dry up, like a desert arroyo ten minutes after a flood. Or to turn bitter, twist his thoughts back to that matchless beauty, his willing enslavement, her perfidy. He kept his mind from Graciela as much as possible. Better so.

Alice led the team out in a circle ending in a pivot, Mose swinging around on the off side and Maggie pirouetting on her forehand with ponderous elegance, and backed them up to the flatbed so that Domingo could attach trace chains to singletrees. She clipped on the cross-checks, looked at them, and muttered, "Now, why did I do that?" Unfastened, untwisted, and clipped them again. "You drive," she said, pleasing Domingo greatly, and walked ahead to open the pasture gate.

Alice did look before leaping. Between helping her last two calves of the season into the light in the afternoon and entering their data into the computer after dinner, she looked into her heart, but she found no plain answer. One thing she could do, she supposed as she trudged down to the pens for the bedtime check, was to consult Robey Whyte, or maybe even her other neighbor Bob McCrimmon, a big operator with lots of employees, some of whom must be without legal status. But things were a smidgen cool between herself and the McCrimmons just at the moment, about the location of the property line where they and Standfast came together. Robey, then. Domingo Roque, who had fallen into the routine of the nine o'clock round, broke in on her internal discussion.

"One those gemelos, she don't feed too much." Alice translated: one calf of one of the sets of twins wasn't getting enough nourishment.

"Does it suck?"

"Yah, pero—no too much. The other is too big."

"Which one is it? We better bring it inside and give it a bottle."
Which black calf, in a herd of black cattle, at night . . . ?

"Is okay tonight. We can feed she, her, in the field tomorrow."
Ducking through the fence of Falcon's pen to check that he had
cleaned up his grain. "Two times every day, no problem, she's okay."

And that, she reflected seconds before plunging into sleep, was just
one example of the advantage of two pairs of knowledgeable eyes over
one pair, no matter how wide awake they might be.

Domingo took no account of his loneliness. That is, he would not have
called himself lonely. Alone, merely. To be lonely, one had to desire
company, which he did not. He lived within himself, had done so for
a long time now. When he reflected on this, as he seldom did, it was
without surprise, or regret. He had been solitary since childhood, alone
among many.

Which was odd. For though his mother was orphaned young, his
father had been one of eight, most of whom either lived and worked
at Rancho Lomas Chatas or married into the town of Santo Tomás.
Dozens of cousins, moving in thoughtless unison like horse herds or
flocks of doves, attuned, sharing a slang and a history, at home in each
other. A tribe.

Except for him. Well, of course, his mother was foreign, from Oaxaca in the far south. Chocolate dark, Indian featured. And a teacher,
more foreign still. And then his father, Fidel, rose to be the mayor-
domo, the foreman who received and transmitted the commands of
the patrón, who consulted with the señoría themselves, man to man.
Which put distance between Fidel and his brothers, thus between
Domingo and his cousins. This was a price he had been paying for so
long, by the time he first recognized it, that he could manage it without strain. Just this: he made damn sure that any deference paid him
as the son of Fidel Roque, he earned; any learning attributed to him as
the teacher's kid, he actually owned.

After his mother died, after Fidel died on the Border, the habit of
solitude strengthened. It protected him in the North, preserved him

from insult; also from the kind of companionship that led to blowing whole seasons' wages in bars and cardrooms and whorehouses. Except for that one slip in Del Mar, it kept him clear of trouble. Though the business in Del Mar had been grievous enough.

It would not be true to say that he missed his cousins, but he thought of them sometimes. What had become of them all, that gang of Roques and Muñozes, all those boys wild with life, that he had fished and swum the river and helled around on horseback with? All those teasing girls? Asunción, kicked in the gullet by a rank horse, drowned in his own blood. Juana Inez, incorrigible flirt, pregnant at her quinceañera, married to one of the possible fathers, and the mother of seven sons like a biblical matriarch at twenty-five. That strange girl Rosario who became a bruja and went to live among the Indians. Hortensia, who was always trying to teach him to dance, crippled in a bus wreck. Macabeo who was nearly as adept a vaquero as he was, but who lost himself in the tequila bottle. Gone, scattered like yucca blossom.

It was enough to make him sad if he thought about it much, so he didn't. But it gave him a very queer feeling to imagine that great hot tangled fleece of a clan now spun out to a single twisted thread adrift on the wind of a far country: himself.

And one other, he thought, with a yearning he could not suppress. Himself and one other.

When he had met her at the Del Mar racetrack, she was a famous beauty, Graciela Gonzalez, sixteen years old and the queen of the fairgrounds. Men ran loco for her, fought over her; her brothers constantly sported stitches and shiners acquired defending her skittish honor. The family ran a couple of taco stands, and Graciela had ample scope to exercise her charms, which were mythic: her sumptuous shape, the cocoa-rose perfection of her skin, her face of a saint in a shrine, smiling blessings on the tortas de sesos and Styrofoam bowls of menudo. But more than just her looks: up close, she projected a terrific vitality, a constant expectation of fun; it was as if she exuded some fragrance, essence of pleasure.

And she caught him. Well, she caught them all, but she chose *him*, and he dropped off the vine into her hands like a big red-ripe tomato. He hadn't had much to do with girls up to then; his classmate Meché Rosales, hand-holding and pecking kisses; the chamacas in the field-labor camps who all ran around together in bantering remudas. Had never been in love. So, as far as he knew, love was like this: danger, fever, disgrace, and loss.

She had him for two years, they had each other in all the haystacks and horse vans at the Del Mar fairgrounds, nowhere too risky. Or if too exposed even for her, she would tease him and run away, be seen next filling tacos as cool as cream. Then she had become pregnant, and he was thankful. They would marry, he thought. Things would settle down into a normal pattern, he would be happy, sure of her. Make love to her at night, leisurely, in a decent bed.

The brothers had invited him to the house to talk about the marriage. He went, and Graciela passed him in the yard with a taunting little wave, going out with a man he didn't know. It was like bathing in acid, that moment, he would never forget the sensation. Like drinking lye. Elías standing on the porch, a scared leer, afraid of him; inside, the other brother, Mauro, getting up from the sofa as if to face a firing squad. Probably they expected him to wipe out the insult pelado style, a knife in the girl's heart, a bullet in his own head. Tear the house apart, at the very least. But for once, he supposed, he had shown himself his father's son. De tal palo, tal astilla: a chip off the old block, this one time.

A coral-pink dawn, wild March wind. Alice and Domingo brought the two Clydesdales out of their pen. Alice turned back to latch the gate, listened.

"What the hell is that?"

Whisper, soft clatter building to a stuttering roar that jammed the air into her ears, and two helicopters swept up from behind the sway-backed hill, passed over the house at very low altitude, and dropped out of sight two ridges to the east. A ringing quiet.

Her ears popped. She found herself alone with Mose, his ears up but standing quiet. All the working horses in the pens were on the run, though, tails high, and Maggie, her lead shank dragging loose, strode purposefully toward the nearest hay shed. Domingo nowhere to be seen.

"What in hell?" Alice said again, hustling after the big mare. "Maggie, whoa, whoa." She caught up with her and took hold of her head rope. Domingo came out of the barn carrying his saddle by the horn and staggered off down the yard.

She followed him, mystified, towing the great beasts. Something frenetic about the way he moved—something is wrong with Domingo, she thought. The helicopter noise had done it; what did that mean? She wondered if it might be dangerous to hang around.

He was in the round pen with the red mare. The rig leaned on its cantle against the gatepost, the gate closed but not latched. He was stripping the mare's blanket off, unrolling the bandages from her legs, every movement fluid with skill but at frantic speed, so that the horse blew uneasily and shifted her feet, hindering him.

"You call those guys on me?" Alice barely caught the words, thought he spoke to the horse; he hadn't looked up or seemed to notice her.

"I didn't call— You mean those choppers?" half-mesmerized by his swift, deft, verging-on-frenzied movements. "Why? You think they're after you?"

A bark of wild laughter.

"Anyway, they're state police, not Immigration Service."

"How you know this?"

"'Cause it said SP underneath, State Patrol."

"Don't matter!" Cinching up, following the mare as she sidled away.

"Why? I mean, why not? Are you a criminal?" It just slipped out.

Domingo froze. He heard and understood the word, and the lightning flare of fury in his head surprised him. He waited, two or three long breaths, until he could see. Turned slowly.

"Güera," he said, "escúchame." And she did listen; she had no choice, standing there between the two massive Clydes, with her ugly mottled face and her blind pale eyes. *"Fourteen years I have worked in this country, never asking more than my wages fairly paid. Never have I stolen so much as a toothpick, never driven too fast, never drunk too much beer, never even pissed in a doorway. As God hears me, I have never done anything wrong. Yet I am driven like a lame dog from place to place in this land. I ask you, why? Is it just? Tell me! Is it just?"*

He spoke so slowly that she understood nearly every word. The whole of it came so softly and slowly, shockingly intense, as if the words carried heat; the narrow frame poised electric, the face all eyes. He scared her weak.

Mentally, Alice glanced behind her, planning escape. But a habit of steadfastness so long imprinted it was like instinct prevented her. Instead, most unwilling, she stepped forward. Mustered her Spanish.

"Indeed, truly, it is most unjust. Nonetheless, those airships do not seek you." Thought for a second and tried again: *"Those police do not search for you."* And she turned her team deliberately and led them up the yard. Because cows have to be fed, she told herself as her breathing evened out, come what histrionics soever.

She chored, and took a bottle of supplement down to the feeble twin in the field, managing to feed it without too much interference from the cow. The sight of all those healthy calves, their fuzzy black coats glinting, cleaner and cuter than they ever would be in their lives again—the smile in the stockman's heart, she thought, holding the calf between her knees and clamping its sticky little muzzle onto the rubber teat. After that she did some laundry, made shopping lists, got her ideas in order about a vegetable garden in case winter ever let up and gave her leave to plant one. Made sandwiches of the leftover salmon loaf, heated some soup.

Left alone in the fight, Domingo found that he believed her. How could he not? He so much wanted it to be true. And then, he asked himself, as if wakening there in the round pen, would they really send two helicopters to gather up one miserable alambrista? Would they? He leaned against his horse and closed his eyes, sick with unspent adrenaline. Nothing happened. The horse settled, lowered one hip, and cocked the hoof. Time passed; nothing happened. He roused himself. Very slowly and meticulously, he unsaddled the mare, inspected her legs, replaced her borrowed blanket, rolled up the bandages, lugged everything up the yard, and put it all away. In the little apartment, he sat on the bed in his outdoor clothes, thinking that now he must leave the place. The horse was nearly sound again. If he could get la ruana to tell him where he was or show him a map, probably he could think of where to go, what to do. After a while he lay back and fell asleep.

When he rapped at the kitchen door later on, she beckoned him in. He stayed by the door until she gestured toward the dinette.

"Lunch is kind of strange today," she said as if nothing had happened. As if, Domingo thought, he had not revealed himself in that unmanly way, not insulted her on her own ground, flouted her hospitality.

"I need speak you, patrona, please." She seemed a little bit shy of him. But he could see she felt strong in her own house. She turned off the stove and sat down with an open expression. The puppy, Glen, had glided in with him and now sat between his knees; feeling for words. Domingo occupied his hands with Glen's ears.

"I want say," he began, "about this house, good thing only. I want say you sorry, because here only happen good for me. What happen other place"—waving it away—"don't matter. In this house—you understand me?" He had wished in respect to her to speak English, but such English as he had was barren for his purpose. *"From your hands I have taken my life."* That was what he meant to say.

"Please do not allude to it. It is as nothing," Alice answered instantly, correctly. So that was all right.

Reassured, he went on, "I thinkin' tomorrow I will go."

Alice nodded. Her face took on a decided, slightly bulldogish expression. "Are you looking for work?" she asked.

"Uh-huh." Now if she asked him where he intended to look, he was stumped. How ask for directions, to where, from where?

"Is this the kind of work you want"—a swing of her arm, taking in the whole place—"ranch work?"

"Uh-huh."

"Because we are looking for someone. Somebody to help me on this place."

"Uh-huh." His brain caught up with his ears. "Oh. ¿Chamba, trabajo? Here?"

"Yes, here. Full-time, standard wages, room and board for you and your horse. What do you say? You want to think about it?"

He felt like he'd found a crisp hundred-dollar bill in the street. Not only was she not calling the bulls down on him—Think about it? He could hardly push the words out of his mouth fast enough. Roque luck, in nuggets.

"Yes, I think yes. Pero, dígame, por favor, ¿en dónde estoy? Where am I?"

So much for consulting anybody's preference but her own. Janet would have a hissy fit. But Alice believed that she knew her man, doubted she could do better on the labor market. She needed his skills, he needed the job, surely the law would be mild to them both. And just in case it wasn't, let everybody do their damnedest to keep the law from finding out.

The next day they drove to Waitsburg and took Highway 12 down the Valley sixteen miles into Walla Walla. Alice had a list of supplies to buy and errands to run. Domingo had a little money and some projects of his own. The twentieth of March and a soft, soft day of rain. In the truck, silence and the rip of tires through the wet; on the hills, an emerald plush of winter wheat alternated with smoothly curving bands of blue-brown fallow. Keeping in mind that the person in the cab with her might be of interest to the police, Alice drove with mincing care, until she realized that hypercorrectness would likely attract more attention than her usual five-miles-over-the-limit dash.

"Where do you want to shop?" she asked as they spiraled down off the highway at Second Avenue.

"La segunda, si hay."

Walla Walla was a bigger town than he had seen in months; Domingo felt fizzed up and nervous, like a Pancho-del-rancho. By the time she dropped him off at the Saint Vincent de Paul store across from the courthouse, he had spotted seven Mexican businesses including a religious bookstore, a shop displaying flounced and ribboned first-communion dresses, and a bakery that also sold CDs and stuffed iguanas and pictures of busty Aztec princesses painted on velvet. It might be, in such a place, that he would meet someone he knew, get some news of Graciela and her apple-tree trimmer. If they were still living in Wapato near Yakima, he now knew that he was closer to them here in the southeast corner of Washington than he had been when he worked across the Snake in Idaho. If they were still in Wapato.

"I'll pick you up here in two hours. That enough time? You got a watch?"

"No, Patrona, but I can—" tapping his forehead. As if he could not keep time like an adult! He watched the pickup turn onto Rose Street.

"*Countryman,*" to a grizzled guy leaning with a heel up against the storefront, waiting for his womenfolks, "*do you know this town?*"

"*Like my tongue knows my teeth, son. To where?*"

"Al correo, por favor—"

Alice worked her way down her list: feed store (sacks of corn-oats-barley, sacks of whole oats, containers of calf supplement, dog kibble), tractor store (replace belt), accountant (sign tax return), vet (pay on account), the Bennett-Briscoe Bank (deposit board checks), Safeway. The regular Friday influx of farm-folk crowded the streets and super-market aisles, and she had several impromptu gab fests along the way and was late getting back to the secondhand store.

"Mexican time," he joshed her, slinging his plunder behind the seat. Not knowing how to take this, Alice covered up by explaining why they were going home via Eastgate instead of the freeway: she needed to consult the people at the locker beef outlet. While she was doing this, Domingo had nipped into the Baskin-Robbins next door and laid out for a quart of ice cream. Alice looked at the sack on the seat.

"You went to Thirty-One Flavors?"

"Of course."

She couldn't help asking, "What did you get?" He displayed the lid. "Jamoca Almond Fudge! Great snakes!"

"You like it? Is, for me, the favorite. Is for lunch, okay!"

This jokiness: she didn't exactly mistrust it, but it was sure new and different. The whole shape of the guy was new on this day—relaxed, open. No chatterbox, but when he talked, his voice quirked and broke as if on a bubble of laughter. Maybe it was relief, after having been in such a fright the day before.

Alice herself felt relieved to have the decision about the hiring over. Her labor halved, that was the calculation she made. She had seen enough of him to think she could rely on his cowboy skills. If he turned out as handy at other work, she would consider herself very well served, very clever. Though (passing through Waitsburg at this moment) she boggled a little bit at presenting the thing to Janet as a done deal. Janet and Philip had so much more to lose than she did if the Immigration Service came down around their ears. Though the trouble would be hers too, in every conceivable way. She had opened a pit at their feet.

And yet she knew that Robey Whyte employed for berry-picking every year a group of chiapanecos of whose collective illegal status she was as sure as she was of her way home. How was that arranged? She needed to talk to Robey soon.

As it happened, Robey and Vera Jane came to Standfast next day, on horseback by the trails. Vera Jane seemed slightly frail to Alice, who got one of those disconcerting second looks at her old friend as she dismounted, laughing at herself for the time she took about it. "C'mon, sticks, down's easier than up," her fingers clenched white on the horn. Domingo was introduced, then led the two horses down to the pens, Alice privately determined that she would drive them and their elderly riders home later.

"Come in out of the wind. Whatever brings you out on such a day?"

"We couldn't stay in one more minute! That house! Kid, it just feels like jail to me!" Vera Jane had on a watch cap, and over that her battered old hat with its Texas roll, tied on with a silk scarf. Bundled up for warmth, not chic. They brought in their saddlebags two dozen oatmeal-raisin squares and a loaf of VJ's famous poppy-seed pound cake.

"Who's that fella took the horses?" Robey, nosey as a weasel.

"The guy I told you about, that I found in the snow."

"He's still here?"

"He was here right through calving, and thank God for him. He's been fierce big help. And Robey, I hired him on yesterday, so I need to talk to you about that, about how not to get in trouble about it."

Robey blew on his smoking coffee. "That might not be the brightest thang you ever done, darlin'. You don't know nothing about him, do ya?"

"I know this: he's a damn good hand and a bear for work."

"He seems like a nice-enough young fella," Vera Jane said. But everybody seemed nice enough to Vera Jane who did not kick her cats or hawk snoose on her floor.

"And you know he's a wetback," Robey said, somewhat quelled. Good hands were hard to come by, no kidding, and Alice knew whereof she spoke. He had great faith in Alice's capacity to manage Standfast. What Allan Andison had not taught her about the cattle business, Robey had. He was deep in her counsels, and knew how hard-pressed she was.

"Yup. Vera Jane, this is luscious. Oh my stars, yum yum. Yeah, that's my problem. I feel like he's just what the doctor ordered, but I'm scared of making a problem for Janet and Phil. So how can I do the payroll stuff without bringing the guv'mint down on us?"

"Well, all you need is Social Security. If he's got a Social Security card, that's all you gotta see. You just write out the paycheck like he was American."

"Really? Easy as that? What's all the fuss about, then?"

"Beats me. That's all I know, and all I wanna know. Works for us, we never had any trouble." Alice felt uneasily that there must be more to it.

But Robey was large with other news: "Did you see them two heelycopters yesterday?"

"See them, man, they dang near tore the roof off the machine shed, they were that low. What was it about, do you know?"

"We thought they were rescuing somebody, didn't we, Robey? 'Course, nobody coulda been still snowed in by then."

Robey relished the suspense a minute more. "Well, they went to the Hashknife place. It was a raid." He loved this.

"A raid! What for? You mean for—?"

"You got it." Couldn't wait. "They found a myth lab. They were making myth right there with all them kids and women in the house."

"You are kidding me!" Alice feigned amazement.

"Nope! Not a bit! And guns, they had a lotta guns and stuff in there too. Told ya." The Whytes hugged themselves, horrified, thrilled to be first with the news.

"Robey, was it you that called the staters? After whatsizname, after Bick pushed you around that time?"

"Oh no, honey," the old wife laid a knotty hand on her husband's arm, "he wouldn't do that. You know, we like to keep friends with our neighbors." Old hypocrites, Alice thought fondly.

Robey cracked a grin. "Hell no, Alice. Them guys, them troopers been watching that place for years, y'know. Years!"

"They have? I'll be damned. Well, so much for true religion and back to the land, huh?"

"Well," cautioned Vera Jane, "I wouldn't say nothing against their religion. But for farmers, well, better sign the whole place over to the government than what they done with it, I say."

Seeing an opening, Robey struck straight for the heart of the matter: "Now, Alice, there's where you and us come in. We need to buy that place, the good half of it."

"Ah," chuckled Alice. "I see it all now. A Plan is in the works. But no way, honeybunch. Doncha know, when they arrest somebody for drugs, they seize all their stuff and hold it till after they're tried. That property won't see the light of day till hell freezes solid, the way the state courts are backed up." Partly she believed this; partly she needed room for thought. Robey, however, wasn't having it.

"Usually, prob'ly, but not this time. I happen to know"—Vera Jane beginning to nod and smile— "half of the place belongs to the bank. Them people ain't paid on the mortgage since Hector was a pup. The Bennett-Briscoe foreclosed on it eighteen months ago; they was just scared to evict. Hell, we can walk in there today and put our money down. What d'ya know about that?" He tilted back his chair and beat a little riff on the table edge with his forefingers.

"Well, I'll be switched. You old wheeler-dealer, you! Aren't you the blue-eyed boy? There's just this one thing," and she rubbed her fingers and thumb together.

"Aw, c'mon, Alice, you can get it somewhere. Sell something, for hell's sake. Sell that piece of creek bed that's all stony, that don't grow nothing. Hell, I'd buy it off ya."

Aha.

Vera Jane, who had no kind of a poker face, went to the bathroom. Alice made a tower of her fists and rested her chin on it. She tried a feint. "You'll stay for supper?"

Robey shook his head.

"I thought you were s'posed to be cutting back." Another dodge; foiled. "You sell those chickpeas?" The garbanzos in question, about forty-thousand bushels, having languished in storage for more than a year. "You did? And now, instead of putting the profit aside for your old age, which is fast approaching," shaking her finger, "you're going off on a toot with it."

"Government'll just steal it if I don't."

Vera Jane came back with her layered headgear on, and Robey unfolded upward one hinge at a time. "I got just one thing to say to you, Alice—"

"That'll be the day."

"—and it's this: first of all, that's good hay ground high up; and two, down there where the house is, is good pasture. It's steep and shady, and you wouldn't want to live there, but it's got a well, and there's grass on the slopes all year round. Your market steers'd do real good there. And C, if you had as much sense as God give a gopher, you'd be jumping on it."

"Robey," said Vera Jane, objecting to God and gophers in the same sentence.

Alice held Robey's eye. "Much as I like my odds against a gopher, let me just ask, since you know so much about it, who owns the rest of the property? Who's the kindly landlord that's let them stay there all this while, selling dope for rent money?"

Robey coughed the name into his fist.

"Who?"

"Jerry Graeme."

Chapter Three

End of March, and the cowboy work started in earnest. Domingo Roque limbered up his rope arm, threw at fence posts, straw bales, the collies, the mortified cats, getting his eye in. Prompted, Alice put in some practice herself, and the yard resounded with the whoosh and thwack of the loops. The red mare, though sound again, was too big in foal to work, and Alice wondered what to give Domingo to ride. Skookum, of course, who had risen greatly in her estimation. But after that, there were only Cattywampus, talented but inclined to buck, and the two thoroughbred broodmares Raevonne and Three Cheers, both open this year but in soft condition, and without a grain of cow sense between them. Apart from the boarders, they were all she had.

"Y de ellos, ¿qué?" Domingo pointed his chin at Jerry Graeme's horses nosing along the creek at the bottom of their pen.

"Oh, those aren't ours. They belong to a guy who owns part of this place. I don't dare use them. If they got a ding on their legs or a scratch on their butts, he'd charge me the whole price of them, and they are not cheap animals."

"He don't use it?"

"Oh no," she said, sour. "They're like everything else of his. He buys the best and wrecks it or lets it rot."

Domingo thought this pretty poor, especially with regard to one of those horses, a stocky, hairy-legged grullo mustang who, when ropes began to sing and rattle on the shed yard, had come up eagerly to the fence, scenting the battle.

"He don't stay here, the guy? He don't help you?"

Acidly, "No, he does not, thank God. He's a son of a bitch. With any luck, you'll never meet him. Are you ready to ride? Let's get the racehorses down from their vacation resort."

There were eleven of them, and they clung to their freedom. The pastures where they spent the winter letting down from racing-fit condition covered two steep ridges uphill from the Standfast homeplace, with tiny rills trickling down between. The gates where they came down for their hay stood close to the yard. Sheltering thickets of sumac and alder lined the little creeks, and there were stands of fir higher up where they could get cover from the wind. The beauty of the site was the necessity for the horses to climb up and down to eat, up and down to drink, so that they kept fairly hard even in their time off. However, they also got to feeling pretty independent, and required careful herding, dogs left at home.

Domesticated in their heart of hearts however, they formed nice cohesive bunches once choused out of the brush. Two holdouts, impelled in the end by prey-species fear of isolation, came scrambling down on their own at last, and fed themselves into the lane of movable panels to the covered arena as if this were all their own idea. Domingo looped them then, one after another, and Alice put their halters on, chains over their noses to remind them of their duty. Stalled separately, they mostly lay down in the clean straw and rolled off a layer of mud before reacquainting themselves with automatic waterers, hay in nets, and grain in buckets.

This operation ate up the day. Domingo thought he had seldom had so much fun in his life. Even the loss of his gray horse and his truck ceased to pain him. If not for the burden of Graciela on his heart, he would have called himself a happy man.

"You didn't let him rope the racehorses?!" Aghast, Janet let birdseed run into the sink.

"'Course I did." Alice shook the feeder to make more room. "You feeding the finches or the garbage disposal?"

"But does he know how? They aren't steers!"

"He does know how, or he figured it out pretty quick. Didn't put a mark on them. He was giggling the whole time. Shall I put this out?"

"Not in your socks." Janet plunged down the steps and up her long backyard to the goldfinches' preferred spot among the mountain ash trees. Beyond them, beyond the unfledged lilac hedge, the ground kept on rising in a long smooth brown wave, steaming gently. Alice thought reflexively of her hay fields. Janet tromped back and kicked off her clogs.

"So he's turning out to be some use."

"Uh-huh."

"Well, shoot. He wears those big old spurs."

"So do I."

"But you take care not to hurt."

"So does he. That's a myth, you know, about Mexicans being cruel to their horses."

"Probably the same myth Robey thinks they were making on the Hashknife place." Janet snickered. Domingo Roque's way with livestock was not the real focus of her anxiety. "How are you intending to pay him?"

"Cash."

"That can't go on indefinitely. There have to be W-2 forms, W-4 forms, quarterly withholding—"

"Don't ask me. Not your business."

"—unemployment insurance, tax declarations, et cet'ra, et cet'ra," pouring wine and setting out shortbread.

"Don't ask, toots. I won't tell."

"Alice, you have no idea what you're dealing with."

"You misery," said Alice equably, taking a cookie. "How'd you like to be pinched really hard? Don't you dare take that superior tone with me."

Janet smiled and sipped. Alice put her left foot up on the chair adjacent to ease her back and drew her wineglass closer. Their mother had died when she was ten and Janet twelve; the sisters had been in each other's pockets ever since.

"You cannot report wages to the government," Janet orated, "either for withholding purposes or for tax deduction, without a valid Social Security number for the person being paid."

"Maybe he has a Social Security card."

"He probably does. But it's crooked, fake. Bought."

"How do you know?"

"Because he's illegal, sweetheart. We're pretty sure about that, aren't we?" Alice nodded, the helicopter episode stark in her mind. "Now, if you just go ahead and use his store-bought number to report, the government is going to say, 'Okay, will the real Melvin P. Glotz please stand up.' It might not happen the first year, but it will happen, believe me."

"But then how come it works for Robey? That harvest team of his, they come straight off the Petén, for sure. They barely speak Spanish, let alone English."

"Seasonal workers get a little different deal, see, the rationale being that they go home at the end of the season, don't draw on our social services and welfare benefits."

Alice brooded, bumping her knuckles against her chin. "Well then, how about . . . couldn't Domingo get a real, legitimate Social Security card? He ought to be getting FICA credit for his work, anyway." Janet shook her head.

"He would have to be a citizen of the United States, native born or naturalized, or a legal permanent resident alien, a green-card holder."

"So how does he get a green card?"

"Oh, Alice, Jesus!" Janet writhed with irritation. "Haven't I ever explained this to you? What do you think I'm always whining about, our students' problem? Look, it's perfectly simple: all he has to do is go back to Mexico, go to any American consulate for the application forms, submit the forms with a fee, two hundred bucks or so, and then wait eleven years for his visa number to come up."

"Eleven years!?"

"Mm-hm."

"Jesus Christ."

"In spades. That's why there are so many illegals. Push the short-bread this way; thanks."

"Oh, but we'll have to do something, won't we? Change the law or something. 'Cause that's making criminals of all these folks."

"Yeah, it is. We're cultivating a fine old permanent underclass here."

"So won't they . . . ?"

"Amnesty or something? I'd love to think so. But I sure wouldn't bet the farm on it." Alice heard, *bet my job, bet Philip's career.* "Listen, there's Phil. Come in here, you gotta see this."

As Philip's tread sounded on the porch, a young pied cat careened into the front hall, scrabbling on the hardwood. The front door opened.

"Mimi!" cried Philip, setting down his briefcase. The kitten danced forward on her hind legs, batting the air with broad six-toed forepaws and uttering glad cries. Philip squatted and she leapt into his arms, tremulous with purrs, thrust her flat triangular head under his beard, and kneaded his necktie.

"My God," murmured Alice.

"Mm."

"That's nauseating."

"Yes, if I were not such an easy keeper, I'd grow thin."

"Don't you give him, like, wifely affection or anything?"

"Can't get close enough. She has claws. 'Hello, darling,' said the long-suffering but recently supplanted spouse."

"Mimi, Mmmmimi," crooned Philip, rubbing the little creature's cheekbones, "has Mama been cruel? Taunted poor Mimi with her lack of thumbs?"

"She opens cupboards," said Janet aside, "hangs from doorknobs. Has to be locked out of the bedroom. *Despises* women, even Nan."

"Who does?" Nan came in from school, a frosting of big snowflakes on her chestnut mane.

"Mmmmimi."

"That little squirt gets between me and my father, she's roadkill. Hi, Aunt Roan."

Philip dumped the kitten briskly. "Good evening, womenfolks; hello, Standfast. Good to be home. Martini in the offing, my little endive?"

"I gotta chore," said Alice, pulling on her jacket.

"What? Won't whatsizname do them?"

"Well, one of us has to get dinner."

Janet made her eyes round. "He cooks too, this paragon? You amaze me. Does he clean up?"

"Well, no, Janet. He's a guy, after all." Snickering, Janet returned to the kitchen, and snickering, Alice went out to her truck. But she was depressed. The Domingo business—she and Janet were at odds. And Philip didn't know.

On Thursday, Domingo answered the phone. "Standfast," he had learned to say.

A male voice barked out, "Who the—? Alice?"

"Wait, please." He held out the phone to Alice, who put down her sandwich.

"Who the hell was that?" Baritone, cawing timbre. Alice's hands grew cold.

"Friend of mine. Hey there, Jerry. Long time, no hear."

"Didn't sound like the kind of friend you oughtta have. How long's this been going on?"

"Where you calling from?" she countered. She had known him, fought him off, since high school. His claim on Standfast was a bruise on the otherwise flawless apple of her possession.

"Listen, honey, I need you to do me a favor." Oh, when didn't he? "I need you to sell my horses and send me a check, real quick like a bunny. Got a pencil?"

"This'll be after you pay your board bill, right?" Twenty months! And not a lick of work out of him, or his horses. "It's up to about six thou."

"Jesus, Alice, see, there you go, breaking my balls! Jeez, what a ballbreaker. No wonder Vinnie dumped you. Don't you see, that is my *home*? I don't *pay* to keep my horses at my *home*."

"Everything on this place either works or pays rent. That's just how it is. Your horses eat but don't work. You can—"

"Okay, okay, okay, Jesus, what a pain in the ass. You really are a pain in the ass, Alice, you know that, don't you? Just keep one and sell the other two. Okay? Will that get you off my ass? And do it quick, I need . . . listen, they're champion stock; you damn better get top dollar, I'll come up there and kick your cute little ass. Got a pe—" Alice clicked off.

"Who that?" Domingo asked. She shook her head, still holding the phone.

It rang. "What happened? Can't you even work the phone, for fuck's sake?"

Good old Jerry.

"What address?" She didn't want to know, but—

"Box 908, Green River, Wyoming. You can figure out the zip, can—" Alice clicked off again, handed the phone to Domingo, took her lunch into the kitchen and dumped it in the trash. Vinnie, she thought. You wouldn't dare call Vincent "Vinnie" to his face, you twerp. You shadow-rider. Her armpits were wet, her ear ached from the pressure of the handset.

Domingo tactfully got another glass of juice. Her cold, ranting voice on the phone: he had not heard that before. She was very angry; also, he believed, afraid, her eyes slitted and her fingers whitely laced. After a while she looked up and read the tilt of his head.

"That was a guy named Jerry Graeme. Those are his horses, the ones we don't use. He owns, sort of owns part of this place. He plays poker for a living, I think. Anyway, he hangs around where people gamble, and I'm always expecting him to lose half of this place out from under me," with a laugh that was no laugh. "Well, he needs money, and he wants me to sell the horses. We'll have to work with them a little bit to tune them up for sale. I s'pose their papers are—" Glancing at a door that Domingo had never seen opened. "But!" brightening up, "I'm going to keep one of the horses for the board money he owes me. Let's go choose which one! No, let's get this part over with first."

Two steps up, an odd little hall with a cupboard at the end, and the door, which wasn't locked. Inside, a small room with windows on two sides, a double bed on an old-fashioned wooden bedstead. Alice dragged a chair to the closet, pulled a plastic file box from the shelf and handed it down to Domingo. Inside, she found the folder containing the registration papers, bills of sale, and performance records of Jerry Graeme's horses. She put the file back and closed the door carefully.

"He live here, these guy?" Shirts hanging in the closet and other signs of occupation, but the dust lay white on every surface. Whereas Alice kept the rest of the place in a state of military cleanliness.

Alice did not feel that she owed Domingo Roque an explanation of Jerry Graeme's interest in her alfalfa fields; in any case could not quite explain to herself how Jerry had maneuvered himself into the house after Allan's death, into the room, into the very bed her parents had shared. Like a cuckoo, she thought. Like a canker in a rose. His mere voice on the telephone spoiled her day. She had hoped and, after a year and a half of absence, allowed herself to believe that she would never have to deal with him again, apart from periodically forking over a quarter of her estimated profit on alfalfa via her accountant.

On the other hand, selling his horses off the place would loosen his grip fractionally.

Alice knew which one she wanted to keep, but thought she would see which Domingo favored, see if he confirmed her judgment.

Going down to the pens, Domingo asked, "Why he don't help you the ranch, the guy?"

"I don't need help," she rapped out by reflex and then, hearing how that must sound, backpedaled, "I mean, I don't need *his* help. He is no hand at all."

"Pues, he got good horse."

"Yeah, he does. He likes to spend money. But he doesn't like to work. Those horses were right spendy, muy caro. He played with each one for a month or two, but in the last couple years he hasn't laid a hand on any of them. He talks good. You ever hear the expression, 'big hat, no cows'?"

Domingo translated thoughtfully, frowned at the notion of dropping good horses in their prime, wasting their skills, diminishing their self-respect. "You don't like he."

"You bet I don't, slick. He's—" So many apt descriptions sprang to mind: a creepy, smarmy, delayed adolescent, a parasite, an alcoholic, a gambling fool, a waste of skin. But also, in his younger days, a charmer, handsome as the dawn, sweet talker, heartbreaker. Everybody's buddy. Till you knew him. "He's way more trouble than he ever was worth on this place," filling her pockets with windfall apples from a bin in the tack room. "Let's go look at his horses. Tell me which one I should keep."

Of the three, the mouse-dun mustang was the greenest. The others, a brown quarter-horse mare and a bold-colored Appaloosa gelding, had won their share of arena honors, calf roping and team roping. The mare had been bad-tempered and nippy when she came, but two years of doing nothing but walk uphill to eat and downhill to drink had cured her sore back; she accepted a snack graciously and allowed herself to be rubbed and stroked all over and to have her feet lifted. Alice thought her a shade too tall for ranch work, though ideal for rodeo. The gelding's great gift in competition had been consistency: out of the chute and on the calf in exactly the same way, same number of strides, time after time, no matter how the calf zigzagged or what the other roper did. A nice animal in spite of his sparse mane and tail, his pink muzzle, and the white sclera of his eye showing all around.

Two years of being let alone had not interfered with the mustang's domestication, apparently. When Domingo grabbed a hank of his mane and swung up bareback, after a snorty moment the youngster walked off calmly, guided by leg alone to circle and stop and turn back. Domingo slipped off and walked around him, approving the short loin and deep quarters, low hocks and flat boxy knees. The best thing about the critter was his feet, big and bell-round, the angles of the hoof and pastern parallel, a well-formed and substantial "understanding" that predicted soundness and a long working life. Like Alice, he hated the trend toward big stout horses on little teacup feet; such creatures had brief, unhappy careers and wound up in dog food cans, a shabby end.

"I like this," he said, knuckle-rubbing the cowlick between the grullo's eyes. "You think?"

"Yes, he's my choice. He doesn't know much yet, but—"

"No, pero, tiene ganas, you know? Entusiasmo. ¿Cómo se llama?"

"Mouse. Because of his color."

Domingo chuckled, "Ratón, Ratón." He found the place behind the girth where tickling caused the horse to sidestep. "You like organize these cow? Tomorrow you can start to learn."

"Where did you get those trout?" Philip leaned back as if to keep himself from licking the plate. "That's a nifty invention, that Andison Amandine."

Nan departed bedroomward, and Nick stood up and began to clear the table. ("How come Nannie doesn't have to fucking wash dishes?" Nick once asked Janet. "Because she's crying about her trigonometry." "If I cried about my homework, would I not have to?" "But lovey, you never do homework.")

"From Albertsons, and thank you. Philip."

"Mm?"

"Alice really feels like she can't manage Standfast by herself."

"She's admitting it? Good. The cape-and-tights routine was getting tiresome."

"Not in so many words. But the thing is, she wants to hire some help."

"The infamous J. Graeme, I gather, has never—?"

"No, and thank God. If only you knew. If you knew how many times he stood by while we two women struggled to do something, and sneered and smoked, and then waltzed in, 'Stand aside, girls, this is man's work,' and then absolutely screwed it up!"

"Does Alice have someone in mind, then? You aren't thinking of giving up teaching—"

"No!" convulsively. "It's that stray she pulled out of a snowbank last month. She's been working with him and thinks he's capable, and of course he has the virtue of being on the spot."

"And the disadvantage?"

"He's a mojado," Nick blurted, before Janet could frame her answer.

"Nicky, you do not know that!"

"It's pretty obvious, Ma. Nannie says he's a good hand, though; better than her."

Janet threw down her napkin and refilled her wineglass.

"Is that the source of your unease, my love?"

"You bet it is, old Philip. I'm afraid if it got out, not only would Alice catch a fine, but I'd be fired and you'd be disbarred, or reprimanded or something."

Philip steepled his fingers lawyerlike, and examined the ceiling. "It's my belief that as long as the employee is getting a fair deal, it won't be a problem. It would be any whiff of exploitation that would do the damage. Anyway, I'm pretty thoroughly firewalled off from the ranch. If there's danger, and I'm guessing there isn't much because it's only one person, but if there is, it's probably more to your position. And Alice's exchequer of course."

"But Phil. It's— Never mind the danger of getting caught; it's against the law, isn't it?"

"It would be," said Philip, "if she weren't trying to legalize him."

"But that's the point—she can't."

"No, love," unsteepling and leaning forward to polish off the last of the wine, "the point is that she be seen to try."

Janet felt she was being overscrupulous and a pain in the neck in the matter of Domingo Roque, yet she could not see a way out of her problem. On the one hand, she begrudged no immigrant a job or an education, legal or illegal. Green cards, she believed, were few and far between among her students, but neither she nor her colleagues in the department wanted to know the immigration status of any individual in the free English classes. They were teachers, not enforcers. Also, those three women shared a deep appreciation of the nation's immigrant roots. "Immigration is our lifeblood," Janet once wrote in a letter to the editor of the Walla Walla paper. A letter that had drawn a flurry of rabidly illogical replies, and one moderately scary phone call.

At the same time, and on the other hand, she believed that what drew immigrants to the country, beyond the primary and pressing need to make some money, was the rule of law. Nobody thought that the guarantee of civil rights operated perfectly everywhere and all the time. But most newcomers seemed to trust in its existence and durability. And so, what happened to their sense of the Law when they were (a.) tacitly permitted to flout it, and (b.) publicly punished when they called on it for help?

A veteran foot soldier of the local Democratic cohort, Janet got out the vote and poll-watched, and barred the classroom door with her body lest any newly naturalized student leave without putting into her hands a completed voter registration form. Apathy about such duties eroded the rock of democracy, she felt; ignorance undermined it. And the open and customary breaking of any law, even a silly one like the one against marijuana, acted like acid on the rock. That Nan and Nick and their friends toked up in the high school basement drove Janet crazy; not because she thought it any worse for their health than beer, but because doing so undermined their sense of both the power and the fragility of the rule of law.

After her fourth-hour class she sat at her desk and diagrammed her dilemma in two columns headed Pro and Con. Under Pro, she wrote:

1. Alice needs help.
2. Domingo needs a job.
3. Domingo is a better-than-average hand.
4. Domingo wants to work for what Alice can pay.
5. Alice can pay standard wages.

Under Con she wrote:

1. It's against the law to knowingly employ illegals.
2. Nobody would believe we don't know the law.
3. Persistent, widespread disobedience undermines all laws.
4. I am in fact sure that Domingo Roque is illegal.

Below the two columns she wrote Other, and under that: "I am not willing to give up teaching to help Alice run the ranch." Then she scratched out "run" and wrote "keep." Then she scratched out "Alice" and wrote "us."

After work she drove on through Waitsburg to Iwalu and on up to Standfast, and found Alice standing in the muddy yard with her hands full of lists. She was tearing some up, folding and redistributing others, occasionally pulling new scraps and tatters of paper out of her pockets. She had on her army surplus jacket of olive-brown wool, a Christmas present from the Westons, which she liked for its many pokes and nooks.

"Hey, sweet-hot!" she sang out as Janet came along, minding where she walked in her school boots. "What brings you up on a weekday?"

"Got a problem." Alice, she thought, looked pretty good for a woman with the whole weight of the ranch on her shoulders; not just her high outdoor color, but the spring in her step, as if she expected to get her day's work done with some bounce left over. "Your new hand around?"

"Yonder he comes." Domingo Roque strolled up the yard, swinging a big loop, sweeping it over his head with a slow wristy motion. "You have a kinda Smokey Bear face on. Is your problem about immigration status, by any chance?"

"It's your problem too, dear, whether you— Buenas tardes, Señor Roque. ¿Se siente bien?"

"*I'm good, thanks. And you, ma'am? And the family?*"

"*We're all well, thanks to God. How's it going with the expectant mare?*"

"*More expectant day by day,*" carefully coiling and tying his rope, "*though the boss knows more than I about this.*"

"She looks ripe to me," confirmed Alice, "in spite of her tribulations. We're taking Silka and the Mouse up the swayback ridge—come with? You can have Tommy."

"Oh, I can't, Alice, look at me," gesturing at her working clothes.

"Yes, come. Those boots'll do; come on, Yanny, you haven't been out in days."

"I have to go make dinner. Besides, the horses will be mud from end to end."

"C'mon. We'll tack up for you. You won't get a speck on you."

Janet really wanted to go. She said, "Okay. But first let me ask: Domingo Roque, do you have a Social Security card?"

"Sure—" without hesitation, putting his arm through the coiled lariat and fishing out his wallet.

"There you go," said Alice to Janet, "no problem."

"—I have two," and he produced them. Alice tossed her slips of paper into the breeze, and Janet said, "There you go. Big problem."

"What I do wrong?" he said, mystified. One had to have a Social Security card to work in the North; everybody knew that. One of his cards had been a present for his sixteenth birthday. The other was his father's.

"You don't," enquired Janet gently, "by any chance have a green card?"

"Ay, no!" Such things were very costly; besides, one had to deal with criminals to get them. He looked uneasily from one sister to the other. What could be wrong now? He trusted Alice, for several reasons, one being that her need of him was so clear. But the other one?

"Domingo," said Alice, holding Janet with her eye, "would you mind bringing up Silka and Mouse and Tom Fool, please? We'll go for a ride up the hill." He went, worried; part of his mind automatically filing away "would you mind."

"You can't pay him in cash year-round—"

"I'll ask John R"—the accountant—"about it. Purely theoretically, of course."

"—because you can't withhold FICA, and he can't file a tax return, and every year he doesn't file, he's in contravention of federal law."

"Ten years no worse than one year, then; as well be hanged for a sheep as a lamb."

"Ten times worse, Roan. And it's not just him that'll get hanged."

"Nah." But Alice paused. "You might get hanged, you mean?" Janet looked away and sighed. Did all her civic religion come down to this, that she feared being caught and punished?

"Did you ask Philip about it, purely theoretically?"

"Asked him straight out."

"Uh-huh." That was how they were, the Westons. "How did he take it?"

"Curiously unworried. That is, he doesn't think he's in the line of fire, though I might be. You'd have to pay, if caught, and of course they would shunt young Señor Roque down south of the Line in a heartbeat. But the against-the-law aspect doesn't seem to bother him. Which is odd, Philip being Philip."

"Odd. 'Course, he's from Wenatchee"—apple country, with illegal labor the bedrock of the orchard industry, taken for granted, a matter for no comment whatever. Janet felt more and more like the heroine of a story titled *My Fight Against Common Sense.*

Domingo towed the three horses up, and he and Alice got to work with the shedding blades and currycombs. Clots of mud and winter-coat hair flew wide. Janet stood back, not tempted to help but itching to ride; she so seldom got a chance during the school term.

It was all uphill to the swayback ridge behind the homeplace, not steep but steady; they walked it since two of the horses and one of the riders were soft. The big eventer, Silka, who boarded at Standfast each winter, now needed to begin legging up for the coming competition season. Silka's real name was long, Germanic, pretentious, and registered in the Hanover studbook, but she herself had no notion of winning or losing. She just liked galloping across country, jumping down every obstacle she came to. Fast, deep, and honest: that was Silka. Also, she produced a very nice foal every three years or so for her owner Mary Friel, who loved her devotedly, as did Alice, to whom she was a regular source of income, a great trail mount, and an occasional schoolmistress in dressage.

Alice told Janet why Domingo was taking on the Mouse, and Janet moaned. Anything having to do with Jerry Graeme gave her the willies. There was nothing to hope for there, except that the kind of excitement Jerry Graeme fed on would never become such a feature of life in Walla Walla County as to attract him home.

Janet had left her with this: "He won't even have a driver's license."

"Why not, for hell's sake?" thoroughly exasperated.

"Because you have to show a legitimate Social Security card or a green card, which we know he doesn't have. What if he got stopped in our truck? Which he very well might. A brown man in a nice pickup: a cop target. And there he'd be, caught dead to rights in the Standfast rig, our brand right there on the door panel."

Alice took her point, dadgummit. Maybe this hiring wasn't worth the risk. But the thought of going back to single-hand made her sag at the knees. Of course, she might hire someone else, someone legal, but who? Old-fashioned ranch hands were a dying breed. And then Domingo filled the bill so completely! There must be a way to work this out, there *must* be. She willed it to be so, clashing the pots in the sink, determined.

Domingo, watching television half-asleep, turned his attention from the high-braced bosoms and sequined sombreros of Univisión to the clatter in the kitchen. Now what? The sister's visits seemed to put some kind of twist on la patrona. He clicked off the remote, stood up yawning, and monkeyed incompetently with the woodstove.

"Domingo," said Alice, rolling down her sleeves and taking the bull by the horns, "do you have a driver's license?"

"Of course."

"Of course!" with a slightly deranged giggle. "Please don't say you have two."

Domingo darted her a look. As it happened, he did have two. He showed her the most recent one, the California one that gave his name as Juan D. Roque M., an address in the Imperial Valley, and his uncle Damián's date of birth, which, if Alice had noted it, would have surprised her a lot as it made him sixty-five years old.

"That's great. That is way cool." He didn't understand her elation, or her words, exactly. "Let's have some ice cream." But what were they celebrating?

Alice meant to explain but could not get the terms of the problem straight in her own mind. So she wound up talking about Janet in a more familial way than she intended, or was wise, probably, to Domingo who was after all a stranger. "She wanted to be a teacher from the age of four. If anything happened to prevent her from teaching, you know, I don't know what she'd do. She feels about her job like I feel about this place."

Greek to him. But he used the opportunity to satisfy himself on one point. "You can tell me please why Mrs. Janet she speak too good español?"

"Why she . . . ? Ah. Because of her students. A lot of them are from Mexico, so they teach her. She teaches them English, and they teach her Spanish. She took French first, at school, but she really learned her Spanish on the street, as they say. She's pretty good, pretty fluent, isn't she?"

"She speak excellent!" sincerely. Riskily, a point nearer the bone: "Why doesn't she like me? 'Cause I think she wants me to leave."

Brought to the question in spite of herself, Alice made a try. "It's nothing personal, believe me. You probably know, it's illegal here to hire people who don't have legal status, green cards. The Migra will prosecute the employer. *She, my sister, have anxious for her job, for the situate of her man. Her job the more, because pays her the government of the state. If Migra discovers you employed by us, she fears scrambled eggs for the family. Also, she dislikes to fracture, I mean, traverse any law. I speak it so foul, pardon me.*"

"*No, very well! Everything is clear now. I was only laughing for the pleasure of hearing my mother tongue. But what about you? Is it dangerous for you too?*"

"Well, yeah, I'll get fined. Plus, I'll lose a good hand, which will put me in a world of hurt."

He took his ice cream dish to the sink. "*You said you didn't need help, I remember. Maybe it's too much risk. If you say go, I go,*" his back to her. Don't say go, he thought.

"Stay," she said promptly. "Your kind of help—it's hard to come by. And since you showed me your driver's license, I can't believe there will be any problem. Just please don't tell me how you got it."

Juan Damián Roque Muñoz, Domingo's father's elder brother, crossed the Border west of Tecate in Abuela Refugio's belly. The night was moonless; Refugio rode her husband's black horse, unshod and nearly silent on the deep dust of the road.

"*Wait, woman, wait.*" Damián senior padded ahead, leading the horse. "*Be strong, be patient.*"

Eight miles by the back roads, groaning and sweating in labor, to Dulzura where in a church basement clinic Damián junior came into the world a native-born citizen of the United States. The grandparents were never able to repeat this trick, Refugio's next three babies coming too quick for travel, and when Damián junior overdosed and died on the wrong side of San Ysidro in his evil-living fifties, all his documents including the birth certificate gained by such courage and craft disappeared, lost to the family.

At the time of this death, however, his nephew Juan Domingo

Roque Menchú had in his possession a still-valid Texas driver's license in his uncle's name, abbreviated Juan D. Roque M. in the Mexican fashion. Eighteen and working as an exercise rider at the Laredo fairgrounds at the time, Domingo instantly stopped shaving his upper lip, cultivated bristling Francisco Villa-style bigotes like Damián's in the picture, and "renewed" the license. Nobody noticed the oddity of the birth date. He had renewed ever since, state by state, with an apparently valid license in hand. He kept Damián's original, for sentiment, and because he might be able to sell it sometime. He no longer affected the mustache, though. Graciela had liked it too much.

Janet gave up the fight. In her heart, she doubted that the Immigration Service would bestir itself to search out one lone wire jumper, unless he proved to be a drug mule, or unless somebody with a grudge ratted him out. A traffic stop would hardly do the trick; Domingo had a license, the Standfast vehicles had insurance, and local law-enforcement deeply desired not to make trouble for themselves by trespassing on Migra turf. Pay your ticket and go on your way, that was their attitude. They were even likely to add, "Have a nice day," which threw immigrants of all nations into fits of hilarity.

And Alice needed help and Domingo needed work, and that might be sufficient unto the day. And to settle the matter, she backed herself off by considering that she ought to spend her afternoons and weekends working on the ranch if her tender social conscience and deep desire for moral perfection did not allow her keeping her big yap shut on the subject of Alice's alambrista.

Domingo missed his dally and swore, and the cow ran off with his rope. But she plunged in among the others, trod on the trailing line, and threw herself. Lay there, the whole bunch moaning in chorus around her. He handed Alice his rein, got down, and strolled slowly into the gang, giving them time to disperse. The down cow's buddy stared at him. Scraped a forefoot, lowered and thrust forward her heavy head and bawled, showing her eye-whites.

Domingo stopped and looked at her sideways. *"Come on, old lady,"* singsong, *"come over here now. Nobody's going to hurt your girlfriend."* He bent down for the rope, still chatting to her, and worked his way along it. The cow on the ground raised her head for a look. Deciding he was not a problem, she rolled onto her chest and stood up, back end first. He scratched her high up on her back a little bit, and around her ears. After a minute he took the bottle of Cut-Heal out of his pocket, unscrewed the applicator, and daubed the cut on her elbow. Took the rope off, coiled it, and hung it on his shoulder. The cow and her chum shambled off together. He turned toward Alice, who came trotting up leading Skookum. Instead of stopping to mount, he caught the horn and swung on up, startling both horses into a lope, his hat falling back and his long hair shiny and flying.

Pretty, Alice thought, and then checked herself. And then thought, What?! Hey, can't a person even just appreciate—? Jeez.

Chapter Four

THEY SPENT A COUPLE OF DAYS SLICKING UP ROSEMARY KEITH'S racehorses. Pulled their manes, banged their tails, and helped along the shedding out of their winter coats. Put them into the covered arena two at a time for exercise, and ponied them up and down the yard between Tom Fool and Skookum to remind them of their business in life. The rough ground on which they wintered represented a tradeoff: on one hand, it was steep, trappy, rocky, and poor in forage, the kind of place where horses used to combed tracks and flat paddocks could easily hurt themselves out of ignorance or careless high spirits. On the other, the same qualities ensured that, as they grazed between feeds of hay, every step they took required more effort of mind and body than flatland browsing. So if they didn't break their legs or wrench their backs (and none had so far), they came back to work in the spring alert, snorty, and with a retained muscle tone, a step ahead on their way to racing fitness.

This spring, as usual, not counting a few nicks and dings, everybody had come through the winter in good shape, except for one little brown gelding. Alice got Domingo to look at him with her.

"Uh-huh," as the horse passed down the long side of the arena at a bounding trot, head and tail up, nervous about being alone with the two-leggers. "De acuerdo. Is a little bit short, this—" pointing to his own left shoulder. This was her opinion too: shoulder sore or wither sore, though the horse had come off the track in October believed to have strained a tendon. Still, he moved more freely now, whatever his complaint, and Alice felt that her client would be satisfied with his progress.

A couple of days before the Keith string was to transfer down to Rosemary's place on the creek flats west of Walla Walla, Rosemary's vet came up to vaccinate them. He was Alice's preferred vet too, Mike Sage, and he brought along the new intern in his practice, a fair-haired sprite named Mindy. To whom Domingo, having shaken hands with Sage, gave a careful three fingers in case something might break. Mindy knew her stuff, however, substituting leverage and tact for height and brawn as they dealt out four-way boosters to Rosemary's racers as well as Alice's working stock.

Since the vet was on the spot, Alice asked him to take a squint at Domingo's horse. The mare looked just right to Alice's eye—big, slow, and sleepy, her social life winding down and her appetite huge. But just to be on the safe side.

"Chugging along normally," Sage confirmed, stripping off his latex gauntlet. "Due next month? Yep. Are you worried about her for some reason?"

"Not very. Just, she got lost in that blizzard at the beginning of February, was out, what, four days?" Domingo shrugged noncommittally; he hadn't figured it out yet. "Around four days, and she covered a fair distance, say eighty, ninety miles, with no food, water, or shelter." Mike Sage looked like he didn't believe her, and she didn't blame him. "So she had a right to lose it. But it seems like she didn't."

"Nope, she sure didn't lose it. Look there." They could all see something like a dimple in reverse traverse the swell of the mare's belly. It started underneath by the bulging milk vein on her near side, moved up diagonally toward the ribs, and vanished. The stroke of a tiny hoof. Everyone turned smiling to Domingo, standing speechless with delight and dread like a father-to-be.

This day of veterinary work, plus feeding and mucking out, plus riding herd and hand-feeding two calves, would make a nice round day's work, thought Domingo, reckoning without Alice's lists. Himself, he had no use for lists, even mental ones: proper work led one onward, task into task, in a natural rhythm, satisfying even when exhausting. He disliked schedules and timetables. Americans were obsessed with time, blocks and strips of it, quarter hours, designated minutes. It was sad. If you like your work, why crank it around to fit the clock? he wondered. If you don't like your work, then you are a slave, of course, and that is a different matter. But to treat one's own self as a slave, the patrón mind driving the peón body, seemed to him perverse.

It was evident to him that throughout his working life north of the Line, work was more closely supervised and regulated but, he believed, less effective than in Mexico. On a schedule, even one as traditional and largely tacit as a racetrack stable routine, some things did not get done, went unnoticed, because other things had to be done or were thought to have to be done at certain times. Not that he would ever leave a horse standing hot or half-groomed. But he might, having found a burr of plastic on the inside of a halter strap, take the halter away to fix it after putting the horse up, and so not be found raking the alley at the correct time, and catch hell.

He liked to remember working with his father when he was young and still going to school at Lomas Chatas: that had been good. Nobody scheduled his father; he was the mero-mero, the caporal. And Fidel in those days never, scarcely ever told Domingo what to do. Domingo copied his father, like his shadow at noonday.

In general, he liked remembering that part of his life, of his education. Learning came without words; correction too: what he had done wrong would be swiftly undone, the correct way shown. He could remember himself a baby almost, standing between Fidel's knees while big hands tore apart a length of látigo he had braided, one hand coming up quick but not ungentle to scrape the tears from his cheeks. And then showing the right way to braid, giving the piece back, taking it again and showing the right way, giving it back. At ten or so, he had learned how to take off a loose horseshoe in one pull, not leaving it dangling for the beast to quick its foot on, learned it almost in his father's lap, the hoof on his own knee supported by Fidel's knee, both their hands on the tongs. He had not had the strength then, but he learned the trick, the technique, and so at twelve he could do it alone.

"What's wrong, buck?" said Alice. Thinking of his father made his face hard.

"Nottin. We finish here? Uh-oh. That list."

"Yup. Lost without my list. Let's go look at the grass on the Dogleg and the hay ground up that side, see how much thistle we have to pull. It's only three o'clock. We can ride Silka and Mouse and pack Ricky and Effy, kill two birds with one stone."

Killing birds with stones: a mug's game in Domingo's opinion. Admitting to himself that it was not rigidity in planning the work that bothered him about the boss. In truth, she tended more to his own circuitous and contingent method. Not the scheduling but the extent, the fucking duration! The list always had another item! And she had more than one list! Her jacket pocket was like the jug in the story that kept filling itself with milk. He came within a hair of complaint. Outworked by a woman? Not he! But as the sun grew stronger, the list grew longer. What would this job be like in July? Santo Dios.

Packing the three-year-olds, now, that was new to him. Neither of the colts had been ridden yet, as far as he knew. He would have been on them at two, not for work but to teach them their duty. Alice just led them around the place behind Tom Fool or Silka, mature horses with both physical weight and the authority of high herd-status. Now she wanted the youngsters to carry stock saddles weighted with sacks of bran. She wanted them to stand quietly, tied to trees, to stand hobbled without a fuss, to balance light loads, in general to manage themselves and their burdens alertly and sensibly uphill and down. Not to bolt when pheasants burst up out of the ryegrass; not to root for a nibble at every gate halt. Much ado about little, was Domingo's assessment, not realizing what his neutral expression gave away.

Eloquent silence, Alice thought. Though possibly there was nothing but echoing space between those long flat-set ears. She doubted this, however; the guy seemed bright enough. He remembered instructions, picked up routines, closed gates, turned off lights, put away tools. Her slightly compulsive rulishness might not suit his natural bent, but it represented a deep strain of her own character. Alice knew herself well, knew that if Domingo had not been willing to do things her way, there would have been no comfort.

There were two gates before the Dogleg, solid six-barred metal ones with sturdy posts, none of your barbwire-and-two-sticks traps. Silka, dressage-court diva though she was, showed her good ranch skills, side-passing for Alice to open these, taking Ricky on his lead line with her. Domingo had more to do to close them. The Mouse, though willing, didn't yet know to move crisply away from the leg, and as he stood irresolute, shifting his haunches and flicking his ears, Effervesce took the opportunity to dip his head toward the grass for a snack. Effy was stolid but hungry; also tall and heavy. Each rooting dive yanked Domingo off balance, spoiling the Mouse's focus on his lesson.

Finally Domingo shook off his right stirrup and dealt Effy a terrific toe-kick behind the cinch. The colt leapt forward with a pistol-shot fart, hit the end of his lead, swapped ends, and wound up facing the Mouse, red-nostrilled, white-eyed. What happened!? Was I struck by lightning!? Alice doubled over the horn, laughing. Domingo returned to his gate lesson, and Effy spent the rest of the expedition eyeing the heavens.

A long trot up the Dogleg let the colts feel the bran sacks flopping like novice riders; a twisty track beside the creek brought them all within sight of the sweep of the high hay fields. They tied the young horses in a grove of mossed and lichened apple trees, the remains of some vanished homesteaders' hopeful orchard, and leaving them calling forlornly, trotted up onto the open ground. The view from here was, to Alice's mind, sublime. Long, long smoothly congruent slopes of the foothills rolled and plunged rhythmic as surf down toward the big river; to the south, the level rampart of the Oregon plateau glowed gray-amethyst as the sunshine weakened. Pausing at a ridge of stone like the spine of a buried dragon, Domingo leaned forward to feel between the Mouse's forelegs: barely damp. Not too soft, this little horse. He himself was enjoying the ride, glad to get up off the yard and out where you could see around you. Alice was too, though by counting and multiplying the patches of Canadian thistle and yellow star thistle as they went along, she had reached a fairly depressing conclusion about the cultivation task facing her this season.

"Where, how far extend this rancho? Up there also?"

"Right to the top behind us," thinking of the volcanic Circ up there. Should that go to hay this year, or pasture for the replacement heifers? "And down to the road there, and beyond it to the second line, the second ridge you can see on the other side."

A fair piece of country, he thought, but broken and dark. Not like Lomas Chatas, where the hills were bare and pale, the wide plains all shades of green. A different smell on the wind here too, damp, sharp with pine. As he still did every once in a while, he felt his guts twist with longing for home. Querido México, mi cielito lindo, golden at this distance. Nostalgia, untrustworthy.

"Y el Columbia, ¿dónde está?"

"See that ridge where the radio tower is? And see the hill behind it shaped like"—she always thought of the shape of a young breast—"the pointed hill, straight on the left side and round on the right? The river runs between the ridge and the hill. That pointed butte is on the west side, it's the edge of Horse Heaven."

Domingo translated. "That will be a good place."

"Not much water. Not as good as this."

"Is more flat?"

"Yeah, it is. But this place . . . if I can make a living here," she leaned over, ran a hand under her cinch. "I will lie, cheat, and steal to keep this place. Kill for it, even."

Domingo stayed there, looking, as she turned her horse back. Marking the river in his mind. He had to get his hands on a map.

Janet came up on Saturday with her bull-hide gloves to help them pull thistle. Alice had already gone out to the hay ground, leaving Domingo to chore, so she rode up with him, taking Bel and Glen and carrying a picnic lunch in their saddlebags. He was as silent as a man could be, without discourtesy.

"You know the way, I see," Janet observed at the second gate.

"We rode up here yesterday, ma'am, to look at the crop ground."

"Ah. And the ground, how does it seem?"

"Lots of bad plants; the boss seemed depressed about their quantity and variety."

"Oh dear, not surprising. The thistle gains on us year by year. May we speak informally? My name is Janet. Domingo, yours? Your dun pony is slicking up a treat."

"He's a springy little model, all right. Not mine, sorry to say. Belongs to that guy who doesn't live here, whatsizname."

"This is the one Alice is keeping? Why did she choose him, do you know?"

Domingo believed that the choice had been his, but didn't mention it: *"He takes an interest in the cows. Also, he's a good shape for the work."*

"He sure is. So, till your red horse comes back to work—"

"This one, yes. And your tobiano, chubby though he is. The boss is generous with horses." Afterward he wondered at the speed with which he found himself facilely using the informal word forms to Janet Weston without any sense of distance at all, as if they were long acquainted. He was even letting these women call him by his nombre de bautizo, his real name, which was dangerous since he was working under his uncle's papers. Alice had read it on the red mare's registration document. He had been too confused to correct her when it first arose, and now it was too late, would draw attention. *"About the boss, a personal question?"* Janet nodded blandly, expecting "Where is her man?"

"Why does she wait to get on her young horses until the third year? Because at two, their bones are hard, and their minds are still soft."

Janet grinned privately. That was perhaps just where-is-her-man in a different guise. She explained, *"Notice that those two colts are warmbloods, know the breed? For jumping cross country, and for high school figures. Very big, and as a result slow to grow. Their knee joints don't fully close until they are four."*

"But even so, why wait till they have all their teeth and a lot of smart-ass ideas? She's just asking for a fight."

"Well, she would be if she really didn't touch them till they were three. But we've been working with them since they hit the ground. They know a lot: how to pony and pack, stand for shoeing and bathing, get in and out of trailers. They can pull the harrow when we drag the arena. They carry all kinds of tack, and of course we've sat on them a few times. Everything but ride them for work, really."

"Thus my question, all the more," polite but firm.

"Well, brother, till you came, she was alone out here after our father died. Nobody around to scrape her up off the dirt if she got ditched." They had reached the foot of the creekside trail. The Mouse showed off his new trick with the gate to an appreciative audience of Janet and collies. She didn't think she had convinced Domingo Roque about their breaking method, but had no intention of trying to explain the Jerry Graeme situation to him, whom she hardly knew. Far less Alice's divorce from Vincent Greer. None of his business, any of that; let him think of her sister as a mule if he thought of her at all, except as the Boss.

Smoke rising in a milky column guided them to Alice at the top of the first field; she had a green-stick fire going in the far corner. Skookum called, and she turned as Tom Fool answered, and waved her hat. She had the gray gelding rigged up to a bright-blue tarp that, when heaped high with uprooted thistle plants, she could fold over and tie, and let him drag to the fire. This field was almost cleared, and Alice picked up her pace a little as she pulled up the last of the pretty yellow-flowered star thistles with their needlelike thorns.

"One good thing," she said as they drew rein, "the purple ones seem to be squeezing out the goddam star." Straightening up, a clump in either hand, "Hey, peach," and to Domingo, "You brought the other tarp; great. Did you bring lunch?" Domingo pointed to the saddlebags.

"Outstanding. Sweep, put that down, it's dead. You nasty dog. Go away; brush your teeth."

It occurred to Domingo, sharing lunch on a spread-out tarp upwind of the fire, that by far the most bizarre aspect of the situation was that he had never stood in such relation to any norteamericano as he seemed to have fallen into with these sisters. They treated him familially, like a nephew or a young cousin (except that in speaking Spanish the younger always used the respectful forms; why?), talking to him and across him without reserve about Nan and Nick, about Janet's husband, the ranch's financial outlook, Janet's classes and colleagues, Alice's neighbors, everything. Even about himself:

"Domingo, you have family around here?"

"No."

"They're back in Mexico?"

"No here, no in Mexico," grazing the sharp edge of a lie, sucking water from a plastic bottle.

A slight pause, and Alice said comfortingly, "Well, it's not like you have no family: this dog has adopted you," Glen having crept by quarter inches into his lap. "And 'course you belong to Standfast now, so Janet's quit worrying about your immigration status, haven't you, Yanny?"

"Pretty much. You aren't very worried about the Migra, are you, 'mano?"

He wasn't at the moment, not while Graciela had an appetite for his money, though he didn't care to talk about that either.

"And of course as far as the law goes, Alice would lie, cheat, and steal for Standfast—"

"As I mentioned yesterday, you remember. Orange or apple?"

"Not that we aren't going to explore every avenue toward legalizing this guy. I'd love to hear that he's married to a citizen or a permanent legal resident, for example."

"Why?" said Alice. "What good would that do? Here," cuffing Domingo on the back, "apple down the air pipe? Drink some water. What difference would that make to his status?"

"A bunch. A citizen spouse can apply to change an alien spouse's status to permanent resident, get a result in about nine months' time. Green-card-holding spouse can do the same. Takes a little longer; less than two years, though."

"Way better than eleven years, holy smoke. I s'pose people marry for the green card fairly often."

"I reckon they do. Reckon we should be shopping for a citizen wife for our young friend here."

Kidding, of course. Halfway across the next field, getting the better of a shallow-rooted Canada thistle taller than he was, he convinced himself that they were teasing, and his hackles eased down. Steady, man. Te estaban tomando el pelo. Just kidding.

"The racehorses are going home today." Alice consulted an inky paper napkin that ruffled in the chill green-scented breeze. She stuffed the napkin into a back pocket. "Let's get them slicked up and looking like winners."

"Okay. You mind tell me what also say those list today?"

"Break down the movable pens, for one thing, and we ought to drag the arena; Arlene comes with her students tonight, remember. Look at the calves, of course. Why, buck? You got plans? Or are you getting as obsessive as me?"

There, now. That type of comment. He did not know how to take her, or how she took him. At times she treated him like an honored guest, at times like one of the collies. Never did she seem to accept him at his own valuation. But that was all right; he was used to that, living in the North. In a way, it was better so. He felt anonymous, almost invisible, and he preferred that distance, the uninvaded space in his head. Used to solitude, armored in it.

Though, when he worked with Alice, the feeling of being separate thinned out. And this worried him somewhat. It felt like a letting down, a slackening of sinews. The constant sense of threat, nearly subliminal after so much time north of the Line: was it passing off, leaving him unguarded? Not in general, no; just up here, with her. Working at Standfast, he sometimes felt light, released. He dreamed of horses that changed color as he rode, of orchard ladders going up into the clouds. Was he worried about not being worried? Good God.

The next time they went to Walla Walla, he bought a little grifa, smoked it in the evening after the last check on the stock. The Free Mexican Air Force flying at low altitude. It didn't help. Although he was not sure what help he wanted.

Silka went away on a Saturday, in maroon traveling boots and a quilted blanket to match, in a maroon and silver Circle J trailer, double high and double wide to contain her amplitude, with a tack room and bunk beds built in. Mary Friel's pickup, too, was maroon and silver, with a crew cab. Altogether, Domingo had never laid eyes on such a fancy rig. The truck alone must have been worth, well, God knew what.

"I'm sorry she's go," he said to Alice, watching the fancy combination trundle the mare away down the back road. "Es muy amable, you know?"

"She classes the place up, doesn't she?"

"Funny thing about her: she's stout, like a stockhorse, but you get that bouncy feeling, like the thoroughbreds have," jerking a thumb over his shoulder.

"You got it, kiddo. The engine's in the back with that critter, definitely."

Meanwhile, Mary Friel having handed Alice a check for board fees, and Rosemary Keith having sent one, the ranch's finances seemed pretty robust, so Alice left Domingo in charge and chugged into Walla Walla with Philip Weston to consult their accountant about their Byzantinely complex joint tax arrangements. John R tended to be offhand about matters that caused Alice to lie awake and sweat. She just thanked her stars for Philip, whose preferred mode in such an interview was interrogative silence, and who never let up on John R until he felt sure that Alice understood matters thoroughly. She was very likely to accede to some plan of John R's in a state of panicky semicomprehension, otherwise, and then go home resolved to give up chocolate, take on another boarder, and turn down the thermostat out of sheer fundamental pessimism.

Silly sacrifices of this type, what Philip called voluntary misery, did the ranch no earthly good but undermined Alice's mental health insidiously. Philip Weston had great faith in his sister-in-law's sanity—her head ruled her heart a good deal more firmly than Janet's did, for example—but he and Janet confided to each other their anxiety that Alice in her devotion to Standfast and its maintenance and improvement sometimes got too tired to look after herself, too tired even to eat. Would finish shifting hay onto the flatbed at eight o'clock, say, and decide to clean the Clydesdales' harness before going up to eat dinner, and then take a last turn around the yard finishing up odds and ends, and at ten, no longer hungry, fall up the stairs to her bed, and rouse out at five to start again, too famine-struck to want breakfast.

Janet faced down her troubles with food, Alice with work. In times of stress, Janet made almond chicken with hot greens; Alice painted the porch. Janet, as a result of this, looked younger than her years, a good solid double handful of a woman, while Alice especially in the last two years had grown gaunt, and her face had gained a decade. At her insurance physical the previous October, she had weighed in at one hundred seventeen pounds, frightening herself. Five foot seven, waistless and broad-shouldered: one seventeen was no proper weight for an adult of cobby conformation. What would become of her, she had cautioned herself, what would become of the ranch if she got too weak to work? If she grew faint and hypoglycemic and fell off the tractor, who would find her? Nobody, certainly not before the tractor ran itself into the creek or snagged down a fence line, and Standfast could not afford such setbacks.

So she had set herself to take in nourishment. She put mealtimes on her list, made extra spaghetti and scalloped spuds so as to have microwavable leftovers; hard-boiled a dozen eggs each Sunday. Stored dried fruit, chocolate-covered peanuts, and a couple of quarts of double-chocolate milk in the tack-room refrigerator along with the horse vitamins, worm paste, and vials of vaccines. These measures had gradually taken effect: she started to sleep better and feel less frantic, or at any rate to distinguish between justifiable and irrational anxiety.

But she still worked all the hours God sent, and Philip, watching her scarf down a lunch of salmon chowder and Caesar salad at the café on the corner of Main and Palouse, told himself that all of their stars ought to be fulsomely thanked for the lucky appearance of Domingo Roque on the scene, problematic though it doubtless was. For one thing, more hands made less work at Standfast. For another, he assumed that at the appropriate intervals Domingo would be saying "Let's eat" and "Let's quit," and so gradually bring about a more balanced life for Alice as well.

"Latte, large, please, and some cheesecake, and two forks. Philip," as the college-student waitress whizzed off, "do you think the Bennett-Briscoe would lend me some money?"

"Sure, certainly."

"No kidding! You think they would? A lot of money, for example?"

"I think I can state categorically that they would. You're the Candy Kid with the Gum Ears as far as the bank is concerned. How much, and what for, if it isn't indiscreet to ask?"

"I am, really? How come? John R is always so dismal about everything."

Philip fiddled with his barbecue sandwich, which he now realized was far too rich for lunch: heartburn on the horizon. "John R doesn't think you have enough debt, is all. He's very pleased with you because—remember, he said this?—you are both solvent and diversified. You just get under his skin sometimes because he personally, though diversified to beat the band, cannot always call himself solvent."

"Isn't liquidty better than solvency?" a motto of Philip's.

"Usually true, always nervous."

"But I'm not that diversified. There's the hay, and then there's the beef, and that's it."

"Well, horse hay, two or three kinds, and cattle fodder; then the market steers, the brood heifers, and the freezer beef as well. And then the horse boarding, and your homebred horses—only every third or fourth year, but the eight or ten thou' is a chunk o' change in a timely fashion. Plus the rental on the arena, that pays for its upkeep. Plus, you pay your bills on time, and own your own water, most of it." He did not mention Jerry Graeme, the leaden drag of that life interest on the Standfast hay operation. All of Alice's and Janet's imagination, all Jean and Allan Andison's ingenuity before them had pitted itself against that mortmain. They couldn't shift it, though, and so they ignored it.

"Well, you know," latte foam rimming her lip, "when you add it all up like that, I guess—"

"So what about the bank loan? You going down to Stateline, the Oasis, play a little blackjack?"

"Oh yeah! Just my style. Here, take a fork to this; it's terrific. Robey's after me about that place beyond us, up back of him, you know, the Hashknife outfit. He has a Plan."

"Uh-oh." Robey Whyte usually did have a Plan, was widely acknowledged one of the most inventive farmers in the Valley. Robey's Plans tended to resemble rhizomatous plants, with runners and suckers linking far-flung objectives. These Plans often involved his neighbors. Robey brought qualities of vision and patience to his schemes that many of those inveigled into them found easy to resent but hard to resist.

"I'm wondering, Phil—do you know what the status of that property is? Couple of those guys are in the county slammer awaiting trial, I do believe. Can they sell anything, even if they want to? Robey thinks the bank's foreclosed on it already. I'm wondering if Jerry Graeme still has an interest there. Robey thinks he does. Whoa!" just thinking of this, "if Jerry has an interest in the property, would he likewise have an interest in the jail time?"

"I will consult the spirits," said Philip, leaning back and jingling the change in his pockets; meaning, Alice assumed, his contacts in law enforcement. "It will depend on the strength of Alcohol, Tobacco, and Firearms' case against them, to some degree. Also their tax situation, the bank's claim, and . . . other things. Child welfare questions, for example. You wouldn't want those children dumped out of their home onto the road, I expect."

"No, but I would sure like us to own some of that hay land if we could get it for a decent price. Of course, Janet will make that sound like I'm chucking the babies in a box and floating them down the creek to drown like puppies. Presumably, if we pay a reasonable price, their wretched parents will find some shelter for them. What a stony-hearted old bat I am."

"Clearly, if they have any equity at all, selling it would be better for them than having it sequestered by the narco-cops. Unless that has already been done. Give me a little time to scratch around."

"Kinda nervous about this. Usually you want to give Robey's Plans time to reveal their various parts and particles. But I'd hate us to get beat out by the government. Or the McCrimmons."

"The McCrimmons? What interest can they have?"

"Those reivers. Ears to the ground, always."

"They're like yourself then?"

"You're calling me acquisitive, are you?" finishing up the cheese-cake.

"You *are* a Scot."

"Philip Weston. Stereotyping, raw prejudice. Shame. Who's that?" Philip waved at someone passing southward along Palouse Street: a college classmate of Janet's, another lawyer.

"I saw in the paper about their divorce," she said. "Sad, huh?"

"Maybe. He seems happier. Let me get this, Standfast, I can bill it out," palming the check. "She's remarrying, someone in the same hot-tub group. Or grope."

"Hardly seems worth the trouble and expense," Alice snickered. "They all know one another so well by now, it must be like all one body."

Philip thought the difference for their friend was significant; thought him a conscientious advocate, if not particularly imaginative. "The kids are hers, not his, so she kept the house."

Don't you dare suggest that he come and stay at the ranch, thought

Alice. I am not Available. I intend to live single all the days of my life. One old-fashioned vaquero and some good dogs and horses're all the society I need.

He said instead, "Standfast, you're looking pretty good," by which she assumed he meant her financial position. Yes, but also the spring sun had brought her freckles out.

At one stroke, Alice found herself afoot. Tom Fool put his forefoot into a hole in the creek bed while playing in the water, and his ankle swelled up hot. Falcon, the very next day, staked himself in the thigh on a spike of alder. He required daily dressing of the wound and a course of antibiotic shots, additions to her daily chores that she resented less than she did being forced to work with Cattywampus.

"Catty's good-looking, all right," she agreed as she swabbed a site on Falcon's rump with alcohol, "and he can work all week on a dime's worth of grain. If he will."

"Pues, how come you don't use he? Him?" Domingo held Falcon's head; rather proud about "how come."

"Because I can't—no le tengo confianza," holding the injection needle cupped in her right hand. Not sure whether she had said "I don't have confidence in him" or "He doesn't have confidence in me." She socked Falcon twice on the swabbed spot, the third time slapped the needle in, and stood back out of range. When he stopped dancing and cussing, she fitted the syringe to the needle and squeezed in the milky dose.

"Don't cry, baby," said Domingo, putting Falcon into one of the foaling boxes. "See, I save you from these cruel doctor." As long as he was there, he looked in on the red mare. She barely acknowledged him these days, barely moved except to shift her weight from one hip to the other. And to eat, of course; he piled loose hay into her empty manger, and when Falcon nickered yearningly, into his too, knowing that Alice would not begrudge it. Alice begrudged nothing that kept her work-force fit, he thought approvingly. He himself, for instance, was better fed and softer slept than many a man on his own ground. And special prenatal foods for his horse, and the vet's attention; none of this taken out of his wages. He had even offered to pay, but Alice said, "She will work that off for me. A good horse is worth its keep." This was a view honored more in the breach than in the observance, in Domingo's experience, up North. In Mexico too, truth to tell, and in regard to humans as well as equine and mechanical servants.

He wondered why she did not want to use that handsome gelding, though. Cattywampus: a strange name; strange colored also, very dark copper brown like an old penny, with the wavy silver-flaxen mane and tail. The same combination, it occurred to him to notice, as the boss's tense curls.

Later in the week, on the way home from the hay fields beyond the county road, strolling down a stony little steep-sided draw, Cattywampus out of nowhere caught a buck-fit. Alice, turning in the saddle to say something to Domingo on the bank of the gulch above and taken wholly by surprise, whacked her wrist on the horn on the first jump and dropped a rein. But, she thought, I can ride this down. Another jump, bigger, the gelding's tail whisking her hat off; another bigger yet, straight at the wall of the draw and, betting on a downhill swerve, she was easy meat for the four-legged reverse and slammed shoulder first into the luckily somewhat soft and sandy bank. Cattywampus crow-hopped gleefully in a circle, trod on and broke a rein, and careered away downhill, showering gravel.

Easy does it, Alice thought, sliding down to the bottom of the gully like spilled water. No panic. Been here before. She couldn't breathe, but had faith that eventually her lungs would resume their task. Sometime soon. If she contained her impatience. I wonder if my medical is paid up, she thought, to distract herself. I wonder if anything's broken. I wonder if shooting the sonofabitch counts as depreciation. The edges of her vision sparkled and faded; however, a tiny shallow breath got in. Ah. Here it comes. Ouch.

Domingo's tall shadow against the sun. "You okay?"

"Uh-huh."

"You okay, how come you don't stand up? You takin' a sunbath?"

"Ha ha."

"Okay, in several moments, I call nine-one-one."

"Let's wait a minute, see if Catty can get hit by a semi crossing the road."

He reached down a hand, and Alice caught it and stood up by stages. Stood for a while holding a hank of Skookum's mane, looking thoughtful. Went and picked up her hat. Domingo shook off his stirrup so she could get up behind him.

"You see my problem with that horse," she said as the paint picked his way down the draw.

"I can fix it."

"Like hell!" Her shoulder hurt, her neck hurt, her wrist ached, she was pissed off. She could "fix it" herself if she were buster enough to stick on and spur and leather the beast until he broke his heart, or his neck. Or if she rode him in a come-to-Jesus headstall. Or if every time he ducked his head, she got off and beat him till he fell on his knees and sobbed. But, hell! She needed a working companion, not an armed truce. Or the walking dead.

"I can fix it," he said again.

Domingo's own horse had a curious history.

"You bought her in Idaho, didn't you?" Alice asked as they dug the post holes for a round schooling pen at the far end of the shed yard. "Was this when you were working for the Foulkses?" No, this was in Boise: he went there to work in the potato processing plants. In addition, he rode exercise gallops very early in the morning during race meets at the Boise fairgrounds. And she was there, in somebody's backyard pasture along the backstretch of the track.

"One day," above the roar of the motorized drill, "I'm fight with some horse want to run—atrás y oblicuo, how is that—?"

"Backwards and sideways, oh yeah, I know. So she was on the track?"

"No, she's a baby, maybe not have two years. In a corral in somebody yard out there behind the track." Each time around, he looked at her—first at her color, later, at the nice little thing herself, very young but already a classic shape. She had a pen to herself, beside a bigger pen where three or four Simmental calves lounged around, and sometimes he would see her pacing along the fence, looking at the calves.

"What, at that age? Wow."

"You can say wow. I'm impression. So one time I see a sign, For Sell. Okay, is deep enough," lifting the drill out of the hole, moving it to the next marker. "So next day, I go with my trailer to ask." The drill roared, threw up a little tornado of black dirt; by gripping the handles between them, they could make sure the hole was plumb.

They were güeros, the owners, so he didn't expect a welcome. *"I'm sorry, but not all Americanos are civilized like you, patrona."*

"And not all Mexicanos are polite like you, let's get that straight." He said things like that and she never took offense; what a prize of a boss, he thought.

They were fairly civil, though; a thin man, his chubby wife, and two skinny little long-haired girls. At first, the price was high. But it came down, almost before he offered. And then the story came out. He didn't get it all, not all at once, because the man spoke fast and the children interrupted and cried. Apparently, they knew nothing about horses, bought the filly as a fawnlike foal, a pet for the little girls. Regally bred, the little creature, but they had no idea about this. How had they gotten their hands on her? A fracaso de negocio, Domingo suspected, some businessman's play ranch gone bust, barnfuls of high-class babies auctioned off; infant royalty one day, canner's meat the next. So they bought her and brought her home. The children soon lost interest in her, and after a while got a calf to raise, a new toy, and put the calf into the backyard pen with the filly. And in fooling with the calf in her cowhorse way, what with the hot weather and her greater length of leg, one day she just ran it to death.

"She killed who?" Alice asked.

"The calf, she play the calf till he dies," with a grunt lifting the drill clear again. "Okay, one more. And, but they think she does this with intention. You understand? I know, ridículo! And so they are disgust of her. Don't laugh, Aliz, these machine don't center."

They believed the filly had done murder, malice aforethought. "And now," the thin guy had said self-righteously, "we won't let the girls have nothing to do with her. We won't have her on the place no more. If somebody don't take her, she's goin' in the can," at which the little girls burst into shrieks and spouts of tears, and Domingo and the father concluded the deal in a wet and tragic atmosphere.

He had one other horse at the time, a brown gelding with high white on all four legs, the last of his father's string, boarding near the stockyards in Caldwell. He put the red filly in with him, old Blas, who took her under his wing. She followed him around like a dog.

"We raise her, Blas and me, you know. But I don't like her name, Poppy. To me sound like papí, like padre. That's why I call her Chamaca like Little Girl." Alice thought the mare didn't care what he called her as long as he called her. As long as he brought her to the work she was born for, the place where all that she was and everything she knew came to a diamond point against all that the cow was and knew, again and again, until the mere contemptuous rake of her ears could make the other grass eater do her will.

"Tonight's the night, I betcha," Alice said after dinner, her hands on either side of the root of the red mare's tail. Under the sleek hide the usually firm muscles of that apple bottom undulated softly, jellylike. "Feel that, how soft? And her udder's waxed up and dripping, her milk's in. You staying up with her? Wake me up if you get worried." She went away, taking Falcon out with her and leaving Domingo sitting on a bale wrapped up in a horse blanket, worried out of his head. Then she came back in, said, "The quieter you are, the better she'll like it," and went away again. As if I didn't know that, he thought, miffed. Do you think I intend to serenade her, sing "Las Mañanitas"? The fact was, about horse obstetrics he knew less than Alice did, but her nonchalance in this particular case graveled him. This mare was all his wealth. Besides, if he knew anything at all about the business, he told himself sulkily, and he did know *something*, after all, it was that bad things happened fast, and that before he could get up to the house, never mind bring the vet, his dear mare might evert her uterus, bleed out and die, or her foal come feet first and suffocate in the birth canal. What good in the world will your mountains of wisdom be to us then, stain-faced wiseass of a gringa? Tell me that. The mare, of course, paid him no attention at all. He sat there, sidelined and helpless. Feeling sorry for himself, he fell asleep.

To start awake before dawn. The foal was out on the straw, rocking to the strokes of its mother's tongue, bug-eyed, amazed at the world. Alice came down around five, he still sitting there, enchanted, although he had had the sense to wrap up the afterbirth in a grain sack for her inspection.

" 'Pears to be all here," poking at the placenta and then wrapping it up again. "What a good girl! Did she have any trouble? Never thought she would," ignoring his fumbling reply. "I'll bring you down some breakfast; you'll want to watch it stand up."

Exactly. He felt so grateful for her understanding this that his eyelids prickled. A Tupperware box of egg sandwiches warming his knees and a thermos cup of coffee sending steam up his nose, he got to see just as advertised the bright little spark sorting out the tangled struts of its legs. Unfolding them singly, then in pairs—the wrong pairs. Then the two fores: bingo! Then a rest, sitting up. Then a try with the hinds, disastrous, and a long rest lying flat, delicate rib cage heaving. Then the fores, the hinds, and he was up, trembling, bent-legged like a spider: a colt, red-gold as late sunlight. Alice came along choring, leaned into the stall, and sighed out, "Oh, isn't he bonnie!" Whapped Domingo on the shoulder: "How about that, slick? Is that alright, or what!" Domingo felt that if he grinned any wider, it would hurt.

"Here comes the proud papa!" caroled Janet. "Oh no! What did I say? What a thundercloud." She searched her mind for a reason, personal or cultural, why Domingo Roque should turn on his heel with a frown and go straight back down the hill. It was never going to be a Hollywood-handsome face, of course, but recently, with the last of the scabs off and more comprehensive shaving, in general it had been at least an open and approachable one. "He sore about something?"

"Not that I know of." They were sitting out in the locust grove, soaking up April sunshine and the grape-soda scent of locust blossom, sharing a box of Kleenex. "Been kind of moody lately. Postpartum depression?"

Janet giggled. "What's he calling the baby?"

"Chispa. That's 'spark,' right? I don't know if he intends to register him or not, but if he does, hadn't he better go with English?"

"What's the sire's name?"

"Gold Bar Rocket. And the dam's Vandy's Poppy Bar None."

"Wow. Fancy. Let's see: Rocket's Gold Spark, Spark of Gold, Sparky Bar None, Sparky Vander Pop, no, too Dutch—"

"You're good at that, Janet."

"I am, aren't I?" complacent. "Any luck unloading Jerry Graeme's critters?"

"The mare's sold, to a member of the Pendleton Fair Court for quite a nice piece of change, as a matter of fact. Hope she keeps sound under the strain."

"Surely she will. What does she have to do besides run-ins, sliding stops, and parades? And she's crowdwise, bombproof, and, anyway, the Round-Up princess must be a better horseman than old Jerry."

"Could hardly be otherwise. Shall we talk about the bulls?"

"Yes. Are we having Kid and Sixteen again?"

"I assume so, unless you have a better plan. This is probably Sixteen's last year." A moment of silent appreciation for the senior bull. "What about one for the yearlings, any ideas?" The bull leased for the young replacement heifers, first-time bearers, would need to be known to throw low-birthweight calves.

"Mm-hm, there's one up at Enterprise called Hamster that I think . . ."

"Hamster. I see."

"Well, Duke of Hamilton or something. I need to study him a little more, though, before I decide. May fifteenth still your preferred date? Okay, I'll lay it on."

That decided, Alice went to rototill the garden and Janet took her pruning shears to the hedges along the lane.

Domingo, bumping along standing on the spike harrow as Effervesce pulled it across and across his and Ricky's grass pen, watched the sisters and cultivated a mood. Why in hell can't I use the tractor for this? Half the time, a quarter the trouble! Though he knew why and approved the reason: it exercised Effy's jumping muscles and it saved gas. "Chee, Effy," irritable, "chee, chee, chee, chee." Effy sidestepped neatly rightwards around the end of the row like the plowhorse he so much resembled. Domingo thought wretchedly, "Proud papa," my sorry ass.

Chapter Five

Nobody told Domingo the roundup family was coming. He guessed it from the advance preparations: heaps of groceries laid in, new towels bought, temporary horse pens set up, a Porta-John rented.

"Let's see," Alice counted on her fingers, "you and me and Robey, and Concha and Beto and probably the two primos, and Lourdes and Vera Jane and Janet, and Nick and Nan and Tammy. That's thirteen at the table, very unlucky, but actually Janet and Lourdes never sit down. And so where will we sleep? Beto and Lourdes in the camper, Concha with me . . ." Domingo braced himself to be turned out of his room, but it didn't happen.

Alice expected to castrate, de-horn, brand, and vaccinate starting on April the twenty-first, but on the nineteenth snow fell, eight wet inches, so she called Beto Vélez in Hermiston and held them off for three days. Just as well, for it snowed again on the twentieth. But then spring really set in, and the white stuff went off in a matter of hours. The ground dried out under milky skies and a steady warm wind out of the south, and a mist of green suddenly appeared in the creek willows and Russian olive along the county road. Beto phoned from Boardman where they stopped to pick up the cousins on the way north: was Alice ready for them? At noon, the camper and the pickup with attendant horse trailers bumped carefully across the cattle guard at the foot of the lane.

Up and then down they came, growling and swaying into the yard, cut the motors, piled out of the cabs. Lourdes Vélez seized Alice in a hug, rocking her back and forth, "Alice-baby, I'm so glad to see you! Oh, you look good! You painted the barn! Look, Beto, don't she look good? Not so skinny."

"She always looks good to me," touching his hat and shaking her ceremoniously by the hand, then embracing her and kissing her on the brow. "¿Te sientes bien, mija?"

"Don Beto. Estamos bien, todos. Y ustedes, ¿cómo? A new trailer, I see—slick! Concha, ¡tu peinado! I do believe you are the Glamour Queen of the West." Concepción had her blondish tresses braided in thin plaits in front, and the rest falling straight down her back, banged off at the bottom. "Beto and Lourdes, this is Juan Domingo Roque. Domingo, this is my friend Concepción Vélez."

"Encantada," tall, stacked, green-eyed, eighteen or so. Smooth oval face, matte rose-brown like a hen's egg, pretty as a Fair Court princess: Domingo caught himself ogling. She had a grip like iron. The two cousins came up, Saúl and Noe Garza, shook one of Alice's hands each, and so surprised Domingo with the full cholo knuckle-knocking hand jive, he almost missed his cue.

These people, he learned, came from Hermiston in Oregon, had a ranchito there, raised ten or fifteen cows a year, quick heavy-horned little corrientes for the rodeos, and Doña Lourdes sold cooking and curing herbs and traditional medical supplies imported from Mexico. According to Vera Jane and Janet, the Vélez connection with the Valley went back decades, Beto having worked for the Andisons, the Whytes, and several other outfits for a long time before launching his own custom ranching business, conducting annual gather-ups for other people's beef operations. The primos were beekeepers by trade, from a wide-ranging Umatilla-Boardman-Irrigon clan, happy to take a cowboy holiday whenever their great-uncle summoned them. The girl Concepción—¡qué taco de ojo!—went to high school and helped Beto with their little ranch. A finished cowhand however, as she showed the next day, never mind the gold disks in her earlobes, swaying fringe on her jacket.

All the next day and the next, as the weather turned from warm and breezy to hot and still. The mud of the corrals dried to dust, beaten up into a pearly fog that hung motionless and surreal above the workers. All day, the thud of hooves, whoop of ropes, desperate bawls and moans, flight and pursuit, triumph and tragedy, and Beto Vélez calling for the next calf with a strange, plangent cry.

Nick and Nan Weston and Nan's friend Tamlyn Evans took over the regular chores on the place, and Janet and Lourdes and Vera Jane cooked. Janet adored the spring roundup, lovely old-fashioned link with the past that it was, and nine banquets in seventy-two hours struck her as a challenge worthy of her. Of course it involved an awful scramble to cover her classes and get her essays marked, but it was well worth that, especially since the cooks could watch it all from on high, uphill at the house, and never encounter the calves' pain and terror, the stink of blood, burnt hair and skin, the brute reality of the business. Never lay eyes on the gallon jars in which floated calves' testes glaucous as shucked oysters, like half-boiled eggs or dissected eyeballs, traditionally the roundup foreman's bonus. Nor would she cook the damn things, no matter what Lourdes said about their therapeutic properties. Vera Jane backed her up, sitting on a stool peeling pie apples: "Listen, kid, no woman should never have nothing to do with them things."

Alice was unfazed. She was an expert castrator, well taught by her mother, fast and sure with a knife as sharp as remorse, and over any qualms she might have had about the job before she turned twelve. Little blood spilled, and the small incisions healed cleanly. Domingo, towing a furiously struggling mother away from her captive child, wondered how Alice would react if he complimented her on really knowing her way around a scrotum. His eye fell on Concepción Vélez, hard after a calf, high in her stirrups, loop singing. Delectable behind rising from the cantle as she loped back. Diosito mío. She had invited him to church with the family on the coming Sunday. But he wasn't going to church, not for any heart-shaped bottom in this world or the next.

As they were changing horses after lunch on Saturday, Concha said to Alice, "How come we don't use those two?"

"The Appy doesn't belong to us, and the other one's that goddam Cattywampus that I can't seem to work the buck out of. Domingo says he can fix him, but Ah hae ma doots."

"That Appy's nice," double-blanketing her old mare to save her back. "He done anything?"

"Lot of rodeo, calf roping. He really had the stuff, two years ago. If he were mine, sugar, I'd give him to you. But he's Jerry Graeme's, so I have to max him out." They worked on in silence for a few minutes. Domingo came along with a fistful of grain.

"Halcón, for me?"

"Your little old Mouse did well this morning, didn't he, buck? Yes, take Falcon; I'll be at the fire all afternoon." He went off whistling "Adelita."

After a pause, Concha said, "How long's he worked here?"

"About three months. Good hand, isn't he?"

"Uh-huh. Cute, too. Lavaba y planchaba. Well, not guapísimo, but, I mean, you know, interesting."

Alice finished rubbing Bigeloil into Tom Fool's ankles and led him away to his pen. There goes my helper, she thought. She came back, scrubbing the whiffy stuff off her hands on her jeans. Concha asked, "He just gonna buck that funny-colored horse out, or what?"

"Dunno. Ask him," showing a little heat, unavoidably. Concha took no offense, accustomed as she was to short answers from women, long ones from men.

She did ask him. During the roundup when Alice took her usual stroll around the place before bed, everybody went with her, a regular paseo, and Concepción came up to Domingo as he leaned over the half-door to scratch the new foal's withers.

"What are you going to do," she asked, "to that Cattywampus horse?"

"Watch him, little time."

"Just watch him?"

"Uh-huh. *First, it's necessary to understand him. After that, I'll try to think of some way to change his mind.*"

"*How about, maybe, buck him till he runs, and run him till he stops?*"

"*Your way, Miss Concha? That's been tried, I'm pretty sure.*"

"*Well, what, then?*" Alice and the others came along outside, and Domingo moved to join them. Disappointed, Concha trailed after him. She thought of asking to see where he slept. But no. Obvious; craven, almost. The thing was, he didn't seem to know how to take advantage of his opportunities. Or maybe he was just traditional, respectful of her, careful of her reputation. There were such men, she had heard.

"*Are you coming to Mass with us in the morning?*" she asked.

"*No, but thanks. You're all leaving after lunch, correct? When I decide what to do about that bronc, I'll call and tell you. If it works.*"

Alice saw them come out of the foaling shed together. Well, that's that. Dammit, she thought. Just when I was getting used to working with him, depending on him. Liking him. Drat that Concha, drat her green eyes.

They drove down to the Westons' for dinner the day after, just the family and Robey and Vera Jane Whyte. Janet showed him a photograph of their father in uniform, and Domingo asked incautiously, "How come he wears una falda?" This after flatly denying, during the postroundup dinner, surrounded by Scots and Scotch drinkers, that bagpipes were in actual fact a musical instrument at all. For which breach of sense the Andison-Weston females offered to tie his espuelas together and flog him with his hat. So he should have known better; but no: " . . . una falda?"

"That is not a skirt," said Janet remarkably coldly, "it is a kilt. He was a soldier, and that is the uniform of his regiment, the Fraserburgh Foot." Putting the full Aberdeenshire twist on the vowels: Freezer-bra Füt.

"Okay, pero parece una . . ."

"Take care, now," murmured Philip, licking sabayon off his mustache, "be warned, señor: if you persist, I shall be unable to protect you." Privately, he thought the whole Scottish business the silliest goddam putting on of airs he had ever heard of. He believed that the sisters must get from their mother this susceptibility to men in kilts, Jean Lyon having fallen flat out in love with her clansman-soldier at first sight.

This was the family story: she met him at a cattle show at Banchory in Scotland, near the Aberdeen Angus breeding center where Jean was studying, an exchange student from Montana; Allan had charge of the military color guard sent down to grace the proceedings. Stout hairy legs and a faceful of freckles, Allan Breac, like in the Stevenson story, with a cocky confiding half-grin—her heart turned over. He saw a wand of a girl as straight as her stick, a funny-valentine face under straight bangs black like the hulking Angus stirk at her shoulder. And that did it for him as well.

Allan Andison and his brother Hugh shared an inheritance consisting of Hamewith Farm near Pitscottie in Fifeshire, and a house on the Lade Braes in Saint Andrews. The house was called Quair Crannies: old, huge, uncomfortable, and worth a lot of money. Neither Allan nor Hugh ever intended to live there; both preferred the farm where they had grown up. When Allan decided to resign his commission, marry Jeannie and emigrate to America, they sold Quair Crannies and then Hugh bought out Allan's share of Hamewith. With the stake thus produced, Allan and Jean purchased their starter bunch of pedigreed Angus heifers, and the original three-hundred uphill acres of Standfast. Which they later, and to their permanent regret, augmented with hay acreage in a deal with Old Man Graeme, Jerry's father.

The whole of this clan chronicle was recounted to Domingo, whether he wanted to hear it or not. And in truth he did want to hear it. For one thing, the telling felt like a ceremony, a social gesture but an unfamiliar one, rousing an emotion so complex he felt he needed to put it away for a while. Let it ripen. For another, how surprising to think of this family being so new on the ground! Take his own case for contrast: though his mother came from the south, his father Fidel represented five generations of Roques at Rancho Lomas Chatas, all belonging to five or six generations of the same patrón, los de Ovejuna. Thus he assumed that the Andisons had always been at Standfast too, part of the landscape.

"Oh no, we're newcomers," Alice said. "Johnny-come-latelies compared to those guys on the Robey Grade. There've been Robeys and Whytes and Stonecyphers and Naylors up there since the Indians gave out. You know Dorothy Creek? That's Robey's great-grandmother, that Dorothy. Or great-great."

And another surprise: the Andisons frequently visited and were visited by their cousins across the ocean.

"Of course. Why wouldn't we?"

Well, obviously, because—he wanted to explain what every Mexican knew, that Americans were superficially warm but essentially cold, unfamilial, booting their children out of the house promptly at age eighteen, even the unmarried girls, sticking their parents into dying-homes to get them out of the way, putting laws and timetables before kinship and patronage. Everybody knew this.

Nearly said so, but realized as he started to speak that he no longer felt entirely sure of his ground, nor of the proposition that Mexico embodied the opposing virtues. Was it not true, for example, that practically every family in Santo Tomás sent or wanted to send a son or daughter north over the Line to earn and mail home money, and did not those sendings very, very often turn into permanent exile? Were not girls, and boys too, made to marry where they did not love, did not widowers frequently abandon a first family when starting a second? And in the specific case he knew, did not Abuelita Fidencia's place in Graciela's ratty household in Wapato more resemble servitude than respect? Domingo held his tongue.

"Would you like to go and live at Hamewith for a year, Nannie? They would work you very hard. But you could go to the university at Saint Andrews, which would be worth two years of college here." Janet looked not at Nan but at Alice who, like herself, had put in a couple of stints on the Fifeshire farm in their youth.

"Don't know about a year. I'd like to visit, though. Too bad we don't still own Quair Crannies."

"God forbid! Drafty old heap, all steps and corners and little corridors and cranky doors, as bad as—"

"Standfast!" said Alice. "I knew you'd say that. Mother used to complain whenever Dad built on something new, 'It's getting as bad as Quair Crannies.'"

"'As squent.'"

"'As squent,' yes, and Dad would smooch her and say, 'Aye, bit ther's nowt quair aboot thee crannies, is ther, lass?'"

Both the sisters blinked rapidly and to the amusement of the old and embarrassment of the young, recounted the scene: The little girls would yell "Da-ad!" and Jean would say, "Allan, you are embarrassing your daughters." And Allan, who spoke elegant north-of-Berwick English as a rule, would sob out a flood of Doric: "Och aye! Ah see hoo et's tae be, the puir auld feyther pit oot en the cauld, naebody tae care noo he cannae wark, ochone!" until the children swarmed over him with kisses and promises of filial devotion if only he would not mention their mother's, or anybody's, crannies.

It was all Greek to Domingo. Except for the way they felt about each other; he couldn't miss that. Nor miss the way he, and his history with them, now seemed one strand among many in this tight-woven circle that was like a wreath of wheat straw plaited to celebrate harvest.

"If you are going to fix him, 'mano, you had better ride him," said Alice, disliking the truculent tone of her voice. "Then you'll know what I'm dealing with."

"*But I already know. It's a problem of respect. He thinks he's the dominant animal. He's happy to work for a while, but only on his terms. There, that's what I mean,*" as Cattywampus scraped his head up and down Alice's back to scratch an itch, pushing her off balance until she had to brace herself against the wall of the round pen.

"But they all do that."

"No, boss, look again. They all push with the nose to say 'It's time to eat' or 'Please scratch my face.' But he—look! Are you a tree, a post? That's how he's using you." Alice turned and swatted the gelding on his bluff brisket. This made sense, actually, now that she had it pointed out to her. The horse's ground manners had always left something to be desired.

"Smacking his nose—it's too late for that to work, I suppose."

"Oh, definitely. It'll take a crisis, something pretty traumatic."

Alice mantled up. "Don't think for a minute I'm going to let you kill him. He's valuable, if only as a canner; look how fat he is!"

"No, no, don't worry. This don't will be cruel. So nice, Miss Nan can support to see."

It better not be cruel, Alice thought, or you don't will be working here.

However, nothing happened for another several days as cultivation, irrigation, and the shifting around of baled hay intervened, the two three-year-olds got ridden in the covered arena, and Chispa followed his dam outside for the first time. But then they had to cut out the dry cows and six yearling heifers for the sale, and then move the whole bunch of nursing cows and calves up off the Triangle to steeper, cooler ground, so Domingo got his chance.

The first couple of times they rode out, Cattywampus behaved himself. Maybe it's just me, Alice thought, or maybe my rig hurts him. But the critter wasn't sore, had never been sore; that of course had been her first suspicion, and she'd had him to the vet again and again. But no, never a trace of heat, tenderness, restricted motion, no time, nowhere. In her own mind, she credited Domingo's analysis: the problem lodged in the beastie's head.

At the ford of Koosh Creek on the third day out, a wide stony shallow crossing, "This would be a bitch of a place to try it out, horse," Domingo thought. But Cattywampus trundled across completely relaxed, only gathering himself to leap up the far bank. But then made use of being gathered up to uncork his Sunday buck. Domingo slid off at once and stood holding the reins and looking the horse in the eye.

"Break me one stick, please, patrona," he said as Alice came trotting back, "largo pero chiquito," holding up his thumb to show her the size. And he started stripping Cattywampus's tack off. Alice rode away and used her wire cutters to pinch off a long thin alder twig. When she got back, Domingo had the horse roped up fore and hind in such a way that by slowly tightening the lines he could bring him to the ground. Cattywampus watched, his ears forward: this was something new! He didn't struggle, but bent his knees, bowed low, angled his hocks, and came softly down on his right side. Domingo bound his knees together, fetlock to elbow, roped his hocks ankle to gaskin, and then removed the Indian hackamore he had thrown on the gelding's head. Then he sat down on a drift log under the willows.

"Now what?" said Alice.

"Probably this take some time. You like sit here? Right now nothing is happen."

Nothing happened. Cattywampus lay quiet, trussed like a bale, a baled horse. Alice dismounted and sat down, holding Falcon's reins.

"Where did you get that rope?" A braided white-cotton line, soft and lithe, nearly two inches thick.

"In the saddle room. It's yours, not used much, though. Maybe forgotten."

"Forgotten by me, for sure." She got up and took two Gala apples from her saddlebag, gave one to Domingo. "What happens when he tries to get up?"

"He can't."

"Yeah, but won't he hurt himself?"

"This horse is not into hurting himself, believe me. If he were crazy, or of a hotter breed, he might work himself up into a heart attack. But this guy? No."

Cattywampus got bored and tried to stretch his forelegs out. This proved impossible. He tried harder: no give at all. Annoyed, he tried to writhe his hindquarters free of the net of rope; fruitlessly. Alice and Domingo ate their apples and fed the cores to Falcon. Falcon eyed the other horse, alarmed but interested. Cattywampus struggled, raising dust. A trio of curious heifers wandered over. Cattywampus lost his temper completely, squealed and grunted, thrashed madly, beat his beautiful head against the turf in a frenzy. No good. He lay still, flanks heaving, sneezing and snorting. Started the whole sequence over again: tried, tried harder, panicked and struggled, got mad, pitched a fit, gave up and lay still, puffing, groaning. Sweat slicked his neck and shoulders, twigs tangled in his tail; his big nostrils cupped and flattened, sucking air.

"Enough, you think?" said Alice, anxious. She was still having trouble getting her socks on, bent out of shape from the last time the animal had ditched her, but she didn't hate him, and she didn't like torture. Or in Catty's case, not prolonged torture. Domingo took his alder stick, got up, and went around to the horse's head. Very softly he touched the twig to the wet neck. At the contact, Cattywampus heaved and lashed his tail. Domingo sat down again.

"No todavía."

A few more bovine kibitzers wandered along, and a pair of magpies flew in and sat commentating rudely in the top of a cottonwood. The fourth trial with the alder stick got no reaction at all.

"You come here, please, Aliz." Alice went and took the stick, applied it as instructed, very gently. No reaction. The horse might have been dead, except he was breathing, and his big moony eye blinked. Domingo freed the ropes, leaving a loop around the neck. "Come, Catty." The gelding lurched up fore and aft, stood with head hanging, dejection's own self. Alice felt sorry for him, but she didn't touch him. Domingo tacked him up swiftly.

"You can think," reading her mind, "sympa—what that word? Yes. But! Don't say nice, otherwise this happen again," he said, coiling and securing the fat cotton rope. "Tiene que rendirse, someterse. Is like—surrender? Because, if no, he goes in the can." This was so manifestly true that Alice gave the poor beast neither a kind word nor a pat all the way home.

The treatment did not take, however. Having watched Catty creep home humiliated, gawked at by cows, the butt of crows and magpies,

Alice could hardly believe how quickly he recovered his old swagger. Physically unscarred, psychologically unbowed, snorty Morgan attitude to the fore. The only question was, did he have sense enough not to bronc up again?

No, he hadn't, and a second session took place a week later, just as unpleasant for him and as entertaining for onlookers, but not as long. In fact, Domingo slipped off in midbuck, and the horse found himself on the ground again almost before his tail unkinked—no fun! And once again, stumbling home lathered, filthy, the talk of the neighborhood.

The third time—well, there was no third time. Only, coming down off the swayback hill one noon, he hesitated a quarter second—and then hurried on, ears lopping, hoping no one had noticed. Domingo pretended it hadn't happened. After that, Domingo rode him, Alice rode him; he never bucked again. When other horses hurtled down the pens in play, tails high and farting like semitractors, jolting out one spine-popper after another, he would look, sigh, and turn back to grass. For him, those days were gone for good.

"And you think that's cured the problem?" Janet said, dubious. "Not sure I want to risk it."

"I wouldn't bet the ranch. But he hasn't offered with either one of us since then, I can say that. It's a question of whether the lesson is painted on or tattooed in."

"I would think so. How in the world did you get yourself to let Domingo do that to him? You're as much against hog-tying and lip-chaining and all that rough-breaking stuff as I am, or so I'd of thunk."

"But it was all so soft and easy. The critter doesn't have a rope mark on him, honest, Yan. You know, if the guy had gone to whack him while he was tied up, I'd have fired him, hell, I'd have enjoyed firing him. But it was all done in a spirit of education."

"Huh. Well, good, if so." Speculatively, "Maybe I should try the method on my rhetoric class."

Janet had a wet cold. She didn't want to teach, tutor, or talk to anybody. She'd already read the first two essays of the latest set from Basic

Rhetoric and they were dreadful, incoherent; the worse because so obviously effortful. "Go home," her officemate said. "But first, pick up your phone, it's your favorite student."

Not again, thought Janet. Not now, not this dopey kid when there are all these hard-tryers to deal with.

"Brandon," mock-cheery, "what's up?"

"Hi, Janet. I was just wondering what I need to do to catch up. Things have been kinda crazy around here and—"

"Brandon, you've missed two-thirds of the class meetings and you've only turned in one essay. I'm afraid you're out of chances as far as this quarter goes."

"Well, I've called and e-mailed to explain—"

"Yes, you have. You've called more times than you've attended class. That just isn't the way to learn to think and write, dear. The best thing would be for you to file for a late withdrawal and try again next time." Or hand over your tuition benefit, Janet thought, to somebody who would put it to use.

"See, Janet," he'd seemed a nice-enough kid at first, not especially nimble of brain but sincere, earnest. Now she thought him a stinker, a trainee-cop ambitious to rise in the ranks by smarm and charm. "See, that's not the way it works. I have to have this grade. It's for my program. I have to. So just tell me what I have to do to pass this class. That's all I'm asking."

"Okay. You have to turn in all six essays and a quarter's worth of journal pages. And attend class every day for the next three weeks, and take the exam."

"And then I'll pass?"

"Then you will have a very small, non-zero chance of passing. And Brandon, that's my best offer."

"Sweet," he said, and hung up.

Alice took Three Cheers to a kindly old Holsteiner stallion in Prosser and left her there, dropping in at the Westons' on her way home. Family conclave in the kitchen. Emotions ran high, but Nick's presence on the scene was having its usual pacific effect. Nick ate continuously, whatever was at hand, beans out of a can, fossilized marshmallows, old salad; it was soothing, his steady mastication, like the munching of cattle.

"Nan what? *Nannie?!*"

"She said something to her Spanish teacher, and he threw her out of class."

"What in the ever-lovin' world did you say, peach?"

"Nothing, just a dicho, a proverb," Nan swirled her curly mane up on top of her head and with a sigh let it fall. "A lot of people didn't turn in their homework, and he got mad and said we were a bunch of burros, and I said 'Los lunes ni ponen las gallinas,' you know, 'On Mondays even the hens don't lay,' and the kids laughed, and he threw me out." Dashing tears from her eyes; Nick was the one who was used to being yelled at by teachers, not Nan. "Maybe he didn't understand what I said, maybe he thought it was obscene or something."

"So he's not a native Spanish speaker, I take it," said Alice, trying to get a grip on the problem.

"Yes and no," Janet said, as annoyed at the school as she was at Nan. "Do you know what 'pocho' means? Someone born here, Mexican parentage, uneducated, speaking both languages fluently but to a very low standard. Sometimes illiterate in both."

"Like Lourdes Vélez."

"Exactly. Not a very nice term, by the way; I wouldn't say it to her, were I you. Nan, buck up now. We'll go talk to him tomorrow, straighten things out. Speaking of los Vélez," she said as a diversion, seizing the cat Mimi by the scruff of her neck and separating her from the chair cushion with a powerful wrench, "did it seem to you that Concha kind of shied her hat at Domingo during the roundup?" She sat down and with her foot pushed out the chair opposite for Alice.

"Boy-howdy!" Alice said. "Did she ever. Her and her outstanding little behind, luring him away— Jeez! Every time I think what my life was like before he showed up, I could cry a river."

"I thought one of the primos got his brand on her last season," said Nick from inside the refrigerator.

"Out of their league now," Nan said, perking up a little. "Ooh! Sigh! The girl has grown up, and out." With little physical vanity herself, Nan easily appreciated what boys saw in other girls.

"Things are not all smooth and shiny chez Vélez, I fear," said Janet. "Nicholas, those are for dinner. No. No. Put them back at once. Lourdes told me Beto's ready to do patriarchal murder. Concha hangs around with the Future Farmers of America boys after school, comes home late, Beto's stuck with the chores."

"Chores can't be much, on their little place."

"No, but the point is, he wants her home. You know, traditional Mexican miss, close to the hearth, modest, respectful, et cetera, et cetera. Meanwhile, Concha wants to go study animal nutrition at Wazoo, be a stockman like you. You're a bad influence, Roan."

"Why shouldn't she, though?" Nan said. "She's a good hand already. You're always saying, Ma, a person should do what they love."

"She should, of course, if she can get a scholarship. But remember, Nannie, that leaves them alone, and getting on. Beto's, what, seventy-something. Lou Lou's hands are bad; she can't bend over very well, though she doesn't complain. With her, it's all about Beto; with Beto, it's all about purity, duty, and tradition. Screaming fights, I gather; household objects hurled."

"Ooh, God. Poor Lou Lou. Still, I think Concha should go to college if she wants to, don't you, Aunt Roan?"

"She should want to take care of them," Alice objected, "among other things."

Nick backed out of the fridge, a stalk of asparagus in one hand, the young cat in the other. "He fucking backs her into a corner, though, if I know Concha—"

"Katy-bar-the-door," his mother agreed. "Why are girls so damn hard to rear? If even Nannie is going to start barging around—"

"But I didn't—!"

Nick said, munching, "It's not her. It's Saenz, the Spanish teacher. He's actually the wrestling coach. He doesn't really speak Spanish at all."

"How do you know that?"

"Xochi and Viviana and those guys told me so. They say he can't even read very much, he gets somebody in the office to correct the homework. Anybody who tries to speak Spanish in class is going to look like a smart-ass."

"Nicky, I've known Principal Roy for twenty years. I really can't entertain the notion that he'd put a nincompoop in the classroom just to fill out the nincompoop's contract."

"That's what he's done, though," resting the cat on his shoulder and patting her as if burping a baby. "Anyway, Nannie doesn't have the guts to call the teachers out; she's way too nice."

"Thanks, I think," Nan said.

"Welcome."

A silence ensued, in which Mimi's ecstatic purring gradually overwhelmed the whirr of the Frigidaire as Janet thought, bracketing her nose and chin with thumb and forefinger. "Well, Nannie, whatever you did, don't do it again," she said with a rather desperate laugh. "He's probably doing his best. Is that Mimi making that grinding noise?"

"Verdammt! She's drooled on me!" said Nick, exasperated with the cat and his mother. "Ma," as if to a child, "please try to understand this. You are a teacher. Bobby Saenz is crap. Aunt Roan's Domingo could teach Spanish better than him."

"No way!" Alice cried.

"He could, I'm not joshing, he's helped me a lot. School should sign him up."

"School can't have him, and neither can Concha Vélez! I found him, and I'm keeping him." She had everybody's attention, for sure. "I may have to raise his wages," she added lamely.

She got out of there before anything else surprising came out of her mouth, backed out of the driveway a little too fast, tapped the mailbox with the right taillight and came pretty close to grazing a passing blue-and-silver Trans Am with the left one. Are you safe to drive? she thought. What is your problem?

The other car turned around at the cross street and came back. Is this guy gonna deal me a ration of shit for stupid driving? Well, I probably earned it. Alice waited at the intersection to apologize. But the Trans Am cruised on by, the driver looking the other way.

Delicately, with the point of his thick blue tongue, Kid, the junior bull, cleaned first his left, then his right nostril.

"They won't fight, will they, Reese?" said Alice, reaching between the bars of the open-stock rig to give old Sixteen a scratch between the eyes. "Not that they ever have."

"Not them. They lived together all winter, got all the corners knocked off the relationship." Reese Pritchard, Angus breeder, down from Steptoe, was an old favorite of Alice's. Allan Andison had liked him, and Alice and Janet trusted him. The one season they had gone against Pritchard's recommendation on a bull for the Standfast herd, Janet must have overlooked something big in the pedigree of the animal she selected. The calves grew too big in the womb, cows couldn't get them out, 8 percent calf mortality, a disastrous year. So even if they didn't lease Pritchard bulls, he was the person Janet went to for advice. This year, he approved their election of Hamster even though Hamster belonged to someone else; that was Reese all over. A handsome, flat-faced Welshman, twice divorced, he had a son and daughter-in-law deep in the business, a good long-term connection. "What say we innerduce the gents to the ladies? No, thank you, ma'am, can't stay for lunch; them other two got a hot date in Pendleton tonight."

Domingo met them at the bottom of the terrace field to open the gate. Pritchard drove through and made a big circle to bring the truck back out and stop with the tailgate of the trailer just inside the pasture fence. Sixteen bawled, a raw, masculine, sexy sound. No cows were in sight, the bunch having grazed around the shoulder of the hill. But love is in the air, Alice thought, closing her knees and shivering, smiling at herself. She got out and corralled the collies while Domingo leaned from the saddle and disengaged the trailer's latch bar. Positioning his horse against the tailgate, tail toward the hinges, he deftly sidestepped the gate open. Pirouette, thought Alice, watching Skookum; where did you learn that?

Sixteen and Kid shouldered their way out onto the grass, the Pendleton-bound bulls testing the internal gate as they tried to follow. Cubic and shiny as chunks of anthracite, heraldic against the green, the two bulls analyzed the breeze, curling back their upper lips to concentrate the scents. Sixteen blared again, and far away a cow answered. Instantly the old bull trotted away on the track around the base of the hill. Kid watched him go, impassive. Dropped his head, sampled the grazing. Suddenly he jumped up, all four feet at once, and set off at a sprightly canter straight over the top of the hill. Alice and Reese Pritchard simultaneously remembered the punch line of a hoary joke about an old bull and a young bull: Hell, let's jump the fence and screw 'em all.

"That Sixteen always gets right down to work," observed Alice appreciatively as they drove back. "What a busy bull."

"He's a lesson to us all," Pritchard agreed. "Who'zat fella up there? You finally getting some help on the place?" Since Allan Andison's death, many people worried about Alice, though she didn't realize it.

"Yeah, so I hope. But I don't know how long I'll be keeping him. He's got the love light in his eyes."

"Uh-oh. Local girl?"

"Hermiston."

"Well," letting her out at the top of the lane, "hanging out with them bulls ain't going to improve his attitude. Best put him moving pipe, it's less stimulating."

"I shall arrange it at once," laughed Alice. "Bye, Reese. See you, when, end of August? Take care now."

Nonetheless, Domingo took off, leaving her flat just before the first cutting of hay.

"Patrona, I need go for little while."

She straightened up, flushed from forcing the mower hitch, now blooming a deeper rose through her freckles so that for a moment her face seemed to him to flash red-gold.

"Man, I can't spare you now," she said, amazed. Half on the road already, hat in hand, duffel on shoulder. Of all times to pull this trick! Raging inwardly, Damn Concha to hell and back!

He raised a palliative hand: "I'm return Friday, don't worry."

"Listen, this is not a good time to go, think of the work we've got . . . ," her dismay patent.

"Is necessary," flatly, a peculiar lizardlike set coming over his face, eyes half lidded. Alice didn't notice this transformation, instead seized on fact.

"You're coming back when?"

"Friday, seguro."

She breathed through her nose, controlled. "Okay, go if you have to. I'll expect you back on Friday." Bent over the hitch again, she watched his boot heels scuff away. She knew nothing, she realized; not where he was going (though she had a guess), not how, not why. Did he mean, for instance, this coming Friday, or a week from—? She slammed down her wrench, yelled "Shit!" startling the barn swallows into a flutter.

Nan walked in, braiding her hair over her right shoulder: "Did you yell 'Shit'? How come?"

"Domingo's gone, just taken off without a word of warning. Of all times!"

"He coming back?"

"So he says. But who knows?"

"He left his horses, didn't he? Then he'll come back."

"Well, maybe. But imagine, not telling me ahead of time!"

"Maybe he didn't know? Where's he going, anyway?"

"Dammit, he did know! Sitting there at breakfast, no, all this week, in fact, as glum as a toad. 'Course he knew. Just didn't have the huevos to ask me 'cause he knows what a rotten time it is for me to be on my own. He's dropped me in the shit, the jerk, and he knows it. Men cannot be depended on, Nannie, remember that."

"What's huevos?"

"Eggs."

"I know, but . . . but anyway, don't worry, I'm here, and Nick and Earache will come after school, and Tammy will do the feeds if you need her to. We'll get 'er done, Aunt Roan."

"Och," said Alice, spreading her arms wide, "bless the yoots of America! If I wasn't greezy, I'd kiss yiz."

Bel growled at Earache. In spite of his nickname, Eric was a nice kid, last name Doyle, a pal of Nick's who loved Nan devotedly. Nan liked him but didn't know what to do with him, so she brought him out to Standfast when she worked there after school. He pitched right in, not skillful but energetic, and Alice paid him, over his loud objections. "The worker is worthy of his hire," she would say, but he would have preferred to offer his labor on the altar of love.

Bel growled and slunk under the porch, and Earache sat blinking: what had he done but reach a hand to her ears?

"What's that about?" wondered Alice, coming out on the porch, still filthy from her day on the tractor, with six-packs of pop.

"I dunno. She practically sat on my lap yesterday."

"She's done that a couple of times lately," Nan said. "Maybe she has mites in her ears or something."

Alice took Bel to the vet, hoping she had a foxtail in her ear, a tick under her skin, a kidney stone.

"She has a growth in her head, Alice. I can't get at it. We could try a little chemotherapy if you want."

"Is she in pain, Mike?"

"No. But she's confused, and she'll get stranger every day till she dies. How old is she now?"

"Eighteen, nearly. She was my dad's dog." Mike Sage had the wit not to say anything. "What would you do?"

"Put her down, right now."

Driving home dry-eyed, the dead collie on the seat beside her, Alice visualized Allan in a Fifeshire landscape, Bel rushing up, tail whirling. "Wha's the guid wee duggie, noo?" Jean there too, farther back. She shook the vision away: sentimental drivel. Still, if anything did come after, she hoped they were all together somewhere.

The young ones were gone when she got home; good. Alice got a spade and dug a hole at the edge of the bluff above the Triangle, between the locusts and the steep slope Janet had planted to iris and day-lily. The collie graveyard. Kit, and Marr, and now Bel, her name scratched on a flat creek stone. Good dogs all.

Her father had put his faith in dogs, her mother in horses. As a combined legacy, Alice felt, dogs and horses could not be beat. But their lives were short, they left you, and left you sad. After chores, she sat on the porch steps, an arm each around Sweep and Glen, a glass of peaty Islay malt between her feet. A knot under her breastbone. The same feeling as when, several years after Jean died, they had to put down her old Susan mare: the last of Bel, the last of Dad.

Alice, you are drinking your dinner! This will never do. Get up, get a sandwich, make a list, get busy! Nowadays, because of Domingo, the freezer always contained two or three kinds of high-class ice cream. She chose Baskin-Robbins Nutty Coconut. This might just be the night to scarf the whole quart. On television, Seattle was playing Anaheim at Safeco Field. Outside in the lilac-gray evening, tree frogs began to sing. Sighing and picking up her spoon, Alice gave her attention to the fortunes of the Mariners. Her list for tomorrow ran: check bunch on terraces, turn hay, move pipe (ride Ricky, pack Effy), yearlings to Dogleg, weed garden, drag arena. All stuff she wanted to do, enjoyed doing. It just wouldn't be as much fun without Domingo.

"Is he back?" Janet, on the cell phone.

"'Course not. Why would you ever think he would be? He'll prob'ly be sending for his horses in a week or so."

"I ain't guv up yet. Maybe tomorrow."

"Maybe never. What did Concha mean about washing and ironing, by the way?"

"It's a way of repeating that babbling sound, blablabla. She meant the sight of him leaves her blithering and drooling."

"Huh. Does it, though? The guy is not drop-dead gorgeous, exactly."

"True," thinking of Domingo's bold Aztec profile. "That type of face last broke hearts in, say, 1521 AD." There is something about him, though, Janet thought.

"I told you about Bel, didn't I?"

"Yeah. Poor you. Are you sad, Roan?"

"Little bit. Remember when the Susan horse—?"

"Yeah."

But on Saturday morning, to Alice's speechless surprise, there he was, coming out of his room welsh-combing his hair with both hands, as she strode down to the yard to chore. Not a word said, then or at breakfast. Chilled-looking, slit-eyed, hungry as a coyote; didn't look much like a successful suitor. Alice tiptoed round him, suppressing Nan the while.

"But can't I just ask where he went?" she whinged as they rode the two young horses down to move pipe on the alfalfa fields, the morning heating up, fleets of blue-white cumulus scudding before the breeze. They picketed the colts between a couple of cottonwoods, and Nan unclipped her white jockey helmet and hung it on a branch.

"It just may be," Alice loosened Ricky's girth a hole, "that it's none of our beeswax."

"But did he really go visit Concha? And if so, are they hooked up?"

"You're taking a kind of prurient interest, aren't you?"

"Well, *yeah*."

"Well, don't. I'm so happy he's back, I don't care where he went. Be obliged to you if you didn't pester him about it." Now, she wondered, peering down the county road: who is that? Dark blue car, silver stripe, male driver. Second time this week. And hadn't she seen him . . . ? Hm. "If you talk to him at all, speak Spanish, for practice."

"Okay, I will. It's weird, though: he treats me like a princess or something. Almost, like, *bows*, or, I dunno. Sometimes I don't know what to say."

"Well, you are, I guess. Princess-like. The daughter of the house. Let's flush this section, there's something dead in there." A ground squirrel, defunct and slimy, slid from the lower end of the pipe. Alice quickly trod it under to keep it from tempting the dogs. "Even if he didn't respect you personally, he would feel bound to treat you like a prize tulip on account of the family, his position with us."

Nan chewed this over. "But that's dumb. We aren't all that big on social position and inherited status and stuff like that."

"True. Doubt you can talk him out of it, though. Enjoy it, therefore, is my advice."

"Okay, but sometimes," her forty-foot section of pipe flexing deeply with every step, "he makes me feel, like, embarrassed or ashamed of myself. Like I'm not coming up to some standard of behavior. I mean, he doesn't say anything. But I feel like I wouldn't want to let him down." Alice smiled secretly. So much the better for you, baby, she thought, if respect generates self-respect.

"Your granddad used to say, 'Earn what's given,'" she panted out.

"Aha," Nan mused, twisting a connector closed. "Would that be that Wisdom of the Ancients I keep hearing about? Well, I'll try to be nicer to the Ancients. I wonder why he keeps on calling me miss though."

What put Nan off, in truth, was that in spite of Domingo Roque's graceful manners, she had no idea whether he liked her or not. Many people did like her, school administrators included; those who didn't were pretty open about why not, and if she just waited quietly, usually they came around. And she herself liked just about everybody. But with Alice's new hand there was some kind of barrier. Thoughtlessly egalitarian, Nan simply assumed that she and Domingo would become friends. Instead, there was this lacquered punctilio. And it seemed to her that he kept the same sort of distance between himself and Concha Vélez; that was why she was curious about them.

True, he touched his hat brim to Alice. But on the other hand he called her by her name.

If not for the silver rally stripe, the dark blue Trans Am would have been invisible, parked beside the Dixie School at midnight of a wet spring night. Even so, the flying rags of cloud parted to reveal it by moonlight only fitfully. The driver, however, was awake and alert. So when the Corvette tore by at eighty, double the legal speed, the Trans Am peeled right out after it, no lights, and shot up the hill past the grain elevator close enough behind to identify the Nevada plate. Under the radar, thought the Trans Am driver. Silent but deadly.

Along the twisting state two-lane as one, down into Waitsburg, slackening speed just feet before the right-angle turn by the machine shop. The Corvette cornered level as a roller skate, immediately accelerating again. The taller vehicle took the turn on two wheels, the driver fighting the wheel, but made up the distance on the straightway over the bridge, drafting in on the Corvette's bumper. Like a wolf shadowing a deer, thought the driver; like a shark under a boat. Dudn even know I'm here. But he was disappointed, had hoped the Corvette, obviously up to no good, would somehow turn back to Waitsburg, implicate the Weston bitch.

Seven miles on up the narrow valley, a low hill, and the mouth of a road bearing off to the east. Falling back a little, the Trans Am made the crest in time to see the other car take the eastbound cutoff. The county road was narrower and not well surfaced, the Corvette putting the Trans Am on its mettle. So concentrated was the Trans Am driver that he nearly ran up on the lower car as it slowed, approaching a ranch road. Slowed and stopped, turned off the headlights.

The Trans Am driver sped past as he had been taught to do when tailing, rounded the curve looking left and right, found a place to turn in a wheat field, and came slowly back. There sat the Corvette. There sat the driver, face a pale blur in the black of the cockpit, looking up the lane toward the house. Could have been dead, could have been a corpse, sitting there so white and still; spooky. What was that about? Didn't get out or anything, didn't smoke.

The Trans Am driver made mental notes so he could find the place again if necessary. If it turned out something bustable was going down here. Wasn't it around here somewhere, the State Patrol made that big meth bust? Yeah. He couldn't read the sign over the gate. Mailbox on the wrong side of the road

An hour and forty-three minutes later, the Nevada car started up, no lights, and pulled across the cattle guard as if to drive up the track to the homeplace. A couple of dogs came tearing down the hill, but before they reached the Corvette it reversed out and laid smoking tread down the westbound lane. Putting a little space between him and Nevada Plates, the Trans Am driver clicked on his running lights and followed. The chase, he thought, is on.

Back to the state highway, through Waitsburg and then Dixie deeply sleeping. Along the north side of Walla Walla, the short stretch of four-lane, then off on Second Avenue, Rose Street to Ninth, down Ninth until it became Highway Eleven to Milton-Freewater. All at a pace that strained the Trans Am driver's skills; luckily, neither city police cruisers nor county cars interfered. Across the line into Oregon on the new wide road, screaming through Stateline, past the apple orchards and battened-down fruitstands, right through town, running every red light.

The Trans Am gave up the chase at the Milton-Freewater city limits, the Corvette's taillights winking away south on the road to Pendleton. The driver turned back to the all-nighter at the crossroads for a slash and a latte. Penciled into his notebook the plate number. Wished he could ask for help IDing—but that would reveal his private operation. He also sketched the design on the ranch gate: a diamond with two crossbars inside it, like an A standing on a mirror.

Chapter Six

JUNE WORE AWAY, HEAT SWELLING ON THE LOWER GROUND, THOUGH THE high pastures stayed cool and chilled off at night. At Standfast they baled and then stacked the first hay; repaired fences and gates; moved irrigation pipe; rode the two young horses on the tracks and through the creeks; rode herd. Hamster the bull came up from Enterprise in Oregon, and set about impregnating the yearling heifers on the Dog-leg. Alice sent some brood heifers to the sale, and sold Jerry Graeme's Appaloosa gelding to a drill-team rider for an excellent price. The mare Three Cheers came home from Prosser pregnant.

Domingo Roque recovered his spirits; hot weather clearly agreed with him. He could sing, a husky true tenor. Alice couldn't, but she could whistle, and the radio would tune them up together sometimes. She liked the sound of him around the place. Didn't mind if he sorted out her Spanish. God knew it needed sorting out. One night in the kitchen, talking about Jerry Graeme, mistaking pato for puta: "That sonofaduck!" Domingo laughed until beer came out his nose.

Nan Weston graduated from high school at a ceremony of which, for insipid banality and zoo-grade crudity, Janet said she had never seen the equal. The graduates acted like prisoners let out of jail, she told Alice, whereas in fact they were nonswimmers kicked off the dock. Not having organized her thoughts about the future, Nan was bound for Washington State University in the fall. Philip and Janet maintained a stance of stoic noninterference in this matter. "Well," sighed Janet to Philip as they sat on the deck after dinner, swifts and bats darting in the warm dusk, "she'll find out."

Philip thought that Nan lacked intellectual confidence. "Wazoo may be just the thing," he said, spooning up early and very costly raspberries, savoring each one. "She may develop a longing for a higher net."

"She may become bored and discouraged and come home pregnant."

Philip went down to change the position of the sprinkler. "Have a little faith in your good work, my vanilla bean," he said, coming back and taking up his dish again. "She's the one who's saved up to go to language camp year after year. She just wants to stick a toe in the water, doesn't want to jump in all at once. You know how she is."

"Yes," Janet said, "clever but cautious."

"Nothing wrong with that."

"Like me."

"Nothing at all wrong with that."

For the first time in a decade, Janet decided not to teach summer school. She didn't want to leave Nick alone all summer. Nick was a brute these days, sullen, secretive, flammable. The things he said, the bloody-minded politics he propounded at the dinner table, made Janet want to smack him and throw him out of the house.

"He's like a three-year-old colt with a half-made mouth, unsteerable," she fumed to Alice. "Not by me, anyway. Better with Philip. But he's using him awfully hard; Phil was up until three last night listening to Nick rant about the world and its problems. He'll have to change the way he practices law at this rate. No kidding," Alice making a face, "he turned down an arbitration case in Boise, his favorite thing in his favorite city, just because he doesn't want to be away from home right now. I don't know what to do, I really don't. Except I should quit trying to reason with Nick, that's pretty clear, 'cause one or both of us wind up screeching."

She did quit talking to him, but she talked to all his friends. A number of Nick's friends were at daggers-drawn with their own parents, or just not being paid much attention to. In fact, several of them were frankly ill-fed, and hung out many an evening in the kitchen at the Westons', ate pretzels and drank Diet Coke while Janet cooked dinner, ate the nachos she made on the side, stayed for dinner, and got driven home by Philip because Nick had a twelve o'clock curfew.

Alice took him in. He might as well work for her as for 7-Eleven, she said; more useful labor under less depressing conditions, and he could learn to drive the moribund Chevette—stick shift, which would stand him in good stead later in life.

Nick had the occasional go at her too, for playing into the hands of those who liked the lousy immigration regulations the way they were, but these forays were not very satisfactory to him. Alice was working too hard to notice, generally, and Domingo, representing the abused wetback, pled poquito inglés. He just wouldn't play the underdog. When Nick suggested that the undocumented workers ought to form a union, Domingo said, "Sound like one way for guy like me to get kill." He showed no resentment, no interest at all in the general lot of his countrymen up here in the North, and declared without undue modesty, *"I am the best vaquero in the state; why should I allow somebody else to decide what I should get paid?"* Against which Nick had no come-back. Also, those lists of Alice's wore him to a frazzle; he wound up asleep in his plate every night.

Further unraveling ideological consistency, Alice the oppressor was likely to defend Domingo the oppressed if she thought Nick was out of line. "That was mean, Nicky, making him out to be half-bright for not being political. Making him out to be 'part of the problem' last night at dinner. Were you showing off for Philip?"

"Certainly not," said Nick, horrified to find his aunt so acute. "I was just trying to get an argument going. I like arguing. But he—how come Domingo never defends himself?" as Janet came in from the car-port with a plastic box of snickerdoodles. Nick waded into them, glad of the distraction.

"Because," Alice, undistractable, "he's too well brought up to argue with his host's son at his host's table. So you're able to impose on his good manners. If you thought he'd brush you back like you deserve, I doubt you'd tackle him. And anyway, he'd be surprised to know he needs to defend himself against you."

"I know! He doesn't take me seriously, kid that I am."

Alice stopped a cookie halfway to her mouth. "No, it's because he respects you, he assumes you're a good person. He assumes, though he may be wrong, that you respect him. Also, he doesn't understand your sarcasm; he just thinks he didn't understand the words. Are we out of milk?"

Janet got up to look. Nick's forehead went bump on the table. "You want to come out to Pataha with us and look at this horse?" Alice was on the hunt for a dressage prospect for Janet.

"Jesus, no. I'm just hoping I'm adopted, that's all," he mumbled.

"Go lie in the hammock, then. Don't feel bad now. Your ideas do you credit. I just don't want you to make an example of Domingo because he's handy." Seizing half a dozen cookies, Nick went out, pointedly not slamming the screen. Janet brought in a pitcher of lemonade. "You see?" she said.

"As long as he has that kind of appetite for your snickerdoodles, I can't believe he's as alienated as he makes out. He's just trying on hats in a safe environment, like we did with poor old Mrs. Motley, God forgive us. It's just a question of you holding off on killing him long enough for him to get civil again."

Janet ate a cookie gloomily.

"This too shall pass," Alice said.

Janet ate two cookies at once and changed the subject. "Domingo was on the Triangle when I drove up the lane. He rode over and gave me a little clinic with that Cattywampus. Grinning like a monkey the whole time, the smart aleck. Did you know Catty could do a school canter? That's about third level."

"That's the message, I s'pose: anything a fancy-pants dressage rider in white breeches and tailcoat can do, the average working cowhand can do."

"What shit. Anyway, he's not average. And besides, let's see his trot-pirouette, canter half-pass with counter changes of hand."

"Yup."

"Reefing the critter around in circles with its mouth open does not qualify."

"Yup. Though he's got those two colts tossing off flying changes without batting an eye."

Janet pushed her jaw out until she looked like a bad collie. "The point is to make the animal appear to dance for its own pleasure."

"Yup. I'm on your side. Listen, shall we get him to come look at this horse with us? He has a pretty good eye."

A gorgeous day for a drive, green-blond wheat and brown summerfallow in sweeping baroque curves banded the hills, sunshine like a benediction. They had a little trouble finding the place, the lane overgrown with alder, sumac, and stinky ailanthus. Half a mile in, a line of sheds heaved and staggered along a narrow bench above the river, trailing away from a rackety frame house. Additions had been tacked on to the house in the same crabbed proportions as the original structure, a lick of staring yellow paint laid on the unprimed boards of one side, but so long ago that thistle had grown up head-high among the rungs of the painter's ladder. They rolled in and parked next to a hay shed with several thousand dollars' worth of solar collecting panels leaning against one of its stanchions, deep in dust. The farmer had imagination, evidently, but not much staying power.

Two dogs came helling out of the nearest hut, not farm dogs but heavy-duty rottweilers. Domingo, halfway to the ground, hopped back inside and slammed and locked his door. Instead of barking, the rottweilers poured out a continuous rolling, slavering yell, never stopping for breath. They assaulted the truck, mouthing the bumpers and tires and hammering the windows with their blunt paws. Nobody offered to venture out; all sat in the truck waiting for somebody to take the dogs in hand.

Janet, direly: "If one of these monsters eats a tire, old man Tillotson will pay."

After a while an angular kid with a prodigious overbite dashed out of the house, caught by the scruff the dog gnawing the bumper, dragged down by its choker the one scratching the windshield, and hauled them both off out of sight, though not out of hearing. At the same time, a bone-thin old man in a bill cap, jeans, and an America Love It Or Leave It T-shirt came out of the house and waved: *follow me.* They got warily out of the truck. He kept waving them on, not looking back, walking like a convalescent, like a man with a chronic bad back or a shattering hangover. Led them down onto the flat by the creek where there was a piece of ground rototilled up, a circle about twenty yards in diameter.

When they got close, he turned on them a false and gap-toothed smile. "You hear about the horse?" Evidently: Janet in her breeches and stovepipe boots, Alice in jeans and ripstop gaiters. Domingo, Alice thought, looking around, had perhaps stayed with the truck?

"Jessie!" bellowed the old guy, amazingly loud. The bucktoothed kid, who turned out to be a girl in her twenties with a totally unformed figure, ran out of one of the sheds with a horse on a long lead shank. "Bring the colt out!" unnecessarily. The horse was a thoroughbred, long-stemmed and long-necked with a pretty Araby head. His mahogany bay coat was still woolly, which was strange in June, and covered with a goodly layer of mud. Even so, they could count every rib.

"He's rough," old Tillotson said, "but you can see through the rough." This was supposed to both flatter and deceive, Alice supposed.

"You can just about see through the horse," Janet snarled under her breath.

Domingo came down the hill. Catching Alice's eye, he cupped his left elbow with his right palm: elbow—codo, codicioso—stingy, miserly. Scoping out the hay and feed supplies, that was where he had disappeared to. Alice deduced that the bay's ribby condition derived not from sickness or nerves but from bad and insufficient feeding.

"Walk him around there, Jessie!" which was what she was doing. The horse was alert, eager even, but docile, keeping the shank slack, turning toward the girl confidingly every step or so. He seemed to have plenty of energy, skinny though he was. Also, Alice gained an impression of stoutness. Puzzled, she said, "So tell us about him, Mr. Tillotson, how's he bred?"

"He's by Lolo," the old man said, sinking his chin into his neck and squinting intently across the creek as if the real, serious buyers might appear over there. "Y'know Don Eslick's stud, over to Prescott? Real good horse. This one takes after him: fast, real fast. And the mare, she was my mare Lovely Star. But she ain't here, I sold her to a guy up in Yakima, big-time breeder, he's breedin' runners out of her. She's a Bold Ruler on her mother's side."

"Is he registered?" Janet asked, forestalling Alice who hadn't believed any of this either, certainly not about the Bold Ruler dam.

"'Course!" offended. But then, hastily, "But he ain't never raced. He's sound, you can see, got no bad habits."

"Let's go talk to him," suggested Alice, "see what he's like up close and personal."

"Git the chain, Jessie!"

"Don't bother, Jessie!" Janet shouted to the girl, and to the old man explained, "If I can't manage him, I don't want him." This seemed to strike old man Tillotson as a novel and pretty stupid idea; he didn't come with them to the horse. The bay gelding wheeled to face them as they approached, flicking his ears back and forth; the girl Jessie did the same, except for her ears, but by not moving fast and not looking directly at either one, they induced both to ratchet down a notch or two.

Jessie said, "Don't worry, he's nice, he just don't care for men very much."

"Sensible attitude," Janet said. "Would he eat a cookie, do you think?" taking three or four pressed-alfalfa tidbits out of her pocket. The horse's ears snapped full forward.

"He ain't never had one," began the girl, "but you can sure—" The gelding took all four at once, though politely, mumbled them around for a minute, crunched, chewed, chewed with enthusiasm, chewed and chewed, nodding his long, keen face up and down and holding up one forefoot ecstatically.

"I'd say that was a success," Alice chuckled. "Got any more, Yan? He's askin' for the recipe."

During the second round of cookies, Domingo came up. Still crunching, the bay backed to the end of his lead rope. "Señorita, please, what he's name?"

"Oh, Lolo's Pride or some dang thing," blushing rosy at "señorita." "But I call him Baby, 'cause he's my baby." She shut her mouth hard and blinked several times. Domingo held out his hand, and reluctantly she gave him the shank. The horse gave a long snoring snort and braced his legs, but nothing happened. Alice and Janet walked around him, looking him over.

"Do you have a brush I could use?" Janet asked, and Jessie went off, apparently mystified, to find one. Meanwhile, Alice got out the fold-up hoof pick she carried in her hip pocket where other cowboys carry their snoose cans, and picked out the bay's feet. He didn't mind about this, just peered around at her when she did the hind ones and rested his upper lip on her back when she did the fores. He didn't mind about Janet scratching the caked mud from his back and his girth. When she went to brush his face, though, he turned out to be madly head shy, throwing himself back so hard he nearly sat down. Domingo backed up with him so he wouldn't feel trapped, and Janet went around to his off side, where he didn't seem so much bothered.

Alice trotted up to the truck for Janet's dressage saddle and her snaf-fle bridle with its classy white-piped brow band. As she came back past him, old man Tillotson waved her down: "Aw, you gonna ride him?"

"Sure, why not? Isn't he broke to ride?"

"Yeah, sure he is, but"—looking like a terrorist whose ticking briefcase is handed back to him by some helpful airport functionary— "whyn't you just put your Meskin boy up on him?"

"Yes, Teacher," Domingo said to Janet, deadpan, "why you don't put you Mexican?"

"Hands off him, you bulldogger. It's my belief this horse was born to dance," she said, and Alice thought, uh-oh.

The saddle presented no difficulties, Alice taking the precaution of girthing up one hole at a time so as not to startle the tummy. The bridle would be problematic. She unbuckled the reins to put them around his neck at the withers rather than over his shy head.

"Let's take the cavesson right off, Alice, don't you think?" Janet suggested. She unbuckled the cheeks from the headstall and ran the headstall up the gelding's neck by stages with many cookies and kind words, until she could slip it over his ears from the back. So far, so good. She buckled on the off-side cheekstrap. When the bit was presented to his lips, he took it like a gentleman, and she buckled the near-side cheek with no trouble.

Jessie, who had held her breath throughout, said suddenly, "Lemme ride him for ya, just for a minute."

Janet grinned her down. "You think he'll dump me off?"

"Well," diplomatically, "he ain't been rode for a while."

Janet scratched the horse where his neck met his brisket, to his evident pleasure. "Let's see how he goes," she said, "before anybody rides him. Do you have a longe line?"

A twenty-foot length of webbing was produced. The horse had been "gypped," run around on the end of this line for exercise, all right. He thought only one gait possible: full throttle. Janet kept shortening the line when he'd get too fast, letting out when he'd ease down. It didn't resemble the focused calisthenics of genuine longe work in any particular; still, he balanced himself well, hurtling around in the deep going.

"What's she want him for?" old Tillotson asked, sidling up to Alice where she stood back out of the bay's orbit.

"Dressage."

"Oh. Ah."

Domingo legged Jessie up jockey style. She had a fine natural seat, though she wanted her knees up under her chin, and a light and tactful hand. She must have been her dad's exercise galloper from Year

One, Alice thought. Then they got to see the bay horse's gaits, and they were fancy, she had to admit: a reachy true walk; a lofty trot, bold and rhythmic. The canter, however, was a fight; Jessie had her hands full with him.

"Don't canter," Alice muttered to Janet. "Looks like he doesn't know it from gallop; he'll take off with you."

"I have no desire to wind up in Washtucna," she agreed.

When Janet got on, her long stirrups must have confused him, probably her real-woman weight did too; still, he cut nary a dido but walked off as stolid as a beer-wagon horse. Now, why do I think of heavy drafters, Alice asked herself, and before she got on she stooped down and measured the circumference of each cannon bone with her hands. And then she knew why he seemed stout in spite of being rake-thin: it was all bone, a massive degree of bone for his breed. While she was down there, she noticed something else. Looked up at Domingo to call his attention to the tiny white dots in rows on the front of each shin; he nodded and made a complicated grimace, pointing his lips at old man Tillotson and squinting, dubious. And her spirits sagged, for she knew by certain infallible signs that Janet had fallen in love with the beast in all his flagrant unsuitability. Lord! Maybe because of it.

"How much are you asking for him?"

"Put him on the hot walker, Jessie!" affecting not to hear. But Janet kept hold of the horse, petting him and leading him up and down, giving him cookies. It appeared that if she sat down, the gelding would curl up in her lap.

"He raised on this place?" Alice said, to disturb the old man's timing.

"'Course!"

"He always been so lean?"

Squawking, "Lean, hell! The horse is racing-fit, 's wrong with you, can't you see that?" Out of his sight, Jessie rolled her eyes. At last he worked himself to the sticking point, "eight thousand," on a big sigh, like a concession, "a steal at that, win it back for ya in a heartbeat."

Dumbfounded silence. Janet kept on rubbing and scratching the bay horse's face.

"Well," she said at last, "thank you for letting us look at him," and she handed the lead shank to Jessie.

Old man Tillotson jumped as if he'd touched the hot wire. "Put him away!" he bawled at the girl. "Put the goddamn horse away, Jessie!" and stamped off toward the house.

"¡Estará loco!" Domingo murmured, surprised. Loco is right, Alice thought; did he really think we'd pay a premium price for this middle-aged meat rack?

"He's real nice," Jessie said pleadingly to Janet, "he's a real nice horse, he's just—"

"I know he is, honey," her voice a trifle husky. "Thank you for riding him for us."

Jessie tried and failed to cover her teeth with her upper lip. "Welcome." She was still standing there with her bay horse as they drove away.

Janet stayed to dinner because Philip was in Moses Lake, Nan had gone to Portland with Tammy Evans, and Nick was off on a JROTC encampment. She made herself a martini and took it out on the porch. "Awful sweet," she said, "considering what he's putting up with."

"Now, Janet, *no*! He's a lousy deal at half, at a quarter what they're asking."

"Did I say anything about buying him? Okay, why is Domingo Roque smiling that nasty smile?"

"Prob'ly because he's never seen a five-year-old horse with a ten-year-old mouth before; it's a kind of miracle."

"Jesus Christ," he snorted, "that guy lyin' about everything, how old, how he's train, how he don't race. This horse race a lot. Pinfire is expensive, nobody don't pay for pinfire no horse which don't race."

"Yes, I saw the scars. But it doesn't mean he was lame; some people pinfire to toughen the bone cover, to prevent injury. It's disgusting, but it's done."

"Some bastards pinfire to make a horse sore and ginger him up;

which do you bet— Look, you cannot trust one thing that old souse said about the critter. You'd be buying a pig in a poke, and a skinny pig at that."

Janet set her glass on the porch railing and studied the olive: "Nice long shoulder."

"Short pasterns!"

"Not short, just thick. And a good angle. And a super back end."

"Yeah, well." There was no denying that. "Funny, though. Croup's flat where you'd expect a peak."

"What did you think, vaquero? Moved nice, didn't he?"

"Música, Teacher," slurping beer. Alice scowled and shook her fist at him.

"Anyway," she said, "a dressage horse needs three good gaits. If you dassn't canter him, how can you—"

"I dast; you told me not to."

Alice had nothing to say. She worked on her beer. After a while she said, "Don't buy it, Yan."

"Don't buy a thoroughbred, Teacher," Domingo chipped in. *"Take it as a maxim."*

"Who said anything about buying? You're the ones who keep saying that word." She sipped. Sipped again.

"She's buyin' it," said Alice and Domingo to each other. Janet laughed dangerously.

"I'm hoping she's forgotten it," Alice said, weeding down the tomato row ahead of him. Meaning the Tillotson horse. "That would be a poor bargain. But why not a thoroughbred? Some of them have spectacular gaits, and since we can't afford a European horse . . ."

"Portales?"

"Not gates; gaits, pasos. Even that one of Tillotson's, for example. Lotta bounce to the ounce. What you got against them?"

"Bat-shit, most of them. Because of the life they lead. Racing, I mean. It makes them think people are no damn good. We make them go to the limit of their strength, again and again. Not what they'd do on their own. They

get hurt a little bit, but still they have to run, and then everything hurts, and still we make them run . . ." Domingo heard himself and straightened up, embarrassed. Picked and crunched a green bean.

Alice looked up at him from her hunkers, smiling a crooked smile. "Slick, you're a fool about them," she said. "Might as well face it."

"Me? No way. Anyway, so are you," laughing. *"Well, I won't tell if you don't. Did you ever ride gallops, Aliz?"*

"Nope. Been run away with a couple of times. Is it like that?"

"Yes y no."

The first one that really gave it up to him was a very tall liver chestnut, thick in the throatlatch, a coarse head and a small, cold eye. He himself just starting as a gallop rider, the trainer trying him out as a favor to his father. "Just trot a furlong, and ease on up, once around. He raced yesterday, so . . ." Domingo did not pick up the doubtful cadence, trying to settle on the beast as it tossed its head and whirled and balked. It wouldn't steer, even at trot, and veered from side to side of the track, its nose in the air in spite of the running martingale. Rather than be dumped off in full view of the backstretch community, he had pushed on around the turn at a rough canter, the beast fighting all the way and panting like a runaway train. Lather slicked the reins, he was on his butt and on his knees by turns, winded and tiring, and at the end of the homestretch Domingo surrendered. Gave up, sank into the horse, his face to its crest and his hands high on the sweated neck, offering the reins. Go where you want, you dumb bastard; just try not to kill us.

In an instant everything changed, smoothed out like deep water after rapids, every stride longer and flatter, the horse doubling like a greyhound, the white rail, the corduroy track streaming by, joy like a river streaming through them, on and on. You darling! Domingo shouted inside himself. You angel thing! You excellent elemental all-over noonday fuck of a thing! On and on and on, all the way around. And they ended up at the clubhouse turn again, dropping down to a trot in perfect accord and turning to walk back with the reins slack, Domingo in love with all the world, nearly sobbing with pleasure.

Certain he would never ride for the guy again, not caring; wanting to embrace the horse, elope with it. Though when he hopped down, it nipped him and tore his sweatshirt.

"How did you get him to run like that?" begged the trainer, leading him aside, he still panting, almost blubbering. "You got a card?" Of course he had no license: just eighteen, already five foot six, and he would never see a hundred and ten pounds again. Race-riding was not for him. But that streaming gallop—he could never get enough. It was as good as sex and longer lasting, a pure and perfect surrender. Worth risking his neck on a hundred hammerheads to feel like that: fully in his body, totally out of his mind.

Janet usually threw a party on the Fourth of July, a potluck to which everybody brought an "ethnic" dish. She baked some salmon fillets and simmered cabbage in cream; Nick dealt with the spuds. Vera Jane brought her famous Dundee cake, studded with almonds and breathing whisky. Nan made a very creditable cream crowdie; Terri McCrimmon won lasting fame with her pierogi, tiny, flaky, and bursting with leek and carrot, with peppery gravy. Earache Doyle, though underage, generally showed up with two six-packs of Guinness Stout.

"What are you making for the Fourth?" Alice asked as Domingo, grease to the elbows, withdrew carefully from amongst the small tractor's innards.

"?"

"For the pachanga tomorrow at Janet's, what are you making?"

"They invite me, ¿de veras?" looking rather scared.

"Sure, of course. It's just the family, well, family plus. Big dinner, fireworks, dancing. Singing, if we're not careful. Everybody you know will be there, all the gringos anyway. Fun! Unless you're invited somewhere else."

How could he refuse? Churlish, ill bred. They were buena gente, these Westons, for sure. Yet what was he to make of this invitation? In Mexico the situation would have been so clear, reciprocal duties of patronage and dependency known, accepted. Here, all was hazy. They employed him; they punctiliously adhered to the terms of his employment, no irregular demands, no ugly surprises in the pay envelope. But they seemed to offer something beyond this: a relationship at the same time more personal and vaguer in outline. Here he did not know the rules, did not know where he stood.

Come to think of it, nothing confused him more than the way things were with the boss herself. He had fallen into the habit of addressing her by her name, just because everybody else did, but sometimes when he caught himself at it, his skin crept cold with embarrassment. Another thing: he liked, positively enjoyed working with her. And he was hard to please! He valued her opinion. Was starting to master her quirks of dialect too. Tell you what, slick = escúchame. I hear that = órale, de acuerdo. You said it, kid = seguro. Apart from never using the tú forms, she treated him like a younger brother. And he was getting used to it. As if from a distance he watched himself settling into the place, pulling its comforts around him like a quilt. Risky, risky.

A good hot day for the party, gray and thick until after the evening feeds, then opening up finely toward the west as if in anticipation of the town's fireworks display. Nick had mowed the Westons' backyard and set up a couple of long tables; through the aromas of the feast wafted up now and then the sweet breath of new-cut grass. Fifteen were invited, most of whom Domingo knew, plus wanderers-in from neighboring yards bringing beer, watermelon, strawberries, platters of sweet-onion slices. They were dancing on the deck to old-fashioned rock and roll, Janet and Philip really acabándose las chanclas, he noticed. People talked about local politics, state politics; the Mariners' awful season; the lousy price of wheat, the plummeting market for beef; the decline and rebirth of downtown Waitsburg; prospects for development in wine, in skiing, in summer tourism. He understood about a third of what was said, regulated his beer intake with care. As he stood talking horse with Alice, Janet came up:

"Dance with me, Domingo!"

"Teacher, I don't can!" But she had only asked out of courtesy.

"Alice, come on, then. Phil's beached," and she led her sister away by the wrist, Alice handing off her beer as she went. The Andison sisters could really bebop, apparently; everybody knew it and stopped talking to watch. The tune was loud and fast, heavy on drums, and Domingo stood gaping, a can of beer in either hand: quick feet, whipping skirts, wreathing arms; Alice's face intense, Janet's sleepy, blissed out. The first time he'd seen Alice in anything but jeans. Nice legs, he thought, considering how skinny she is.

"Them girls been dancing together since they're small," explained Vera Jane Whyte, coming up beside him, incongruously shawled. "You not dancing, young fella like you?"

"Doña Vera, my feet are bricks," and she giggled like a maiden. It wasn't his feet that were itching; it was his fingers, for guitar strings. He could have played that tune, he thought, Do, Fa, Sol, Do.

At ten, the whole party trekked to the park with blankets, cushions, coolers, and plastic chairs for the oldsters, to watch the fireworks. By the light of the first few rockets, Domingo saw a man he thought he knew from California and went over to check, passing the fire engine on duty and, with a start, a car he remembered, a car with a stripe, parked under the blood maples, and somebody leaning against it in uniform, wearing sunglasses in the dark. The firetruck, okay: wheat harvest-ready covered the hills all around; but why the policía?

Meanwhile, cannily as he imagined, Robey eased the conversation around to the Hashknife property.

"Y'know, Alice," she sitting cross-legged at his feet in the velvet dark, "that place is up for sale now." Alice glanced around at him, bristly eyebrows, snaggly grin, devilish in the rockets' red glare, and regretted her last Labatt.

"Vera Jane, is this fair? Control your man, would you, please?"

"No, no, nothing serious. I'm just letting you know so you can be thinking about it. Relax. Watch the fireworks, go ahead."

Alice turned back. Three green stars whooshed up, burst in golden rain; another green one hung against the cyan sky with swinging gold pendants like birch catkins, catkins of fire. A barrage of red stars, deafening.

"I been talking to Bob about it."

Alice fell backward, dead, defeated. "Okay, why are you doing that? Janet, come over here, help me. Whyever are you bringing Bob in on the deal? Jeez, Robey, we're s'posed to be having fun here."

"I'm havin' fun," McCrimmon said from the other side. "Just listen, Alice, will ya?"

"Because it's too big for just you and me," Robey said. "D'you know how far back up the crick that place goes? It's the old Graeme place, remember that. Graemes used to run four, five hundred head of stock on that place, not Angus neither."

"Why would the breed of cattle make any difference?" asked Philip, rowing toward them on his bottom with a plate of raspberry cupcakes. A scandalized pause. "Razzies!" yelled Vera Jane, to deflect everyone's attention, and then under cover of mass munching gave Philip a clue: "Honey, you know why: 'cause your Angus will rustle for forage where Herefords and Charolais and Simmentals and big beef like that think there ain't any." A faint memory came over Philip of having been told this before. Perhaps more than once.

Robey forged ahead: "Them sections away upstream back right up against Bob's place. McCrimmons got their own water, so they wouldn't bother you any more than they do already—"

"Which is a lot!" Alice broke out. She groaned and harrowed her curls. "All I need is them extending their empire around my top fields. Ole Bob has offered to buy us out three times since Dad died—haven't you, Bob? Whose side are you on, Robey?"

"Keep yer hair on, Alice, don't get yer shorts in a tangle! Now, what's so dang funny? Listen, will ya. Here's the good part. The sections south of you, over the ridge, they're high, but they're nice level benches, good ground. I was telling you about them, remember? Too high for alfalfa, but timothy, brome, orchard grass. About fifty-two acres total, that's another hundred ton a year, dorlin'."

"If the weather's perfect, and the crop goes premium, and the market holds—"

"Heck sakes, what a pessimist," McCrimmon said.

"Realist, Bobby, and so are you. Nothing's sure, you know as well as I do."

"How did you get into farming at all anyway?"

Alice calculated, lying flat. How many man hours per ton? She'd have less help, with Nan going to college; would she even be available in the summers? Would Nick, would Janet? Would Domingo stay? That would be crucial. And first and foremost, would the bank really lend her the money?

Meanwhile, Janet said, "What's your interest in this scheme, Robey Deal-Maker? You just want the dregs, gravel reef, hot old dry creek bed?" and Vera Jane burst into giggles, rocking back and forth, her shawl ends to her mouth.

An earth-jarring salvo lit everything up in Old Glory colors. Robey leaned back perilously, one arm around Vera Jane, the other flung out like P. T. Barnum. "Behold," he crowed, "the owners of Vera Vineyards!"

As if it were not enough—party food, late hours, wicked beer-hangover, Robey's maneuverings—as if these were in fact forerunners of trouble, Jerry Graeme called.

Alice didn't know who it was at first. She was on horseback at the top of the Circ, looking over onto the Hashknife land: weedy fields and reeling fences, but God's own sweep of a view down the Valley toward Horse Heaven. Disgusting mucusoid sounds in her ear; her gorge rose.

"Uh. Yeah. Listen." Buzz, click, snuffle. She squeezed the handset against her ear, trying to guess what was going on, imagining nastiness.

"Jerry? You okay?" Actually, *how* he was didn't matter to her; *where*, was the question.

"Yeah, listen. I'm authorizing, hereby, I hereby authorize you to sell my half."

Alice took the cellular unit from her ear and peered at it.

"Pardon, what? Say again?"

"I said," same prelude of nauseous sounds, as if he were freeing his tongue from mucilage, "I hereby authorize you to sell my half." The emphasis on "hereby authorize," as if to bind her legally. *My half?*

"Your half of what?" with a dreadful premonition.

"My half of the ranch, you slut!" A horrid whine; Alice's hackles stood up. "What the fuck do you think? My half of the fucking ranch, I auth—hereby authorize you to sell my half! Jesus Christ!" Heavy breathing; then, very soft and rapid, "I hereby authorize you to sell my half of the fucking ranch, you should get fifty, between fifty and a hundred grand, aye ess aye pee." Panting. Then at shocking volume, "DO YOU FUCKING UNDERSTAND!!"

She nearly dropped the phone. Carefully, "Jerry, you don't own half of this ranch. You own a life interest in some of the hay ground. Do you want to sell your life interest?" He hung up.

Up there, alone with the clouds and the crows, Alice stared all around her, sure that something hideous threatened, visible, palpable. She ran Tom Fool hard for home and called Philip from the safety of the kitchen. He was engaged. She pulled on a sweatshirt while she waited, perched on the stepladder, shivering in midsummer heat, hands clamped between her knees. Philip rang back; she described Jerry Graeme's call: "You wouldn't believe how crazy and weird he sounded, Phil, and sort of . . . sick."

Philip thought he would believe it. "Where did he call from?"

"I don't know, I didn't look. Jesus! He really scared me!" She poked at the cell phone. " 'Out of area,' it says."

"How did he get your cell number?"

"I don't know. He used to live here, for Christ's sake! My God, can you believe that? Of course, he wasn't nuts, then, just awful."

Oh no, indeed, Philip thought. Had always been nuts, a head case from the word go. "Do you have a phone number for him, by any chance, or an address? I'll see if I can get in touch with him. Cheer up, Standfast. This may be a golden opportunity, you know."

"But Philip," calmer, coming to the nub, "could he sell his life interest to somebody else, somebody who isn't us?"

"Now, as I am sure I have mentioned before, property law, like the sexual life of the camel, is stranger than anyone thinks. So I shall examine the documents, and perhaps seek ancillary advice and counsel. But I'll say this: if he sells, he sells to us."

Hot weather hurried on the wheat, white-blond and thigh-deep on the Palouse hills, fragrant as baking bread. Just before wheat harvest began, Alice and Domingo cut hay on the high ground at Standfast, trundled the mowers back downhill, and the following week cut the alfalfa fields for the second time. Guardedly hopeful, Alice triangulated the thermometer, the barometer, and the sky. "Make hay while the sun shines," she said to Domingo who responded, "A Dios rogando, con el mazo dando." If rain fell on the mown grasses as they lay drying in windrows, they would mold in the field or in the bale.

Twice more during this time Alice saw the racy dark-blue car with the broad silver band, once in the alley behind Janet's bungalow and once coming out of Waitsburg on the highway. That time she pointed it out to Domingo, but neither of them caught the license number.

They baled hay on the high ground and left the bales to cure; tackled repairs on the pens and corrals; trimmed the fruit trees behind the house, worked on the garden; turned the dung heap to compost it. Trailed the Angus herd to new grazing every third day, and dragged the pastures behind them. Moved irrigation pipe. Played with the young horses. On Saturday mornings they set jumps and cones in the covered arena for Pony Club lessons; on Tuesday evenings the drill team came to practice. A full life, full to overflowing, thought Alice—a sentiment she would have shared with Domingo had he not been lying asleep on the sports pages.

They spent three days setting a stock tank on the Forty-Acre. Laid pipe from the creek to fill the tank, and then fenced off the creek to keep cattle from tromping down its banks and filling the watercourse with mud, spoiling the stream for trout and steelhead. The question of the Hashknife ground worked away in the back of her mind. She wanted to ask Domingo what his plans were, but couldn't find an opportunity, a tone.

Finally, heaving the last of the tools into the truck bed, "Are you going to stay here?" Alice demanded, and then thought, crude!

"Up here?" confused. "Pero, why? We got one hay deliver today, no?"

"Yeah, no, I mean, *is it your intention to continue in my employ?*"

"Yes, please, of course," regarding her narrowly. "Why you askin'?"

"Because—did you hear Robey and Bob McCrimmon talking to Janet and me at the fireworks, about buying some more ground for hay? No? About fifty acres, they say." She leaned her butt on the truck's bumper and folded her arms. "Philip thinks the bank will loan us the money. I'm asking about your intentions because . . . because I don't think I can operate that much more land on my own. But with you, I can." She looked at her boots. Now, what did that sound like? she thought.

Domingo took off his hat, sailed it into the truck bed. Thumbed the sweat from his eyebrows, considering. "Yes, patrona," slowly, "I will stay here. I like here. Is a good place." Serious, this was. A long-term, maybe a permanent commitment. And no exaggeration: this *was* a good place. Not neighborly to Yakima, to Wapato, but close enough.

What would it be like, he wondered, to say, to *feel, I belong here?* He tried it a couple of times: Yo soy de Standfast.

Alice realized they were out of ice cream one weeknight when the dust raised by her neighbors' wheat combines produced a great bloody battlefield of a sunset. She viewed it from the porch for a while before strolling down in the afterglow to break the news. Domingo was fooling with Chispa and his mother in their temporary pen by the machine shed.

Elbows on the gate, "Se nos acabó la aiscrin," she intoned.

"¡Choque, horror!" Chispa fled when coaxed, barged in when ignored. Domingo worked away, soft brush in one hand, rubber curry-comb in the other, on the mare and on the colt when he got in the way. The siren song of the red mare's foal-heat was causing some of the geldings nearby to make fools of themselves, rampaging up and down the pens, squealing like litters of shoats and throwing off artistic bucks. Not Cattywampus, though.

"You notice that?"

He nodded, unsurprised. "Momentito, voy a la tienda. You comin'?"

She made keyboarding motions with both hands.

"Okay, aiscrin, y ¿otro?"

"Just ice cream. Here"—holding out a bill—"get two, one chocolate," and went indoors to fire up the computer.

He went, but he didn't come back. Alice worked at her data entry, one ear out for the chug of the pickup; switched off at ten thirty and went out on the porch for a stretch and a yawn. Full dark now, and a full moon ruddy with the dust of the harvest. Sweep moseyed up. No Glen; down by the gate, probably.

The telephone rang: "Standfast."

Long pause. "Miz—Andison?"

"This is Alice Andison. Who's speaking?"

"Miz Andison, this is, I'm a Walla Walla County sheriff's officer, and I have your boy Wan Roke here—"

"What's happened? Is he okay?"

Sounding surprised, "Yes ma'am, he's okay."

"Then what's the matter? Has there been an accident? Hello?"

The speaker seemed thrown off stride, as if she'd interrupted a rote recitation. "No problem, ma'am, no problem, I'm just checking, just calling to check—" This time Alice clenched her teeth and waited. "That it's okay, that he has your permission to, to be driving your truck. To be driving your truck at this time of night." Long exhale.

"Yes," succinctly, "he does. Is he there? May I speak to him, please?"

"Ma'am, uh, no, this is official equipment. But if he has your permission, he can—" Click.

"What in hell!?" peering at the handset distractedly for the second time in that many weeks. What in *hell* was going on? Where were her sandals, what vehicle could she take, the dicey Chevette, the flatbed loaded with hay? And go where? From Waitsburg he could be home in twenty minutes. She would wait; in twenty-five minutes she would call the sheriff.

In twenty-five minutes the pickup growled up the lane and into the carport. But she got nothing out of Domingo.

"¿Qué te pasó?"

"Nada," jamming the ice cream into the freezing compartment all anyhow.

"Then why did they stop you? Tell me what happened."

"Nada, güera; ¡no me preguntes!" Unforgivably rude. But he couldn't stand the sight of her whiteness, and yearned with all his soul for a long scalding shower to sluice away his rage and fear, sweat it out like a fever.

In the morning, dripping Cholula sauce on his eggs and beans, he warned her off with a flat mask of a face.

But she wasn't having it. "I'm not kidding; I want to know what happened down there last night. Tell me right now."

Domingo jerked up, shoving the plate away, but she caught his wrist in a fierce grip, not to be broken without a fight. He sat again, rigid. Alice let go. At last he sighed, relaxed, put his head on one side and, fiddling with a teaspoon, confessed all. In English, for the benefit of the idiot-woman.

"He's estop me on the highway, before the semáforo."

"Before the traffic light in Waitsburg? This was before you got to the Seven Eleven?"

"Uh-huh. He's waiting behind las torres, el almacén," meaning the grain elevators by the tracks on the north side of the town; Alice nodded. "When I pass, he come after."

"Were you speeding? How fast were you going?"

"Uh-uh, forty, thirty-five, twenty-five," slowing down from highway speed as he crossed the city limits.

"So where did he stop you?"

"Estacionamiento where is closed the restaurant."

"And what did he say? What was the problem?"

Domingo rolled his eyes: was it not obvious? "I don't do nothing wrong. He look my license, the registration, the seguro; everything is correct. The lights, the placas, correct. You know this! Okay, he say come out, I come out. He take, took out everything—"

"Wait a minute, he searched the truck?"

"Throw everything out, Aliz, everything from the truck, everything from me."

"He searched *you*?" He leaned back. God's name, could she really be such an innocent?

"He cannot find nothing wrong," sparing a second's thankfulness for the half-ounce of grifa hidden in the Guadalupano scapular around his neck, not in his wallet. "So he have to call you, for be sure I don't steal you truck."

After a pause, Alice said, "Promise me you weren't speeding." He raised his right hand. She shook salt onto her plate, wet her finger, dabbed some into her mouth. "You know," she said, coldly furious, "I think I'll give the sheriff a call."

Domingo started up again as if to head her off from the phone. "¡No le hablas a nadie! Patrona, por Dios, ¡no le digas nada a nadie!"

Startled, but madder by the minute, she began to explain, "Look, sport, this guy stopped you and searched you and searched the vehicle for no reason. That is not okay in the USA, however it may be in—I mean, this cop is out of line, and we can pin him for it, we have good grounds. And we *should*! People in authority must not be allowed to get away with that kind of—"

"This cause a lot of trouble."

"Doesn't matter! Citizens gotta stand up and, oh. Oh. Damn. I forgot." Yes. Civic virtue for her, deportation for him. "Man, I wish you were legal here." And she felt half sick with outrage. A fierce tension headache clamped onto the back of her skull, so that her voice shook a little when after another electric pause she asked, "Does this kind of thing happen to you very often?"

"No. Only sometimes," relieved. It looked like she was going to be reasonable, in spite of her crazy initial reaction.

"I apologize for my country."

"Aliz, is not you fault."

"It is, partly, if I don't try to correct the problem." What a weird idea, he thought. Responsibility stopped at the ends of your fingers, as every child knew.

"So this happened before you got to the store, and afterward you went right on and bought ice cream?"

"How better to annihilate the memory?"

Alice forced a smile. "How, indeed?"

She didn't call the sheriff, though her conscience smote her and although the sheriff was a friend, an old fishing buddy of her father's. Nor did she describe the incident to Janet. Because, never mind the danger of prosecution as an illegal alien, she believed that Domingo felt the encounter, all such encounters, to be shameful to himself. To have your face rubbed in the fact of your vulnerability, impotence: heart-scald every time, and no balm for it but the passage of better hours and days. Even telling her shamed him; she repented of forcing him, said nothing to him or anyone, sank the whole business, as far as she could, in time and work.

So did Domingo, as far as he could. Though he asked himself once or twice, on the brink of sleep: why didn't the deputy check for the green card? How did he know to call Standfast? God's name, he even knew the phone number. And where have I seen that face before?

Chapter Seven

One simmering forenoon Alice picked up the phone in the foaling shed to a voice she almost knew saying, "Ask Eslick."

"What? Who's this?"

"About Lolo's Pride. Ask Mr. Eslick." And hung up.

Alice had been relieved that Janet pretty much forgot about old man Tillotson's bony horse. She had looked at three or four others since then, including a couple of nice warmbloods; big noble movers, but vastly out of her pocket range. One scopy, ram-faced homebred up Ritzville way really tempted Alice to put money down, but Janet was not as fetched, was still looking.

Alice finished raking up loose hay, thinking about the phone call. She almost knew who it was, almost, and then she did know: whatsername, Jessie, the bucktoothed girl who loved the bay horse. Well, this is interesting, she thought. She weeded the garden, conferred with Domingo about irrigating the Forty-Acre, made a grocery list, drove into town, picked up Judy Ellen Eslick Toutle from her job at the chiropractic clinic, and took her to lunch at the Modern.

"Alice, how neat! Sweet-sour, please," to the fair-haired girl in the mandarin jacket. "I 'bout never see you, except the Fair."

"Yup. You guys going this year?"

"My square dance group is, we're doing an exhibition. And I'll prob'ly ride the trail classes, and of course Dad's halter babies. You going?"

"Yep, same deal, just about."

"So," pouring tea, "What's up? Wanna buy another horse?" Alice had Tom Fool from the Eslicks, out of Judy Ellen's brother Frederick's calf-roping string. "You ever get that gray horse of Fred's to go in the trailer?"

"Oh yeah, eventually. He just didn't like to rodeo, I think. He's fine on the place; a real servant, as my dad would say."

"Nice man, your dad," Judy Ellen said.

"You said it, sis," said Alice, and sniffed. She separated her chopsticks and made a couple of practice passes. "Listen, I want to ask you something: did you ever know a family named Tillotson, farming up near Pataha, our side of the creek?"

"Yes, I did." She sat back and made her hands into claws. "Hope they're not friends of yours." The sweet-sour pork and the shrimp wontons came, and they set to. Alice told about their adventure up at Tillotsons' and about the phone call.

"Okay," said Judy Ellen, "put that together with what happened to us. About fifteen years ago when Steen—you know my sister Christine, right? That's right, she graduated high school the same year as Janet—when Steen and I were still living at home and Frederick was just a little guy, Steen bought this big old mare. Thought she'd make a good rope horse 'cause she was so solid. She was . . . what's that breed of German horse, Trekker something?"

"A Trakehner? My stars!"

"That's it. And she was in foal when we got her, by some stud over on the soggy side of the state," cheating on her chopsticks a little bit with a forefinger. "Well, she died foaling, but she had twins, and we bottle-raised the babies. Steen was real disappointed, of course. But she thought the twins might turn out good, 'cause that's a real stout breed, you know."

"No lie. And so both twins lived?"

"Yeah, they did. We named them Hawthorne and Melville because of Mrs. Motley. Remember when Mrs. Motley showed us that movie *Billy Budd*, and all the girls cried so much she had to leave the lights off and send the boys home early? Anyway, well, Hawthorne ran through a fence and ripped his chest all up, and Dad sold him to the canners. And then Steen never got around to competing Melville; she got married and moved to Richland. Melville didn't have much 'cow' anyway, though, God, was he stout. So then Dad didn't know what to do with him. He was still entire, and royally bred, but of course nobody wants to breed to a twin. So we started using him as a teaser for our thoroughbred stud. You remember him: Lolo, that we got from Canada."

"Sure I do. Lolo got a lot of good colts around here. And I bet I've seen Melville out at your place: little chestnut with a bottlebrush mane?"

"That's the guy." Judy Ellen helped herself to rice and wontons. "Dad still had him up till last year, but he got a tumor or something, went into a slow decline. But he was a good teaser, real sweet and sensible in spite of the frustration."

"But what about Tillotson?" Alice pressed.

"I'm getting there. Old man Tillotson just showed up one day, no breeding appointment or anything, no phone call. Pulled in with this big ole ugly mare in a trailer, just sailed right onto the place without a by-your-leave. In fact nobody even knew he was there, I guess, till I came around the barn and saw him. But I had the three yearlings in my hands and they were jumping around and pulling me every which way, you know, like they do. So I stopped there by the top corner of the barn to try and settle them down. So he didn't see me. He had the mare out of the trailer, tied up on the side. And old Melville was right by there in his pen. And of course he starts horsing like crazy; she was in season, oh yeah, no question. And he gets down on his knees by the fence—the stud, not the old man—and stuck his head under the bar, and then he kind of jammed his shoulders under the bar. And he's thrashing and scratching around, and making all this noise, 'Ho-ho-ho, hang on, honey, I'm a-comin', you know. And the old guy is standing there, watching. And then, the damnedest thing," leaning forward and lowering her voice, "that stud just shimmied his way right on under that fence. And he's up and on that mare before you could say squat!" Judy Ellen cackled lewdly, but quietly. "And of course old Tillotson didn't make a move to stop him. Just stood there with the long whip in his hand and a big dirty grin on his face; free stallion service, he's prob'ly thinking. And I couldn't move, with my three crazy critters pulling me to pieces."

"Oh, Judy Ellen, that shifty sonofabitch."

"You got that just about right. So then old Melville gets done and hops down, and along comes Dad from the house. So I yelled at him and he comes running, sees what's going on down in the yard—mad? I guess!"

"Rightly so. And Don is not a forgiving man." Alice eyed the last wonton but decided against it.

"Putting it mildly. But I didn't hear what he said. I was scared if I tried to lead my babies past the stud they'd really get away from me, so I put them back in the field, and when I got down there Dad was just catching Melville up to put him back in the pen. And the old man kept saying it wasn't his fault if folks didn't know how to keep their horses in. Grinning like a possum the whole time. Except he kept on calling the horse Lolo. So Dad says, 'Anyway, this isn't Lolo; it's a teaser.' Well, Alice, the old guy goes, 'What?! Shit!' and starts waling on Melville with his whip. On poor old Melville, just for doing what comes naturally! And of course that's all she wrote for Dad, he threw the guy in his truck, practically threw the mare in the trailer—ooh, it was ugly. 'Course, you know what he thought he was doing, don't you?" She reached for the check, which Alice deftly snagged. "Getting his mare two covers for the price of one. 'Hey, not my fault if Eslick's stud gets out,' you know. But then to beat up on good ole Melville!"

"The geezer is a slime bucket, is my impression."

"Honey, you don't even know. Chapter two: a year later he writes Dad a letter asking—*demanding* compensation, because his mare got in foal by Melville, and he lost her breeding services for the year, unquote. Can you believe that?"

"Yes, I do. That old bastard has more crust than a five-cent pie. What did Don do?"

"He wrote back—really, it was cool—this very polite letter (that's after he wrote the obscene one and tore it up) saying here's our lawyer's name, and if Mr. Tillotson thought he had a case, he could blah blah blah."

"So did he?"

"Nah. It was all a trick to get money out of us. I doubt the mare even settled or anything. Melville probably didn't even know how to do it; he usually never got the chance to actually follow through."

"Well," Alice drawled, "tell you what, sis: I think she did."

She gaped. "Get out. You gotta be kidding."

"I sure wouldn't bet the farm on it, now. But that horse we looked at out at Tillotsons' is about ten years old, no matter what the old man says, and real stout, more bone than any thoroughbred I ever saw before, and he calls it Lolo's Pride."

"You are kidding me."

"Plus I think it's raced; been pinfired anyway."

"Aw, but Alice, it couldn't, 'cause he couldn't have registered it without the breeding certificate."

"Well, that is kind of an obstacle. But we just need to suppose that Mr. Tillotson is a little bit more of a crook than we already know he is. He had a sample of your dad's signature, right? From the letter he sent."

"You mean, you're thinking he *forged* Dad's name on the papers?"

Of course he had. The more Alice thought about it, the more obvious it became. And the more disgusted she got, about the trick played on the Eslicks, about the abuse and neglect of Tillotson's good-doing bay horse. And something else, something about the air out there along the Pataha, where a lot could be gotten away with, passed off as just the way one family managed itself and its property, nobody else's business.

There was even less pleasure in their second meeting with old man Tillotson, but more satisfaction. They took the precaution of bringing plenty of muscle, not only Domingo but Nick Weston and Earache Doyle, lured by the prospect of impersonating thugs in a good cause.

They took copies of Lolo's Pride's registration papers secured from the national thoroughbred registry, among them the breeding certificate with Don Eslick's name forged on it. They took the two-horse trailer with the partition removed in case the bay gelding proved hard to load. And Janet called Jessie Tillotson and told her they were coming.

The same thing happened, dogs and all. This time, however, the old man took fright at the number of vehicles, the grim faces, and didn't bellow at Jessie to bring the horse out. Jessie led him dancing out on the long lead anyway, a teary smile coming and going on her wind-burned face. At this, old Tillotson boiled over, threatened to get his gun, call the sheriff, sic the dogs. But they had him four ways to Sunday, and he knew it. He could go before the state racing commission and be barred from all tracks, or he could lose the horse to the Humane Society on Janet's complaint. Or he could sell the horse to Janet for twenty-five hundred dollars, a great deal more than it was worth in its present sad state.

Alice, Domingo, Nick, and Earache hung around looking mean. Janet stood quiet, holding her check at breastbone height while the old man cursed and fulminated. Nobody else, once the proposition was stated, said a word. The wind blew, lifting the horse's black forelock and Jessie's sandy one.

At last the old man ran down. He must have really looked Janet in the face for the first time, and scared himself. He tried to snatch the check then, but Janet held on. Now she had him hooked, and she made him stand and listen.

"Pay attention," in her classroom voice, precise as a mink after a fish. "I have a lot of friends in the Palouse, lived here all my life. And I'm thinking you should get out of the horse business here. A stinker like you, word gets around. For example, if ever I heard of you selling a horse around here, ever again, I would go to the buyer and tell everything I know. Everything. I promise.

"So I want you to think of this check as the last money you'll ever make on horses in the Palouse. Now we are going to get the horse loaded up, and ourselves loaded up. And then I'm going to give this check to Jessie. So you can just go on in the house now, and think about how many people around here know what a skunk you really are."

Alice supposed they were lucky the ancient didn't have an apoplexy and fall over dead on the spot, them liable. But in a surprisingly short time he caught enough breath to curse with, which he did all the way up to the house, remarkably loudly, and stood on the porch yammering and waving his sticklike arms slowly like a mantis.

The bay horse loaded like a charm. Janet made them leave Jessie alone with him to say good-bye. Then she gave Jessie the check, who folded it and placed it reverently in the pocket over her flat left breast. Alice felt like saying, "You come too." Jessie kept mashing the water out of her eyes with her thumb and smiling around those big teeth of hers. "Come and visit him, Jessie, any time."

Jessie whispered, "Sure."

"¡Qué songabeach!" marveled Domingo, turning onto the highway.

Alice muttered, "I feel like a vigilante."

"I feel good!" Janet sat back expansively, all ginned up with righteousness. "Even if the beastie throws me on my head, even if Tillotson sues for harassment. I feel like a million bucks in unmarked twenties." And she said, "I am going to make curried prawn crepes for dinner."

Scouring up the lane in an antique red Corvette: aggravation its own self. Alice felt her bowels uncoil.

After a day of bucking bales of alfalfa into the dutch barn, the classic summer task on the place, they were cooling off under the locust trees before dinner, Alice in the hammock and Domingo and Nick flat on the grass, drinking beer.

"Fuckin' *car*!" Nick breathed, getting up. Domingo slanted his eyes toward Alice, who made a God-give-me-strength face. On the driveway, a tall man levered himself out of the cockpit like a folding rule; six foot three of him in full urban-cowboy gear complete to the snakeskin boots with graven-silver toe caps. Country-music idol, that was the look. Nick went toward him, partly to do the honors of the place, partly to examine the car, but Jerry Graeme passed him without a glance. Seeing this, Domingo lay back down. Alice stood up, though, preferring to meet trouble on her feet. Jerry Graeme lowered himself into the hammock, careful not to rumple his outfit, lay back and closed his eyes.

"Sweet Alice. Miss me?"

Always offensive. Always slim, now thin. Subtle ruin. Calm, though, not raving as the phone call had led her to expect.

"Good to be home." Crafty! Alice swallowed bile. Wait, she counseled herself, and watch.

"Who's the guy?" opening eyes still beautiful, big and pale green like citrine with a dark rim, dark lashes. Nick wandered back, doubled himself down against a channeled bole.

"Which one?"

Jerry Graeme made a contemptuous little pout. "The kid is Janet's kid, right? The Mexican."

Domingo's voice came like a breeze through the grass: "¿Quieres que me vaya?"

"Quédate."

"Now what's that all about, in English?"

"He asked if he should leave; I told him to stay."

"You should tell him to go."

"I don't think so."

He turned his sleek silvery head away wanly. "You never did have a brain in your head, did you? Where's Janet? I've kinda missed her. She's a nice little piece of ass."

Nick sat up, alert. Jerry Graeme worked himself out of the hammock and went toward the house, crooking a finger at Alice, a motion rude to Nick's eye, obscene to Domingo's. Alice followed him, having no choice. As they reached the steps, the two collies, who had been cooling off in the creek, rushed up to let her know there was a strange car on the place; all mud, sand, and flying spray. The dude had to hump it indoors for the sake of his clothes. Chalk one up for the dogs, thought Alice.

He got himself a beer; once he was out of the kitchen, Alice made an iced tea. He lounged on the couch, stretching long legs out.

"So what's new? Besides your tame beaner."

"You. Where you been?" She had no interest in this. What she wanted to ask was, Why are you here now, and when can I look forward to your going away?

"Around. You saying you been thinking about ole Jerry? The Cisco Kid not enough for you?"

"Missed you last year at calving. Not so much this season." Nor ever again, Alice promised herself.

"We-el," stretching luxuriously, turning sideways on the couch as if to take a nap, "you can just send him back where he came from, the kid too. I'm back to put a little juice in your jeans."

"Will you be staying for dinner?" she asked, angling for information in the guise of politeness. He was not in the least deceived. A dreadful, nasty, triumphant grin stretched his mouth.

"Honey," opening those green eyes wide, "Honey-baby, I live here."

Dinner was awful, everything burnt, but hunger overcame repulsion; Domingo and Nick took theirs onto the porch and finished it off with the help of more beer than was good for them. Then they fed the stock, and then played catch for a while in the cooling twilight, Nick in his ragged cutoff shorts leaping around like a stag, Domingo cannier, more economical of movement. Alice could see them from where she sat, trapped inside with the Incubus, the Cuckoo's Egg, the Wolve, all the names Janet had ever made up for Jerry Graeme made flesh, lolling at the table, picking his teeth.

It got too dark to see the baseball. Nick stuck his head in the front door: "We're going to town for a while, Aunt Alice, okay?"

"Okay. Oh, Nicky, wait," springing up and running out. "A word in your shell-like ear," she murmured on the way down to the Chevette, pulling at his belt loops to get his attention, "stop in at home on the way back and let them know Jerry's here. In fact, you stay there tonight, don't come back up till I tell you."

"Okay, gotcha."

And to Domingo, "When you come back, when you go to bed, lock your door."

"Maybe it would be better if we didn't go. Is he a friend of yours, the man? His manners are bad even for a gabacho, pardon me."

"Nick will explain."

Scared, Alice went back to the house, in at the kitchen door, and took the Carborundum and her big slicer out of the drawer. Jerry Graeme had moved to the love seat by the front window; as if putting his dibs on every chair in the house, marking his turf like a dog. Claiming the house and everything in it. Claiming her; he always had done that, without the slightest encouragement on her part, nor as far as she could see any liking on his. Just for the annoyance value.

She went out onto the front porch, set the sharpening stone on her knee, and began to hone the long blade of the carving knife. Of course he couldn't stand his own company for long; brought out a chair to save his pants, sat behind her and talked to her about old times. He knew a great deal about her, and smeared it all, her parents, her sister, her first and second boyfriends, her marriage. All the Standfast horses, the collies. He had but to mention a thing to smirch it, one of his few skills. All the while Alice slowly stroked the blade over the lisping stone; all the while, as the steel grew brighter and keener, hearing her whole history tarnished and slimed.

"Guess that must be getting pretty sharp by now. Who you fixing to cut, Alice? You always were a great little castrator. Ask any guy in the Valley; they'll say, 'That Alice is some ball cutter.' Ha ha. Quite a reputation."

He began to talk about Standfast. He wanted to see "the books," the "bottom line." He could of course, if he cared to risk his tall knees under the computer desk, key up her last year's numbers in a trice. She decided, mentally drawing a line in the sand, to defend the computer with her blood if he should move on it. Probably, though, he didn't know how to operate it; didn't know enough to ask for the passwords for starters, not that she would have revealed them. Besides, she thought, I bet you know as much about spreadsheets as a pig knows about Sunday; which made her think of Robey, which steadied her. Jerry Graeme asked a great many questions about ranch operations, cultivation, and profitability, not waiting for answers, which in any case she would not have given. She had never known him to take such an interest in the place.

Alice plucked a grass blade and laid it across the sharp edge of her knife; the leaf creased and hung down limp on either side. She went inside, ignoring Jerry Graeme, put the Carborundum away, and climbed the stairs to bed, the slicer by her side, a big thing with a wooden hilt, a wide blade curved like a saber. Couldn't sleep, however; the locked door cut off the draft, her room stayed stifling. Sweat trickled off her, as if her body wept. Dragged herself down to chore in the cool of the morning, more tired than when she'd lain down. The blessed ordinariness of Domingo Roque, unconcerned, making up grain feeds in old coffee cans, revived her.

Jerry Graeme stayed at Standfast, each day making himself less welcome. Alice felt herself grow haggard and snappish. He stayed up late, turned the television volume high, but she could hear him moving around the house, opening closets, rummaging bookshelves. In the morning the furniture would be slightly out of place. He rose at the crack of noon, ravaged the kitchen and the downstairs bathroom, the whole place reeking of his over-ripe cologne. Twice he drove off in the red Corvette and twice, to her sick dismay, he returned. She hardly dared leave the home yard, but she had no choice; the work was in the fields.

Domingo too lost sleep. *"He cruises the place at night, boss, know that? He counts the hay, the horses. Last night he opened all the cupboards in the shop. He acts like a thief, in my opinion."*

Alice tried to remember if she had always felt so put off by the man; hadn't she gradually gotten used to him when he had come back before? But her repulsion grew by the day, along with a paralyzing sense of threat. He talked and talked; well, he always had. But now he repeated things, strings of things, with buzzing fricatives as though his teeth, his foully gray and decayed-looking teeth, didn't mesh properly. He didn't take in anything that she said to him, little as that was. An alternative history in his head, in which he owned Standfast and all it contained, absorbed him.

One night he put his hand on her shoulder in the kitchen. She had her big knife right by her. "If you like that hand, take it off me."

"Aw, hey, Alice," making big hurt eyes, "your bean eater cutting me out? What would ole Al say? You know your old man meant us for each other, don't you?" She didn't know what made her sicker, Allan's name in Jerry Graeme's mouth or the notion of having anything to do with Jerry Graeme in a physical way, ever. And then, in a completely different tone, perfectly ordinary, "Where's Bick?" And then waited for an answer, which was also unusual.

"What—you mean Bick at the Hashknife place?"

"Yeah, where's Bick?" It was so nearly normal, conversational, that she answered without thinking, as if passing on gossip to a neighbor:

"Somewhere wearing an orange jumpsuit. You didn't know? The state police came down on those guys last winter for operating a methamphetamine fac—" Good God. Hadn't Robey just mentioned the Graeme connection? Alice whirled around, soup flying from her ladle, in time to see the whole surface of Jerry Graeme lose focus like a landscape at the start of a mudslide, go from terribly good-looking to flat-out terrible, wasted, shriveled. He reeled away, stiff-legged, out the front door; she heard the Corvette grumble down the lane.

Turning at the top of a swath, Alice caught sight of a rider: Domingo, Falcon loping up the track. Back from Walla Walla a bit early. She braked the tractor, turned the key, jumped down. He came up and dismounted.

"How was town?"

"Aliz, listen, he's there, he's in the bank when I go."

"Who?" Though she knew.

"The cabrón, you know." He'd cleaned up for town, but now his shirt stuck to him wetly again; he'd ridden up to the hay terraces the fast way, along the dry creeks.

"What," afraid to ask, "was he doing there?"

"He's sitting in the back, he's talk to one bank guy with the corbata," signaling necktie. "I try to hear, but the caseras start to look me funny."

"He was talking to a bank officer? Which one; did you see?"

"The sign say Castillo, something like that. Patrona, what you thinking?"

"Oh, God," she said wildly, catching herself on the tractor's big rear wheel. "I think he's trying to sell the place out from under us! But no, now, wait. I don't think he can do that. But I'll bet the farm that's his plan. Janet was right: I should have let him kill himself with the harrow that time!"

Domingo caught her under the elbow and eased her down on the step.

"Patrona," he said, squatting down, "what we gonna do?"

"Damn if I know," desolate. "Listen, I don't think he can do anything without my consent, without my signature. And I'm not signing. That's flat. I don't care what he does." She looked at Domingo, at the dark and hawklike focus of that face. "Don't beat him up," she said.

"Why *not*?"

"No, *don't*, man," gripping his arm hard, "it'll just make things worse. Domingo, *no*."

He relaxed slightly, patted her hand, held it there. "Aliz, you do this, okay? You don't sleep in the house where he is. You better take my place, down in the barn. I can go in the orchard; he don't care about me. No, is no problem. You do this, okay? Odderwise, I'm getting too escared."

"Well, okay. Okay, I will. But swear you won't beat him up."

"Only if you say me."

She handed off the hay swather to Domingo, took Falcon, and called Janet on the cell from the Circ, where she felt safe and almost sane, out of range of encroaching craziness. "When is Philip coming home, dammit? Things are getting weirder and weirder up here." Philip was in Yakima, in court.

"He usually calls between the session and dinner; do you want him to call you up there? Some new outrage? Or are you just reaching the end of your tether? Would you ever come and stay with me, Roan? I hate you being up there with the creep. Drunk as usual, I suppose?"

"No, he isn't, it's something else—something's made his teeth black and his eyes weird. Yan, I'm betting he had a stake in the Hashknife dope operation, and not just as a consumer. Now his supplies are cut off; that's why he's so desperate—anyway, damned if I'll leave Stand-fast, *damned* if I will, Janet. Let him run me off? Fuck that."

"No, I don't mean—never mind, listen, want me to go talk to Sheriff Harley? Could we get a warrant or something?"

"Don't you s'pose that red car will have been noted in town? If he's arrestable, they'd have arrested him."

"Has he been in town, though?"

"That's why I want to talk to Phil. Today, when Domingo made a run down there to take my deposit to the Bennett-Briscoe, he saw Jerry Graeme deep in talk with one of the bank officers. Subject unknown, of course; he couldn't get close enough to hear. But my question is, can Jerry sell that life-interest property without reference to us? Can he do that? Do we have any recourse, any control at all? I'm feeling really snake bit about this. It's more worrisome than the queer way he's acting toward me."

A long pause, and then Janet said, "Boy, do I not like the sound of that last part."

"Well," in a subdued tone, not having meant to let on about that, "Domingo's right here, and the dogs."

To Domingo, she said, "Keep away from him, 'mano. Don't lose any more sleep following him around. He's probably harmless, but if he isn't, there's no reason for you to get in harm's way."

"Hm," blandly. Alice didn't press. By herself, she felt neither strong nor brave.

The following Thursday, Domingo saddled his chestnut mare and put her back to work, a slow stroll up to the terrace field and back, to look at the cows and calves, Chispa skittering and snorting around her. She pointed her ears at the cattle, but Domingo kept his distance because of the bulls.

Alice spent the morning on the hay rake, and they moved pipe in the afternoon. A hundred and twelve degrees at four o'clock, and the flatbed still to be loaded with bales for delivery on Friday. It had to be done, and it was done, but very slowly. Not a pleasant day, despite the sunshine; the dry-pea harvest was on in earnest and the sour green stink of smashed pea vines burdened the breeze.

Domingo disappeared after dinner. Alice hoped he had gone to bed early but suspected he was somewhere uphill from the house, on watch; Glen trotted off through the orchard in that direction after she and Sweep settled on the porch. Alice had a backlog of data entry to do but didn't want to draw Jerry Graeme's attention to the computer, so she brought some mending out into the evening light. Jerry Graeme sat behind her making ugly commentary in his sweet baritone. By luck, she was in the kitchen getting tea when the phone rang.

"Philip says Jerry can't do anything," Janet whispered, keyed up. "He called Vern Castile at the bank: you were right, he was trying to mortgage the place out from under us. But he can't. Phil says we'll take a loan if we have to, and try to buy him out of his life interest. Are you okay?"

"Yes," said Alice, "thanks for calling. Jerry's right here," so close behind her his breath moved her hair, "want to say hi?" Janet gasped. Smirking, he held out his hand for the phone. The slicer sang from its sheath. He drifted back out of the kitchen.

"Is Domingo with you?"

"I think so."

"Are the dogs with you?"

"Yes."

"Do you want Nick to come?"

"No."

"I think he'd better."

"No, love, really."

Janet paused as if she were trying to peer up the telephone cord. "Okay," she said at last, "but we're coming up tomorrow night, all of us."

"Okay. That's good. Sleep tight. Don't bring the kids." As if the place, their own place, were contaminated.

Jerry Graeme flopped onto the couch, sighed, "Alice, Alice, Alice, Alice, Alice. What am I going to do with you?" His boot heels on the arm, paper-white face luminous in the shadow. "The thing is, darlin', I need a little money." When did you not, she thought but did not say.

"What do you guess," he said, lacing his fingers behind his head mock-idly, "what do you suppose this old place is worth on the open market? 'Cause Christ knows, you aren't getting any younger. The place is too much for you, about time you moved off here and into town." Still, she said nothing, while outrage bubbled up and then sank down in her like magma. "So what do you guess it's worth, lock, stock, and ready to rock?"

Alice took her time. "It's priceless to me and Janet, I'll say that; Philip too, pretty near."

"What's old Philip Weston got to say about it?" disconcerted.

"They're a unit, Philip and Janet. Married, you know."

His eyes seemed to roll up for a second. After a while he said, singsong, "I need some money; I need some money." Alice's mouth dried. Even across the house from her he did not seem far enough away. Her hand closed on the hilt of her heavy knife.

He told her his plan to mortgage Standfast. Three or four times he went over it, as if the deal were done. Alice just kept shaking her head no. Ten minutes passed; he stopped talking in the middle of a repetition. Lay there open-eyed, vacant. I would pity you, she thought, if I were not so much afraid.

At five the next morning, when she came downstairs in her shorts and sneakers to go out and chore, the wretched man was still on the couch, eyes still open, empty. Had he lain there awake all through the short summer night? When they came in to breakfast, he was gone, asleep, she supposed, in "his" bedroom. For small mercies, ye gods above be thanked, thought Alice, the one thing worse than the idea of Jerry Graeme in control was the notion of him out of control.

Domingo drove the load of hay to a quarter-horse breeder across the Oregon line in Milton-Freewater. Alice went up to the hay rake. The cockscomb of white cumulus along the crest of the mountains turned misty, transparent with heat; the Blues looked like heaps of cinders. A great day for hay. At twelve thirty she finished the field, cocked up her rake heads, and towed the rig down to the homeplace. The flatbed was back, and Domingo lay asleep on it in the shade of the Dutch barn, worn out with night-watching. He woke up at the sound of the tractor, walked up to the foaling shed, turned the hose on himself, and when Alice came up, on her.

"Oh yes," rotating in the fine spray, "Mil gracias. Paradise."

"What we doing after lonche?" He coiled the hose, and dropped onto the bench by the door.

"Taking the yearlings up to the Forty-Acre, aren't we? Scootch over. You got a better plan?" His shoulders had left a wet patch that dried on the corrugated metal wall as she watched.

"*We should stay around here, I think. Whitey's building up to some-thing.*"

"Such as what? I doubt he'll do anything on the place any harm, except me or you, maybe. Since he believes every nail and bale belongs to him."

"*Maybe today; maybe tomorrow.*"

"Why do you think so, buck? He give some sign during the night?"

"*Because he's fucking crazy, please excuse me, and you not giving him what he wants is making him more so all the time.*"

"Damn right I'm not giving him what he wants. I'm also not ar-ranging the work on this place to suit him. Period."

"*You're the boss, of course.*"

"Ah, good, you noticed that," kicking the wrong dog in her distress.

They walked up to the house for lunch. Still no sign of Jerry Graeme. But as they mounted to ride up to the Dogleg afterward, he appeared in the yard like a white haunt, startling the life out of Alice. Gorgeously dressed in a guayabera—a wedding shirt, dark gray cotton embroidered in shades of salmon and rose. Gorgeous but curiously lifeless, like a store mannequin, with his cap of smooth silver hair, his smooth still-handsome face. Many a woman would have found him magnetically attractive; she supposed many a woman had. But all Alice had ever wanted to do was to get her leg over a good horse and ride away from him.

"Beat it, homeboy," a voice like a match striking. Domingo took less notice of this than of the blackbird's whistle.

"Hey, asshole. Understand English? Beat it; fuck off." Domingo spat between his foreteeth, a long arc down the breeze.

"Coerce the dogs, will you, cousin?" said Alice. *"And I am with you before you reach the crooked field."*

"One shout, I come on the run. And I'll leave you Sweep." He sorted out the collies, moved off slowly, Cattywampus's haunches rolling defiance.

"Last chance, Alice," Jerry Graeme said.

"Last chance for what?"

He opened his arms wide: *I'm all yours.* She shook her head. "Not tempted, Jerry, not now, not ever." Domingo was right; the creature was as mad as a snake in a gunnysack.

He dropped his arms. "Oka-ay." As if to say, *you asked for it.* And he made a gun of his right hand and jokily shot her. Then mimed a heavy two-hander police pistol and blew her away, with sound effects: "Boosh, boosh, boosh, boosh, boosh."

Alice blanched; the pupils of her eyes expanded galvanically. Falcon settled back and raised a forefoot.

"And this is *your* last chance," hoarsely, "you get off my place today, now, or I call the sheriff. Understand English? Be gone when I get back. Be outta here when I get back." She didn't stay for his reply; her horse sprang away up the hill, Sweep rushing alongside. As they came to the turn in the road out of sight of the yard, Glen dashed out of an alder thicket, dashed in again. Domingo rode out of the thicket: "See, she coming. You satisfy now?"

They were out all afternoon, their task complicated by the attitude of Hamster the bull, who fell in with nobody's plans, maintained his own agenda, and set his own pace. On the bluff at the top of the Forty-Acre, riding around the bunch a last time to make sure they were settling, Alice thought she saw the red Corvette far off on the state highway.

"¿Se fue, Patrona?"

"Not sure. I want him gone so much that—no, can't tell, it could be the school bus for all I can see from here. Let's go home and face the music."

No pillar of smoke rose up before them as they jogged homeward in the deep dust of the tractor trail. Riding into the yard, she thrilled to the sight of no Corvette blocking the driveway; in fact, Janet's Toyota pickup stood there instead. Nan ran down toward them, her hair wild and her face cream white.

"He's wrecked our house, Aunt Roan!" she sobbed out. "He's ruined everything, everything! Oh God. Mother's crying so hard." Then in an instant they saw it all: the hammock hanging in tatters, the old lawn chair chopped into firewood. Water cascading down the porch steps.

"Take care of Nan," vaulting off and tossing Domingo the reins.

"Hija, come here, please! Come help me with these horse."

The flood on the porch came from the house in pulses, propelled by the broom Janet wielded in tears, her denim skirt kilted above her knees. "The son of a bitch," she quavered out, "has shat in your bed."

"Aw, hell," Alice groaned. "Okay, I'm calling the cops." But by that time the red Corvette was far away.

Chapter Eight

"Mauu."

"So you say. But has either of you caught a mouse today, done anything to earn your kibble?" The laconic cat walked away, disgusted.

"Mngeerrrroo-giaow. Wowow," explained the chatty one, Einstein.

"Well, get off there, this bench is for folks first, cats second." To Domingo, "Can you really play that?" One of the few unshattered objects left in the house was Jerry Graeme's own guitar, a grand old Guild D-50 bought in San Francisco and after a month abandoned, forgotten. Just like Jerry, Janet said, to buy the Stradivarius of guitars and then leave it under a bed in a flood. A flood caused by himself, at that.

Little had been saved from the wreckage. Allan and Jean's relics, stored in the attic; a framed snapshot of the little girls and their mother riding triple on Susan; all the computerized records providentially backed up onto the Westons' system the week before. Alice's underwear left in the washer, unnoticed when its hoses were slashed. The sight of Nick Weston, man of a thousand dirty words, rendered speechless, arms around his mother, flotsam wreathing his ankles.

"Hey, bucko! You can play!"

Domingo blushed through his plummy summer color. "What is 'baco'?"

"Short for 'buckaroo,' I believe, which is American for 'vaquero.'"

"Oh. No significa horse-buck?"

"Nn, well, that too, maybe. Many a vaquero's like a bronc that won't be rode. Some don't submit to authority gracefully," giving him a meaningful look. Which he returned with interest. "Yup, okay. If I'd paid attention to you, Jerry wouldn't have had a chance to wreck the place. On the other hand, you wouldn't have gotten your mitts on the guitar. Got a nice tone, doesn't it? Or is that all you?" Janet had suggested selling the Guild; that was before the insurance guy appeared, along with the deputy, a different deputy from the one Domingo had had trouble with, he was relieved to see. They declared the contents of the house a total loss and Jerry Graeme a "person of interest."

Alice fought off Janet's plea that she leave Domingo in charge of the ranch and stay at the Westons' during the refit. The work was up there, she insisted, and anyway the madman might return. Domingo declared with cheerful savagery that he hoped so.

"That's exactly what I'm worried about," Janet said. "Besides, you can't even cook up there."

"We'll keep cold stuff in the tack-room fridge. Beyond that, you'll have to feed us."

Alice borrowed a sleeping bag and camped out uphill from the fruit grove on a little plateau long devoted to summer sleeping and meteor watching. At dawn the three-note calls of quail woke her, strangely harsh for so refined a bird. The moon hung like a dime in a lilac sky. The crisis was past; the place was theirs again, more theirs than ever. She stretched out her limbs four ways, flat on her back in the warm waving grasses, the stored heat of the ground coming up through her bones, drunk on the wine of possession.

Mid-August, and the flies were bad despite a second release of natural predators, tiny wasps that preyed on fly eggs and larvae. Horses stamped and thrashed their tails, thundered madly up and down the pens, and rolled the dust of the wallows into their sweated coats. Farther uphill, cooler, the cattle suffered less.

When the time came to take the bulls off the herd, Sixteen and Kid gave little trouble. Old soldiers, they knew the drill, probably remembered that a good feed of mash awaited them at the pasture gate. All the same, Alice and Domingo double-looped each bull and convoyed him down to the open-stock rig, one on either side like a ceremonial guard. Hamster was another matter. A rollicking little character with a sense of humor expressed in ponderous bucks, he ducked and shimmied among his admiring heifers, soon infecting the whole harem with unwisdom. Forefeet scraped dust; phantom horns hooked. Snippy moos in the hot collies' very faces. The bull's owner, meanwhile, squatted on the ramp of her trailer in the gateway.

"Shoulda brought them something to eat," Alice sighed, stroking sweat from her eyebrows as they stood their horses in the cottonwood shade, taking a breather. "Wonder if it's worth going back down for."

"I wish my other horse," said Domingo. He leaned to stroke the Mouse's wet shoulder. "This guy is tryin', but—"

"Yes," she agreed, "but he's not quite ready for the bull. Well, let's see what Tommy can do." Walking the gray horse out of the shade, she showed him Hamster, let out the reins, sat deep in her saddle, and set her left hand on the horn. A hand too tall for this work, Tom Fool, but he had the advantage of a quiet mind and great natural authority. Now if that enthusiast Glen could prevent himself from interfering . . .

The two grass eaters squared up, took each other's measure. A thousand pounds a side, give or take; the gelding's height imposing, but the bull's weight of muscle animated by a brute will to dominate. To kill, even. He was polled, and Alice was glad of it. Horns would have tipped the balance of risk. Hamster determined to hold his ground; Tom Fool determined he should not. At first it was a chess game, the bull cruising among his little bunch, hiding out behind this cow or that; the horse easing him toward the edge of the herd. Hamster didn't like that. He darted out and around, leaving his pursuer stuck in the middle. Another try, same result.

Alice brought her horse to the mark again. This time the gray cut through the herd fast, head low as if driving his own kind. Heifers quickstepped out of his way. Coming face-to-face with Hamster, he lowered his forehand, bent his hocks, juked right-left-right with the bull, tight as his shadow. Hamster reversed and trotted away, whipped around, scratched up dust, and charged. Defying instinct, Tom Fool bounced forward, his ears pinned flat. Unexpected, that big white hurtling shape! Those long yellow teeth! The bull veered off toward the fence, and now Domingo could get between the duel and the bunch, get his loop on. Then Alice got her loop on, and they held Hamster between them. The dogs strolled the rest of the herd away up the Forty-Acre.

Shown the open gate of the rig, Hamster lumbered up the ramp to his treat with a philosophical shrug of humpy shoulders. The gate clanged shut; the owner, another woman of the mule type, Domingo noted, reached through the steel slats to free the ropes.

"Bye, Mizelle, thanks! Take care on the road." Alice didn't like to brag on her horses, but she felt Tommy had shown some real stuff. She tugged at his roached mane: "You are a good horse."

Yes, Domingo thought. And this Mouse is, will be a good horse. But for cutting out cows: wait, Alice! You've seen nothing!

"This is all set to go, Alice, as soon as all parties sign," Philip said when at last he called.

"Do you mean we'll be clear of that crazy bastard forever? For real?"

"That is the plan."

"Oh Philip, really, like *really*? I kiss your knees, I do. How much?" He told her. "Jesus Christ! In a lump?" But this was entirely reflexive. In fact, the price of Jerry Graeme's life interest exceeded by not much the cookie-jar stash she and Janet had been feeding for two decades for this very purpose.

"Don't be so Scotch, Alice. This is painless dentistry. It's what all the scrimping is for."

"You're right, of course."

"And John R will love you to death."

"More good news. When can . . . do I hear Mimi?"

"Well—yes." What a racket. She must be sucking his collar buttons. "Shocking; poor, faithful Janet. When can we close the deal?"

"As soon as the other party's lawyer can locate his client."

"Oh no. I knew there was a hitch. I knew he wouldn't— Do you trust that lawyer?"

"Sure. He's okay; don't worry about that. Just keep the money handy, and be ready to scurry on into town with Janet and put your John Hancock on the line. We may have a fairly narrow window of opportunity."

It was decided in family conclave that Domingo Roque should drive Nan Weston and her impedimenta up to Pullman to start at WSU at the end of August. They got off early, before the sun made its weight felt, and Janet called Alice in a very strange state of mind.

"Are you laughing or crying?"

"Both. We're going to the batting cages tonight, to take our minds off our half-empty nest; want to come? Or, no, you're on your own up there since I borrowed your top hand. And your truck. God, Alice, we've really hung you up! I am sorry!"

"Nuts to that. He'll be back tomorrow. And Nan will be back at semester break, don't forget, with thirteen weeks' worth of alarming stories, purple hair, and a tattoo. How is Nick taking it?"

"Can't tell. Eric Doyle is in mourning, however. Positively weepy. He and Tammy Evans were here for dinner, awfully quiet. She's off to Central next week, you know. What will Nicky and Eric do then, I wonder?"

"Pine and sigh. And then sing hey, nonny nonny. Pretty resilient, boys are. One thing I'm sure of: your phone bill is about to take a big bounce."

"You think?"

Alice was right; the bounce started that night. But Domingo was gone for three days.

Once back, he gave a highly satisfactory report: Nan was installed, classes confirmed, books bought, bank card functioning, dining hall and library located. Sound system operational; roommate vetted. Alice didn't ask where he had been in the interval. She noted the mileage counter; that was enough. A number of possibilities crossed her mind. He might have gone to visit Concha Vélez in Hermiston. He might have gotten lost. He might have set out to steal the truck, but thought better of it. He might have been running drugs. Of these, she discounted the last three as being ridiculous, unlike the man, or her notion of him. Concha, on the other hand, seemed possible. Alice held her peace, waited.

"I put these calf in the round pen, okay?" jogging Chamaca around to the weather side of the machine shed, making her jump, her ladder clash, and her paint can teeter. "He scouring too much. I put him some hay. This looks good."

"You like this color?" Flecks of pine-green exterior latex augmented her freckles. "I got kinda tired of red. How's she like being back at work?" Real work every morning for the red mare now; Chispa confined, caterwauling.

"I need tell you something."

She stopped painting, chuckled, "I think you do."

"When I'm to the university with Miss Nannie, I'm thinking about my other horse; I tell you about this guy? Also my trailer, my troca, which I abandon at the Foulks, you know. So I'm thinking I will go and check if . . . because, *because there was one other vaquero there, a white guy, Len Loftus, a very good hand. All the rest of those burros . . . Anyway, I thought Loftus might have preserved my gray horse and my truck. But he has moved on. And nobody there knows anything about anything; no horse, no truck, no trailer.*"

"*Some person sequestered your effects? It's injurious, disgraceful!*"

"*Yes. But not unusual. In any case, I misjudged the distance from Pullman to Lewiston; it's very far! And my ears were down, because of my loss. And so I came home. If this worried you, I regret it.*"

"It did a little bit. But I figured you had a novia over there."

"Not me," absently. "I think you going to look good, green."

"Oh, for heck's sake. Well, her too."

"¡Ay, párate!" not in time to prevent the mare from testing the paint with her upper lip.

He really appreciated Alice not running him over the cheese grater about being away with the pickup the extra day. It was exceptional in his experience to be granted such latitude. Not that she didn't care, oh no; clearly she had been waiting for an explanation. But in patience, not in anger. She trusted him, apparently. The knowledge made him happy out of all proportion.

Third cutting of hay, a gamble, the endlessly scrolling white skies and oven breezes starting to break up in bursts of hail, heat lightning, dust storms. Alice challenged herself to let the mown grasses lie in windrows on the high ground an extra day. It was a fine crop; she must not allow anxiety to stampede her into premature baling and stacking.

Meanwhile, here came Labor Day and the Fair to keep her from fidgeting. Even though neither oldsters nor youngsters any longer held 4-H memberships, the Standfast family always attended the Southeastern Washington Fair in Walla Walla, as they did Dayton Days in Dayton, Waitsburg's own Days of Real Sport, and the Caledonian Games at Athena in Oregon. The last few years they had given the Pendleton Round-Up the go-by as being too far, too national, too touristy. But the smaller and more local festivals retained all the features of clan gatherings: familiar faces, friendly competition, odd foods, too much beer, and sunburn. Ritualized promenades, sidelong sizings-up of the marriageable. But their chief interest was in seeing Rosemary Keith's horses race, and in the horse show.

Nan caught a ride back from Pullman for the long weekend and entered Skookum in Western Pleasure, Amateur Rider, she being too old now to ride as a junior. She and Alice and Janet always competed in the Trail Horse classes just to see how their working horses shaped up against the competition. Philip and Nick steered clear of the whole event, beer and cold cuts and quiet at home their consolation. This year Alice shanghaied Domingo for the second day, when they were all competing and therefore unable to valet and groom for each other. So as usual Standfast was amply represented.

The first day they had taken just Skookum, plus Cattywampus because the two were buddies, not intending to compete Cattywampus. But Boyce Yamada, the ring steward, asked if someone from their outfit would ride turnback for the cow cutters, so Alice and Janet took turns on Catty, who worked like his heart was in it, sure enough.

"Domingo must have said a word in his hairy ear," Janet said, but Alice said, "No indeed, I think he's really mended."

Skookum placed twice in his Pleasure Horse classes, second in the amateur, and fifth in the open division. Then to Nan's delight, they won the Amateur Trail class. She hadn't trained for it, but work on the ranch had made him confident and obedient, and that sufficed.

Something about a blue ribbon fluttering at the headstall! Next day, all fizzed up, Nan entered the Open Trail class.

"He can play with the big boys, Aunt Roan, don't you think?"

"Sure can, peach, if he works for you as sweet as yesterday."

"Okay, that makes all four of us, then," wielding her sweat scraper to the detriment of the passing crowd's clothes and sunglasses. "Money in the bank; Standfast rules!"

"Who four?" said Domingo alertly. The three females looked at him. "Ay no. No, I'm tell you," surrounded, pinned to the trailer.

"No chicken at our place," Nan said.

"Jesus Christ! No way! I don't know nothing! Okay, okay, okay, don't looking me no more, ay Chihuahua."

"Good, I'll go sign you up," Janet said. "Keep an eye on him, Alice, don't let him weasel out."

"Wait, Yan," hurrying after her. For her ear alone, "You think it's safe to put Domingo out front like this? What if somebody asks the wrong question, or—"

"Oh sure. Local law aren't interested, and the Feds concentrate on big busts. Packing houses, feedlots, big agricultural operations—two hundred at a sweep, that's what they go for. He's safer here than on the streets of Tijuana."

"He is? Why?"

"He won't get hit up for little bribes everywhere, for one thing."

"I prefer use my horse," Domingo grumped to Nan.

"Catty goes great for you, though; you're in his head."

"Is not like her." As it turned out, though, Cattywampus was good enough.

In addition to the usual obstacles for the amateur trail class—wooden footbridge, ranch gate, rows of old tires, and so forth—the open class featured some refinements: a tent with an oscillating fan inside it, a nanny goat with twin kids in a pen, a crate of chickens covered with a sheet, a machine that blew up a balloon and then let the air out in a long fart, a grove of potted palms. And the real killer, the Pit, a big sheet of black indoor/outdoor carpeting, laid flat on the tanbark and resembling a glittering abyss, hell's own gate.

The Pit proved the undoing of many a horse of blameless life and unblemished reputation. It did for Skookum, who took one look, backed into the tent, and was disqualified. Tom Fool carried Alice across it after powerful urging but, unhinged by the experience, refused the rows of tires, of all things, and offered to kick the goat. Vera Jane Whyte's old gray Solomon, nearly blind, crossed the Pit without a blink; also dead to the leg, however, he stopped to eat part of the palm grove, and was led from the arena in disgrace. Every horse entered had something to say about the Pit, and mostly what they said was no.

Janet came in with her new mount, whose racetrack career had prepared him for nothing in the world like this: the arena, the dark far-off ceiling with its fans and lights, children romping up and down the bleachers, smells of bratwurst and curly fries, and he all alone in the midst of it. Giving a great despairing whinny, which no one answered, he set about jumping down everything that was presented to him. Over the footbridge without setting foot to it. Over the lines of tires, the spectators beginning to titter. Over the Pit in one bound, over the end of the goats' pen. Goggle-eyed through the palm grove, leaving the fronds thrashing. With difficulty prevented from leaping the five-barred in-gate; did leap the Pit again, and hurtled out the exit, Janet hilarious, the crowd wild, loving it.

A post-entry, Domingo came in last, wearing Nan's hatband of silver conchas for luck, Standfast's last hope. All went well until Cattywampus winded the chickens. He squatted and threw his head up. No more than that, but he was close to the rail and must have caught the cheekpiece of his bridle on it. When he drew back, the bridle with its split-ear headstall and no throatlatch came right off and hung by the reins against his chest, and Domingo had no control of his head at all. The audience went still.

Get off, Alice thought, leaning on the in-gate.

"Get off," muttered Janet. "Nannie, run get a halter and lead rope."

Domingo reached slowly around Cattywampus's neck for the headstall, slowly coiled the reins, and hung the bridle on the fence. He rested his hands on the horn. Cattywampus walked on, past the chickens, around the farting balloon. Through the palm grove without hesitating.

Next came the Pit. Pin-drop silence in the hall. The burly gelding halted, his toe clips at the edge. Lowered his head and gave a blasting snort. The sleek hide of his flank dimpled to the spur steadily pressed in. Hind feet came forward but his fores hung fire on the edge of the void; the spirit was willing but the flesh had better sense. Teetered, all four feet in a space the size of a cookie sheet. Lifting a forefoot, he gave the black stuff a delicate touch.

Solid!

Tension drained from him; he strode boldly across. "Aw right!" yelled someone in the quiet stands. The tires: he paced them, a foot in each. The ranch gate: done them all his life. No bridle? No problem. The second time over the Pit he simply ignored it. They left the arena at a slow lope, real charro stuff. "Folks, that's J. D. Roke on Cattywampus, let's hear it—" drowned in a rising tide of yells, whistles, and applause.

"Did you see that?"

"Saw it, don't believe it," Alice said. "Who is this guy? Who are you, anyway? That was just magic. Go on in there and get your ribbon, boy."

"Is what I don't want. You get that bosal? Teacher, please take this horse."

"Isn't he pleased at all? Where did he go? Everybody's asking me about him."

Alice and Janet looked at each other: maybe this hadn't been such a good idea after all. "Shy, I guess. Best let him be, Nannie. Just a real private person." To Alice, "I didn't know he was going to *win* the damn thing, for heaven's sake."

Alice shook her head. "I don't think we're any too bright, for such intelligent girls. Dang, I'm glad I saw that, though. Here's your hatband, Nan. Lucky in spades."

Toward the middle of October, the weather changed for good. On a day of fine rain clothing every twig and grass blade in silver, of wind bringing an astringent tang of conifers down from the Blues, they set out to drive the culls to the finishing pens to ready them for market. Eleven of them: old animals, poor milkers, bad bearers, those who had failed to conceive a second time, bound for slaughter, to be replaced by yearlings in the spring. Some of them she would be glad to see off the place, Alice reflected as Falcon spurted forward to ride in a pair of ruffians determined to get back to the main bunch. Others, though . . . she never named her cows, but she knew them well, especially the old reliables, and when she sent these away to have their brains curdled and their hides yanked off like gloves, well, she never really hardened to that.

Some of the culls had a date with fate purely on grounds of attitude, one in particular. He was clever, that was his trouble. There had to be one in every crop, it seemed, a calf with ambition, that opened gates, pushed down fences, led his comrades into deep mud, fast water, other people's grain fields. A brainy cow, just what the rancher doesn't need. This year it was a steer of good weight and shape, with a crafty expression and two stupid but loyal cronies.

Pleasant as it was not to be breathing dust anymore after such a long dry season, the task lengthened out of toleration as this rogue animal broke back, broke back, taking his two pals with him, giving the whole little bunch bad ideas. The riders got them, finally, down onto the Triangle, where there was good feed waiting in the pens, and where they were used to answering Alice's holler to go and eat special treats of mash and vitamin supplements. She rode in and called, Domingo manning the gate, and the bunch trailed in docilely enough. All except the three miscreants, who held up at the top of the field, bawling, and suddenly the other eight seemed to realize they were in a trap, wheeled around, and pushed back out again, jamming the gate along with Domingo and his horse back against the fence.

This happened twice more, until by dint of combined driving and calling the eight unimaginative ones were penned, and settled down to munch. Domingo got down and surveyed the Mouse's hock, scraped in his collision with the gate. He and Alice had reached that stage of disgust with each other's incompetence that doesn't bear speech, the horses hung their heads, steaming, and the collies declined further involvement.

"We don't seem to be much good at this," said Alice, whacking the wet off her hat against the gatepost. "What say we knock off and go eat?"

Domingo checked his cinch and swung up. "Come on," doggedly. "Nos faltan tres, no más."

"Okay, if you're game. Once more unto the breach, dear friends, for Harry, England, and Saint George. Prob'ly nothing but beans for lunch, anyway."

With the whole Triangle at their disposal, the three rascally calves held out for quite a while, but in the end seemed ready to give up the game, began traveling in the right direction at last, toward the smaller of the two corrals, the dogs and the riders on two sides of them, the creek on the third. But then in the very gate they turned again and stood at bay. Sweep and Glen ran in, sure of victory, but the ringleader bolted through them and charged Domingo, his two buddies at his shoulders. Domingo shouted and fanned his hat, but on they came at a dead gallop. Panic stricken, the Mouse froze, and in an instant the phalanx of steers plowed into him like heavy cavalry.

For several seconds Alice, coming at a run, saw nothing but square black bodies and flailing dun legs, no sign of Domingo at all. Then the steers moved away, replete with mischief, to graze; the young horse lurched to his feet and trotted off distraught.

"Fockinhell," on hands and knees, bloody. A gash at the corner of his eye, a coursing nosebleed.

"Take it easy, kid. Don't get up just yet."

He knelt up, holding to her stirrup; coughed, spat, and sneezed, spraying gore. Got to his feet and stood swaying, a hand on the horn.

"Anything broke?"

"Está bien."

"I don't think so. Take this horse—"

"I'm okay."

"No *sir*, no argument. Take this horse, go up to the house, *go inside*, I'll be there in a minute."

She prevailed, and Falcon carried him up the hill. Alice caught up the Mouse, looked him over, and walked him uphill, put both horses away.

"What's the damage, buck?"

Groggily, "This little one broke, maybe," pointing at but not touching his left collarbone. Bleeding all over the sofa. "I'll bring the Chevette up," figuring he would have a hard time climbing up into the pickup.

"I don't going."

"No argument. Broken bones are nothing to fool with. See if you can get your jacket on again."

"You can fix it," desperately, but she was gone. I'm not going, he thought, sick with pain. No doctor, no fucking hospital. However, Alice forced him, a bag of frozen peas for his face, a rolled-up towel under his left arm. "I don't take medicine, Aliz. Is for nothing, this go-to-town." She ignored this, drove carefully.

Doctor Timmons, a Whetstone classmate of Alice's, presided over an emergency room empty except for a weeping child with a pencil eraser stuck up her nose. They parted company, Alice to fill out forms and Domingo, cursing in two languages under his breath, to limp after a nurse through the swinging doors, and she saw him next flat on a table, having the cut beside his eye sewn. A little bright-eyed Filipina nurse stood at the head of the gurney with her hands over his ears.

"What happened to him?" asked the doctor, making a knot.

"Bunch of cows ran over him, him and his horse."

"Looks like it. Bull rider's injuries. Belong to your outfit, does he? Tetanus booster, Elsa." The nurse went out. "Couple of ribs cracked, looks like, collarbone, possible concussion. We'll keep him overnight just to be—"

"I will not stay here," low but definite.

"See if you can get him to hold still, Alice." She moved around to the nurse's place. Domingo looked at her, upside down, dying-cat eyes, and swallowed expressively.

"What kind of problems are you worrying about, Tony? Seizures?"

"Seizure, hemorrhage, punctured lung, stuff like that. Probably not, but . . . why, is he scared of the hospital? The food is good here, the nurses are good looking. Even the guy nurses."

"Dile al pinche médico que no me quedo aquí en el pinche hospital."

"Did he say what I think he said?" The doctor lowered his broad beam onto a stool.

"Yes, I'm sorry. It was all I could do to get him here; might be doing you a favor to take him back home. If you could see your way clear."

Sighing, "It's probably okay. But if not, your place is pretty nearly off the end of EMT services, so . . . ." Another knot; the Filipina nurse came in and gave Domingo a tetanus shot. "There's the secondary problem that you can't really immobilize ribs and collarbones; you have to immobilize the whole patient for a while. That sound possible to do?"

"Did you comprehend what this good and kind medical said? See here, you mustang! Comport yourself like a man, no vulgar expressions."

He would have liked to den up in his own little room, but couldn't get down there under his own power; Alice made him stay at the house in case he fainted or fell in a fit. She fussed with quilts, extra pillows.

"No necesito ser mimado, Aliz."

"Mothering's just what you do need, you poor little dogie-calf," plugging in the heating pad for his knee, "but you'll have to make do with me. Stay put. See you at dinnertime."

A bad three hours; no painkillers because of the concussion. No reading, no sleeping. Crashing headache. Grizzling rain outside, gray light indoors. At least, he thought, I am out of that goddamn death house.

Alice blew in dripping, aggravatingly spry. Turkey and gravy, hot in minutes.

"No. Okay, thanks. My little horse okay?"

"Yeah. Well, sore, but nothing much else. His brains are probably scrambled."

"He have ánimo, don't worry. What happen those calf?"

"The sonsabitches got lonesome out on the field and went into the pen on their own. Funny the Mouse isn't hurt. They must have all jumped over him and landed on you."

"I don't want to remember. How come I have to stay here?"

"So I can keep an eye on you, make sure you do what the doc said."

"Fockin' médico!"

She looked at him curiously. Fed the fire in the stove, cleaned up the kitchen, worked on the computer for a while. The rain shushed down, a steady lulling fall. After a while she went out again to check her stock.

Coming in, she found Domingo fooling with the big guitar one-handed. "You help me, please, Aliz."

"No, I will not. Don't be taking that sling off. Do what I say, or I will take you straight back to the hospital."

"You can't," scornfully.

"No, but I can call the emergency medical techs and get three big guys to come and stick you in a truck and take you down there in two seconds."

After a considering pause, "You don't do it."

"I sure will."

"You are nice woman."

"Not particularly. Here's the deal: give me the guitar and go lie down, and I'll give you some medicine for your headache. Why are you so scared of the hospital, anyway?"

"Not escared," he said, easing down among the quilts again, taking the pill. "I hate it. My mother dies in there."

"Well, mine did too. Also me, almost, but I don't"—wrapping herself in a Pendleton blanket, one of the new ones, she settled in the wing chair—"hate it, exactly. Though I guess I'd do about anything to avoid going in there, whatever the reason. I don't blame the docs, though; they did their best, God knows."

"What happened," Domingo asked in a low voice, *"about your mother. If you don't mind telling."*

"She went to have her appendix taken out. It's the same word en español, no? No problem, easy operation. The next day, she got out of bed to take a little walk down the corridor, and a blood clot went to her heart, and she died. Just in seconds it happened. We were just children, Janet was only twelve. It left a hole in our life." Alice had a clear memory of being out with the cows with her father afterward, his ringing parlor tenor, "O'er the hills tae Ardantennie," cut off short. The next line being, "Just tae see ma bonnie Jeannie." "It was quick, she never knew anything about it. That's a blessing, I guess. She was a good hand, my mother, a horseman, crazy about my dad. I miss her, still. What would you say to a little . . . hot chocolate?" What she wanted was a tot of malt. Not a good idea, though; she could so easily become maudlin.

"I'm stupid from this pill. Oh, mine? Cancer. Not quick. She liked horses too. Not for work, but for companionship. A good woman." Then Alice thought he went to sleep.

Around ten, though, out of the blue, out of the dark beyond the fire: *"Why is there no man here with you?"*

In fact, there had been a man with her for eight years: Vincent Greer, Walla Walla boy, Philip Weston's college roommate and best friend.

Many of the qualities Alice admired in Philip, she had loved in Vincent; in addition, she lusted after him so much her hands lost their grip. She married him after graduation, moved to Portland, and set up housekeeping. Went to work in an office on Burnside, typing and filing, while Vincent finished his law studies at Willamette.

"I mean, do I look like a secretary to you?"

"No more than I do."

"Well, no! Though it was kind of fun for a while, city life. But after a year, I guess Vincent could see I wasn't thriving. Like a calf that's not getting enough nourishment, you know."

Vincent assumed that this experience would uproot Alice from Standfast, expand her horizons, addict her to live theater and gourmet coffee. Alice thought Vincent's time in Portland would reconcile him to wheat and heat and silence. Grievous miscalculations, both.

"We moved back to the Valley, to Waitsburg, and I taught high school, and worked up here as much as I could. My dad needed me, because by that time Janet was teaching full-time. He never said so, but—well, you've seen what single-hand is like."

Vincent Greer tried to establish himself in Walla Walla, first in one of the old traditional law firms, then in partnership with Philip, finally on his own. It was not what he wanted, not the kind of law he wanted to practice. He felt thrown away, boondocked, so he worked out adjunct arrangements with practices doing poverty law and environmental law in Seattle, San Francisco, and Los Angeles, was away months at a time. After four years, Alice shifted to the substitute-teacher list so she could work on the ranch full time.

"So you livin' alone here?"

"Well, with my dad. But I didn't feel like a, you know," shifting uneasily, turning sideways in the chair, her knees up, "like a wife very much."

Domingo clicked his tongue in sympathy. After a while, "Lotta woman in Mexico like this, guy come up here for work. Sometimes he don't come back, but . . . sometimes he come back, but she already make her life alone, you know? There is no more . . . how can I say, cariño?"

Affection. No more tenderness. Yes. She remembered that. Heartache, still, to think how punctiliously she would leave Standfast on the dot of five to get dinner for Vincent at their pretty cottage in Waitsburg; how he reproached her with it. Jesus, Alice! You can hardly tear yourself away to come home, can you? Call this marriage? Well, she reproached herself. He was right. She had married him under false pretenses.

"And then the baby died."

Domingo drew a sharp breath through his teeth: *"What happened?"*

"I was teaching school. And you know, teachers catch whatever bugs the kids have. So I got a flu in my eighth month. Great big fevers for six or seven days, I didn't know what was going on. My little boy was born dead. My little Lyon. I s'pose that's why I'm so fond of the Weston kids."

And her womb scarred closed. She recovered slowly, Vincent not at all. He blamed her for riding while pregnant; he blamed Allan, the hospital, the doctor who treated her, the school where she taught. Indicted the very wind that combed the wheat. And was gone, within a year, with little discussion. The divorce was fast; they had nothing to share but the house, quickly sold.

"When did these things happen?"

"Seven years ago. And six years ago my dad had a heart attack. So then it was just me and Jerry Graeme. And now just me. And you. What luck, you turning up! *You being with me, am I not the favorite of fortune?"* In daylight she probably would not have said this; and of course, she didn't know exactly what she *had* said. "How you doing? Want another pill?"

"You want another child?"

"More than to live, almost." For a while she avoided foals and puppies and kittens, couldn't trust herself not to pool up and snivel. Under the blanket, her hand on her belly. "But for me, it's not possible anymore," matter-of-fact. "How old were you when your mom died?"

"Sixteen."

"Oh, man, I'm so sorry. Did you have family then?"

"I was alone."

Thank God Alice avoided the usual platitudes: *she's in a better place*—none of that foolishness.

He had not seen his mother's face when she died, his own being hidden. Just the pressure of her hand, lessening to mere weight. The terrible blank end of everything. No one now in all the world cared for him at all.

She told him otherwise, always. Your father loves you, he does, never doubt it. Promise me.

I promise.

Strange, though, Fidel's love, even his love for her: cold, commanding. Punishing. Hurtful to Fidel himself, it seemed. Love is a wound, he seemed to think. Such a weakness, a man, if he wishes to call himself a man, must dissemble. Amor chueco: crooked, lamed love, made fierce by being dammed and blunted. Love just the same, do not doubt it, she said. Promise me.

After the funeral, he sold his books and his prepa uniform, left a gift for the family where he boarded in the town, thumbed a ride out to Lomas Chatas with a face swollen as if battered; it was a wonder anybody picked him up. A vaquero family who barely knew of them had taken over their house, but his mother's school was empty, locked up, a couple of scantlings barring the gap in its hedge of prickly pear. He knotted his school necktie to the big wooden doorknob. Pressed his forehead to the faded paint of the portal. Two days later, he joined his father on the Border.

Love him; look after him. Promise me.

But he had failed her there.

Chapter Nine

HE WOULDN'T GO TO THE CLINIC TO HAVE THE STITCHES REMOVED. "You can do it," he insisted, blockading her in the kitchen, brandishing the little scissors from the sewing box. Even the Clydesdales wouldn't budge him, that was clear.

"Dadgummit! Why are you so cabezón? Oh, all right. Sit there, by the light." She poured a finger of whisky, to steady her hand and to sterilize the scissors in. Bending over him, "Blink, and you're a one-eyed jack. Jesus, *cowboys*!"

"When we going to sell those guys?" Upbeat, for a guy who hated cold rain as much as Domingo did; interesting also, Alice thought, how thoroughly he seemed to have bought into corporation Standfast. Alice knew why he was asking about the calves, though. She too was anxious for some real cowboy work after weeks of loading, stacking, selling, trucking, unloading, and restacking hay.

The calves looked good, marketable. "Two weeks, I'm thinking. We'll bring them down tomorrow. Think you can stand a day in the saddle? I'm candy-assed from all this hay work."

"Repeat, please."

"Soft in the butt," rising in the oxbows and smacking her behind. "Go throw a line on that heifer by the sumac for me, the one that just stood up."

"The black one?" with a grin, loping down the terrace, rocking his loop back and forth to build it.

Alice measured the beast around the middle with her arms. "Better than five-fifty, I'm betting," as it ambled off. "Not bad for a heifer; probably the steers are at or above six hundred. Two weeks of finishing, most of those guys will make market weight and then some. Another two weeks for the females."

"¿Por qué las novillas no ganan como los novillos?"

"Because I don't give them that stuff to suppress their heat, their uh, uh, celo, can that *possibly* be the right word? It sounds like the cows are jealous. Their estrus cycle. Some folks do, but we do not."

"Uh-huh, okay, why not?"

"Because," rather declamatory, "we suspect that what affects the reproduction of one mammal, a cow, may also affect the reproduction of another mammal, a woman," having said this before, most ringingly to the members assembled at a meeting of the Palouse Cattlemen's Association. Alice had meant to drop a private word in the chairman's ear, but Janet forced her hand by bringing the question up in open session. An awful stramash ensued, hard words all round, and the Andison sisters stalked out in righteous dudgeon. Many people, still sore and shy of Alice, snubbed her firmly even now. Janet resigned her membership, ate only Standfast beef.

This having been explained to him, Domingo wondered aloud what the fuss was about. Plenty of other outfits used the stuff. There was no law against it, right? Who was to know . . . ?

"I would know," coldly, riding down again to set up the finishing pens. "I'd be selling what I wouldn't eat. I couldn't look myself in the mirror."

"Pero, Patrona, si todo el mundo usan pesticidas para los tomates, las frutas, los chicken," taking the pragmatic, rather than the idealistic position. Though God knew why she expected idealism from him. Victims were the ones idealism most appealed to, and there wasn't a victimish bone in his body.

"I can't save the world," she began virtuously but modestly.

"You rich, you don't mind lose the money."

Now, that was annoying.

"I am not rich! That's one reason I can't just decide to hold my heifers off the market awhile. The big outfits—there are economies of scale."

"What might that mean, in a civilized idiom?"

"Hey, I don't understand economics in English, kid, much less in— damn, here comes the rain again. Did I leave my slicker up there on the fence? Yes, I did."

Alice hated being called rich, especially before her calves were sold, when it seemed to her that the whole enterprise hung by a thread. Rich, for God's sake! Or at any other time, matter of fact, with the place sucking up all of her strength, all of her time, whether she made a profit or not. And cash poor always, budgeting for necessities, penny-fretful if her yard boots sprang a leak or the toaster went tits up.

On the other hand, she thought, the ground she trod on was her own. What could Domingo, stray that he was, call that but riches?

Alice had had this dream three times: she found she had become Standfast. Its steep ridges and watercourses and long contoured hay terraces formed her body. She was of great extent. Hot, silent. Slowly turning under the sky. Always she woke up smiling, never told a soul.

"You want to get a look at that mare of Domingo's, kid."

"Good, is she?" Janet dished up chicken pie.

"She is a step up, no lie. Kinda scary."

Domingo put down his fork, denying nothing. He could have told them so, long since. All the same, he delighted to hear her praised; especially by Alice, who knew what she was talking about.

Philip asked, "Is this the horse that killed the calf?" and Nick said, "Jeez."

"It's a shame the calves are all gone to the sale. She could do you a demonstration with the cows, but of course the big'uns are slower, not as much of a challenge."

"In what—another slice, my chou-fleur, small slice—in what, if you can explain to the likes of me, resides her excellence?" Domingo looked at Alice, who said, "Tell Philip how your horse works."

"Ah. She don't, doesn't . . ." much preferring to speak about the red mare in Spanish. For himself, he didn't care about awkward infantile language, but she deserved the most elegant expression of which he was capable. However, in deference to Philip: "She attack the calf. She is more fast than every calf. She's playin'! Sometimes she goes on her knees, almost."

"She bores in, like Sweep. I've actually never seen a horse work that close, she gets nose to nose, I mean there's no margin for error at all. What's in this, raisins?"

"Currants, and citron."

"Jeez," said Nick again, at his plate. "Could I have a little more, though?"

Alice felt that neither she nor Domingo had done justice to the red mare's drive and virtuosity. "She's the best damn cutting horse I've ever seen, live," she said flatly. "She has this aura, this flow or something, I dunno. When she zeroes in, she looks like she might *eat* the critter. Fun to watch, hard to ride; though ole Slick makes it look easy, cracked ribs and all," tipping her glass at Domingo.

"Muy amable," raising his own. He was dozy with wine and warmth after a long day fighting a fierce northwesterly gale. November, the hills taking on their winter palette, dun and silver stubble, the mauve-brown of fallow fields. The heifer calves were gone to the sale; Silka was back home, trailing clouds of horse-show glory. Next week, Rosemary Keith and her son Campbell would bring the racehorses up. Ahead loomed the unfencing of the Hashknife piece, slogging labor in dirty weather; painstaking too, for wherever those old fences were down, yards of barbwire lay coiled in ambush for plow and harrow and the legs of horses. And razing the house at the bottom of the pothole valley, which the Alcohol, Tobacco, and Firearms investigators had left a trashed-out shell. Burn it, was Domingo's advice; but Alice meant to save the window frames and doors, the bricks of the chimney, the tin roof. They needed to reline the well out there too. Holy God. Listen to him now, making lists in his head like la Patrona.

"Nick, we're taking down the old house for scrap next Saturday. Want to help? You can swing the hammer."

"You bet. I like destruction." In fact he liked doing just about any work with them. They were so teamed up they were almost pretty to watch. Plus, they never groused at him for not knowing how to do stuff, and talked to each other all the time in Spanglish, funny as hell. "Look. Domingo's falling asleep. Can I have his dessert?"

"Unconscious, not dead," fending off Nick's raid on his flan. So sleepy he forgot to ask Alice whether she too had seen the low car with the silver stripe, parked at the Seven-Eleven.

The three English teachers tramped into the wind up the path along Mill Creek, scarves straining backward. At the footbridge they turned around. Scarves strained forward; however, conversation became possible.

Janet gazed at the creek sliding glassily over its step dams. "I wonder if you can adopt an adult," she said. "I'd like to adopt Domingo Roque, who works for my sister. What a find! He's so good with Nick, like a big brother from another planet. A planet where all anybody wants to do is work like hell all day, and play catch in the evening. They took Nicky on last summer, Domingo and Alice; he came home on Sundays dog tired and perfectly civil; it was a miracle."

"Whoa! Can I send my problem child up there?"

"They should open a re-education camp," Eileen chuckled, "for sons of the middle class. Y'know, when Mexico throws away a person like that, we gain big."

"D'you think," Jolie said, "he'd want to be a citizen? Or does he just want the green card? Does he realize he'd have to give up Mexico, I mean really, under oath?"

"I asked him that, just the other night. Know what he said? 'You always know who your father is, but if he doesn't take care of you, you don't develop much of an attachment.'"

"Isn't that a parable for our times," said Eileen, patting cold hands together. "Let's go to La Tolteca for lunch, to show solidarity."

"Can't," gloomed Janet. "That damned criminal-justice student is coming to see me, Brandon Galante."

"What, again? Still? That was two quarters ago, wasn't it? The guy who felt he should pass Basic Writing," Jolie reminded Eileen, "without actually writing."

Eileen plied a Kleenex. "Not a happy chappy," through it. "What does he want from you after all this time?"

"Still," Janet said. "I'm starting to get a little nervous about him. He still wants me to say he passed Basic Writing."

"And?"

"I will not say it."

He never laid a rough hand on a horse, Alice thought, but he damn sure punished the machines. What ailed the man? Foul language, thrown tools, wary cats, Glen skulking and whimpering. Whole evenings passed in bleak meditation; no guitar. She plumped down on the other end of the new sofa.

"Say, slick." He quit cracking his knuckles in rotation, raised his eyebrows. "Tell me who's hurting you and I'll go beat them up."

Not even a snicker. So long since she'd kidded a grin out of him, she couldn't remember which side the gold tooth was on. But after a while he sat back and said, "I need go way for little while."

"Okay," equably. "Better now than in the summer. When, and how long?"

"You going to town Saturday, you can take me to the bus. Two weeks I'm back."

"All right. You okay for money, need an advance?" She knew he sent money away somewhere, had seen him coming out of the post office folding the money-order receipts. Going to see Concepción Vélez, probably; but why the thunderclouds, if so? Domingo leaned toward her, smacked the middle cushion.

"You hella good boss, Aliz, you know? *I am under great obligation.*"

"Well," said Alice cheekily, "I've got your horses. Don't forget that, primo. So I know you'll be back."

The day Domingo left Standfast, the wind backed into the southeast. A warm tumult of air swiftly peeled off the snow from the week before, causing the cattle to galumph and bawl excitedly, and then lie down all together on the Triangle like a reef of black boulders. All afternoon the storm gathered force, skirling in the fence wires. Branches cracked and crashed down, buildings moved subtly. Coming back from her evening check of the yard, Alice heard a rhythmic clash of corrugated tin start up, part of a shed roof pulling loose.

The barometer needle whipped over counterclockwise. She didn't get much sleep, dozing and waking, conjuring the roof to stay on. At five, as she brushed her teeth, the phone rang. A lot of teasing calls lately, ring and click. But no: Robey Whyte, from the hospital.

"What are you doing down there?"

"I brought her in. She fainted. She ain't *never* done that." Alice disliked both the news and the doleful sound of Robey's phlegmy old voice. After chores, she took the pickup over to Robey Grade and fed their animals. Gathered as many eggs as she could find, hens darting and fussing. As she crossed the backyard, Vera Jane's demon white rooster bounced up at her like a gamecock, caught a hurricane gust, and thumped into the siding. He lay in the pansy bed stunned, possibly dead; Alice was too afraid of him to check.

When she went back there in the afternoon, the wind now streaming smoothly out of the west bearing rain and snow together, all was fine. Both of them said so, several times. Lunch had been eaten; the kitchen, the whole place was spotless. A good fire of applewood leapt up the chimney in the living room where Vera Jane sat crocheting, perfectly fine. Alice expected Robey to come out to the truck with her, but he stayed in the shelter of the porch, hunched up, sorry as a molting crow.

She drove home and called Janet. "Something's wrong with Vera Jane."

"I know. What happened?"

"Robey took her to the hospital in the middle of the night. They're back home now, though. Giving out nothing. What do you know?"

"Nothing, not a thing. I've just been a little worried lately; I don't know why. Should I go up there, do you think?"

Alice tested her feeling about this. "Maybe not today. Not just yet. They seem to want a little . . . interval."

"Yes. Okay. Meanwhile," a vast sigh, then a sound like a tractor starting up, "Nick caused an uproar at school. He's thrown out, suspended. Gawd, Alice. Who'd be a parent?"

Me, thought Alice. Let's see, he would have been about seven now, her little Lyon Andison Greer. Plenty old enough to be hating the whole horsey, dirty, exhausting business of farming, and to tell his mother so, thus wrenching her heart warm and throbbing from her bosom. "What's he done, darlin'?"

What Nick had done, according to the principal, was to slander another student in gross sexual terms to a crowded and breathlessly receptive cafeteria.

"So Nick's out for six weeks for damaging this boy's exceptionally fragile psyche plus starting a food fight. We're probably getting a bill for the damage as well. The other boy is big, handsome, popular, a three-sport athlete, and showily pious. We'll be lucky not to get sued."

"You know," said Alice, "the kid's got possibilities."

Domingo Roque, not at the Vélez place in Hermiston as Alice assumed, instead huddled in the dubious comfort of a bus shelter in Wapato, eyes on the door across the road. In the duffel between his numb feet lay a present, also a new snapshot of himself from a machine at the mall.

Jesús niño, he thought. How could he have blurted it out like that? That fucking pill! "You want another child?" As if a dead child were a puppy, to be replaced by another puppy. Lucky she had mistaken the time of the verb, or she might well have thought he was offering to get a baby on her himself, right then.

But his situation at Standfast was all upside down anyway, nobody behaving as expected. There was Alice acting like a true patrón, taking an interest, offering money, time off. Completely out of gringo character. And himself, the dependent, trusting in her, but unable to explain, enlist her help. He squirmed on the narrow bench as if poked. There was, he feared there would always be, something so shaming about his position. Discreditable to a man. He wanted very much to confide in Alice, but he didn't know where to start, he didn't know where he stood. "For me, it's not possible," she said flatly. But then, *"You being with me, am I not the favorite of fortune?"* A strange, strong thing to say, even from friend to friend.

An electric bell shrilled out. The double doors opened, children poured forth, their bright faces and bright-colored clothes thrilling the clear dark air.

There. The yellow light behind her. He stood up. She spotted him; her face changed.

Nan drove herself home from Pullman, the backseat of her new old Civic full of dirty laundry and improbable Christmas presents. Her hair cut short and bleached white, startling Janet. Her coming home in this altered state wrung her mother's heart in a way that her leaving had not.

Those first-semester grades impressed her family but not, evidently, Nan herself. Philip noticed that she had less to say than when she went away, not the development he had hoped for. "Way to go, Nicholas," was all she offered on her brother's plight at the high school; Nick couldn't tell whether she meant it ironically or not.

She hung out with Tamlyn Evans, home from Ellensburg with the Chinese pictograph for "peace" tattooed on her wrist, about which her parents gave her no peace, and a more road-worthy car than Nan's. In it they trolled the county roads with other Christmas returnees, descended like locusts on each other's families at mealtimes, and reveled in the strangeness of being home, of transformed relations with parents and siblings. Tammy said it felt like she was wearing her little sister's clothes. Nan said she felt like a larva that had pupated into a larger and glossier maggot.

"What's it like, you guys?" Nick demanded. He had every good reason for wanting the straight skinny on higher education, since their parents had been promising forever that if he could just hang on through high school until he got to college, he would find his tribe. Nan made a noncommittal sound and slouched farther down on the porch swing, which was uncomfortable, stripped of its cushions. They were drinking beer in the cold, she and Tammy and Nick and Ear-ache Doyle, and their gun-nut buddies Trey and Joel Jussum. Strewn around the Westons' front porch, some of them underage, giving scandal to the neighborhood. Though not really: the neighbors were all indoors toasting their toes before blazing televisions. It was privacy the homecomers were after, not provocation.

"The hot poop. Come on, you," giving the swing a push with his foot. His sister paused the bottle until she stopped oscillating. Swigged, and tilted the neck toward Tammy.

"Not as bad as high school," Tammy said, "would you say?"

"I would say that. Not quite as bad." Nick frowned: not what he wanted to hear. College guys refuse to grovel, is that it? he thought about saying, to try to salvage something of his more and more apparently self-deceiving and rose-colored assumption about undergraduate life. Though guys groveling was not really what Nan was about, as far as a kid brother could tell.

Trey Jussum, accepted into the WSU animal science program for the fall and nervous about it, forestalled him. "Bad how? Too much homework?"

"A lotta that." Tammy took her hands out of her pockets to work the church key. "Nobody comes after you if you ditch a class, but you can't, like, make work up," somewhat hangdog, having failed fresh-man Lang and Lit. Nan knew about this, and said in palliation, "Every required course is a mob scene, cast of thousands. Even the discussion sections are big."

"Yeah, and plus they expect you to, like, read all that shit." In truth

Tammy felt only slightly out of her depth at Eastern, but she knew that this remark would get Nick's goat, so she directed it at him with a stupid, doped-out expression to maximize the effect. Nick turned toward the street, a vivid flush crowding his freckles.

Nan felt that for his sake she should perhaps not complain any-more. But her own powerful sense of disillusionment got the better of her. "There's no conversation. I guess that's what pisses me off. It's all, like, scoring. It's all about getting laid and getting·ripped, how often and how much and who with—"

The Jussums looked at each other. "Sounds great!" Joel laughed, and Trey said, relieved, "Yeah, I was gonna say—"

"Here comes JoNelle," Nick muttered.

The Jussums' sister parked her black Toyota pickup across the street and came up the walk, tall and limber, eyes downcast. Nan moved over to make room on the swing, and JoNelle sat without a word and sank her chin soberly into the collar of her vest.

"That fuckin' truck," Trey said. He and Joel threw down rock, paper, scissors to see who had to ride home in the load bed.

Before conversation could resume, Janet bumped the front door from inside, and brought out two round pans that smoked in the chill air. "A little ballast," she said, setting them down on the wall, "lest you sail home listing to port or starboard."

"What is it?" said the Jussum brothers together.

"Sort of a Tex-Mex pizza. Here, napkins." She went back inside.

Quiet reigned while they tackled the hot, crisp, drippy stuff. "Damn, that woman can cook," somebody said.

Nick jumped as if stung: "She can also write, and think, and teach—"

"And yet, and yet," Nan swept in smoothly, "she cooks. It's some kind of miracle, isn't it? She must love us very much," with a repres-sive stare at her brother, and then surprised him by taking another slice, even though she was, or was trying to be, a vegetarian.

Nick became aware that JoNelle was looking at him. He felt him-self grow warm with a peculiar emotion, a sort of radical uncertainty.

"You shoot your mouth off," JoNelle said to him. What did that mean, You shoot your mouth off? Was it observation, fairly rude, or exhortation? Go, guy: shoot your mouth off! They were in the same grade at the high school, though JoNelle was two years older than he. And Nick was a year ahead of his age cohort, but at the moment, instead of feeling Advanced, he felt young, and at a disadvantage.

He wished JoNelle would go away. At the same time, he wanted to her to say something more. But she didn't. Clad in silence. Nick envied her, wondering about himself. He experienced his own potential to do something remarkable as a formless force caged up within him, battering to get out. He wondered what Domingo Roque thought of him.

Some of 'em fuckers, thought the driver of the racy Trans Am, watching from half a block away, engine idling, are under drinking age, sure as dammit. Debated with himself whether to walk up and bust them, right there on the Weston porch, maximum embarrassment, or wait till they got on the road and collar the driver, or hold off and try for something even more flagrant and damaging. Something that would connect Teacher Janet with the drugs up at that ranch, the sister's ranch. He knew there were drugs up there, he could taste it. The stop on the Mexican guy had been a disappointment. A mistake, true, but a logical one: why would somebody from that particular outfit be coming into town in the middle of the night if not to sell banned substances? It had to be. And the woman, the sister, when he phoned up there, knew all about it!

Also, the Corvette with the out-of-state plates, spotted twice this month: he needed to tie that in. Was the ghostly driver the buyer or the seller?

No. He would wait, he decided. Plenty of time. He'd keep the pressure on Teacher Weston to change his grade—that would make this whole operation unnecessary. Or maybe get his advisor to waive the requirement—if so, ditto. Or—why waste all this effort?—he could make an airtight case, start off his career with a bang.

Yes, he thought, rolling on up and hanging a U-ie at the stop sign. That'll teach the Teacher.

Christmas came, and the Westons and Whytes came to Standfast for Christmas dinner. The weather settled to dull, raw cold. At New Year's, the McCrimmons invited Alice for Hogmanay as well as the Whytes, the Westons, the Ruthvens, Murrays and Marrs from Dayton, and the Pagliais, honorary Scots. They staged a wine tasting of single-malt whiskies, ate all manner of good things, none of which resembled a haggis in any particular, danced reels and strathspeys up and down the glassed-in porch, and sang "Auld Lang Syne" at midnight. Alice said to Janet that their Fifeshire cousins would have scorned this as a celebration. In Scotland, Hogmanay starts after dinner and goes on for six days. American Scots were degenerate, they agreed.

Domingo stayed away and stayed away, so Nick came up and worked for Alice on weekends. There wasn't much regular work beyond choring at this season, and the pulling down of old fences she could pretty well handle on her own, but Alice found that she missed company. Working with Domingo all these months had broken the back of her solitude; she no longer felt content to be alone. Not that she was scared, in spite of continuing strange phone calls, which she'd come to think of some sort of technological glitch, the phone company's problem. Just, she enjoyed doing things more when he was there to notice how well they were done. Besides, she had a few things in mind to consult Domingo about. Chispa, for one thing, that studdy little rip. She wanted Domingo to set a date for getting him gelded.

"Did you call up los Vélez? Do you want me to?" Janet asked, alarmed, when Domingo had been gone six weeks, calving coming on. "Aren't you getting anxious about him?"

"Yeah, but I don't want to spy. If he's in Hermiston . . . though, you know, I was wondering whether he might have gone to Mexico."

Janet wondered the same thing. "It's a common thing to do, get away from the cold, see your family."

"Except it would be so risky for him, without documents. Anyway, he says he doesn't have family. Though I know he sends money some-where."

"Probably has a wife down there. I'm starting to get a bad feeling about this. If he tries to cross back and gets caught, would we ever know? Or would he just disappear?"

A wife? Alice registered her dismay at the idea. "Maybe that's what all these weird phone calls are about."

"Maybe. Do you answer the phone even when the caller ID says Unavailable?"

"Yes. I've been chatting with a lot of siding salesmen and cult re-ligionists as a result. And of course Old Ring-and-Click, whoever he is, but no Domingo Roque. To tell the truth, I'm not really worried. I'm pretty sure he'll be back in time for calving. His horses are here, for one thing, and I don't know, he strikes me as"—Janet listened attentively—"I think he's sound right through, like a Braeburn apple. You like him too, don't you?"

"I do. But then I like Cruz Betancourt and Frankie Padilla."

"What does that mean?"

"It means I'm a lousy judge of character. Well, you can keep Nick for calving if Domingo doesn't show. Let's see if unremitting heavy labor will teach him sense, or at least to shaddap."

Alice put the phone down. Why should I care if he has a wife, what business is it . . . ? Alice, is he, are you . . . ?

Puttering home one fog-bound afternoon just at the end of Nan's winter break, she driving, Nick in front and the Jussum brothers in back, they got pulled over by a sheriff's officer on the long ramp down into Waitsburg. The county cruiser passed them westbound, reversed across the highway, and came storming back blinking the headlights and oinking the klaxon. A buffed-out deputy not much older than they, it seemed to Nick, and evidently not fully conversant with the law regarding traffic stops. No reason given for the stop, and the grounds for searching the vehicle as lame as a drunk's excuse.

They had been target shooting at the gun club in Walla Walla, and the Jussums had brought away a coffee can full of brass shell–casings for some project of JoNelle's. Leaning in, the deputy spotted these, and made Nan open the trunk. Which was empty of guns, the twenty-twos being locked up at the club, but he searched anyway, pulled up the mat in the trunk, got them all out and felt under the seats. Nan kept quiet; they all did; all knew that something about the business was out of kilter.

"Whaddya think he was after?" Trey Jussum wondered when they got on the road again after the formulaic dismissal: have a nice day.

"Strange guy. Anybody get his name?" Strange enough that Nan mentioned it to Philip, who made a mental note: Galante.

Confident though Alice told herself she was, on February first she woke up ready to fire the man, dump his stuff out in the snow, sell his horses to the canner, mad as hell. She felt . . . something like grief.

But that very afternoon as she rode down toward the mailbox, an unfamiliar pickup stopped at the foot of the lane. Someone vaulted out of the back and the truck pulled away, leaving the little dark figure of a man stark against the snow. Soon surrounded by leaping dogs.

"I estill work here?" Wherever he had been, whatever doing, had not improved him; he looked small, beat down. I will have to feed you up before I can use you very hard, Alice thought.

"I sincerely hope so," she said. "You cut it pretty fine, buck. We've been a tad worried about you."

"*I regret it very much. Is all well here, and with the family?*" polite, through chattering teeth.

"*Everything blooms with us. Also, your horses are stylish. We must consult about Chispa, but perhaps not soonestly. Will you manipulate the mail? And I will bear your fardels upward.*" She felt better. Much, much better.

Domingo handed up the contents of the mailbox, and his duffel. Back up the hill they went in the azure twilight, he holding to her stirrup, over the creaking snow toward the house. The sight of the warm yellow house-windows beaming between locust boles, the diamond-cut profile of the swayback ridge beyond, made his eyes water. The comfort of it! As much a home as he was ever likely to have.

Horrendous, the first week's calving; she felt she was paying for all her good luck the year before. Very, very cold, wind-scoured, fraught with birthing troubles. The three of them were up around the clock for three days, had the vet out. In spite of all they could do, one of the cows died after a spendy caesarean section for twins. They saved the twins, two heifers, but lost more sleep bottle-feeding them every two hours. Toward the end Nick went back to high school almost willingly. Alice felt flogged, sore all over.

"Plánchate la oreja," Domingo instructed her as he set off to Walla Walla for grain and calf supplement. Flatten your ear, take a nap. Fond hope, thought Alice. She had to wait for the knacker to come and take away her dead cow, which had frozen solid out on the Triangle, and feed the twins in the foaling shed, and medicate the newest of the calves that had a weeping eye from being crowded into a fence by its idiot mother. That done, and half-frozen even in her thermal gear, she scrambled up into the stacked hay to pull down some bales of grain hay for the racehorses.

They weren't where she thought they were, those bales. Found them, though, after some fuddled searching, up on top of the alfalfa in a part of the stack the kids had made at the end of the cutting season. She climbed up, noticing that the bales were improperly stacked, one on top of another instead of offset like bricks. Tomorrow's extra-credit chore would be to stabilize that section. Dang kids. Paid good money too.

Something seemed to be peering at her under the eaves of the shed as she began shoving bales down: over her left shoulder, a veiled half moon rising from a notch in the hills. Moon of ill omen. Stepping backward to get a better look, Alice dropped with a yell down the slot between the alfalfa bales and the grass hay, seventeen feet onto the concrete pad of the shed. The stacks stood close together at the bottom, broke her fall, but as she lay there, winded as if thrown, the badly made alfalfa stack swayed and buckled, dropping a dozen sixty-pound bales down into the crevice, down onto Alice.

At first it seemed she would die of dust, of coughing, and there was scarcely room to cough. After a while, though, it appeared that if she wasn't greedy about the air, she could keep on breathing. A great relief.

Her right elbow hurt fiercely, the one under her as she lay on her side. So did her right knee and hip, she discovered, taking stock. None of them with the pulsing, sick-making pain of fracture. This is good, she thought, trying to buck herself up, since I don't have room to puke either. She tried what she could move, and found it was not much. Couldn't draw up her knees, couldn't pull her left arm down to her chest. Couldn't check her watch or reach her phone.

Opening her eyes, she assessed the situation. She lay on her right side on the concrete floor of the hay shed, wedged in a space the size of a child's coffin. She tested the bales around her; tested them harder, strained at them till a sparking red fog settled on her eyes. Stopped, gathered her strength, and tried it again. Nothing moved. Cattywampus, she thought, I beg your pardon with all my heart.

Alice detested enclosed places, always had. Hide-and-seek had never been her game. She noted with clinical objectivity the onset of claustrophobia: sweats, drooling nausea, high breathing. A tendency to scream and cry. Which she couldn't afford to do, she told herself. Air was scarce, hard to suck in; the solid mass of the hay compressed her so that she could only draw little panting breaths. To steady her mind, she recited a list of curses in Scots dialect, but it was short; she had forgotten so much since Allan died. This seemed to her terribly sad, and she felt that since she was hurting and suffocating and freezing to death and was alone and orphaned and had lost even Allan's cuss words, she had a good right to cry. But she couldn't. Couldn't drag in a breath big enough. Then she thought, Alice! Who will take care of the place?

Cowboy up. Think.

It was only as the light faded that she realized there *was* light, very faint, creeping in from beyond her head, beyond her extended arm, through a tunnel no bigger than a mouse-run. She wanted to look at her watch. Made a sinew-cracking try at pulling her left arm in. To no avail, and the effort left her light-headed, her heartbeat throbbing in her ears. It must be getting on for four, she thought, when she could think again. Full dark pretty soon, twenty minutes or so. Domingo, Janet, Robey, somebody, come.

She played the penultimate moment over in her head, craving the quarter second of rank stupidity back again. Pretended it was summer, saw herself reminding Nick and Earache and Nan to stagger the al-falfa bales. Saw herself taking Domingo's advice, piling onto the couch for a nap. She noticed gratefully that things didn't hurt as much now, then with a surge of panic thought, Christ, I'm freezing to death. The bales settled minutely, pressing her down.

Think. Keep going. She thought about the horses; to keep down panic, she gave herself the task of mentally tracing their bloodlines. Raevonne open: what stallion to take her to this spring? Other catalogs. The six Lipizzaner founding sires, the three thoroughbred ones, the three Angus ones. The four great battles for Scotland, the four great Romantic poets.

It's getting worse, less air, more weight.

Keep going.

All the poems she knew: first the short ones, Yeats's four-liners, Dorothy Parker, Ogden Nash for light relief, then Housman's beautiful lyric about the cherry trees. "Xanadu," which got away from her; two verses of Ted Hughes's piece about the hawk in the beech hanger that Janet calligraphed and framed for Philip's office. Les Murray's "The Quality of Sprawl"; very difficult, free verse. Surprisingly, quite a lot of "Paul Revere's Ride."

No light anywhere now. No feeling in her hands or feet. Tiny breaths. Keep going.

Descended to coarse limericks, of which she remembered a large number from college, a couple made up by herself and Janet, one not bad either, " . . . who could fuck on the run, at the point of a gun, or on fire at the edge of a cliff," what was the first part? Gotta ask Janet, she always remem—

"Aliz!"

Terror long held at bay rushed in and froze her larynx: "Here!" like the squeak of a newborn kitten. "Here, here, here!" Oh God, he wouldn't be able to hear—

"¿Dónde estás?"

"In here, under the hay! The whole goddam stack fell on me!"

"Okay, you breathin'?"

"Yeah. Though not to excess."

"Pues, don't go nowhere. I'm back in one minute."

One minute stretched to fifteen, Alice counting them like rosary beads. She heard him crunching around out there in the direction of her head. "What are you doing?"

"Say when you see these light." He had a flashlight, the big lantern from the tack room, she guessed.

"Nothing. Nothing. Nothing. Yes!! Right there, I saw it, go back!"

God's name, he thought, she'll have been flattened like a lizard. He put the light on the ground so she could keep her eye on it, and went for the truck jack and the one from the Chevette, also some lengths of four-by-four from the scrap pile. That was how he got her out, by jacking open and bracing the mouse-run until he could pass a rope in to her hands, poking it in to her on a length of bamboo from the garden. The supple cotton rope he had used to re-educate Cattywampus. He extracted her like a calf from a cow, through a passage about the diameter of an RFD mailbox.

As if spring-loaded, Alice shot free, scrambled up and ran, fetched up against the wall of the covered arena opposite, coughing and retching, dragging in searing icy air. In stocking feet, her boots still under the hay somewhere. "Thanks," she gasped out when she could, dragging a sleeve across her streaming nose. He hauled her up, held her steady. "No hay de qué. Go in the house. I feed these guys. Go right now, Aliz, sin discusión." He wanted to see if she could walk, and in the right direction. Satisfied, he put his tools away.

Her live weight on his arm. Lifting sacks of oats out of the pickup: completely different sensation. He stood in the feedroom door, breathing steam and thinking the unthinkable.

Nothing got done about the hay for another week. The last calves came steadily; the weather changed, warmed a little. "Okay, tomorrow I'm tackling that stack," she said, firm after a good dinner and with a full night's sleep in prospect. "I need my damn boots, and my cell phone." Highly surprised, then, by her visceral reluctance to go up among the tumbled mass of alfalfa bales. Domingo was already up in there, tossing them around with gay abandon, remaking the grass stack on the far side of the shed.

Brute up, Alice.

It wasn't so bad, after the first few minutes. Then not bad at all. It was *her hay*, doggone it. Wouldn't do to be afraid of it, certainly not to let on, if she was. With a shout, Domingo pitched up one boot, then the other.

"¡Diosito mio!" looking at the place where she had been trapped. "Come and see, Señora Lagartija."

Mrs. Lizard. "No, thanks. Been there, done that, using the T-shirt for a boot rag."

Two hours to restack the whole shed full, plus a little speed contest with the last dozen bales, and Alice flopped down panting in a cove of hay, out of the wind. He climbed up, sat down opposite, and took in a deep draft of that sweet midsummer smell on the cold dry air.

She had something on her mind. "Do me a favor, slick, don't mention to Janet about me getting stuck down there. I'm much obliged to you, but it's better she doesn't know."

"Sure, but why?" The gaps in communication between the sisters interested him.

"She'll get a torque in her shorts, I mean se molestará. About me working up here alone."

"Okay, but you very intelligent, you wait to fall under these hay until I come back from vacation."

"Yes, that was pretty clever all right," Alice snickered. "How is your girlfriend, by the way?"

"Don't got no girlfriend," instantly.

"Well, why not, for heck's sake? Don't you like girls? 'Cause they sure do like you." She felt herself to be on the prod about this, for no good reason.

"Uh-*uh*, Patrona."

"It's true. I see those women in town, the way they look and don't look."

"I don't think so."

"Concha Vélez follows you around like the Glen dog."

He had to laugh at this. "No soy pichonero, pues."

"What does that mean, pichonero?"

"Means some old guy like little girl. Concepción Vélez don't have eighteen years, I'm thinking."

"What old guy? You can't be more than twenty-five yourself."

"Uh-uh. Thirty-five. What that's word? Senior citizen."

This settled Alice's hash. Finally she said, "My stars. I suppose I have to start calling you señor."

"No, but I ask you one question, personal?"

Warily, "Okay."

"Patrona, how come you don't, don't me hablas de tú?"

"You mean, like, use the familiar forms? That's easy: I don't know the forms, plus I don't know when it's correct."

"Easy: from you to me is correct."

"And from you to me?"

Caught out, he checked her face; how much did she understand? She wasn't angry, it seemed; just interested. "Es que . . . you don't mind I speak Spanish?"

"Go slow."

"Okay, in my country, from me to you the familiar forms are not correct, would not be correct. Up here north of the Line, we of México sometimes use these forms to insult those gabachos who insult us. They don't know that these forms are improper from low to high, so for us it's like secret revenge. Understand, so far? But in addition, everything up here seems to us to be too informal, too familiar. Not respectful. It's very strange to us. Sometimes the boss tells the workers to call him by his name, like I do you. This never happens in México, never. There, the boss speaks most formally to the least of the workers. However, up here we get accustomed to it, we get in the habit of informality, not meaning any offense. Is this clear?"

"Admirably. How crystalline, your speech. So I must not be dessicated when you call me the devil of all devils?"

"Uh-oh! You understand that? I don't realize it."

"Yes. And several other things."

He studied her. "You not mad."

"No, buck. Porque somos compas, ¿no? Compañeros, vaqueros."

Domingo thought, that cannot be what she wants it to mean, that there is no social distance between us. Yet instinctively he accepted that she believed it; Americans were strange that way. Besides, considered from a different angle, it was quite true: they were fellows, after all, in an old and honorable craft. That much was indisputable. And compañeros too, together all the time, sharing all work in all weathers and conditions, to the extent of holding each other's horses while they went into the woods for a whiz.

"Oh, I forget," raising up to fish the damaged cell phone from his hip pocket. He reached it across to her.

"Ah, thanks. Well, that's a gone phone, I'd say. Could you teach me the familiar forms, do you think? And remind me when to use them?"

"Of course, si quisieras aprender. *Did you hear what I said? 'If you would wish to learn.' That's very polite, but also familiar."*

"Familiar and polite at the same time?"

"*Yes, of course. To show respect to friends, and to those we love. This doesn't happen, here?*"

"Among some people it does, some classes, people of certain ages. Too bad it isn't more common. It's the rule in Mexico, is it?"

"I hope so. Okay, I will tell you," inexplicably, even to himself, "long time in the past I like one woman. And she likes me, but then she don't. But she don't let me go. She don't like me, but she don't wants, she doesn't want to let me go. This is my situation."

And that, thought Alice, explains the money orders.

Maybe.

Chapter Ten

One Tuesday in February Domingo went to Walla Walla, leaving Alice to her computer. He parked at the John Deere place in Eastgate, and when he came back out to the pickup found Jessie Tillotson perched on the running board.

"Hi, remember me?" She looked like a kitten too old for drowning, left in a ditch, Domingo thought.

"Señorita," he replied, pulling open the door, "go in, please." Ill-dressed for the season; those sneakers—she might as well go barefoot. He started the truck, turned the heater on high, pulled out, and buzzed down Isaacs to Mr. Ed's where he picked up two coffees and a queso burger to go. He didn't have to ask her anything; it was all pretty obvious. He parked in the lot at Lions Park to let her swarm around her breakfast. She would have said she couldn't eat, she was so cold, but the smell of coffee and the heat fogging the windows brought her appetite on.

"I ain't got no money," wrung from her, the warm and greasy sack on the seat between them. Domingo shook his head.

It pained him to watch her eat, not because of her teeth but because the wolf in her belly warred with her wish not to make a pig of herself. Afterward, dabbing up crumbs with a finger, she asked, "Miz Andison here? This is her truck, right?"

"She's home. How come you came here? For work? You got a job in Walla?"

"I got nothing!" She'd just chained up the rottweilers and walked away from the old place, up onto the state road, hitchhiked fifty miles in the dull cold, a skinny girl in a worn-out Levi's jacket. No friends, no prospects; she just ran.

"You come for visit us?"

"Oh no. I just seen the truck, and I remembered . . ."

Domingo laced his fingers on the wheel; he didn't want to scare her off, her nonchalance pitifully transparent. "You come to Standfast? We got lotta place for you."

Jessie hesitated. What did she know about him, or them, anyway? Her way was too easily made straight. But she believed in destiny; a Pisces, for whom nothing was coincidental. "You think Miz Andison wouldn't mind?"

"She doesn't mind nothing," with mild confidence. "Plus, we got a lot of work right now. Maybe you want to help us?"

"Sure, anything!"

But when he urged her in at the kitchen door, she wasn't so sure. For one thing, the house seemed exotic to her, its random windows and spaces, strong colors. For another, having met Alice Andison but twice in her life, she retained an impression of a not especially welcoming type of person. She had no claim on her acquaintance at all. But Domingo, pressing her inexorably onward, called out, "Aliz, come see who is here."

Alice appeared in her slippers, narrow specs on her nose. "Why, Jessie Tillotson, my dear, hello! How in the world are you? How are things on the Pataha? Did you come to visit your horse?" reaching for the girl's bluish hand and holding on to it. Speechless, Jessie heard Domingo launch into explanation as they propelled her to the dinette; sat mute while he put coffee in front of her and Alice went to turn over Allan's things saved from the flood.

"Here," she said, shaking out a plaid jacket and holding it for Jessie to put her arms in, "you'll swim in this, but you're taller than either of us, so maybe it won't get in your way."

Alice divined that Domingo expected them to take the child in.

What are we, a charitable institution? she thought irritably, although this was exactly what she would have done herself in the same circumstances. Something about his presumption in bringing Jessie Tillotson home to her charmed while it annoyed. This is a working ranch, not an orphanage, dang it. It's becoming a habit, picking up waifs and strays. Bring us your tired, your poor, for Pete's sake; wait'll Janet hears.

Jessie realized with a surge of water to her mouth that she was about to be fed again.

After lunch, as the others made ready to go out, she offered for any work that was going. But Alice said that since she had spent yesterday on the road and last night wandering around Walla Walla in the freezing rain, the best thing she could do was to crawl under the covers and make up her sleep. And so she did, in one of the upstairs bedrooms, in conditions of warmth, cleanliness, and security that kept her awake and wondering for a long time.

"You know, she don't, doesn't have nothing," Domingo said as they went down to the pens.

"Never has had, is my guess. The money for those goddam solar panels should have gone for braces for her teeth. God, that kid could eat an apple through a picket fence."

"I'm thinking she will work, Aliz."

"I bet she will. I have been lucky that way before, picking up guys out of snowbanks, et cetera," feeling her saddle blanket for moisture. "Making yourself right at home here, aren't you?"

"Yes," frankly. For some reason, she beamed at him. "I do the right thing, pues?"

"You did just right, mijo. Let's hope her godawful old man doesn't come after her. At least," callously, "not till we're calved out."

Domingo smiled back. *"You talk tough, lady,"* he said, *"but you are soft. A merciful heart."*

"G'wan," Alice said. "You're the guy that brought her home."

After dinner Jessie asked if she could call her married sister in Puyallup. "Carrie," she said, and couldn't get another word out. Standing there with her mouth open in one long soundless sob. Domingo took the handset, said into it, "Wait a minute, she's comin'," handed her a dish towel, and when she finally drew a breath, gave back the phone. "Carrie," she cried at last, her gaunt young face glazed with tears, "Carrie, I got away!"

She stayed until the middle of April, and Alice was grateful. Though inexperienced with cattle, Jessie could ride anything; put on one of the veteran horses, she made a journeyman cowhand, even tried her hand with the rope. She and Lolo's Pride got reacquainted and she rode him among the cows, he flinching and shying but reassured by what Janet called her "adhesive" seat. Janet had renamed the horse Starry Vere. Jessie didn't get the Melville reference, but she felt it was a classy name, and of a piece with the strange wonderfulness of Standfast.

"I can't cook worth a shit," she told Alice, "but I'm a cleanin' booger," and so she proved to be. Shy of Domingo, she plucked up nerve enough to argue him down about the feebleness of thorough-bred intellects, and declared herself "happy as a pig in a puddle" to help fit and trim the Keiths' horses.

That was where they lost her. Rosemary Keith took a look at her, said, "How'd you like to go racing, sister?" and that was the deal done. "She has that exercise-rider look," Rosemary said. And she felt that Campbell ought not to be leaving his new family for months at a time. So when the racehorses went away, Jessie Tillotson went with them. Then Mary Friel came for Silka, this year taking Effervesce too to make his debut in horse-trials competition, and the place seemed to settle down comfortably around them, their own private park and playground.

Alice recorded on the computer: cows, multipara, 32; live calves, 29 (17 bulls, 12 heifers); barren, 3; stillborn, 0; mortality, 1. Cows, primi-para, 8; live calves, 7 (3 bulls, 4 heifers); barren, 0; stillborn, 1; mortality, 0. Two cases of postpartum paralysis, but with persistent physiotherapy both recovered. The makings of another pretty good year, she thought cautiously, knocking the tabletop.

In the first week of April, to her incedulous glee, came news that

Philip had actually turned the trick, pushed through the Jerry Graeme business, and the ranch was theirs, every tree and stone, free and clear. Alice and Janet agreed that they were having a hard time realizing it.

"Not counting the new ground that we got out of the Hashknife deal, of course," Alice explained to Nan when the family gathered to burn the canceled life-interest documents. "That's between us and the bank, and will be for another thirty years. By that time I'll be way too stove up to run the place, so you or Nick or whoever—what are you drinking? Come on, fill up for the toast," thinking, as she tipped another two fingers of Talisker into her own glass, that whoever took over the running of the place, it would not be Nan. Not if the mere suggestion brought on the evening dews and damps like that.

Gathered in the grove of locust trees before the house in the dusk of a bright cloud-chasing day, Philip doing the honors at the fire pit, they watched as the heavy legal stock of the contract took flame, old onion-skin copies peeling away and flying up in rags of soot. Well, thought Alice, if not Nan, then who?

The flames died. "Standfast!" and all raised their glasses and drank. Domingo thought it very fine, the whole ranch family gathered, Nan on her last day of spring break, Robey and Vera Jane Whyte, the collies with their strong sense of occasion. Himself, in a strangely emotional state. Everyone poured out the last drops of the brindis to quench the fire, and went inside. It was cold again, and Vera Jane needed to sit down.

Alice felt light, buoyant. Not just from the delightful augmentation of her annual income, nearly enough in some years to cover the mortgage payment on the Hashknife ground, pleasant though that was to contemplate. But besides that, she felt half crazy with relief that she never, ever again would have any contact with Jerry Graeme. An idea bloomed in the back of her mind: tomorrow, by God, she would move into that room, Allan and Jean's room, take it back. By God, she would.

"Why," Nick was asking, leaning on the counter with a stem-glass of wine in his hand, "did Gran and Grandad let him stay here, anyway?"

"I think that was part of the deal they made with his old man. Who must have realized Jerry would never have the grit to farm on his own. And Jerry didn't seem psychotic earlier on, did he, Roan? More nasty than insane. This can go on the table," Janet passed over a dish of red cabbage and chestnuts. "Remember when you scared him off with Doric, that time?"

Yes. Janet at fifteen, tears on her face and murder in her eye, rushing past her in the barn, pursued by Jerry, some nauseous fleer about menstruation, and "Ah'll nae hae ye fouterin aboot ma sester!" screeched Alice, rake at the ready. The right words coming into her mouth as naturally as spit.

"What's Doric?"

"A very old dialect of Scots English. Grandad used to use it some-times, remember? Deadly at close quarters."

"That and the wee yin's dung-fork did for Jerry Graeme. Your Auntie Roan's a bonnie fighter, laddie. Let's see, who is the senior gent? Ask Robey to come and carve these ducks. Jerry always had some *car* taking up space and tools—"

"Remember that MG? He finally got that up and running pretty—"

"Alice, wise up. Jay Frazier did it for him, while he stood around smoking. The deal was, Jerry was going to take Jay on an all-expense-paid vacation in return. Which turned out to be every whorehouse and card game between Walla Walla and Reno. Jay slept in that little car many a night. He never wanted to talk about it very much." Sud-denly remembering Nick, who asked with an innocent air, "Are there whorehouses in Walla Walla? I'll get that," nipping into the office to answer the phone out of the kitchen hubbub. Came back, frowning. Looked at Janet and shrugged.

Robey and Vera Jane's vineyard venture dominated the conversa-tion at dinner. The plan to plant vine-stocks on the low, hot benches along Iwalu Creek had run on the rocks, literally. Heavy machinery, gas-powered well-boring screws were found to be necessary to pen-etrate the stone and gravel drifts of the ancient river plain.

"It's setting us back a little bit, no use denying it," Robey admitted, "but Joe Scan says he expected it." That was Josquin Levesque, their daughter Vicky's husband, the only one of the four sons-in-law he liked.

"Josquin know what he's doing?" asked Alice, voicing everybody's thought.

"Yeah, he does. Vicky went over there to France, you remember, when they got married. She says the place where they're at, Joe Scan's folks and grandfolks, she says it's just like here. Hot summers, cold winters, dry and stony, facing southwest. Says, when the rocks roll downhill there, folks carry them back up, stack them around the plants. The *vine stalks*," relishing the word. "They keep the *vine stalks* warm."

Vera Jane's lack of appetite gave her scope to deliver a lesson on viticulture, which the company took in with a fairly open mind. A quarter century of below-par wheat prices had the whole valley thinking in terms of alternative crops. Soybeans had not thriven; chickpeas found few buyers. Oilseed, in addition to covering the hills with nauseous Day-Glo yellow blossom, quickly glutted the market. Wine grapes might be the saving thing.

"You don't want to have cows more, Don Robey?" Domingo inquired rather jealously.

Apologetic, "Oh, we'll fatten a few calves every year, o' course," which was a pretty bare bone to be throwing to a cowman like Domingo, Robey felt. But then Alice had the right kind of land for cattle.

"Aw, honey," crowed Vera Jane, "we're so old! We just can't do that work no more. And the kids don't like it. So we're going with the raspberries and strawberries. And if the grapes go, that'll be even better. 'Cause that's a family thing, you know, wine grapes."

Alice didn't want to talk about Jerry Graeme at all, in any context. She *was* a bonnie fighter, even at twelve, but he defeated her. He never touched her. That, she could have complained of. But he talked, when he could get her alone. Told her what he wanted to do. Coaxed. Displayed his equipment. First his tongue: "Look, now," and out it would curl, long, narrow, and whiteish. "Won't that feel good?" Later, when he was sure she wasn't going to tell anybody, showed her the other thing. By that time she knew to carry something sharp all the time, hoof rasp, bot knife, the scissors for cutting baling twine. He never touched her. He just dirtied her.

Domingo didn't think he had understood Vera Jane. "What said the old señora for family grapes?" he asked Alice as they were watching Three Cheers's colt-foal be born, a bit early and just as well, big as a bacon hog. That remark had struck Alice too.

"Let's go make old mare a nice mash, what say? I think Vera Jane was talking about who's going to take over their place when she and Robey retire." Or die, God forbid. "Vines kind of bind families to their land, seems like; at least, there are vineyards in Europe that have belonged to the same family for two, three hundred years."

"So who is going to take this place after you?" realizing a quarter second too late how brilliantly tactless it was to ask.

"You go right for the throat, don't you?" She was sensitive on the point. Which was odd too, Alice reflected, because she couldn't remember having considered the question before, and now twice in two weeks.

Allan must have thought about it a lot. That was what all those little jokes were about, when she or Janet would get serious about some boy or other: bring us a lad for the farm. Bring me a man for Standfast.

Well, Dad, we've let you down there. Neither Philip Weston nor Vincent Greer was such a man, though at least Philip settled in the county, intended to from the start. Poor Vincent, though, married with two disastrous words to a woman he did not quite love, a place he didn't much like, and a job he despised, a view of himself he couldn't approve.

Gie me a lass wi' a lump o' land, Allan used to sing, the Scots lowlander's ideal bride, but a prize no longer valued in the Palouse. The Whytes had three other daughters, not one of whom, not one of whose husbands cared at all for their place except as a vacation resort, or so it looked to Alice. If Vicky had not met Josquin studying agronomy at WSU, who knew what the future of that farm would have been, or Robey and VJ's outlook? Sell to the developers, move to Arch Cape on the coast, stare at the ocean. That seemed to be the program, and a thoroughly unattractive one it was to Alice, though she wouldn't have said so to those of her neighbors who were actually facing it.

Anyway, plenty of folks did not have even that option. "In this business," Alex McCrimmon lamented to her during one dismal season when even his agrochemicals sideline barely eked out their grocery bills, "you just work as long as you can, and hope you don't last too long after that." Now Alex, Bob's brother, was a whiner and a rank depressive, as everyone knew; still, that crack had the ring of truth. Would she herself live another thirty years, last out her new loan? Something could always happen; something *had* in fact happened last February that might very well have put paid to all her striving. In which case, what in the world would have become of Standfast? Lucky for her, for them all, that Domingo had come back from town on the cusp of disaster.

"Domingo," leaning over the wall of the foaling box, watching the foal get up to suck, its little navel-string dangling, "did I ever thank you que me diste socorro that time when I fell under the hay? Thanks. I really appreciate it." He looked at her, startled. Had he heard right? Socorro?

It started out Edenic, that day, a warm green-gold dawn in which not a leaf stirred. As they were choring, a big hawk flew very low over the yard, looking for new hunting. She whistled as she came, and her tiercel, wheeling far up the thermal over the swayback hill, answered. That hissing scream, so high and wild! Alice shivered, spoken to.

It was Friday. They went down to Walla Walla and ran around with Alice's list. Domingo nipped into the post office while she cruised the Safeway. They got halfway home before realizing what time it was, and that they should have stopped for lunch in town.

"Let's try the new place in Iwalu," suggested Alice, always desirous of supporting new businesses, especially eateries. Janet had mentioned it, the Yellowhawk Café. Totally remodeled, she reported; new menu, trout and steelhead the specialties of the house, oh boy. She and Philip were planning to go every Sunday, keep the place afloat single-handed if necessary. In a land dominated by golden arches, a genuine local restaurant got her excited.

So they turned in there, Alice and Domingo, by way of giving themselves a treat and having their town clothes, their town faces on. The landscaping was certainly new and imaginative, though the low breeze-block building defied disguise. A dry creek lined with smooth stones, a "landscaping feature," ran across the front, young sumac bushes and birch saplings strategically disposed. Inside, flocked red wallpaper and tasseled lanterns had given way to pelts, antlers, and Bierstadt's Yosemite.

Nobody in the dining room, Alice was sorry to see. A girl in a fringed skirt and vest waited tables; a couple of guys at the bar in the back, one of them big and wearing a WSU Cougars jacket, the other weedy, in a T-shirt that announced, Shit Happens. The place smelled good, though. They took a booth by the front windows, looking past the neon Bud sign at the fiery-green little leaves and yellow catkins on the birch twigs, tossing in a soft wind.

"We go back early from here, we can fix the gate for the Triangle," Domingo began.

"You have a list too? Great snakes. This is getting scary. We better combine . . ."

She hadn't taken in any of the warning signs; he neither. Maybe there hadn't been any. She did see, from the corner of her eye, the waitress start toward them with menus and glasses of water, and then turn back. The silence at the back of the room didn't register as a threat; she didn't even see the two men at the bar move until they were there, beside them. Domingo's face suddenly set.

"Alístate," he said, and the big man snatched him out of his seat like a bale off the back of a pickup.

Alice squalled, inarticulate.

"Come on, slut, you're outta here," snarled the weedy guy. He dragged at her elbow, nearly fell when she cannoned into him getting out of the booth under her own power, and grabbed the strap of her satchel as she charged up the aisle.

To judge by the jerking of the Cougar fan's thick shoulders, Domingo was not going quietly. Alice shot a look toward the waitress: no help there, she and the cook stood wedged in the kitchen door, neutral.

"¡'Lístate!"

"Shut the fuck up!"

She plunged after them, half-dragging the skinny sidekick who kept trying to take charge of her. In the vestibule Domingo got a hand on the doorframe and fought matters to a standstill for a moment in the small space, the gumball machines sustaining a lot of damage, and Alice caught up with them just as they shot outside, caught a glimpse of Domingo's face, large-eyed but calm, turned back toward her.

Alístate. Get smart? No: ready. Get ready. The thin man tried ineptly to drag her arm up behind her back, and now they were outside in the sweet spring air, and there came a sound, a crunch like a heel on gravel. The big guy fell on his behind in the dry watercourse, boot soles in the air, one hand to his face. Between his fingers ran runnels of blood, fire-engine red.

"Hey," said the sidekick faintly, starting toward his hero. But Alice was lista. She caught him by the arm with both hands, yanked him toward her, and with a technique she didn't know she knew drove the side of her foot into the side of his knee. She would remember the snap, the sensation, for months. He toppled with a grunt, and that was the end of his ambition.

Straightening up, Domingo turned toward her that face of wild calm. She went to him crabwise. Looking neither right nor left, he escorted her to the truck and held the door for her. Got in without haste and started the engine; drove leisurely out of the parking lot and onto the county road, careful to check for traffic in both directions.

Alice looked back at the sorry tableau in front of the Yellowhawk Inn, augmented now by the noncommittal faces of the waitress and the chef peering out through the Budweiser sign.

"You okay?" in an ordinary voice.

"Pull over, let me out. I'm sick."

"No, you not."

"I'm gonna throw up."

"No, you *not*." *Pull yourself together, woman, for the love of God.* Left to himself, he would have driven on home five miles under the speed limit, schooling himself to feel nothing. But she—he would have to look after her. He turned off into the park above Iwalu village, a tiny place overhung with willows and cottonwoods, one picnic table and a fire pit, the creek there narrow and swift. Alice was out of the cab before he set the brake. He hustled after her.

"Don't cry, Aliz. You cry, they get the victory."

"I'm not," she said thickly. Almost, he wished she would cry; he didn't like the looks of her. Though they were the same height, her gaze, wide and limpid, seemed to touch just below his eyes. He saw that her pupils were wide open, shocky, sweat on her upper lip. Her freckles in high relief, as marred a thing as ever he saw. "I'm not gonna cry. I want to kill somebody."

But he felt horribly sorry for her.

His right hand ached mightily, exacerbating the mess such an encounter always made of his guts. How ironic, he thought, if I shall be the one to vomit.

"Better get your hand in the water," Alice muttered. He walked along the edge of the creek, found a spot where he could squat and lay his palm on a stone and let the cold water take the swelling down. She stood by the truck, fists in pockets, grim, and did not cry. Not a word out of her. He looked back once or twice, but she looked away.

"Let's see," when he came back. She took the hand, cold and dripping, puffed and bloody on the knuckles, into hers, and held it and looked at it a long time. With his free hand, he pressed her head against his shoulder. She gave a big sigh between a gasp and a sob, just one.

After a while she drove them home, very calm. He hoped she could see to drive with her eyes like that. In the carport she stopped still, arms clamped against her diaphragm.

"Báñate," he said, "hot as possible."

That thin-irised gaze, off target. "I better not call the cops."

"No." So now you know, güera, he thought, cruel, ashamed of himself.

They told nobody, not even each other. Except that Alice said over the wine one night, "There's not enough hot water in the world . . ." and he answered, "Sí-món."

They were farming hard now, a long mild spring with early heat bulking up the grasses, putting weight on the calves. They pulled a lot of thistle off the new acreage, burned the whole plot over to kill the weed seed, chisel-plowed and chain-harrowed it. When finally it was sown with a good mix of horse-hay grasses, smoothed and tamped like a new lawn, Alice felt that she had done her level best for the piece and, obscurely, that the ground itself must be pleased to be back in production after so many years of fallow idleness.

She did not see much of Domingo for a couple of weeks, being on the tractor day and night, as it seemed to her. He, meanwhile, rode herd, chored, and built some loafing sheds in the horse pens. She left the young stock to him too: Ricky, Raevonne's four-year-old son, to start over poles and little jumps; yearling Chispa to teach trailering, ponying, ground manners, and other things colts need to know if they want to remain entire; the new dark-gray foal to groom and lead and fool with under Three Cheers' benign gaze.

April drew on in steamy heat. Lourdes Vélez called up to say they were on schedule for the Standfast gather-up, and Alice began to wonder, in view of that conversation up in the haystacks, how Domingo and Concepción would behave to each other this year. In the event, though, all other concerns sank into insignificance under everybody's realization that Vera Jane Whyte was seriously ill.

"When did she get like this?" whispered Lourdes to Alice, out of hearing of the trio of solicitous cowboys getting VJ installed on the porch. Robey having all but carried her up the four steps. "She was okay last year, hoppy as a kid goat." A slight, no, a substantial exaggeration, thought Alice, feeling that she had no right to her sense of shock but a very good right to the rockslide of guilt that came with it. She should have seen, should have known. She found Janet in the same state later in the morning up at the top of the orchard, her knuckles against her mouth.

"Alice, how could we not—have you been by there?"

"No. Been on the goddam tractor." No excuse. "Have you?"

"Not in a couple of weeks. Dear God. Does Robey know?"

"I don't think so. Not in a deep way. Do you suppose *she* does? Come here." They put their arms around each other.

"This is the worst thing I can imagine," groaned Janet. "I just want to sit by her, sit there and never move from her."

"We have to stand it, big yin."

"I know. I just don't know *how*."

The gather-up went well enough, no accidents or injuries, and Vera Jane clearly enjoyed it. She did everything that was put into her lap to do; she just didn't get up, or eat. She did not seem to be in pain, or even very tired, still announced the juiciest bits of gossip with "Oh, kid, kid!" She just looked reduced, bleached. As if a scrim hung between her and those around her. As if she were slowly vanishing. Domingo asked nothing, having learned from Alice in one eloquent look all that she felt and feared about her old friend. But he thought that if he were a pious man, he would be lighting candles.

To Alice, the whole deal was wrong. Here it was, spring, heady scents of sage and alder like incense on every breeze, calves gamboling all over the place, the slope in front of the house swaying with jonquils. Herself turning sideways before the bathroom mirror, surprised and pleased by the reappearance of her nice snub breasts and a genuine convex belly. Robey's vines creeping out along their wires. The notion of expanding the Standfast herd to fifty, not yet a sure thing, but in keeping with the season of bloom and increase. And in defiance of all that, there sat Vera Jane not so much dying as diminishing, going smaller and smaller, as if they were all drifting away and leaving her behind on the shore of a wide, rolling river.

For some time Domingo had been wondering whether he should breed his mare again, or wait to see whether Chispa developed any cow sense. If Chispa showed no interest in, as Domingo put it, "organize these cow," then if he did breed the dam again, there was no point in taking her back to the same sire. It was Concha Vélez, in fact, who brought it up to him, in a significantly sisterly tone. Making it clear that she was grown up now, that her little bronca of last year had been just ebullience of girlish spirits, a mere pase de capa in the bull ring of her youth. She knew, she said, of a fit match, a Umatilla County stallion much praised locally, of fine family, sound and sane—might she send him the web address?

Alice advised him to consult his own preference: would he rather work with the mare, or try to duplicate her? If he decided to breed her again, though she might not pass on her superb cow-cutting gift, the worst he could expect would be another nice working animal. What did he have to lose? It was up to him.

With Alice's help, he set about investigating the Umatilla County stud electronically. The computer! He had no idea about it, sat with his ankles wound together and his palms shoulder high, scared to touch anything.

"¡Qué idioma nuevo!"

"Yeah, but the vocabulary is very small. For a bilingual like you, no problem."

"Don't abandon me, Aliz," grabbing comically for her hand. "Maybe this machine attacks me."

"I'm right here, que no tengas miedo. *Did you hear that? I'm becoming splendid!*"

She did a thing, undid it, did it again, undid it, and let him do it. Showed him the *Oh Shit* arrow on the toolbar, the novice's panic button. He started to relax a little. They worked on it after dinner two or three times a week. After a while he could turn it on by himself, find bookmarked sites while she finished up in the kitchen. Didn't need his hand held, though sometimes he pretended to, just to kid her.

It turned out that the horse Concha had in mind had won all his honors and decorations in reining classes, not in cow-cutting competition. Also, the beast had a short breeding season because he spent his days on the horse-show trail rather than on a ranch somewhere, which Domingo and Alice both thought was the only proper life for a horse. Of course, that did not mean that he *couldn't* do ranch work. But Domingo had a settled contempt for all denizens of horse shows, rodeos, and charrerías. Play-horses and shadow-riders, fine for level, well-dragged, well-lit arenas, but put them out on a steep hillside in a cold wind spitting rain, with big, rude, barging steers—ay Chihuahua.

In the end he doubted that he could do better than Chispa's sire again. So after they cut out the barren cows for the sale, and trekked the rest of the bunch up to the Circ out of the unseasonable heat—the second week in May, that was—Domingo borrowed the pickup and the two-horse trailer, and hauled his Chamaca southeast through Oregon, across the Snake into Idaho, and on past Boise to the spread near Mountain Home, where he left her to the amorous attentions of Gold Bar Rocket.

When he got home to Standfast the next night, Ricky too was gone, sold away into California to Alice's intense gratification. It turned out that one of the judges imported for the annual Walla Walla dressage competition—this part of the story blowing by Domingo, zip zip—eyes out as always for young equine talent, was being squired around by a Waitsburg rider who knew Alice and knew of Ricky.

"Man, he practically sold himself," Alice reported. "You know how nice he goes, and how sweet he is to handle."

"It's true, he loves everybody. Also, he's a good color, big . . ." forming dapple-shapes with both hands.

"Yeah he is. And likes to jump."

"¡Órale!"

"Wait, lemme tell you! When I went to put him back in the pen after we were done playing with him, I forgot the damn three-gang was still in the chute," meaning the three units of the spike-tooth harrow, detached from the tractor. "So, does he fall all amongst it and break all his legs? Heck no. He runs down and jumps it. The prospective buyer standing right there. And it's all of twelve feet wide. And then! He turns back and jumps it uphill, just for fun. I could have asked a million dollars for him."

"Chis! You get one million?!"

"No," laughing, "and ain't it a shame! But if I did, slick, you'd get half. 'Cause you made a real nice ride out of that young crackerjack." And now, she thought dolorously in the seldom-visited part of her mind where she worried about her animals after they were sold, if they just don't try to tune little old Ricky up to Grand Prix in two years, I'll be happy.

It was about that time, between the bulls going out to the cows, and the first cutting of hay on the low ground—about the same week that he finally learned to put the *s* to the third person singular—that Domingo fell in love with her, or realized, admitted to himself that he had.

At first he told himself he didn't know what was going on when the palm of his hand wondered what it would feel like to press the springy curls on the crown of her head, or cup the boss of her shoulder, smooth and sunburned. He was watching her read the paper one day after dinner, late in the spring, watching without thinking her beautiful round spangled arms sweep the pages over, when she looked up and touched him with a long look and then a sweet, grave wink.

He fled the house. Ox! You're crazy, doomed! Are you a man? Drive this under.

Foul memory sloshed over him, the whole wretched business with Graciela: led, used, conniving at his own degradation. He *refused* to let go like that again. Besides, Alice was white, and older than he, and not even pretty. But the whole time it was as if he were describing someone else.

He leaned his arms on a bar of the round-pen gate, bounced his forehead a couple of times on the next bar up. Was it fair, was it even *possible* that lightning strike him *twice*?

Furthermore, Alice . . . did she feel anything for him? That was a question. What, otherwise, might be the burden of that wink?

Only two things he knew, but he knew them for sure. He was no ox. And she was no mule.

Alice stood between Skookum and Falcon toward the end of the afternoon of May the twenty-fourth, working a dandy brush under Falcon's belly, scuffing the brush off on the rubber currycomb every third or fourth stroke in the time-honored way. When her brush arm tired, she changed hands like a juggler. Sometimes she dropped the brushes, though. As she did now, just as Domingo came around the back end of Falcon carrying a bridle over his shoulder, saying, "These bosal starts breaking right here; you want me—"

Alice paused, one hand on a piebald, one on a liver-brown shoulder, and he stopped—everything: talking, moving, breathing. The pause drew out, became something sweet, a singing note on phantom fiddle. To Alice it felt like liquid electricity played over her skin; if she looked down, she would see it dripping in luminous gouts off her elbows. So, she thought, you saw that wink. And she watched his face change, felt hers change, the same recognition: "You want me."

"Yes," she said, her voice breaking on a bubble of delight, "I want you."

Domingo held out his hand and she took it without a second's hesitation. He drew her arm slowly behind his back and held her there. Brought her close to him in the afternoon's thick heat, between the two big warm beasts, his shirt damp with sweat under her hands. Alice lowered her eyelids, expecting to be kissed. Instead, her face was softly pressed, and lashes stroked the orbit of her eye. And then she was kissed, meltingly and deliberately. He put his arms all the way around her and kissed her cheek and her neck and then just held her.

"Oh boy," she said.

Stepping into this embrace, Domingo felt his life swerve out of control, fishtail on a sharp bend. Yet he kept on. He believed that Alice was true in herself, and trusted her. That was the wellspring of love, for him. So he kept straight on, pressing kisses on her yielding mouth, yielding himself more and more luxuriously to the—

"Ay, Skookum, pig-infant! Your family disgraced forever! Wait, love, I will bring the fork and barrow."

Chuckling, Alice led the two geldings to their pen.

She dropped down on the bench in front of the barn. The metal wall breathed heat, and she felt grubby and sweaty; still, she had hopes that Domingo would come sit by her, and say "amor" again. He came, with a towel wrung out in the tack-room sink for their refreshment.

"That rooter in latrines," he muttered, sitting down, picking up her hand, and resting it on his knee. Slowly he stroked the damp cloth down the inside of her arm, down her palm and the back of her hand. That arm, and then the other one. With a finger, pushed open the collar of her polo so he could press the towel coolly to her throat, the sides of her neck, her burning cheeks. The most delicious thing she had ever had done to her with her clothes on. A ridiculous grin occupied her face; she couldn't help it. "Ranch romance," she murmured, "nothing like it."

It took a few minutes for him to arrange his thoughts because every time he looked at her, he kissed her. Meanwhile she held his hand and sat as close as she could, in spite of the heat. She thought him splendid, apt to every need, the inner man beautifully tender and receptive. My dear luck, she thought, waiting without impatience.

"Do you mind this kissing? One word, and it stops; we go back to the way we were."

She laughed aloud: *"Man, would you crunch my heart?"*

Domingo regarded her fondly. *"Your Spanish is improving."*

"My excellent instructor," calm eyes smiling. *"Sweetheart, I think for us there is no reverse."*

Truly, he thought, that was no swerve but a pivot, a hinge. A portal swinging wide. He put up a hand to her face and passed the callused ball of his thumb over her narrow lips. Many kisses, and Alice's toes turned up inside her sneakers.

"Listen, heart," against her ear, *"I loved you in January, or in December already. For a long time I've wanted to tell you."*

"Are you serious, man? Why didn't you say something?"

He laughed through his nose: "Because is crazy, of course! Is crazy enamorarse del mero mero," a rude term for the boss: "devil of devils."

"Well," she said, a little later, "me too, you know."

"What? Yes?! You also don't say nothing!" If true, what a pity she had not spoken; he might have dragged himself off to Wapato in a sturdier frame of mind, armored in such news.

"No. I thought maybe you wouldn't feel the same way about me. I didn't want to you to feel, I don't know, pressure about it. What if you felt like you had to go away? Then I would lose my friend, my compañero too." Coming in a rush, this required concentration to unravel. Alice left room for it. Then, firmly, "Domingo, answer me one question."

"Pregúntame."

"Are you married?"

"No-o!" a shocked, falling-rising note. "I told to Teacher; you don't remember?"

"Yes; but not in Mexico either?"

"Amor, pero nunca. No right now, no before, never. Why you asking?"

"Why do you think? Because I refuse to share. *Because for me, there is none but you.*"

And this gave him immense pleasure. But he had to wonder, what did she mean by it, exactly? Not proposing that they run away together, was she? She wouldn't throw off her family for him, that was sure, nor give up Standfast. What, then? It sounded to him like a promise, a pledge. That she pledged herself to him, woman to man, just that. Which was much; more, almost, than his parched heart could soak up. But she wasn't swept off her feet, like in a telenovela, and she didn't seem to mean for him to be.

It felt pure and simple to him, both necessary and sufficient, like water in a dry country. Ranch romance: that was what she had in mind. Not coy tremblings, nor renegade sex that made you forget to feed the horses, but love for all seasons, getting on with whatever needed doing. She put her hand in his hand, she kissed him back, and the gates parted on a prospect of wide fields and skies, work and rest, heart-friendship, rootedness and deep content. Could that happen? Could love be that way, frank and fair as blond wheat in sunshine?

Chapter Eleven

DOMINGO DROVE TO PULLMAN IN THE RANCH PICKUP TO BRING NAN home from college because Nan's old Honda had gone west, sideswiped by a drunk in the stadium parking lot, totaled. He towed the two-horse, and they crossed the Snake to Moscow and went on south through Idaho, picked up his red horse and brought her home. He was gone for three days.

Alice took the separation hard. She wanted to be with him all the time now, *all* the time. If she saw him far off, up on the swayback ridge or somewhere, the hairs on her arms rose; There you are, she thought. She manipulated her daily list of tasks so that they would be together. "Work shared is work halved," not fooling herself.

Work lay heavy on her while he was away on this errand. She baled hay, made fence, rode herd. Aha, reminding herself, prostrate at dinner time, yes, this is what single-hand is like. It wasn't work that leveled her, though, not only work. Released, her feeling for Domingo swept her like a range fire. The coolly rational, squared-up part of her felt like flotsam rolled over in a big surf, big glass-green combers golden inside, blood-warm, plunging in foam, resistless. Come back, she called him in dreams, come home.

He did come home, dropped off the mare and the trailer while Alice was out with the Clydesdales loading bales, and took Nan on to the Westons' in Waitsburg. Got back to the place about dinnertime and went looking for her. A note on the refrigerator: "D: estoy con los

Whytes, volveré las 6:30, besos, A." He was chopping chiles when she burst in, barely got the knife out of the way. A rib-cracking abrazo, Alice couldn't breathe. If I die here, she thought, good.

"¡Me extrañaste!"

"Missed you montones. How's la yegua roja? How's Nan?"

"She's okay, also she. Or 'her' is correct? She, Nannie doesn't talk too much, you know? Maybe she's too tired."

"Been having exams, I s'pose. What's cooking? Us! Oh boy, muchas smooches."

Domingo's cup ran over. All the white-line miles had given rein to doubts, which now thinned away to zero. He was home, enfolded, cradling the big guitar on the sofa while dinner was cooking, distracted with happiness.

"What's that song?" Alice yelled over the sizzle of onions frying. "'If I die, don't . . .' what?"

"'Don't bury my clothes.'"

"Don't bury your clothes? Why not?"

He put the instrument away and went into the kitchen. "Because I might come back."

"Oh, good."

"How come is good, amor? You don't escared of a, a spirit?" standing close behind her.

"To me, you are welcome, love, in any form." She felt him think this out, and then slowly cleave to her from the floor up. His arms around her middle, his long nose against her ear.

But she had bad news about Vera Jane Whyte. VJ was at home, but visibly slipping away. The four Mayan brothers and their sister Rigoberta, Robey's berry-picking crew, had come in to take a ceremonious leave of her while Alice was there. They knew, if Robey did not. He nursed her like he would a runty calf, patient and capable, but Alice had a feeling he expected Vera Jane to get up one of these days, grab her basket, and go pick some peas for dinner.

Out in the hammock after cleanup, Alice told Domingo, "You know, she's almost our mother. She took us on when Jean died, even though she still had her own girls at home. Taught Janet to sew, helped me with my geometry—yeah, she did; a good head for math. Chaperoned us. The first time I went on a date, she drove us to the movies, sat through the film in the parking lot, and drove us home. She really pulled me through when Lyon died, she and my dad."

"Who is Lyon?"

"My baby that died, was born dead. I told you about that, no?"

Yes. She'd told him about it, and the story went right to his heart. He never referred to the child. Felt shy even of pointing out that his own mother had lost her firstborn at birth, but gone on to raise and love a second child, himself. So it could be done. She sometimes spoke of the little boy, rather flatly. He had a feeling she had schooled, was still schooling herself not to make a fuss. A well of tears, there. As for himself, he could think of no worse thing than to lose . . . and it could so easily happen, he thought. A child was so little, so tender that if nobody paid attention to her, took care of her . . .

"Vincent—my husband—he wanted to think it happened because I was working stock when I was pregnant. But Vera Jane absolutely told him off. Said it was from teaching school, all the kids were sick, passing some germ around. Saved my sanity. Insofar as I'm sane."

Sane? None saner, querida, he thought, watching the amethyst dusk charge her dear stained face. Looking her griefs in the eye: mother, father, marriage and child, and now Vera Jane, her foster mother. Facing her losses, owning them, not despairing. Not like himself, wizened and cold at heart, his life raveled down to a thin thread of purpose. Always braced against the next stroke of luck.

He pressed a heel into the grass, setting them swinging. Alice turned to him, her skin where he touched her singing with capsaicin from the chile-oil on his hands. "Put your arms around me, buck. I'm kinda low."

She smelled good. She always did, to him: soap in the morning, sweat, animals, and hay in the afternoon, cooking at evening. He didn't know what to say to her for solace. The hammock ropes creaked. A burst of squeals and thuds sounded from the horse pens. Glen, with difficulty dissuaded from joining them in the hammock, flopped down panting underneath.

After a while Alice said, "Ma made me a horseman, if I can claim to be one. And Dad and Robey made me a stockman. But if I grow up to be a good woman, it'll be because of Vera Jane. I keep trying to tell her so, but it won't come out."

"No," said Domingo, understanding that. Simple heart that she was, Vera Jane would surely be more mystified than gratified by such a communication. "If she don't know this, probably you cannot explain. Y además, ella no quiere que llores."

"'. . . doesn't want me to cry,' you're right, I reckon. 'Cause it surely would be too wet to plow, a conversation like that." He was a man acquainted with sorrow, she remembered, and found the knowledge comforting. "I suppose we oughtta go look at the horses, mijo," really preferring not to move. In case the tears on her lashes might fall.

"Pretty soon," he said, swinging them again. "Maybe you can tell me little bit about those guys. They marry a long time, I think."

So she related the twice-told tale. One fall, Robey's Uncle Naylor broke his kneecap and couldn't ride, so Robey's dad sent over to the next ranch east for the Stonecypher kids to help them bring their cows down off the summer range in Asotin County. They needed to trail their beef herd sixty miles or so down to the Whytes' homeplace where the winter hay was. By "the kids" he meant Sid and Van, who were sixteen and fifteen, stout young guys, good hands. And so, when on the first day of the drive Mother Nature launched a full-on blizzard, and Naylor, who was supposed to meet them with hot food and hay and bedrolls in the pickup, got stuck and lost and stuck again and didn't reach them until after midnight, the Whytes felt pretty apologetic but not worried. But then the second day turned out worse than the first, and as dark came on they were still a long way out, and had to spend another night in the open, the horses left saddled, suffering, and the hands piled on top of each other in the back of the truck, unbedded and unfed. So the third day when Robey, who was riding the drag, began to recognize the landmarks of home, he caught up with little

Van to tell him it wasn't much farther, just to lighten his misery. But the kid pulled the scarf from his face, and was not Van but Vera Jane. And she said, "If I ever get warm again, I'm gonna kiss the daylights outta you, Robey Whyte!"

Domingo laughed silently, like he did. "What sayed don Robey?"

"Robey claims he fainted dead away, and when he woke up, they were married."

"What old they are then?"

"He was sixteen; she was fourteen, I believe."

"¡Órale! I like this history a *lot*! You believe is true?"

"Oh yeah. It must be," said Alice, cheered. "Gotta be."

Nick and Earache took over the irrigating entirely, leaving to Alice and Domingo the hay sales and the herds. The boys bucked bales too, loaded the flatbed, built stacks in the Dutch barns two storeys high. Hurling the bales around one-handed like Frisbees. Alice and Domingo, watching, in silent unison massaging their backs.

"Those guys work like the devil," Alice said as the two made off with their pay, "and never seem to wear out or eat aspirin. How do you s'pose they do it?"

"Juventud," said Domingo, examining his own envelope. "You give me more money, Aliz. For what? For kissing?" not entirely in jest.

"Usual six-month raise for—what?! You think I need to pay for kisses, you rascal?" entirely in jest. "You think I can't throw the heel-catch on any man in this county who takes my fancy?"

"Of course." He knew she was fooling, not insulted; she seldom took offense, never over trifles.

"I just didn't see one I wanted, till you came."

"And don't need to throw on me, 'cause I've been running toward you for three months at least."

"Lovely man," to his confusion. "But I wish we could be putting something into Social Security for you. I feel like I'm cheating you twice a month."

"But I couldn't draw it out, even if you did. Dollars to the government,

wasted. Anyway, I don't care about money. Come over here, beloved. Kisses for free," against the fragrant alfalfa stack, kisses and little bites, a rising fire. Breathing hard, Alice leaned back, liking the looks of him when he was roused: how broad the nose, how full and smooth the lips, the eyelids! She thought, There is one good way for this to end. But not in the hay. I am a grown-up.

"Juan Domingo," her palms flat against his chest, "will you stay with me tonight?"

Of course, he did want money to some extent. He had a use for it, for certain quantities of it. *Poverty is not shameful*, people said in México, *but it's very inconvenient*. More than anything, though, he wanted Alice, oh yes. Like he wanted to drink water, breathe air. He wanted to own her, assume her like a garment, every soft/hard inch and part of her. Also he desired, rather shamefully, to know if she were freckled all over. He wanted her from crown to heel. Were it not for the probability that taking her to bed would wreck everything.

"Are you coming to the church?" Domingo shook his head. They clopped uphill, morning shadows long before them, dust rising golden. "Then would you mind choring at Robey's? He'll be down at Janet's until six at least, even if we don't get him to stay for dinner."

"Con gusto. ¿Dónde va a ser el entierro?"

"Ah. It's not a burial, it's a memorial, for all her friends and neighbors to be together and remember her. She's already cremated, like she wanted."

"Holy God. I live among savages. What a barbarous practice."

"What? Are you really shocked? But why? Don't you cremate in Mexico?"

"In Mexico," stiffly, *"we bury properly. Dust to dust."* Otherwise, how could the spirits of the dead return on their festal day? Not that he believed in spirits, not in their actuality or locality anyway. Though his mother touched him, sometimes; he felt her fingertip press where his shoulder met his neck on the left side. And when the old snake-

mask covered his face, he could be sure that Fidel was somewhere in the neighborhood. *"That way, at least the living know where to go, to take . . . in any case, we do not bring jars of dirty ashes into the house."* He was in a filthy mood, for other reasons, and spoke fast, no quarter given.

"Well, you used to, your ancestors did, I believe. Preserve hearts, anyway," equably, stopping and turning Falcon back. "Mine did too, wrapped them in sheets of lead. Were you expecting paradise, honey-love, our first time?"

Rimrocked, Domingo felt a black flush crawl up his face. That a woman should speak to a man of, of . . . At the very least, he had depended on a decent silence on the topic.

"I'm out of practice, you know. Pero, la práctica hace el maestro, no?" leaning over, her hand in its bull-hide glove on his thigh.

He almost stammered with surprise and relief, and rising lust. "Sí, así dicen," automatically. So they say. Alice just waited then, leaning on his knee as the horses stood quietly, head to tail. Radiating a sort of friendly lewdness. If this is getting fucked up, he thought, it's fucked up in an entirely new and different way.

"Hey, buck, kissing on horseback—"

"Makes work for the dentista. I know. Sin embargo, I risk it."

"Everything is so sad now," Alice said later, farther up the trail, "you are about the only thing that makes me want to get up in the morning. Or go to bed at night. I hope I am not embarrassing you."

"Yes, you are, but I don't care. Tell me one time more about doña Vera: she wants to cremation?"

"Yup, that was her plan, her request. And so Robey's already put her ashes out on their top field, the one that's in barley right now." Domingo turned his face away, revolted.

They rode on, up off the trail onto the edge of the hay field. Chispa, being led saddled but not loaded, considered giving old Cattywampus a nip at the root of his tail, then thought better of it. Single-file along the edge of the field—the led horse requested not to make a pest of himself by dancing his way into the ditch on the low side—and then turning north on the crest of the ridge. No crops up here, only bunch-grass and sage, too high almost for the sage, crowns of basalt breaking through the hill's thin skin of soil. They stopped to blow at the top.

"This we can cut in three weeks if this hot, heat continues," Domingo suggested, crooking his right knee over the horn and nodding down at the field they had just crossed, "and maybe one little rain. What you watchin'?"

"There he is again. Unless I'm crazy." She pulled down her hat brim, squinted toward the county road. "Dark blue, with the gray stripe. How many can there be?"

"I don't see it. Yes, maybe. Ah! You know, that car's at the park el Día de la Independencia. I remember the driver with gafas de sol, in the night. Also, one time at the Seven-Eleven, I forget to say."

"What, on the Fourth? Really? 'Cause I think that's the guy I nearly ran into coming out of Janet's driveway that time. Now, what's up with that? I'd like to know who he is. Next time we see him, let's wave at him."

Let's hope we don't see him, Domingo thought. "We going to continue, look at the other side?"

"Might's well."

Alice felt lamed with grief. New sorrow brought the old ones storming back; she knew this of old. Poor Janet; Vera Jane will never get us singing "Go Tell Aunt Rhody" in two-and-a-half part harmony again. Let us not weep aloud in church, that's all, and shame the family. She stood in her stirrups for a minute, sore in the saddle after last night, and thought for relief about Domingo. Her palms remembered the steely flex of his back; the crest of her upper lip remembered his tongue. She cheered up slightly. Let this sad day pass. Let the night come.

Riding back from Robey's after chores, Domingo mused with pleasurable horror on the Americans' way with their dead. Sickening, really, like being thrown out with the trash. The Mexican way so much better. Socorro lay in the old burial ground by the church of Santo Tomás

Apostól del Oriente, which probably annoyed her, renegade as she was. His father in the city cemetery in Nogales. He knew where they were with exactitude. To her credit, both of Alice's parents were at Mountain View Cemetery in Walla Walla. But she had said that she sometimes felt they were too far away from her. She wished, she explained, that they were here on their own land.

She herself would like to be cremated and her remains distributed in the little orchard uphill from the house. "Scattered," that was the word she used. He shuddered, having looked it up: "dispersar," with its connotations of dismemberment, drift. Utter non-being. And she had asked him, half-laughing but even so, ¡caray!, about his own plans. Plans! How shape one's face to such a question? What a people, these of the North!

For to plan for death was surely to diminish it. Which was not the same thing as embracing it, not at all. The reverse, in fact. To embrace the inevitable, to acknowledge its power, was both a salute and a defiance. One must die, yet would one live as if immortal, freely as a god, not cravenly planning for the end. In fact, to plan for one's end reduced the very idea of it to ordinariness, a mere change of address, tidying up. He shivered the notion away; it dared fate, such a lack of respect, diminution of awe. Made the whole of life vile, mean, spiritless.

Of course, regarding himself he had no present anxiety. If death had not found him in the snow, or under a ton of bistecas on the hoof, the old man wasn't looking for him at present. It must be that I have unfinished business, he thought. Some of it, at least, with Alice.

Coming in after looking at the horses that evening, Benny Goodman on the oldies station, "Dance with me," she said. She loved to dance, and she loved him, and wanted them together. Domingo stood up resignedly and she took him by the hand, but he wouldn't move, except to shift his weight from foot to foot. Not even lifting them.

"You don't like to, 'mano? That's sad!"

"Sure, I do," he said, shifting hands. "Look, I gonna show you. Put this here, this here," her arms around his neck. His around her, palms low on her back. Barely moving, "One O'Clock Jump" raving around them. "See? Nice."

Alice giggled into his collar.

After a while, after "Bugle Call Rag" and "Stompin' at the Savoy," "Is this really dancing?"

"Sure. You don't like it?"

She couldn't stop this snirtling laughter, silly as a drunk. "We might as well be in bed."

"Correct. That also," Domingo said, leading the way.

"There he is again," said Alice, four days after Vera Jane's memorial service, looking at the shotgun-side mirror, "right behind us." The navy-blue Trans Am with its wide silver stripe, provocatively close, tailgating the pickup.

"You know who is that guy?" Domingo said, suddenly sure. "Es el policía, él que me paró el año pasado." He checked the speedometer. "I think maybe he wants me go too fast."

"Well, don't. Are you sure it's the same guy, same cop who stopped you? Because if so, this is harassment. That is the car I've seen on our stretch of the road, who doesn't live out there. Around Janet's place too, come to think of it. Now, why in the world—?"

"You think I better stop?"

"Heck no. He's off duty, won't be wanting to spoil his day off." Unless he was plainclothes, a narco-cop. Or Immigration Service. But no, she thought, he's a county mountie. At least, so he said on the phone that night. Anyway, he would have arrested Domingo that very time, if . . . "Slow down a wee bit. Let's see what he does."

He stayed there, a shade too close for good manners. Domingo slowed scrupulously to thirty, then to twenty through Dixie. Perhaps he would pass them where the highway widened out? No. Maintained the same distance all the way to Waitsburg.

They had a twenty-pound sack of Walla Walla Sweets in the bed of the truck, bought for the Westons, but "Don't go to Janet's. I'll take her the onions tomorrow if she doesn't come up. Let's see how far this geek will go. Are you scared, brother?"

"No way," coldly choused up. "Tú, Aliz?"

"Uh-*uh*."

He put his hat on the seat, raked his hair back. "He's a little more close."

"Don't speed up, though. I have a plan, if he sticks with us through Iwalu. Kind of hope he does."

He did.

"He follows us on the ranch? He have authority?"

"I'm betting he won't chase us if we go up our lane. But don't turn in there, go straight on past. You know the back road, by Robey's?"

"Of course, six miles more, on the curve," an unpaved road deep in dust at this time of year, off which their own back road angled away to the north. The turning wasn't marked; everyone who needed to knew where it was. But a grid of pipes set into the ground at their back gate kept Standfast stock from wandering out onto the Robey Grade.

"You know how our road is deep and high-centered inside the cattle guard?" Domingo's dogteeth glinted. "Can you make that turn at, say, forty? I want to jump the grid."

"Okay," pushing the end of his seat belt toward her. "Bockle me op."

He had to drop down to thirty-five for the turn onto Robey's road, but didn't signal the turn, and the Trans Am was so close behind it slewed and nearly stalled. As soon as the pickup's tires hit the unpaved surface, Domingo gave it gas. A rooster tail of tan dust spurted up after them, through which the low hood of the other vehicle showed from time to time like a shark driving in for a kill. A wild ride, Alice holding on two-handed as the truck rocked and bounced on its stiff suspension. Lower down, the driver of the coupe would be sitting easier but flying blind. She threw a glance back: there he came, lights on, windshield wipers squealing, and then the brown pall hid him again.

"¿Ahora?" softly, easing up to forty-two.

"Go for it."

He swung the wheel left, stood on the gas. The pickup roared like a crop duster, airborne over the cattle guard, bucked down and threw up a solid wall of dirt. Alice felt with hopeful joy the rib of rock in the middle of the trail scraping along the truck's underside. Then a heavy crash behind them, catastrophically prolonged as the Trans Am struck high-centered on the rock and the driver revved the ruts on either side deep, deep out of all contact with his wheels.

The pickup beetled on up the steepening track in low gear, its occupants giggling maniacally. Even at the house, two miles from the back gate, they could hear the car's big engine whine, hysteric, and see the hanging dust cloud suddenly darkly augmented. The longer the intervals between these bursts of mechanical rage, the greater their comic effect.

Eventually it was clear that the coupe wasn't going to get off the rocks by itself. "I'm sure he has a cell phone. Oh my stars!" pulling up the tail of her shirt to wipe her eyes, "probably he'll call a tow truck or some friend to drag him out," Alice surmised. But no, and after a while Domingo came up the yard leading the two Clydes in their pulling harness, his long ojos de chino narrowed to slits by a wicked grin.

"Now what are you up to?"

"We have to help this guy, no? Like, neighbor? Otherwise, it's cruel. Pero no laughin', serious."

"I s'pose we do. But why not take the truck back down there, pull him out with the winch?"

"Winch is broke," blandly.

"It is? Since when?"

"Since right now. You want me help you up?" She did, of course. They were six feet tall, those horses; even Domingo needed to step in a loop of trace chain to mount.

"No laughin'," he murmured as they came in sight of the gate where, like a cartoon of depression, the dust of the Trans Am's mad struggle to get free hung above it in the still, hot evening air.

"No, no. Just neighborly help. What if he takes out a gun and shoots us?"

"Don't worry." Now the driver could be seen, squatting chin on fists, mirror shades pushed up into his high-fashion haircut. "Está pendejo, no loco."

"Need a little help?" called Alice brightly as they came up. The driver's clothes resembled but were not in fact a uniform. He sprang up, lithe with fury, pulled down his sunglasses, and turned away without a word.

Domingo dismounted and helped Alice down; they crouched and peered under the stranded car.

"Yup, she's stuck," Alice declared, chipper as a squirrel. The young man turned even farther away, his fists rammed into his pockets. The muscle of his jaw bulged; dark bristle pricking through pale skin, she noted . . . Basque, black Irish? Domingo had forgotten to look at his name tag, that time last year.

She had to walk the Clydesdales singly through the narrow side gate, avoiding the cattle guard; meanwhile, Domingo lay down in the dirt, crawled under the back end of the Trans Am, and hooked tow chains around the rear axle. Alice brought her team into position on the far side of the grid, tails to the stranded rig, Mose tramping and bowing his neck.

"Easy, easy, easy," she sang. Maggie's collar hung a little forward of her shoulders; the old girl knew her business.

Domingo fiddled with the chains. Because of the pipe grid, the horses were too far from the car for singletrees and doubletree; they would have to make a straightaway pull, tows to traces, with the chance, yes indeed, he thought happily, a very good chance of pulling the chassis out of alignment. He looked over; the driver of the car still studied a far-off creek bottom, ignoring the rescue effort. Climbing out of the cattle guard on the Clydes's side of it, Domingo gave Alice a grin of the kind that might be taken for a squint.

Alice spoke Maggie's name under her breath, and the big mare came up snug into her collar.

"Mose." He was already there. She stood between them, facing them, stepped back, a short shank in either hand.

"Hup!" sharply. "Hup, now, hum up!" The great creatures stepped forward together, lowered their haunches and laid to, ears flat and toe caulks scraping.

"Maggie, Maggie," Alice encouraged her. But the Trans Am merely shimmied a little on its transmission, and Domingo thought with a stab of delight that the axle might pull out, that the vehicle might actually *break in two.* Unfortunately, Alice stopped the horses, a hand on each brisket. She patted them, reorganized them, and called them again. The second time, massive quarters bunching and driving, they managed to wrench the car free and drag it across the grid amid a horrid bawl and squall of rending metal. The driver, still facing the other way, hit himself in the head with both fists.

It was the work of a few minutes, then, to unhitch and loop up the chains and walk the team one at a time back through the side-gate. Domingo legged Alice up, got up himself. Neither looked at the driver. Though they could hear him for quite some time creeping back down Robey's road, whine and clang, parts falling off, scrapyard concerto.

"Which part did you like best?" Alice asked at dinner.

"The part of, el nopal, he keeps driving, such expert, when he's estuck! No, I change my mind. I like better those big horse pulling for you. You appear very small, Aliz."

"Compared to those Clydes, everybody does. Why do you call him a cactus?"

"Because he's as tall as one of those saguaros and just about as intelligent."

"I hear that! Hey, can we tell Philip and Janet about this? I don't feel bad about this, like I did—"

"Sí, por cierto. I enjoy this. Lástima que no tomemos video."

Janet took Robey Whyte a casserole and a supply of ginger shortbread, and stopped in at Standfast. "Describe the guy to me," she commanded, humping her twenty pounds of sweet onions into the Toyota.

"Let's see, six foot something, all buffed out, dark hair. One of those haircuts with short back and sides. No tan; he must work out inside. Mirror gafas, like the staters wear. Early twenties, I'd say."

"And you said Domingo recognized him?"

"Yeah, he"—realizing she was about to break a confidence—"had a run-in with a county cop last year, thinks it's the same guy." Janet didn't seem to be getting much of a kick out of their prank. "Why are you making that grim face, cookie?" Her anxiety about Domingo's immigration status suddenly came back, double.

"I think I know who it is, and I think he's trouble. Disaffected student, has it in for me. Been stalking the kids, possibly. Jeez. I've never had to deal with such a thing before, in all the years I've been teaching." She crossed her ankles and folded her arms, hands in her armpits, leaned against her little red rig. "He could stroll into that office with his wee sidearm, any day of the week, and blow away the whole Basic Rhetoric department. I think I'll stop teaching Americans."

"Domingo believes: stupid, not crazy. Nopal, he says."

"One can hope, I suppose. What kind of problem did Domingo have with him?"

"Better ask him."

"He tell you about it at the time?"

"Under duress."

"Him all over." Janet frowned at the toes of her clogs. "I might have to pin him down. We might have to, if Philip thinks we ought to do anything about him, about young Probationary Deputy Galante."

"Pin, I suspect, will be the operative word in Domingo's case."

"Mm." In Janet's experience, some people blathered out stories of harassment, mistreatment by the police, with unseemly readiness. Others would recount incidents of raw racism only if they knew you pretty well, by way of advancing your knowledge about the general condition of those with little clout in your own dear free and democratic nation. Some covered such wounds with a rough scab of bitterness, and some flatly refused them any headspace at all. Domingo Roque, she would have bet, was of this latter type. She caught Alice's peculiar smile, presumably about the deputy's discomfiture. Though maybe not. "Roan," a rush of collies signaling Domingo's approach, "is anything—?"

Now, what, he wondered, goes on with las hermanas? A sister fight, God forbid? Janet gave him a most peculiar look as she drove off down the lane.

Light dawned.

"Uh-oh. You tell her about, about you and me?"

"No, my honey. But she's noticing something. She is not the least bit dumb, my big sis. Come here, old Sweep; doesn't anybody do your ears for you anymore?"

Hunkering down to restrain Glen, "You feelin' happy about it, corazón?"

"About you and me? Alegre, contenta, feliz." That straight gray gaze. He embraced her awkwardly, the dogs between. Alice felt weighty between the legs, engorged, like an egg-heavy hen.

"Dinnertime can be late?"

"Yes," she said, "please."

"Bye bye, love," Domingo muttered to the guitar, getting in the way of the table being set. "Bye bye, sweet caress. What that means, sweet caress?" She showed him. "Oh. Really? *Show me one more time. I am slow to learn.*"

Humid, elastic, and smooth—twenty years old, in other words: that was how she felt. And how in the world was she expected to deal with such feelings and sensations now? For God's sake. For her that time was past, she had thought. Yet here she was, here *he* was. Alice scanned her reflection in the window above the sink.

She had no quarrel with her own face and shape. No beauty, of course, but she looked exactly as she felt herself to be. Wouldn't have changed much. The outside pretty much declared the inside; best thing for a person whose word must be her bond. But he . . . what did Domingo see? Because he could not get enough of her. And this, for Alice, was a situation totally without precedent. She did not know how to behave. She felt like a snake in a shiny new skin, knotting and coiling lazily in the spring grasses, admiring herself from different angles. She felt like a freak, off her trolley, a balloon escaped from the fair. Waggling its silly string up into the clouds.

She bothered him; they bothered each other at work. Coming into the machine shed one day to find him kneeling over a mess of greasy engine parts, his boot toes touching each other under his narrow behind, it was all she could do not to hurl herself on him right there in the gravel under the workbenches. Working alone, she caught herself grinning, sometimes broke out in sniggers, putting the hunting cats off their game. And when the sun went down, broken sleep, dreams of stampedes, cataracts.

Though she could swear, could *swear* that somewhere along the line he had been teased and humiliated, shamed in the body. And if this were so, Alice would have liked to locate the woman responsible and shake her back teeth right straight on out of her head.

"They're hooked up, Ma. Aunt Alice and Domingo." Janet dropped her dressage saddle but caught it before it hit the concrete.

"What does that mean?" settling her Passier over Starry Vere's withers, wedging the waffle-pad well up into the gullet. "'Hooked up'?"

"Tss," said Nan, holding the bridle ready. The afternoon heat went right to the bone, even up here at the lesson venue, a beautiful foothill farm with walnut and chestnut groves and braiding streams; Starry's bay coat plucked up in salty points on his shoulders and thighs.

"Did Alice tell you so?"

"No. But it's pretty obvious. Not that they trade spit in public or anything. I mean, or *anything*: they don't even touch each other, that I've ever seen. But . . . you don't think so?"

From the indoor arena came the Prussian voice of the clinician: "Outside rein, ja? Outside rein, inside leg. More. More. More, now ask for canter. Galop! Now, vat vas so goddam hard about zat?"

"She hasn't said anything to me."

"Would she, though?"

"Uh-huh. Eventually. Other side, sugar, that's his head-shy side." Starry was getting calmer about the bridle. Nobody bothered his ears.

"So, what do you think about it?"

It surprised her, Nan's asking. As for the news itself—

"Well, I'll tell you the parts I'm sure about. I think she knows her own mind really well. Doesn't let her feelings run off with her," making a mental exception with regard to Vincent Greer. "And I believe Domingo is a good man. I mean, good at heart. Obviously intelligent, well brought up." Nan leaned on the off-side stirrup, and Janet gathered her reins and mounted. The bay horse stood rock-still, drugged with heat. "There just seems to be a bit of a mystery about him, that's the fly in the Fura-Zone. Why? Are people talking about them?"

"Not that I've heard. They aren't, you know, *flagrant* or anything. Besides, there's always a lot more raw stuff than that to talk about around here."

"There is? You mean, besides the plumber's wife Super Glue-ing his hands to his penis?"

"Ma, that's *old*. I mean like, Tiffany Sheehy walking out of the high school and directly into bed with some guy, apparently. Some guy she didn't know, who kept waiting for her outside school, every day, until she just finally caved in and got in the car. And he drove her straight home to his place, one of those farms on the west side that used to be asparagus and now is vines? And jumped her straight into bed."

"Good night, nurse. Whatever are you telling me? How old is this girl?"

"Seventeen, I guess. And the next day, they drove over to her house, and she went in and got her stuff and put it in the car, and now she's living with him."

"And her parents have no objection? You would think Child Protective Services would take a hand."

"You would think so. But nobody seems to care much about Tiffany. Except this guy. And then I just found out that Malina's dad shot her court horse—"

"He *shot* her *court horse*?!"

"Yeah, because she refuses to give up Jeddy Lathrop. And do you know why her family hates Jeddy? Because they're Adventist and he's, like, Catholic or something. I mean, come on, that's *medieval*."

"Nannie, the world you kids live in! I'm so glad you don't take such things for granted. At least I think you don't; do you, lamb? Not notice how bizarre and awful they are, I mean."

"No, yeah. I'm hoping things are just passing through a crappy node around here. That's a chicken, Starry; no threat. That other stuff makes Aunt Roan and Domingo look so clean and natural. I think you can go in now, Ma; Anna's just cooling out."

"When's your go, tell me again?"

"Hour and a half. Plenty of time. Is Herr Juergen going to get all over me about old cowpony Skookum?"

"He has the greatest respect in the world for a working horse," turning in to the arena as the other horse came out, a stout gray whose rider clapped her rhythmically on both sides of her neck. "He only yells if the rider doesn't work. Hi, maestro."

Domingo woke up from siesta lying prone, palms under his shoulders, looking at he didn't know what. Ah. The view resolved itself into Alice's fleecy nape, the sunburnt and peeling rim of her left ear.

"You toast you ears again. Remember the sombrero."

"Five more minutes," on a yawn. He got up swiftly; she heard him dressing, sat up herself, drawing the sheet modestly over her front. "What?"

"You don't—?" touched his nose, and went out. Then she smelled it, strong on the hot breeze, like buttered toast, burnt toast. "Oh, God, no." Dragged on sticky clothes.

Domingo stood on the porch scenting like a bird dog. "In the hay?"

"No, sombody's wheat, I think. Can you see any smoke?" Burning hay grasses didn't smell like wheat. Wheat was oily, made a blaze hot enough to melt the tires off a combine and charbroil beef on the hoof.

"Sí, mire," pointing eastward toward the gap where the road parted the hills, where a roll of dark smoke smooth as a dolphin's back marred the Wedgwood blue of the sky. McCrimmons', thought Alice. And as long as it's already over on their side, please, please let this chancy breeze stay westerly, keep the fire away from my grazing.

The phone rang: Bob McCrimmon, his voice high with strain: "Hey, Alice?"

"Bob, you got a little fire over there."

"Yeah, we do. Thing is, we got about fourteen head of whiteface cows on your side of it. Least I think they are," exactly fourteen, and exactly where he said they were, trust Bob for that.

"Want us to drive 'em out for you?"

"If you would, we'd be grateful."

"Call it done. You take care."

Domingo came inside. "Mister Mac?"

"Yeah. Some of their cows are on our side of the fire; let's go see if we can get them out. You hitch up the two-horse? I'll be down in a minute." She hunted a couple of old sweatshirts out of the outdoor-clothes locker.

"You want Tommy?" as Chamaca, already saddled, hopped nimbly into the trailer.

"I'll fetch him; you go get your jacket."

"My—?"

"Your jacket, go get your chamarra, hurry up!" He went off, baffled, calling the dogs, and came back with his Levi's jacket as she jammed home the door latch of the trailer.

"Go east, like you were going to Dayton."

"We going to the fire? We need other thing, sand, water, shovel."

"I'm hoping not to get caught in it. Let's just go see what we can see."

Turning right out of their lane, "Where this fire, he says, fock! *Did he say where the fire was in relation to us?*"

"Right at their south end, it sounds like, right where they expected to start cutting tomorrow. In other words, our northeast line. Please please please let the wind hold steady away from us. One good thing, all their trucks are over there already. But so are the combines, of course. Not good. Pray for rain."

"A waste of breath," peering under the visor at the flawless blue.

Twenty minutes later, where the road swung around a curve northeastward toward Dayton, the slope on the left side suddenly went from blond wheat, ready for harvest, to smoking char. Domingo tapped the brake and whistled.

Around another curve, and dark gray smoke could be seen welling up the sky beyond the hills and billowing away northward like the rollers of the inland sea that once covered the Palouse. The breadoven smell became a stink. Collies in the pickup bed whined through the hatch, and the truck lurched slightly as both horses stamped a warning.

"Here, turn in here." A little meadow at the mouth of a deep draw separated McCrimmon land from Standfast. Allan and Jean had put in pens and a loading chute here long ago when they first leased the piece, the country between it and the homeplace too broken and dry to drive stock over.

The sides of the draw itself were steep, on the Andison side nearly sheer, with a trail of five or six switchbacks up to the top of the bluff that horses liked to take at a dead run. On the McCrimmon side, it was an easier grade but a higher hill. Good grazing on both sides, or had been until today, the range divided by fences on top, then by the draw itself, and by a little creek that ran down it and collected in a pond at the bottom, at the far end of the meadow. The pond could be seen from the road, its runoff forming another smaller creek that watered the cowpens. Today deep green midsummer brush hid the trail on the Standfast side of the coulee. But the long northern slope of McCrimmon land lay black and webbed with smoke.

Nary a cow to be seen, anywhere.

"Gimme your jacket," Alice said. She took it and her sweatshirts to the pens and sozzled them in the water. Domingo came up with the horses.

"Uh-huh," he said. "Listen that?" Under the shush of the changeable wind hummed a steady bass note almost below hearing. A drone in the bones, coming up through the boot soles, it felt like. They shrugged on their wet gear, mounted, and rode toward the mouth of the gulch, just as a great suave oily bank of smoke curved up over the McCrimmon side. Jesus! Alice thought. They'll be barbecued, if they're there.

"You take our side. If you find them, try to drive them down here to the corrals if you think it's safe. Or if not, see if you can work them down the other side to the Sheep Camp, it's a long way, but if the wind stays—"

"No way," as the horses swirled apart.

"What?"

"The fire is over there," he said, coming alongside. "You better go this way, better for me—"

"What?"

"Aliz," as to a child, "you go up this way," pointing at the Andison side, "and take the dogs," taking hold of her rein to start her in the right direction.

Alice lost her head entirely. "LISTEN, you!" very loud, "hands OFF! You go THAT way! DO'S YER TOLD!"

Domingo's face went perfectly blank, the way it had that day at the Yellowhawk Inn. He let go her rein, flinging up his hand so that both horses shied. Whirled and dashed up the bank to the switchback trail, Glen at his horse's heels.

Alice turned toward the northern slope, feeling queer in the stomach. Taking hold of her horse like that! Hadn't happened since she was ten or so. Do's yer told! He hadn't taken it well, any more than she ever had.

She had to urge Tom Fool; nor did Sweep much like the look of things. However, they built up a head of steam, and surged up over the top ready for what fire or cows soever. Nothing there, though. The hilltop was black and hot underfoot, the air full of drifting smuts and long reeks of smoke streaming northward. Fence wire down, posts burned away. Transparent flames licked along the edge of the coulee to her south, eating their way down toward the creek against the breeze.

She looked southward across the draw for Domingo, or any live-stock. Saw no sign, nothing moving. Far to the east, on the flank of the next big swell of ground, toy machines and tiny people crept along the edge of a wheat field, ministering to a fire that boomed like a big surf.

Alice patrolled around, looking into all the hollows and gullies where cows might hide out. Wringing wet inside her steaming clothes, her gray gelding snorting and twitching. They found no cattle, neither quick nor crisp. At last, as they worked their way down the far side of the hill, Sweep located two Charolais heifers lodged in a pothole, a small steep-sided pool, an inch of water over a fathom of mud. Sens-ing rescue, they blared in unison and churned their legs desperately to show how stuck they were.

"Aren't you clever lasses!" she congratulated them, for they were the only uncharred objects for miles around. One of them was in just knee deep; she looped its neck, dallied the line, and Tom Fool dragged it free. The other was another matter: sunk in sucking mud to the hips behind and over its right elbow in front, wall-eyed, straining its head from side to side. Getting in deeper by the minute.

"Boys, this is gonna take some engineering."

She lay down in the puddle beside the frantic creature to try to poke a loop down around its invisible forefoot. The heifer thrashed unhelpfully. The freed cow came tromping back to watch, bumping Tom Fool off his mark. The stuck one roared its cudbreath in Alice's face, and Sweep ran across her back, trying to keep order. "What am I doing in the cow bidness, anyway? Sweep, you fool." These two were all she could salvage, and they didn't even seem to be part of Bob Mc-Crimmon's lost bunch. She hoped Domingo was faring better.

The breeze strengthened and swung around to blow straight east-ward up the coulee. Little crackling scarlet tongues ran merrily back up the north side, eating up the sage and star thistle and ryegrass and cheatgrass. The closer the burn got to the apex of the draw, the more Alice worried that it would jump the creek to the Andison side. There was a good deal of dry forage on the ground on her side. And down that overgrown zigzag trail on that nearly sheer slope, Domingo would need to drive any stock he found up above. Or harry them several miles in the other direction, over broken ground and downwind of the fire.

Alice penned her two Charolais. They didn't want to be driven, balked and groaned, rolling their eyes. Scared of the dull hum of the fire and the pricking wind. Got them corralled at last. Sweep went off to cool his belly and his scorched pads in the creek, and Alice dismounted and pulled off her sweatshirts, caked in mud and speckled with tiny burn holes. Tight-strung, this air, and she was too.

She wanted to see Domingo come down to the pond right now. Would he forgive her? He must, of course he would. Love does not crumble under such piddling assaults. But would he *understand* her? She prowled up and down, coughing in the smoke as the wind backed again. "Come on, buck." Getting worried now.

Were those the little square shapes of cows, high up at the top of the bluff, instantly swallowed up in high brush? Just for a second she thought she spotted Domingo's straw hat in a gap of leaves. At the same time, smoke thick as nightmare mounted up over the *southern* side of the draw. The change of wind had blown the fire across the creek at its apex, onto the Standfast range. Alice's skin felt tight enough to split. Sweep scuttled a few yards toward the pond, crouched, and cried.

A ringing pause. A soft bat of wind on her left cheek, ripple of movement down through the brush on the sheer southern slope. A sullen boom as the fire leapt the coulee. The whole southern bluff exploded in crimson flame. Tom Fool shrieked, wrenched at the reins, dragging her backward. She flung herself into the saddle, drove him at the fire with rope and spur. No good. He wouldn't brave that hell, and she couldn't force him. Couldn't force herself. Had she really seen Domingo at the top of the trail? Whatever she had seen was in the fire now, burning. She would have to go in and look for him afterward, look for whatever was left. They took shelter behind the trailer, the horse coughing hollowly. "No, no, no," she moaned into her hands.

Half an hour, an hour crept past. Alice sat on the fender of the trailer, holding her gray's reins and wiping tears and snot and sweat from her face with the tail of her shirt. Gradually the heat diminished. At last she could move clear of the rig, holding a wadded-up sweatshirt to her nose. On the meadow the smoke was thick but exhausted looking, half of it steam from the creek, pallid and swiftly rising. Nothing to be seen of the draw. Even the near shoulders of the hills whited out.

But there! Nosing blearily out of the steam came a Hereford heifer, a white fume rising off its dark-red back. Followed by six more, followed by Glen, rushing back and forth like a terrier at a tennis match. Sweep raced in joyously, jumped over the young dog two or three times, and got in the way of the next bunch, seven more heifers all lowing and steaming. Domingo, appearing last out of the moil of white vapor, had to swing his rope to keep them heading penward. Stunned with relief, Alice nearly forgot to open the gate.

"You okay, boy?" He looked okay, though grim. Singed; soaking wet.

"Yes," stonily. She had to control a puppyish impulse to lick his face.

"I saw you at the top of the trail just before the fire jumped over there. What happened?"

"The cows knew what was coming, so they left the trail and ran straight down the hill into the pond. When the fire came, we were all under water. Cows smarter than cowboy." He got down and studied Chamaca's legs.

Alice backed off, chidden, feeling that she deserved it. She ran her horse up the north slope again, to get a look across at the fire on her own property. It seemed to be going nowhere, the wind veering against it once more. Farther up there, the ground turned stony, not much for flames to feed on. Anyway, nothing she could do about it except get her stock out of the way, keep an eye on it.

Reached by cell phone, Terri McCrimmon said that she and her sister-in-law would take the gooseneck trailer on down, load up their heifers plus two. "Appreciate it, Alice. Prob'ly we'll wait to repair the fences till after we're all cut, okay? If there's anything left to cut," the thud and rumble of the wheat fire audible in the background. And they didn't need help, thanks, the fire teams from Dayton and Waitsburg were out there.

Home again, flintily correct in all communications, Domingo unhitched the trailer and applied ointment to the dogs' sore feet, which they immediately licked off with apparent relish. Alice rode down for the mail, took a shower, and went looking for him. Attracted by the faint creak of hammock ropes, she strolled into the locust shade and sat down cross-legged on the grass.

For a long time no one said anything. Cut to the quick, Domingo silently derided himself for allowing this to occur, for going soft in the brain, playing the fool for her, her bed-toy, nothing more. Here is an end to that, buey, he thought, furious and wretched. To Alice, being at odds with him felt like a case of the flu, the seat of her emotions not her heart but her stomach. Maybe later, she thought, that will be funny.

She liked, if they had to fight, their relative positions, she on the ground and he with his back against the high end of the hammock, slowly swinging. It reminded her of being in the round pen with a green horse, one that would soon tire of rushing around the perimeter in the grip of pure instinct, stop, recollect its individuality, and turn toward her. Engage her.

The creaking stopped. *"Are you finished with me today? Because if so, I will go into town."*

She caught the formal "usted," a sharp stroke. "Please don't leave, while we are mad at each other." She could have said yes, dismissed him; she could have said no, accent on his dependent position. This was unexpected. "We," "mad at each other"? What can you have to be angry about? he nearly said aloud, but stopped himself. It was enough, perhaps, for her to acknowledge that *he* had grounds. He didn't expect an apology. In any case, nothing she said could heal him of the stupidity of having, for a while, allowed himself to love her.

"My mother told me the only reason to yell at somebody is if they're far away. And she was right. I'm awful sorry I yelled at you, and I never will again. I hope you will forgive me."

"Of course, don't mention it," caught back by, as much as her words, her sheer calm. No drama, no tears. It couldn't be deeply felt, could it, so deliberate? Yet he believed her sincere, possibly because he deeply, deeply wanted to. *"Don't sit in the grass; please share this hammock,"* his manners a pace ahead of his feelings.

She picked herself up and sat in the hammock, but at the other end, saying nothing. Steadily, she watched him. She had that on her mind that required his most open and complaint attention were it not to go painfully, destructively awry. Were they not to lose each other. She would not stand to be bossed around on her own place; that was the gist of it.

Alice timed it well. Exactly as he thought to ask, but before he could ask, what reason have you to be mad at me? she said, *"A man cannot work with a mule as he works with a horse."*

"Pero, ¿qué? What this means?" surprised into snorting laughter.

"Because the mule does not submit to the man. The mule believes herself to be the man's equal. Sometimes, his superior."

He didn't know what she was talking about, she must have got the Spanish wrong. Or rather, he almost did understand. But anyway, to the devil with it. If she wanted to talk in riddles, that was her privilege, she was the boss. Maybe she thought he had forgotten that; well, perhaps he had for a moment. But it was present to him now, branded on his heart.

"Sometimes, the mule kicks the stuffing out of the man. To remind him." She stopped. She didn't know how much explanation he would stand still for. This would have to be sufficient.

Domingo said nothing. He looked away down the shallow slope toward the triangle pasture where irrigation water arced and fell in glittering fans, a rainbow at every sprinkler head. The ferny boughs of the locusts swept leafily back and forth in the hot wind; a trio of crows rowed past overhead, croaking companionably. After a while, he turned back. And Alice was still there, holding him in the steady, warm circle of her regard. He reached for her.

"Amor, amor," she said. She squeezed him, carefully. "I almost got you killed up there today."

"Better me than you." But for the first time, with a little cold shock, it occurred to him that he might have been at fault. For surely, had she fallen in with his suggestion, well, followed his orders, she would have been the one caught in the fire, not he. Was she hand enough to have ridden out that wild stampede down to the pond, was her gelding horse enough to have carried her? Maybe. But did that excuse . . . ?

"I don't see it that way. Does this hurt? Ow, I'm sorry. What are we going to do about this, our little problem?"

"Don't worry. From now, I will obey your every command."

"What shit. Be serious. Kiss me, though."

"¡Cuidado, mujer! This hamaca falls us to the ground. My opinion: next time, we can throw one money. You know? Cara o cruz." She guessed he meant, flip a coin. Gently he tugged the lobe of her ear, *"That no harm come to you, that's all I want."*

"I know. Best of men. But, listen, corazón," touching the bump where his collarbone had healed, deciding she need not mention that he would have sent her into the fire, "I'm no housewoman. If that is the kind you want—"

"No, but," part of him remained bewildered by his change of feeling even as the rest of him roused up, "what do *you* want?"

Alice's bleached lashes veiled her eyes; under his hand the skin of her upper arm turned grainy and smoothed out again. "Tú," she said. Instantly he leaned back so she could get up. She went into the house panting already, to the bedroom, shucking off her clothes. Lay down under the sheet, closed her eyes, and flexed her knees, thinking how it would be: the thump of one boot on the floor, then the other; chime of his belt buckle. His weight on her, massy and hot. And that was exactly how it happened.

Except that this time, she came so strangely, soft but immense, like a vast slow caving in and sliding down of a creek bank into a flood, trees and all. On and on and on. Afterward she couldn't speak, just lay where love flung her down, till feeding time.

Well, she thought, warm syrup in her veins. Land sakes, Araminty. Don't that take the rag off the bush.

After the fire, a cell of threatening weather, vast blue-white thunderheads piling up and tumbling down, sheet lightning on the southern horizon. The whole uphill third of the county held its breath. Alice went up to McCrimmons' with Robey to drive bankout wagons for three days, help them get their wheat combined and stored before rain spoiled it. So it was more than a week before anybody on either side of the burned-out fences could think seriously about remaking them. When Terri called up about it, she said, "It'll just be me and Deenie, Alice, is that okay?" Perfectly okay with Alice; her gripe was with Bob only. She knew that, when they put their stakes in up there, if they weren't certain where the property line was, she and Terri would just split the difference.

They met up at the top on Monday right after chores, Domingo and Alice and Terri and her sister-in-law Jeraldine, with two pickup loads of posts and coils of wire, digging tools, fence jacks, and coolers. Worked at the line steadily till two, ate lunch, and finished up by feeding time: two and a quarter miles of good, tight fence right down to the gate at the county road. The McCrimmons talked the whole time, especially Jeraldine, a bouncy girl with a laugh like a power drill engaging, about everything in the world as far as Domingo could tell, from local gossip to Hollywood scandal to farm policy to God knew what, foods their husbands would and would not eat, types of underwear they could or could not stand to wear, as if he weren't there.

"You women work like Mexicans," he said to Alice on the way home, by way of compliment.

"Thanks, buck," she said. And she parked the pickup all the way inside the foaling shed. "Unzip," she suggested, toeing off her sneakers, wriggling out of her jeans. Threw a leg over, impaled herself on him, looking him keenly in the face as she sank down very very very slowly.

Domingo took her ass in his hands.

Very very very very s—Santo Dios.

Janet Weston had explained to him—in Alice's hearing, so maybe joking—that a type of woman existed who, offered a crown of diamonds or a set of truck tires, would take the tires every time. Of this kind he was acquainted with three: Alice, Vera Jane Whyte, Jessie Tillotson. Mules for work and stubborn as hell, although, as he now knew in the case of Alice, at least, in no way neuter. A kind he had never come across before, that tilted over on its edge the ideal of womanhood he had been brought up to appreciate and respect, also, necessarily, his old ideal of manhood. Altered, not diminished.

From time to time he noticed the effort required to navigate this unfamiliar man-woman landscape. Especially in daily contact, one so easily lapsed into old attitudes and assumptions, carelessly gave or took offense. Though offense was too strong a word. Unresentful, Alice was, had never before, for example, "kicked the stuffing out of him." A crooked look, her head on one side like a collie, that was the worst it had ever come to. But one needed to be alert for this, and cultivating this new attitude wore him out, as exhausting, consuming as the . . . whatever it was that dragged them up out of sleep, reduced speech to stammers, clamped them together like stoats in spring.

Chapter Twelve

IN THE MATTER OF THE OVERZEALOUS PROBATIONARY DEPUTY, PHILIP HELD his hand. No point, he believed, in lodging a complaint with the sheriff's office if this could be avoided. In his experience, such complaints seldom had the desired effect. Far better to frame his concern informally as a quiet heads-up to a superior, a word to the wise. Even this might be avoided if the kid himself would back off.

And in truth, the fellow's encounter with rough justice at Standfast seemed to have been a corrective of sorts. He still patrolled Waitsburg and environs, still ate his jelly doughnuts at the old café on Main Street. But he did not shadow Janet or Nick anymore, or stake out the Weston bungalow as far as Philip could tell. Nor did he make himself visible to any of them in his uniform, as he had been prone to do previously. Off duty, of course, he was easy to spot. The mauled Trans Am, only partially restored, announced its presence like a pipe band. Alice heard it once or twice on the county road, still good for a laugh.

The Fourth of July party that year was blighted. Robey Whyte did his best, but left before the fireworks; sneaked away before dessert, in fact, and the party never really recovered its momentum. Domingo took this to heart. They were discussing Chispa's progress and prospects, he turned to pass a platter and fill a glass, turned back and the old man had vanished. He seemed okay, and then wasn't there.

"He doesn't eat what I take up there," Janet said to Alice.

"What do you take?"

"Dutch chicken, off the bone. An invalid could eat it, an infant." Too fancy, Alice guessed, and vowed to take a more active part, somehow.

Out on the porch, the air was hot at seven o'clock and queerly dark. "I have a bad feeling about this," Alice said. Though the sky was clear, the breeze seemed furtive; lilac leaves clattered, the wands of the bridal-wreath bushes thick with snowy bloom waved like sleeved arms, minatory.

"The barometer's fallen off a cliff," agreed Janet, setting down her platter. "Had we any sense, we'd go on and set up inside this minute. Good thing there's nothing eggy-creamy on the menu; it's curdling weather. Hello, Cam!" as Campbell Keith came around the side of the garage with his bumptious young wife in tow, "Hello, Juno, my dearie! Hand over them beans, go get a drink!"

Nan came to the porch door. "We're putting the corn in now, Mom, okay?"

"Yes, bean-blossom, perfect." To Alice, "She's in an odd mood."

"We're all in an odd mood. Our barometer's fallen off a cliff."

"That's what it feels like. Why are the McCrimmon girls so quiet, do you know?"

"Terri's mom's cancer's back. Goddarnit, if these traditional shindigs are going to be wakes for departed and departing friends, to hell with them!" Alice burst out, dropping several forks. "Mom and Dad, and VJ, and poor old Gertie Franck, and now here's Rosemary laid up—"

"She'll be back, at least; she's all gristle and attitude. It's Robey—"

"He didn't want to come?"

"Hm-mm. I even sent Nick up for him. If he won't come for Nicholas—"

"Huh. Yan, look how dark it's getting."

"Dark as the inside of a goat," said Alex McCrimmon, coming out onto the porch, heaving his big shoulders around inside his shirt as if they itched. As it turned out, they ate their picnic inside, sweltering, doors and windows shut against the siren wind, drifts of gray dust on every sill.

Playing a borrowed electric bass in a pick-up band at the Waitsburg fairgrounds, Domingo Roque missed dinner entirely, nursed a gritty beer in the lee of the grandstand as the horses for the canceled last race of the day, Arabian fillies, were led past him back to the barns. Terrific cracking gusts bent the old locusts and maples; tarps, tents, and folding chairs took flight. Arab mares flourished like kites at the ends of long leads. Dust fogged the air; he couldn't see across the road. The race-meet closed down around him. Everybody who had cover got under it. One of his bandmates offered a ride; gratefully Domingo doubled himself into the cargo space behind the seats of the pickup and directed the driver to the Westons' house.

Deputy-trainee Brandon Galante in his cousin's scuzzy old Escort, laying back a block and a half per standard operating procedure, watched the Mexican from the ranch in question squeeze free of the musicians' truck and enter the Weston bungalow through the screened porch at the back. Uh-huh. Things were coming together. Easing into the alley, Galante parked and settled in to surveil. His own private operation.

There you are, Alice thought, shivers of pleasure puckering her skin, her very brain. Domingo spotted her across the jam-packed living room and detoured through the hall into the kitchen. Where had he found that shirt the color of chiles habañeros?

"Corazón," secretively.

"*I love you so much, my tongue stands motionless! How went the music, then?*"

"*Very well, while it lasted. What is there to eat? Lots of mexicanos, so there was dancing.* How come los güeros don't dance?"

"Because you morenos show us up, is why. Here, hot ribs; you'll like 'em." She sat beside him with her feet on the side rung of his chair and pressed her nose to his shoulder. Domingo held her hand with his left and worked on the ribs with his right.

"Get out of here. Nobody don't dance better of you and Teacher. Mmh. Para chuparse los dedos," showily sucking sauce off his fingers.

"Yeah, but lots of American guys are shy about it, though. We had to teach each other because no boys would dance with us, you know, when we were young." She got up to get him a couple of napkins.

"Why not?"

"I dunno, well, we lived so far from town, and also Janet was so pretty it kinda put them off. And of course," matter-of-fact, "everybody thought I was a guy until I went to college, practically. Who did you see at the—" A burst of laughter from the living room; Tamlyn Evans and Nan came and got pitchers of iced tea from the refrigerator.

"Hey, Domingo. Cerveza?"

"Sí, gracias," and she tossed him a can. He would never, he thought, accustom himself to the truncated greetings, the crude thrustings into conversations in progress of these northerners, not if he lived here ten decades. Then again, sometimes he feared that he *was* getting used to it, in which case he could never go home again, a foreigner among his own kind. Feeling not quite at ease, he wiped his hands, enticed Alice into the pantry, and shut the door.

Juno Keith craned her neck. "Who was that in the kitchen just now?" she whispered to Janet.

"Domingo Roque, Alice's beau. Also our foreman." This fell into a gap in the conversation. Janet braced her back against the arm of the couch. She saw the notion that her sister was desperate enough to get it on with a Mexican farmhand form itself in the air above the group.

"Dang handy!" yelled Jeraldine McCrimmon a tick late, and laughter and talk swelled up again. A hand deposited another smoking ear of corn on Janet's plate: Terri, who bent to her ear and asked, "Is he a lover, a brother, a buddy?" Their ninth-grade formula for the perfect boyfriend.

"Let's go on to Robey's," Alice suggested as Domingo drove them home. "I am not too happy about that old man."

The house was dark, no kitchen aromas, only the rusty-iron smell left by the dust storm. Gloom like sorrow palpable. Sitting in his rocker by the cold hearth, Robey raised his head when she came in, and she looked him in the eyes. It was like peering down a two-bore well. Alice pressed her hands to the sides of the arched doorway. Domingo's weight and warmth behind her, crowding her, seemed at that moment a thing most desirable, beyond price.

"I never thought she'd go before me," Robey said. Domingo went away, rattled around in the kitchen.

"Close your eyes for a second." She clicked on the two lamps, sat on the couch. "Darlin', this won't do."

"I got no gift for livin'."

Could that be so? Had it all been Vera Jane, that broad-gauge energy, interest, optimism? Alice thought that they brewed up the vital spark between them; a good match, that had been. But now here sat Robey feeling as if his life were outside his body, feeling one-armed and one-legged. Slack in the face, even his white cowlick limp. Where were his girls, anyway? Probably, he'd have put up a front, not to infect them with despair.

Domingo came in with a cup of coffee, holding it by the rim so Robey could take the handle, which he did mechanically. His high-cut nostrils flexed, though, and so did Alice's: unless she was much mistaken, a ball of malt was backing up the Maxwell House. "Have you eaten today?" she almost said, but trod on her impulse to mother. Not useful in this case; insulting, patronizing. Then all at once she saw her line.

"You've got other gifts, though, and I need 'em. I know you don't want company. And we haven't bothered you much, have we?" This was hardly true. One of them, Alice, Janet, or Domingo, had checked in every other day without fail. Robey shook his head, however, having been essentially alone. "But I need help, and I don't know where else to turn."

"You got help," slightly more animated, glancing àt Domingo.

"Is too much work," Domingo weighed in, quickly grasping the strategy, "these new land." Having planted the thought: it was your idea, the Hashknife purchase, and now Alice is in trouble because she fell in with your Plan, he took himself off to feed the hens and the Christmas calf.

"We're not getting around to it all," Alice said, just short of a whine. "You know I wouldn't bother you, Robey, if I could think of anybody else."

Robey sipped his coffee. "What about the kids?" craftily.

Alice was ready for this: Nan, summer school; Nick, working for Philip. "If you could just bring your horses over and stay, well, through the Fair would be best. That would be great." She had another arrow in her quiver too: if he wanted to supervise Josquin's vineyard operations, he could ride down there quicker from Standfast than from home. Getting him on horseback was the key to him, she thought. "And plus," her ace in the hole, "since you'd be working for room and board, that helps us a lot."

Robey gave an incredulous snort. Cheap! But of course deep down he believed she was every bit as Scotch as that.

"He will come?"

"Maybe. Dang, we should have left him these beans and ribs."

"Uh-uh, the refrigerador is full."

"Is it? Dammit. Well, we braced him up a little, that's the main thing. Gave him something to argue against. And he might take to the idea after a while."

Then she had another thought: if he did come, how would he deal with the ranch romance? She had no notion of Robey's views on such matters, though doubted he minded fornication as long as it didn't touch his family. But then, she was his family, as good as. Then again, if she had been a man, probably no problem, nor would he have objections on grounds of race. But the notion that she, the boss, was letting herself down with the hired help—that might get under his skin.

Well, if so, she must manage it, that was all.

Under a limpid sapphire sky, Venus hanging like a lamp in the west, they strolled down to check their horses at bedtime. Alice meant to bring up, once again, the question of gelding Chispa. She disliked having a stallion on the place. What with Pony Club, 4-H, and two private instructors renting the arena, too many visitors came around with fingers like carrots incautiously thrust toward any and all horses, even if you pointed out the danger of digits, even little children's whole hands, being munched. And stallions tended to make a separate peace with selected humans, if they made peace at all, and Chispa, though young, had hair on his chest. In the modern climate of litigiousness, it was a worry she could do without. But when she opened her mouth to speak about this, what came out was, "Please come and live with me in the house."

Domingo understood the subtext, that she meant to preempt whatever objections Robey might have about them as a couple. He didn't mind, though. In the beginning he had meant to preserve a space for himself, a fall-back position, just in case. But not anymore. He was as sure of Alice as he was of his feeling for her. And if, as he must, he reserved a part of his mind from her, if he moved into the house maybe he could make up for the dereliction by pure physical contact. Really, it was nothing to him now, where he lived, as long as she was within his reach.

And besides, as completely as he loved her, he so very much wished to avoid further discussion of Chispa's balls.

"You've got blue marks under your eyes, and so has he. Folks'll notice."

Alice smiled fatly at the raspberry canes.

"At this rate you'll get emaciated again, and there'll be nothing left of him, poor rat. Moderation is a virtue, Alice. Are you putting any in the basket? You've eaten every one, so far."

"You're a fine one to talk."

"Look here, I haven't eaten any."

"About moderation, madam." Janet and Philip had had, from their first meeting at Whetstone, a raucous and exigent physical relationship. Alice remembered any number of times having been forced onto the tiny balcony of the dormitory room she shared with Janet, there to smoke many cigarettes in weather you wouldn't put a collie out in, to give those two scope for their desires. Otherwise they would surely have thrown each other down in the juniper bushes by the dining hall in full view of everybody, been expelled from college, herself responsible.

"Oh. Well. Yes." Later, further down the row, Janet said seriously, "Is it wise?"

"Wise. Hm. Remember the time we were burning over that field, and the fire piddled along all morning not going anywhere, but when we went to get our sandwiches from the truck, it flared up and ran across the whole field and burned up about half of Robey's windbreak? It's as wise as that."

"You're saying you're out of control? Not exactly your style, Roan. Though . . ."

They picked on down the row, one on either side of the frame, and started up the next.

Alice said, "Are you thinking about Vincent Greer?"

"Yeah, I am."

"But it's not the same. Okay, I was damn sure out of control about him, I could hardly keep my little paws off his body. But the problem with Vincent and me was that we lied to ourselves about each other, and we lied to each other about ourselves. There was no truth in us, except for—"

"Sex."

"Yeah. And that is not enough."

"Lied how? Listen, you're still eating more than you're keeping."

"I need to keep up my strength, you said so yourself. I let Vincent believe that he could take me away from Standfast. He let me believe that he loved me. I told myself that, because he was like Philip in some ways, he would be like him in all ways, I mean, that he would be satisfied to live out here. He told himself that, even though I wasn't you, I was almost you, and he almost loved me, and if he could be near you, it would be all right."

"What?!" Janet dropped her basket, berries rolled free. "What are you saying?" She stared at Alice over the arching canes, wide-eyed under her wide hat. "Alice Lyon Andison, what are you saying?" And she plumped down in the long grass between the raspberry frames as if her legs wouldn't hold her up. "I don't believe it. I couldn't stand to believe that for one second. Take it back this minute."

Alice picked on imperturbably. "Baby, it's fact; it's data. Don't feel bad; it's not your fault, it's ours, Vincent's and mine. When two fundamentally honest people lie to each other on that scale and get away with it, it shows that they want to be deceived. Get up, Yan, you're squooshing the berries, those chinos'll never be the same."

"Now wait a minute. Did Vincent actually tell you that? About me?"

"No, 'course not. I just knew, you know. Within a year or so. He had to get out of here partly because he had to get away from you, otherwise he was gonna go crazy. And I told myself that I could stand to be second best if I could have him. Which was nuts. The point is, okay, I'm crazy about Domingo, but I'm not kidding him that he can turn me into some other type of woman or take me away from here, or kidding myself about that."

Janet stood up, shaken, and began to comb her spilled raspberries out of the grass. She wished a speedy end to this conversation, no further revelations. But she said, "Then what about him? Who does he send money to, that's what I'm wondering. Has he told you that, by any chance?"

"No, but he will, when he can. Do I detect sarcasm? I'll pinch you good and proper, you twerp. It's me he likes, that's all I need to know."

They worked on. The day was cool for midsummer, the grass of the bungalow's backyard grown long, clover and oxalis blooming in it, drawing bees. When they finished picking, the sisters stood together under the ash trees looking uphill at the fields, golden wheat stubble and dark summerfallow in smooth bands, like a great banner loosed on the wind. "He could break your heart into a thousand tiny shards," Janet sighed.

"Och aye. But who needs a heart if it can't be broken? Tina Turner notwithstanding."

"Where did you pick that up? Complete and total shit."

"You taught it to me," an arm around her neck, planting a smacker on her cheekbone, "a long time ago."

"God forgive me," groaned Janet. Then, the corners of her mouth crimped, "What's he like?"

Alice grinned; her knees gave slightly. After a while, "He's got this kind of . . . attacking style."

Janet laughed her sneezy laugh: "Oh, the *tootsie*!"

Not a spit of rain fell after the solstice that summer. Humping her irrigation lines through blazing mornings, Alice wished that Robey would get his mind around her proposition and come. She had not lied, it turned out, about needing help. Nan really was in summer school in the Tri-Cities; Nick really was working for Philip full-time. Various long-deferred projects, added to regular farming and herding, crammed her workday. She needed to add a wall of corrugated material to the north end of the covered arena. They were building two more loafing sheds for the penned horses and repainting the weather side of the foaling barn. The deck at the back of the house languished half-floored. She wanted to clean out and paint the tack room, extend the pipe fencing all around the yard and the pens, and she thanked her stars that Janet had taken the refurbishment of the house into her own hands, along with all the noncomestible gardening.

In mid-August, they released another set of fly predators, hardly needing to; the long spell of desert heat had the good effect of dessicating fly eggs. Heat also made for growth, and they were able to cut hay again toward the end of the month. Even that late grass made pretty fair crop, leafy, aromatic, generally free of foxtails, and of course in such weather it cured up without a sniff of mold. Nick took a couple of days off work to help them stack it and, dangling her legs over the twenty-foot cliff of bales with a bursting sense of achievement, Alice believed that things could not go better with her, not if they tried.

And then they did: Robey phoned up to say he had organized some of his grandkids to stay at his place and proposed, if she still really needed him, to bring his horses and his traps to Standfast in a couple of weeks. "Aw-right!" said Alice, and Domingo immediately began to calculate which items on his list might usefully be handed off to a competent elderly wrangler.

He bought some good-looking avocados at Klicker's one day on the way out of Walla Walla, and Alice invited the senior Westons for dinner: chicken soup with zucchini, tomatoes, and corn from the garden, slivered tortillas for noodles, chiles, and cilantro scenting the steam.

"Hot food for hot weather," said Janet appreciatively, dripping over her spoon.

"So my mother told me," Domingo agreed. It was pleasant, being alone with them; for one thing, he could understand almost everything anybody said.

"I never used to cook with chiles at all," Alice said, "but now I use them year-round. We didn't use to see fresh ones in the market like we do now, since so many of you mexicanos came up here to live."

"I remember putting canned ones into a tuna casserole one time, wildly daring, when we were young."

"I don't remember. Was it good, chick?"

"Well, you ate it. But you ate everything that didn't run away. Dad couldn't get it past his teeth, I seem to remember." Domingo said nothing, unable to approve such a use of the sacred vegetable.

Philip came from the house with a pitcher of agua fresca. "I wonder if you realize," he intoned portentously, "how new it actually isn't, this cuisine."

"It's new up here."

Domingo and Philip wagged their heads in unison. "No, indeed. It is restored, even unto the forty-sixth parallel."

"Whatever can you mean, you strange creature? Thank you, sweetie, that's plenty. Didn't the immediately previous menu run to dried salmon and pemmican, the odd camas root?"

"He's talking about Mexico own this country in the past. Correct, don Felipe? *In the sixteen hundreds, Spain claimed and Mexicans traversed all the west of this continent almost as far north as the Columbia. Probably in those times, chiles, frijoles, tomates were more common than ice cream and hamburgers.*"

Alice looked searchingly at Domingo, Janet interrogatively at Philip: "Did you get that, Phil?"

"Some."

"Did Mexico really own the whole West? I mean, more than Texas and California?"

"Of course, Aliz, think about the names: Well, not all, but Arizona, Nevada, Montana. This belonged to us for two hundred years, maybe two-fifty." He believed he was on firm, okay, *nearly* firm ground; besides, they were not the kind of people to cripple a good discussion with an inconvenient fact. Anyway, he felt familial with them now.

"So what happened?" Alice, who knew her local history fairly well, wanted to see what he would say. "How come we aren't all speaking Spanish?"

Philip leaned across and patted her arm reassuringly. "We stole it fair and square, Standfast, don't worry. All the paperwork is in order. No court in the land would find against you."

"Uh-huh, you steal some and buy some," Domingo agreed, leaning on his elbow; then, provocatively, "but now we taking it back."

"True! Talk about cultural imperialism . . ." This from Janet, laughing.

"¿Estás de acuerdo, Teacher?"

"What's not to agree? It's obvious. Look at what we eat, listen to the radio, tejano music on the country-western stations. Look at Cinco de Mayo. Look at those five Hispanic-owned businesses on Main Street in Walla Walla. It's a regular reconquista. And all without recourse to guns or armies, or even lawyers, God forbid," giving

Philip a nudge. Alice regarded Domingo affectionately: his English so much improved! And revealing a pleasure in the give-and-take of conversation. But she didn't share his confidence. Revolutions have their price.

"You don't mind it, Teacher?" he teased. "Lotta gabachos prefer all mexicanos return to Mexico."

"Not me. As long as you guys buy into one-man-one-vote and the rule of law—"

"That's the question, of course," Philip asserted. "Can people accustomed to operating through networks of kinship and patronage instead of by external rules—"

Alice opened her mouth to explain, but Domingo nodded, "Uh-huh, corrupción, entiendo."

"—learn to trust the impersonal institutions of law and governance enough to make a real life here?"

"They do!" Janet was definite. "Question answered. Within one generation they take the system to their heart, if the students at the community college are any example."

"Of course. Is the best!" Domingo nursed a deep romantic faith in the rule of law while, Janet was pretty sure, doubting just as deeply its efficacy in his own particular case.

"Not best, 'mano, not necessarily."

"No, Teacher?" greatly surprised.

"I don't know, it might not be good for everybody. We just like it because it works well for the majority of us. Probably if something that worked better came along, we would all change to the new way in a week. To heck with tradition! You know how we are."

Yes, that he did know. He admired the law-abiding tendency of Americans, from a safe distance. But how coldly utilitarian, such a life, how barren of excitement, of art. The operations of chance suppressed, and chance was the wine of life! Yes, okay, it functioned, this country. But, sometimes boringly, stultifyingly. People would say, about mexicanos who made it rich in the North, his wallet is full, but his soul is empty. In his own case, sometimes he almost relished the doom of deportation that overhung him. That sword that hung by a hair, that salt in the soup of his life.

The last of August, stratocumulus streaming eastward, the Perseid meteor shower muffled in high overcast. No rain fell, but neither did the sun come out. Alice forgot her hat on a fence post, and the raging ultraviolet burned her through the clouds. Meanwhile, Chispa lipped the hat off the post. He tossed it, ran from it, stomped it as if it were a snake. Chewed it to tatters. Domingo leaned on the fence and watched. It might be that the colt had some of the mare's good stuff, he thought.

Alice came back, and she too watched for a while, her chin on Domingo's shoulder, her hands in his pockets. Then she said in an objective tone, "Mexican gentleman encourages his horse to eat his girlfriend's hat."

Domingo lifted his summer straw from his head and passed it backward onto hers: "El caballero mexicano hace el gran sacrificio. *Mark me, heart: someday it will be a matter of pride to say, 'This horse is of Standfast.'*"

"Think he's going to make our name? That would be nice. Listen, how's about a nice siesta. A nice lo-ong siesta. Then we'll be able to stay awake for the star shower tonight, in case the sky clears."

Which at last it did, in time for a blazing silver sunset in the gap between the dry-pea harvest and the start of fall cultivation. At ten o'clock that night the mercury was still climbing, humidity still dropping.

The best place to view the meteor shower was a grassy platform along Dorothy Creek, uphill beyond the orchard. They carried up a piece of a tarp and an old quilt, and a bedsheet against the bugs. The cats accompanied them, and the collies of course, though they soon grew bored and rambled away. Sometimes the star shower was a complete bust, Alice cautioned, but sometimes a light show. This time the latter: a silent spectacular, mystic. So long extended that in the end they fell asleep, side by side and hand in hand under the sheet, like effigies on a tomb.

A roaring explosion brought them bolt-upright: after midnight, still hot, the sickle moon low, and a fan of radiance over the grove of apple and pear trees below them: lights must be on in the house.

"Wh—," instantly Domingo's hand covered her mouth. "Gun," his lips against her ear, hardly making a sound. She stared wildly. *Gun?!*

A second echoing crash bounced them to their feet, inside Alice's head all one long groan of terror. Run! If only she could get her feet to move, she was for the hills. Of course they would be sitting ducks up there, no cover for miles. Where, then? And who? And why? Thinking three things at once, uselessly.

Domingo had not moved his mouth from her ear, now whispered, "You got a rifle?" Yes, the twenty-two, for coyotes. She nodded, her arms around him and her face against his, felt more than heard the next two thudding blasts, close together.

Domingo's mind doubled and chattered like a trapped weasel. "Cabinet," Alice moaned soundlessly as if to transfer her thought through the bone of his head. He knew where she meant, in the tack room in the foaling shed, already moving across the creek, across the gullied ridge above the house, away from the orchard trees and down among the sumac and alder thickets, the covering young birch and aspen. Easier going, it would have been, farther up on the open ground, but utterly exposed, starlight ghastly on the wide fields.

Shotgun, that coughing roar? For all Alice knew, it could have been artillery, range five miles, a concussion like that. The twenty-two's effective range was short, its shells tiny, no defense at all. But it looked like a weapon, and it was all she could think of. Domingo dragged her, they dragged each other, breathing open-mouthed to make no sound.

Away back up the creek on the Dogleg, the bunch of cows made humanlike noises; down below now, all was still. A faint mist of dust, thrown up by the penned horses in their panicky rush away from the shots, hung over the yard, slowly rising. Silence clotted in Domingo's ears.

Two hay sheds separated them from the foaling barn, the three structures standing between them and whatever horror was going on in the house. Could he deposit Alice in the haystacks somewhere, try to draw the danger away from her? He didn't fool himself that she would stay there, any more than she would stay here in the inky shade of the woods, no chance of that at all. There was a stack of grass-hay bales in the foaling barn; he might be able to hide her there long enough to . . . what? Try it, anyway, think of something. They could sneak up along the far wall of the barn, then only a few steps in the open to reach the door. Could they chance it? Where was the shooter? Who?

Another explosion up toward the house, with a twanging metallic aftertone, and they were flying along the alley behind the hay sheds to the wall of the barn, passing through cool and warm belts of darkness, flattening themselves against the metal wall still smelling of sun, Domingo letting go of her hand to squat and peer one-eyed around the corner. Nothing. Single file, then, along the moonlit front.

Inside, Domingo turned left, remembering to avoid in the dark the piled-up saddles and gear taken from the tack room during the pre-paint cleanout, seeking a pitchfork, anything, a bale hook handily embedded in the stack, snatching the reata off his rig by instinct as he passed. Alice turned right, terror clothing her cold and dry like a second skin, sneakers soundless on the tack-room steps, the cement floor swept ready for priming, to the cabinet behind the door, her hands cunning as ferrets to the twenty-two where it hung by its webbing sling, the particular smell of gun oil, the box of cartridges on the high shelf, one round for her hand and one for the chamber, kneeling in the space behind the door with the little rifle, heavy for its size, on her knee, the bolt lever up and back, a shell in the chamber, the breech closed in a series of tiny oily clicks—

The lights came on.

A booted foot on the top step, she could see through the gap between the door and its jamb, gray lizard-skin boot, fancy stitching. A knee in dirty jeans at the level of her eye. A crisp sound, crisp sounds. She looked up: red eye, moving jaw. Jerry Graeme, eating an apple.

The whole eye, blood red.

"Hi, Alice."

She froze, jack-lit. Casual as a picnicker, he lodged the apple in his mouth to free both his hands for the sawed-off, the wide black bore of its right-hand barrel coming to bear on her through the hinge gap. Pinned her there, the red eye and the black one.

Alice opened her mouth to say one dear name.

She heard something. He heard it, the low whoop of a swung rope, turned the terrible beam of his eye away from her, and then she could jerk the stiff trigger back as the loop sailed out of the dark. Simultaneous: the twenty-two's flat crack, the butt punching her hip bone, shattering blast of the shotgun, blackness.

Deafened, she dropped the rifle and scrambled for the lights, up down, up down, nothing. A wild leap took her from the tack room to the barn door, the rotary switch for the big overheads. Light flooded down.

Domingo wrestled an alligator on the dirt floor of the barn, straddling the brute: Jerry Graeme, facedown and foaming at the mouth, bucking and writhing. Flailing with his free hand, the shotgun just out of his reach.

"¡Quítale la escopeta!" hoarsely, and Alice jumped for the gun, but she couldn't make her hands seize it, had to jerk off her polo, use it as mitts to lift the terrible object. Dumped it in the grain bunker. As she sped back toward the phone, Domingo threw his hands high like a roper over a trussed calf.

Nine one one. Ring. Ring. She poured it all out at once. Then again slowly, then again after the contact was broken, trailing off, her jaw aching from the pressure of the receiver, shaking, freezing, soaked with sweat. Domingo stood over his enemy, vacant-faced. He didn't know what to do next. Tied up and helpless, Jerry Graeme yammered, radiating madness. Looking bigger horizontal than vertical. Dark venous blood pooled under his knees. Alice quit looking, dragged Domingo away.

They sat on a bale, squeezed together. "The sheriff's coming," Alice said, and then cried out, "Oh God, they'll get after you!"

"No me importa, no me fockin' importa," purged of emotion, of consciousness almost; he felt invulnerable. But shadows and sparks edged his vision, as if he hadn't taken a breath since the start of the whole horrible sequence.

Twisting his head from side to side, Jerry Graeme tested his ropes, clenching bound hands. Searched for them with his blood-suffused eyes. They sat in a cove of the grass-hay stack, out of range. Jerry spat, foamed, mad as a trapped rattler. The motion of his head like a snake's striking.

Alice really wanted her shirt. She planned a route to it that avoided the scan of Jerry Graeme's eyes, the sight of curdling dark blood. Retching, she made her way to the grain bin. Freed her old lilac polo from the weight of the shotgun, dragged it on. It itched, full of crimped oats, but as if at a distance.

From jammed-up instantaneity, time ran down to zero. Each second elastic, infinite. It seemed as they sat marooned on their bale that nothing else had ever happened, would ever happen. Jerry Graeme wept percussively, like a dog being sick. They went on forever, those sick-animal noises. Then not, had never been. The quiet pooled out beyond thought. Four-by-four engines grinding up the lane, the rhythmic flash of light-bar colors had always been.

Domingo snapped awake. "They coming," and went out to guide the EMTs. Cast adrift, Alice hooked her fingers under the baling strings. Her head seemed to want to expand into abstraction. She hung on.

The sheriff came in, Harley Carmichael, in off-duty clothes but with his uniform hat on; he had Domingo by the arm, a deceptively friendly grip. He looked around, motioned the medical techs in. "Miz Alice?"

"I'm over here."

He came over, his small belly like somebody else's burden gallantly borne, and let go of Domingo, who stood swaying until Alice pulled him down beside her. Carmichael dragged up a bale and eased down, clasped his hands comfortably between his knees. Like a preacher at a deathbed, Alice thought.

"Hey, Harley. Sorry to bring you out so late."

"Not a problem."

The medics' radio gave a squawk. Jerry Graeme lay like down timber. One of the EMTs began slicing away his fetters, and Domingo started up, too late.

The sheriff put out a firm hand, but said mildly, "He violent?"

"Who? That one is, when he's loose. This one—it's his rope they're chopping up."

"A perfectly good rope, well broken in," sinking down despondent. Carmichael, himself a fair-to-good recreational calf roper, grunted sympathetically.

"Wanna try and tell me what happened? Don't I know that guy?" nodding toward the long, limp form being gurneyed to the ambulance.

"You ought to, God knows. He practically paid rent at the jail when he was young: Jerry Graeme, remember? Or was Buddy in office then?"

"Me, before Buddy. Yeah, gotcha. Good-lookin' kid, but hard on the bottle, as I recall. Big hat, no cows. What's the connection with your outfit, remind me?"

She covered a jaw-cracking yawn. "It's a long story. The short is, his old man sold my folks some land, with a life interest to Jerry, I guess because he knew Jerry'd never amount to much on his own. And so we've been stuck with him since he was a kid, in all kinds of ways. Well, I won't bore you. The thing is, he sold out to us in April, but not . . . willingly. Under pressure. Seems like he owed money to somebody who wasn't the patient type, something like that. Anyway, so I was hoping never to lay eyes on him again, 'cause he was crazy as a rat in a drain, always, you remember." The sheriff smoothed his mustache one-handed, noncommittal. "But especially after he came back from Vegas last summer, and tore this place all up—"

"Say what?"

"You remember. Well, we called it in, anyway, and Deputy Smoke came out. Jerry took a hatchet to the house, turned all the faucets on, drained the well, the whole nine yards. He was on something, I think, or maybe just more nuts than ever before. The only reason he didn't burn us out is that he got himself to believe he owned the place, or half of it." Alice yawned again. "Kept on saying, 'Sell my half.'"

"Uh-huh. What about tonight?"

She sat forward and Domingo sat back, willing to be ignored. "Tonight. Okay. We were up the hill, looking at the meteors."

"Who's 'we'?"

"Domingo—this man and I. I'm sorry: this is Domingo Roque, our top hand. Domingo, Sheriff Carmichael. Before moonset sometime. And we heard these explosions—"

"Okay, you were where?"

"Uphill from the house, beyond the orchard. Out on the grass-flat up there, you know. It's where we always go for the meteor shower. Usually my sister and her husband come; it's their anniversary, August twenty-seventh, but they went down to the hot springs instead this year." She pulled herself up, shocked. The sheriff glanced at Domingo, who stared darkly and levelly back.

"Okay, shots fired: how many?"

"How many, buck?" He spread out his fingers on his knee, littlest first: one, one, two, one. "Five, total; by that time we were down here by the hay sheds."

"Yeah, so why did you come down here?"

"'Cause there's no cover up there." Her voice jumped a gear, she wrestled it back. "And I think Domingo planned to hide me somewhere."

"House is all shot up," announced the deputy, coming in, fastening his holster as the ambulance made its slow turn on the gravel outside. "Looks like maybe he filled your tractor full of buck too."

"Thanks for sharing that, Darrell. You might wanna take a note here. Go on, please, Alice."

"We came in here to get the twenty-two. I don't know what we thought; it looks like a weapon, something. Anyway he, Jerry, came in with the shotgun."

"And where is it, the shotgun?"

"In the grain bin." She couldn't seem to say any more. The deputy, whose name was Darrell Smoke, went to look, came back with the sawed-off wrapped in a feed sack, nodded to the sheriff, took it outside, and came back.

"Miz Alice?"

"Oh. I shot him. From behind the door," pointing her chin at the tack room. "He looked at me so I couldn't, and then Domingo got a loop on so I could, and I shot him. With the twenty-two. In the knee." She nodded and kept on nodding till she ran down. She and Domingo looked at nothing; the sheriff and the deputy looked at each other.

"Got a loop on?" inquired Smoke.

Domingo said, suddenly furious, "What I'm going to do? You tell me!" Those two white faces, staring stupid as Hereford steers. "What I'm supposed to do? He's going to kill her!"

They all realized about the dogs at the same time. Glen met them in the lane, foaming at the mouth and dragging his hindquarters; as top dog, Sweep had exercised his right to the lion's share of Jerry Graeme's lethal treat, saving the youngster's life. Sweep himself they found by the gate, stiff, looking like he had tried to vomit his tongue. Domingo lifted him into the pickup bed, sure that he was dead, while Alice phoned, routed the vet from his slumbers.

"We're gonna lead you in," said Carmichael. "Don't y'all pass us, now," and they made for Walla Walla in convoy, leaving Standfast all lit up on the hillside behind them. At seventy on the twisting two-lane state highway, Domingo barely kept the dark-green sedan in sight, roared through Iwalu alone in the dark, hoping not to be picked off by some overalert local policía. The deputy conceded some speed going into Waitsburg, but not much, so that as the ranch pickup passed through the town, all Domingo could see of him was the light-bar's periodic glare on the stubble fields ahead. Glen thrashed and cried in Alice's embrace. She braced her feet, unbelted.

⌒

Lights were what Brandon Galante saw too, parked in the alley two blocks back of the Westons' bungalow and four blocks from the highway. Having picked up the Corvette hours before at the Walla Walla city limits, he'd followed it into Waitsburg and then, sure where it was going, turned off and staked out the Weston house. Sometime, Nevada-Plates was going to give the Westons up, he was certain. Maybe tonight. He waited, dozed, fell asleep, woke up, and got out of the car for a leak on somebody's back fence.

The whiney burr of the cruiser's interceptor engine alerted him. Then the lights, flashing red/blue/red/blue against the school's brick façade. Galante yanked up his zipper, plunged into the Trans Am, fired up, and laid tread down the alley, his soul rejoicing. Hot pursuit! This must be it! With the presence of mind to leave his lights off.

In consequence he nearly rear-ended the Standfast pickup when he caught up with it on the highway beyond the town. Caught up with and instantly recognized it, pumped twice with his right arm. Chill, chill out, he counseled himself. Lay back. Don't blow it. Silent, invisible, deadly. Dudn even know I'm here.

Though, what was going on, he did not quite understand. Could not know, of course, until—he pictured several cinematic conclusions. But, frowning, weren't things in the wrong order here? The good guys running, the bad guys chasing? He couldn't figure it out. Well, whatever, he thought, the guy in the cruiser better not horn in on my damn collar, not after I made all the damn connections.

To his right at intervals the dome of yellow light above the penitentiary flared in the gaps of the wheat hills; to the left, the foothills of the Blues massed blackly. They crossed Coppei Creek flying and burst up between the bluffs onto the flats north of Walla Walla, the airport beacon swinging around. Having made up the distance, the pickup was only five lengths or so behind the county cruiser, and now Brandon Galante grasped the situation: the cops wanted the pickup to pull over, the pickup was refusing to do so. Refusing a direct order from an officer of the law, from an agent of the duly constituted civil authority. Their ass was grass, and he, Probationary Deputy B. Galante, was about to mow it. Sweet.

On the freeway now, sweeping curve around the north side of the city, and Galante made his move, pulling up little by little alongside the runaway truck—more slowly than he wanted, the Trans Am still not a hundred percent—to force the pickup onto the shoulder. Or right off the road, if the driver was stubborn enough to— He punched the gas, sacrificing the half-rebuilt engine, felt with a bounding heart his vehicle surge forward!—

Suddenly they weren't there. He was alone, doing ninety-plus, screaming westward through the dark toward Touchet.

He realized right away what had happened: they'd taken the Second Avenue exit while he was concentrating on his vehicle. The sheriff's department sedan too, though; why? Braking, slewing, travel-ing sideways to the detriment of his tires, he clanged around the end of the concrete divider and roared back eastbound. Over the Second Avenue overpass, and there they were! Off the freeway, heading south on Second. Another screeching deceleration, another strictly-speaking illegal U-turn, back westward again, fighting the heavy car around the off-ramp. He sped south, making a lot of noise (muffler, tailpipe?) that racketed off the newly cleaned brick of the big downtown hotel, ran the red light at Rose Street, horn blaring. Shooting across the intersec-tion, he glimpsed them again, far down to his right on Rose, past the old cannery.

"No problem!" through gritted teeth, "no problem!" Horsing his car around right onto Main, right again onto Third, left onto Rose. Nothing was visible. He stood on the gas, poured it on down the straightaway, ignoring stoplights. Really making a lot of noise now. They might hear him coming. Well, let them, let the bastards know what was coming to them. The right-left curve on Rose Street, the railroad tracks. And there they were, opposite the mall, stopped. Or turning? With a yell of triumph, he bore down.

Mike Sage, the vet, led them into one of the treatment rooms, the sheriff holding open the heavy door.

"Darrell," to the deputy, whose shift was nearly over, "you're done here. These guys will drop me home." Big old softy, thought Darrell Smoke, who liked his chief. Don't want nobody see you puddle up over a dog. He got into the cruiser, buckled his seat belt, started up, and backed out from behind the Standfast rig.

As he did this, Brandon Galante's raving Trans Am made the two right-angle turns off Rose Street into the clinic parking lot almost as a one-eighty, swerving wide, spouting up gravel and flowers from the landscaping. Still no headlights. All Smoke knew was the howl of an overdriven engine, the sudden acidulous reek of marigolds, a helluva crash, his cruiser twirled sideways, and echoing silence.

The deputy turned off the ignition. Tested his neck. Yep. He unbuckled the belt and got out. Light from inside the clinic showed him his rear fender mashed in, tire flat. The Trans Am had come to rest at an angle on the other side of the parking area, having climbed the pipe fence on two wheels. Like it had tried to fly up to heaven, he thought. As he stood there, one of the pipes of the fence pronged up from underneath, through the long graceful hood, like a finger pointing skyward.

After a minute or two the Trans Am's door creaked open. Brandon Galante fell out by stages, sunglasses first.

"Hey, there, Brandon," said Smoke.

Galante stood up, staggered, crushed his Ray-Bans with his first step, hesitated, and strode firmly on. "My collar!" just like on television. "Drugs?"

"No, dogs," said Darrell Smoke, unleashing his Sunday punch.

Because of the way Jerry Graeme had stood in the doorway, turning to look over his right shoulder, the little slug from the twenty-two shattered his right kneecap and breached and rattled around inside the capsule of the left one. That limber stride of his was gone for good. Alice wanted to hear that he himself was gone for good. She wished him not just disabled but in Florida, or Australia. Domingo believed the man might very well die, remembering the frightful thinness of those arms he had struggled to bind, the sickening turn of loose skin on the bones, the slack band of the big gold biscuit of a watch. Those eyes.

"What will they do to us if he dies?"

"Love, I don't know."

They occupied their minds with repairing the damage. Bought mattresses, trucked the blasted ones to the dump, had the John Deere guy out to assess the effect of a burst of buckshot on the small tractor. Replaced the tack-room door and the light fixture in there. Swept up the snips and ravelings of Domingo's lariat, dug the blood-soaked dirt out of the floor of the barn. Buried poor Sweep.

Alice seemed to have lost the capacity to make a firm fist. She chored listlessly, didn't cook. Seemed content to live on Coke and Raisinets. Janet had offered her a hooker of whisky that morning, in effect giving her permission to get smashed; she hadn't taken it up, but felt as hungover as if she had. Walled off, at one remove from reality, from herself. Domingo thoughtlessly taking a bite out of an apple brought her right down on all fours in the dust.

Janet called in the afternoon. "Roan? Listen. He's dead."

Alice thumped down on the steps of the deck and stared at the phone. "I've killed him," she said.

He expected her to go to pieces. In fact, he almost hoped she would; he felt like it himself; it would have been a kind of vicarious release.

"It's okay you want to cry," unnerved by her quiet.

"You said not to. 'You cry, they get the victory.'"

"In this case, is okay: somebody crazy tries to kill you, you gotta defense. You don't remember how to cry?" He twisted his fists in his eye sockets to get her started. Alice laughed helplessly, couldn't stop. Each time she calmed down, he did it again, set her off again. They were up above the orchard retrieving the tarp and the quilt left there overnight. He had spent a couple of hours on the baler, the vibration still deep in his bones. This was good; it was like white noise, it blotted out worries about getting copped and deported, soaked up the dregs of the cocktail of terror and rage from last night.

He hardly knew what he wanted, spreading the sheet out in the deep grass under the pear trees. "Shoo the bees away," was all Alice said. He undressed, and undressed her. He made her think of a puma, a big tawny tom crouched between her knees. Mimicking that gutteral rutting yowl. A warm breath came off the Palouse, singing in the grass, bending the tall stems and blades over and over and over, rolling and rising like the waves of the sea. A long, long breath, and Alice went out with the tide.

"¿Qué nos van a hacer, pues?"

She opened her eyes. Leaves and fruit patterned a sky of tender aquamarine. She desired fervently that this pattern, this peace continue. Let there be nothing before them but baling and stacking aromatic hay, moving pipe, gathering cows. Let it be as if no vile thing had happened.

One thing was clear, however: she could not go on viewing the world from a supine position.

"Well," sitting up, plucking and chewing a grass stem while Domingo sorted their clothes, "possibly nothing. According to Philip." All evidence pointed to a well-planned if crazed attack: the poisoned meat for the dogs, the murderous homemade weapon, the raggedy red Corvette parked down the country road, traces of three different kinds of high-grade dope in it and in Jerry Graeme himself, causing a cardiac episode that, according to Janet's nurse-friend in the emergency room, had resembled not so much failure as explosion. That, plus the shambles he'd made of Standfast the summer before, plus Deputy Brandon Galante's somewhat incoherent report of the red Corvette's midnight visits to the county in the last six months. "Philip thinks we're in the clear as far as charges go—he thinks we will not be prosecuted, entiendes?"

From the way the deputies and office staff treated her before and after her interview with the sheriff, Alice guessed that, quite on the contrary, she and especially Domingo might have achieved some sort of local-hero status.

Harley Carmichael asked her whether he had understood right, that whatsisname, Roque, had roped a man armed with a sawed-off shotgun, virtually in the dark, with one swing, in one try? Alice said, yes, he had understood right. Quite a long pause ensued, during which the sheriff rotated his thumbs and gazed out his office window at the statue of Columbus on the courthouse lawn. He looked back at Alice who, thanks to utter prostration of spirit, appeared perfectly relaxed.

"He legal?" as one obliged to ask.

"Pending," and thank you, Janet, for that ready lie.

"How long's he been with you?"

"Two years, thereabouts. Helluva hand, no bad habits, good-natured. Throws a rope better than anybody from here to McAllen, Texas."

"It would seem so." Amiable but searching, "Anything else you want to tell me about him?"

None of your bidness, Harley, Alice was tempted to say. Though in fact it was his business, maybe as a peacekeeper, surely as an old friend of Allan's. She found that, in addition to appearing relaxed, she was re-laxed. "Dad was always after Janet and me to bring him somebody for the ranch, you know. And much as I admire Lawyer Weston—"

The sheriff suppressed a smile. So that's how it was. Well, well. "Sure miss your dad," he said.

"Yeah. I believe they'd have taken to each other, Dad and Domingo. He and Robey Whyte hit it off real well."

"That so?" Filing this for possible follow-up. "How's Robey doing these days? Sorry about Vera Jane."

Alice sighed, eyed Columbus's peculiar pants through the window, and said, "We're trying to get him over to stay with us for a while. Put him to work."

"Best thing, prob'ly. Okay, Alice. Go on home. Call you if I need you again."

She felt almost sure, after that, that the sheriff's case was closed. It should have relieved her mind. She drove home from the vet clinic, Glen on a bed of towels in the footwell, weak but recovering.

Alice, you are lower than a toad's ass. Why?

The truth was, her conscience was squeejawed with the burden of Jerry Graeme. She had loathed him from childhood onward, and let him know it. Now he was dead, a mean and dirty death. After a trash dump of a life, from what she could tell. Alice wondered if he had ever had a friend, ever deserved one, or known enough to want one.

Jesus. Did *she* have to take custody of his memory? She found herself driving thirty in a fifty-mile zone, half on the shoulder. Not even Janet would be sappy enough to entertain such a thought, undertake that task. The man was botched from the cradle upward. But she couldn't throw off the weight of her part in his end.

"You speak with that police about me?" Domingo prompted her later in the day.

"*They* spoke to me about *you*. Very impressed! They kept asking, 'Did he really do that with the rope?' You're kind of their hero."

"Pero, Aliz," brushing this aside, "about those Migra?"

"To the sheriff, yeah, I did. Well, I told a little lie; I don't know if he believed it. But I don't think he's interested in you in that way. Honest, I don't."

It wasn't just lack of interest on the sheriff's part. Harley Carmichael had somehow let her know, without directly saying so, that whatever his legal status, whatever the Immigration guys might think, Domingo Roque was a special case. Had all but said, "He's *our* Mexican."

Chapter Thirteen

ROBEY FINALLY CAME TO STANDFAST IN A RUSH, JUST AT FAIR TIME. "Gotta keep this outfit outta trouble," he explained. Dumped his wearables in Domingo's old room in the foaling barn, his working gear in the tack room, and turned his horses into the round pen. Not quite chirpy as a cricket, Alice thought, but moving a tad brisker. He couldn't make himself go to the Fair with them, though, which was a pity since Domingo's red horse did herself so proud in the cow-cutting that three people made serious, very serious offers for her. However, folks kept looking at Domingo himself and asking Alice about him until he had to go hide out, pretending to read pamphlets in the Christian Science booth, and Alice refused to talk about the Jerry Graeme business anymore.

Robey fit right in, a lucky thing, since the fall roundup for pregnancy checks now came treading on the heels of the haymaking. Mindful on the one hand of Alice's motto that work didn't care who did it, and on the other of Robey's age and possible physical limitations, Domingo marshaled his tact. But he found it wasn't needed. Robey Whyte was a good hand, good help. True, he did not reliably throw the heel catch. Few wranglers could; it wasn't a matter of age, but of eye and hand and, of course, horse. However, he fished like a champion, dropping his loop deftly in front of a hard-traveling calf just in time to pick it up by the forefoot, time and again. Alice used him hard, wore him out, and fed him high. He began to flesh out a little. Not much to say for himself, at first, but at least he stayed around after supper, reminiscing with Alice and listening to Domingo fool with the guitar.

"Whozat?" he said one evening, nodding toward the lane, toward the Jeep rocking up it between the hedges of wild rose and clematis. Domingo went indoors and whistled, and Alice logged off e-mail and came out on the porch.

"It's Bob and Terri. Hey, McCrimmons! Come up and set."

Terri came along carrying an awkward carton, sat down with it on her lap in the chair Robey set for her on the lawn. "Got something for you, Alice," Bob said. "Heard about your trouble."

Terri's carton jostled. She put it on the ground and opened the flaps, revealing a pair of collie pups. "Aaawww," said everybody. Terri tipped the box up gently and tumbled the two rotund little bodies out onto the grass. They were about the size and shape of two-pound cans of coffee, the same dense weight. Two little blue-eyed bitches, Cath and Bee.

"Our good old Candy, you know," Terri said proudly. "She got nine this time."

"Nine!"

"Yup, and every one a pip."

Domingo, sitting on the steps, felt himself smile like a clown, for the first time in days. Glen crept out from under his knees to inspect the puppies. One of them, the bigger one, screamed and peed in terror; the other waddled straight up, laughing, and slapped him in the eye. Glen didn't look like he thought much of them, tell the truth. Fat and short-legged like that, they would hardly be much help on the place. And as for companionship, he had Domingo, so . . .

Alice handed around iced coffee and slices of poppy-seed pound cake that one of the Whyte girls had brought the day before. While she was in the kitchen, Domingo found himself the object of covert scrutiny as well as direct questioning. Word must be getting around, he surmised, about himself and Alice. He had a feeling that Robey's being there with them sanctioned him. *Not that I need anybody's goddam permission,* he thought, but then deliberately unclenched his hands. He was an outsider; he supposed they had a right to wonder.

Their questions, meanwhile, probed the events of that night. Finding Domingo's language adequate, Bob McCrimmon waded in like a prosecutor, until Terri got embarrassed. "Bobby, he wouldn't know," she muttered about Jerry Graeme's financial interest in Standfast—that had been the last query.

"Wouldn't say, anyway," Robey stuck in, "would ya, buck?"

"No espik inglés," agreed Domingo.

A pen had to be set up for the puppies; they were fed, and Glen was fed again, to reduce jealousy. The McCrimmons took their leave, Bob graceless ("If you weren't so stiff-backed, Alice, people'd be nice to you more often"), Terri warm and kind as usual.

"I'll look around," Robey said, taking over the last check on the horses.

Alice and Domingo stayed on, breathing in the cool. Nine o'clock, mauve twilight, little owls trilling. Alice sat on the step behind him and draped herself over his back like a sweater.

"You saved me again, boy," she said, thinking of that night. "I don't think I said thanks."

"We save each other, this time."

Last year, last winter, when he pulled her out from under the haystack, she had told him that now they were even. She had rescued him from the snow, he had rescued her from the hay: quits. That was the way she seemed to see it, as a debt discharged, a bond dissolved. But to his way of seeing such things, it was a bond redoubled, indissoluble. They were in each other's care, in each other's charge, especially now, whatever might befall. Love or no love.

"Did anything as bad as that ever happen to you before?"

He considered. No, never; not even his nightmare second border crossing in Arizona, when he and a forty-year-old grandmother from Nayarit stowed her girls and their babies under the motel beds and held off the drunken and murderous pollero, Domingo armed with his hoof knife and the granny with the family bean-masher.

"Me neither. Not even finding my father in the dutch barn." Dead, as if sleeping, with his knees drawn up and his boot soles one above the other, in his shirt of green McLean plaid from the Pendleton mill.

Not even, thought Domingo, Fidel dead in the sale-pens at Nogales in a rich stink of cow shit, blood, and mezcal.

After a while Alice brought herself to say, "Amor, do you feel like you, you need to get away from this place, all this craziness?" meaning mad Jerry Graeme, and equally mad though cub-handed and comical Brandon Galante. "Because if you do, I won't blame you, you know. Feel awful sad, of course, but sure wouldn't blame you. 'Cause none of it is really your fight."

She would have drawn back then, to give him a little room. But he had hold of her hands and didn't let go while he thought, while he framed what he wanted to say.

"Listen, beloved," at last, *"this is the way I'm thinking. We're bound to each other, aren't we? I am to you, surely."*

"I am to you," slowly and carefully, that there be no misunderstanding, no comedy, *"to my heart's heart."*

"And so I'm bound to this place of yours. And may it always be yours."

"And you with me," fervent.

Domingo absorbed this. Then he raised and kissed her palms one after the other. He believed her, God help him. Against his better judgment and in the face of all prior experience with the whites, he believed her.

Later, in bed, Alice said, "Even considering the possibility that it's rightly yours, I mean Mexico's?"

"Insofar as it's mine, I grant it to you, in perpetuity."

Later still, "Domingo, sometime will you tell me about your people, your parents?"

"Sure. Why you asking?"

"Because I think they must have been good, to make so good a man."

He had to go out on the deck then, to sort himself out.

Philip and Janet back from their morning constitutional, he held the front door for her, and Mimi rushed between them and adhered to Philip's pant leg.

"I little imagined, as a bride," Janet said, "that I would be supplanted in your affections by a six-toed cat. Are you as worried about Nick as I am?"

"Oh yes. He's a bit better when he's working up there at Standfast, of course. But he loathes the thought of going back to the high school."

"Just hates it. And mad at me because all I can advise him to do is put his head down and slog through it. At least he still thinks you're worth being related to."

"Not so much, though, lately," Philip said, transferring Mimi from his shin to his shoulder.

"What? Why not? Meow yourself, you little twit," clicking on the coffeemaker and cleaving a Hermiston melon with a headman's stroke of her big chopper.

"Because I can't find a way to get legal status for Domingo Roque."

"Oh, Phil. Oh dear. Is there really no way?"

"No way at all, at present. Well," he held the young cat like a baby, chucked her under the chin, "there's something called a 245i exemption on the horizon. Don't mention it to Alice, there's no guarantee—"

"I told her to tell the sheriff Domingo was 'pending.'"

"And so he is," Philip said, "if you think of pending as hanging, dangling."

He could tell her about his mother all right, but not about Fidel. Every time Alice said "boy," he flinched. Though he knew what it meant, "chico," nombre cariñoso. But it sounded like "buey," ox. And that was him, Fidel's ox.

When did it start, that change? Everything he knew, almost, about his vocation, about horsemastership, stock-ranching—it all came from his father. Imparted nearly wordlessly but with cherishing care, his mind caressed, his character ornamented with knowledge and craft. But then later, despised. Never struck, when other boys' fathers beat them like dogs; that was not Fidel's way. But the weight of his father's scorn bore him down, made him sullen, ugly.

Others noticed it, his own evident capacity contrasted with his father's as-evident contempt. If there was work at Lomas Chatas that Fidel did not care for, or had too much of la cruda for, "This ox will do it for you," he would say, motioning Domingo forward without even looking his way. And Domingo would do it, whatever it was, and well. But grimly, the work sour, his skill savorless. And other men noticed. That was where the snake-mask came from, blank and cold, untouchable. At first it was hard to maintain; harder, later, to shake off. He would find himself in ambush behind it at school sometimes, as if it were part of his uniform. Once as he lay in bed, his mother in tears smoothed it away with her hands.

What had he done? He could not understand, couldn't puzzle it out. Had he not always striven to be a good son? He was all they had, after all. From childhood he dedicated himself to be all that they could wish, Fidel's vaquero, Socorro's scholar, hombre bien educado, a credit to his name. Had he not gone on studying with his mother after finishing primary school, on top of his long days on horseback? During his two years of preparatorio in Santo Tomás, had he ever failed to return to the hacienda on Friday, to put in his weekend as a working hand? His father's despised right hand. Only for the three weeks when Maria del Socorro lay dying in the hospital in town had he flouted that rule. Surely that might have been forgiven him. And in any case, Fidel changed to him long before that, even before the silky hairs of his first bigotes decorated his lip.

He had tried to let the matter heal over in his mind. Dwelling on it brewed up a dark cloud between him and his life, spoiled his pleasures, unsteadied his hands. Besides, the memory of his mother lay in his heart like a trove of rubies, a fire-coal; it was enough to go on with. Just . . . sometimes he thought of Fidel, his falcon pride and his terrible baffled love, with a rush of grief and . . . what was it? Something like pity.

There was so much to do on the place at this time of year, the three of them could work all day without seeing each other. So it was as a kind of treat that Alice laid on the cutting of firewood. The chain saw frightened her; of all the machines on the place it was, she believed, the only actively malevolent one: its stink, its baleful whine, the way it jammed and shot out deadly splinters and punished momentary lapses of deference with amputation. This was why, though the small tractor might work as well, she always hitched up the Clydes to the wood wagon; if she hurt herself with the saw, the horses would bring her home.

Working with the men lowered her anxiety level considerably. Domingo enjoyed it, though she bothered him with safety goggles and such foolishness, because it meant driving all over Standfast from one crotch of the hills to another, eating substantial picnics, and fooling around with the big horses. And Robey would ride, and would lead Chispa, who could carry their lunch and learn to manage his hobbles and his temper when they stopped to work.

In this pleasant way, even with time out to go over and prop up two of the sheds at Robey's and supervise the capping of the well at the Hashknife place, they got their wood cut and stacked, the last of the hay in, and the irrigation pipes stowed in time to bring the calves down for finishing in the first week of October. The garden that year bid fair to go on forever, the sweet corn and the tomatoes to keep right on coming till Christmas. But at last the weather began to break up, and with lowering skies came a dip in the jet stream, arctic air that stripped the leaves off the trees almost before they could color. A pity, Alice thought. But it just happened like that, some years.

Nan went back to the university; dragged herself back, her aunt would have said, wondering about her. Philip left for Anchorage and stayed there, his arbitration case drawn out and out. The others drew together, Alice and Domingo still fighting off the memory of that night in August, Robey struggling to cobble together a life on his own, Janet involved in a departmental fratz of some kind, Nick miserable at school. Janet brought Nick up to Standfast to make dinner every other night. Nick's heart was not in this, but he went along for the comfort of it.

That his problems at the high school were coming to a head was clear to everybody. He wished, often, that someone would mention this. What a relief it would be to bellow "Mind your own goddam business! Leave me the fuck alone!" throw an old-fashioned tantrum, swear, slam doors, etc, etc. No one said a word, though. On the other hand, he did not feel abandoned, rather, kind of loosely clasped. Given a little wine to drink, which went straight to his heart rather than his head, steadied him, gave him courage to entertain certain wild and scary schemes about his future.

"What," said Janet to Alice one night as they washed dishes, "about that Jerry business anyway? Are you feeling better?"

"Awful, when I think of it. I can't get him off my conscience."

"What?! Ye daftie! Why? The man was a waste of skin."

"This from a woman who cries over Bambi."

"Bambi's innocent. That creepy bastard—all our life, since we were kids, for heck's sake!"

"I know, I know. It's not logic, it's how I feel, that's all I'm saying. He never had the ghost of a chance, you know. Screwed from the start, made in the wrong image."

"Alice," hands on hips, "you've got a jelly doughnut for a heart. Listen, when he was still living here, what, three years ago? He kept sliming around, you had to lock the bathroom door. You couldn't say enough bad about him. And now you're reproaching yourself? Please!"

"I'm not thinking I could have done anything to, like, help him. It's just that now that I'm free of him, I can see what a waste his life was. I'm not brooding over this, mind you."

"I should hope not, indeed," said Janet sturdily as she hung up the dish towels. "I know lots of folks whose lives are being wasted who are honest and kind, who don't even blame anybody. They just keep on keeping on. With them in front of me, I'm not wasting a tear on Jerry Graeme, believe you me."

Alice did not shed tears herself. It was the sense of having witnessed a nauseous deformity that stayed with her. Nobody to blame, but . . . the pity of it!

⌒

They brought the calves in for two weeks of hand-feeding. A good crop, and Alice sent them to the sale with high hopes, though not without the usual sternly controlled pang of betrayal. Then they drove the cows down from the higher ground. This gave the two puppies a chance to watch Glen work, sometimes fumbling along after him on the ground, sometimes carried on somebody's saddle. Glen ignored them. Having abruptly become boss collie, he found he had a lot to learn.

When the cowboy work was mostly done, Robey moved back to his place. He seemed anxious to get home. Alice wasn't sure what to make of this; did he feel more attached to the day-to-day of farming, or did he want solitude to nurse his depression in?

"Maybe he's tired," suggested Domingo, dour as a Scot. "You work him hard, man." She didn't know whether he was kidding or not.

She didn't know, just at the moment, what was up with Domingo at all. Sometimes he was with her wholly, sometimes just as absent. For hours at a time he didn't meet her eyes, other times held her in a deep unblinking stare while she worked at the computer or read half-asleep on the sofa after dinner. Also, he forgot to do tasks on the daily list, substituted others. He dragged the horse pens twice on consecutive days, for example. One night he came into the shower with her; thrilling but disconcerting, and it didn't happen again.

Philip came home at last, mildly triumphant, with a whacking big check in his pocket: a transfusion for the college fund. Mary Friel brought Silka and Effy up for their vacation. Silka seemed just herself, calm and splendid. Effy had not done very well in competition, but neither had Mary pressed him very hard, pleasing to Alice who objected privately but strongly to competing three-year-olds of whatever breed in whatever field. In the middle of November the Keiths' racehorses came back, barefoot and tired to the bone from their season of racing. The two broodmares and Three Cheers's little Brave Wolfe came down off the rough ground and the thoroughbreds went up there. With them came Jessie Tillotson, moved into one of the upstairs bedrooms, and made her first orthodontia appointment.

Two feet of wet snow fell. This thawed, then froze. All the leaves that were left showered crisply down onto the frozen ground and then onto the snow, on the layers and layers of powder snow that followed. Alice caught a cold that sank into a bubbling cough. For three days running Domingo commanded her to stay in bed in the morning; she groused but obeyed. On the third day, he snaked back under the covers fully clothed after morning feeds, fitting the cold parts of himself to the warm parts of her. "Is raining," he whimpered.

"Free water," muttered Alice automatically, though this was the wrong season for it. Rain in the summer: free water indeed. In winter, rain damaged the mountain snowpack that subirrigated her pastures through the hot weather. Maybe it would stop, or chill to snow. Jessie Tillotson could be heard humming and whistling in the kitchen, with occasional pauses in which Alice pictured her resetting her new retainer, twanging the rubber bands. "Oh, the dear girl," sitting up and welsh-combing her curly mop as the aromas of coffee and bacon seeped under the door. Domingo leaned over the side and fossicked under the bed for his socks.

"High Idle don't, did not come down to the gate," he said.

"Uh-oh."

"He's okay last night. You want me go find him right now?"

"Let's get our breakfast inside us, and go together. I don't much care for the looks of this sky." She felt a little better, had slept better. He had been right to ground her, probably. However, three days off was all she could stand.

In the hour or so that it took them to swarm around breakfast, gear up, and saddle up, the temperature dropped ten degrees or so and a battering north wind arose. They led their horses to the pasture gate over a gritty crust of ice an inch thick. Jessie came along as they were mounting, bundled up until she looked fat.

"I'm thinking I'll look in on Mr. Whyte," interrogatively.

"Tell you what," yelled Alice, swinging up, the wind snatching her words away, "let's don't anybody go anywhere alone today. We won't be but two, three hours, depending on what we find up there. Then one of us can go with you in the truck." No use checking on Robey by phone; he always said things were fine, regardless.

There were no graded trails or even two-tracks on the rough-ground pastures, just paths that the horses themselves had trampled out along the ridge tops between the brushy gulleys. Even these crests now lay under snow and a skin of ice. The six thoroughbred geldings bunched by the gate followed the mounted horses for a few yards into the wind, but soon gave this up as resembling work and turned back to the remains of their hay. Domingo and Alice crunched steadily on up the hill.

She didn't worry unduly about High Idle. The colt had always been lucky, for one thing, and besides, he was a sagacious little soul, of all the racehorses the most likely to stand still if he got into trouble, and wait for two-legged help. Meanwhile, Domingo and his Chamaca took the wrong way around a stand of alder and slid into a deep snowy hollow on the low side of it. Alice waited for them to reappear beyond the grove and climb up onto the ridge again. This didn't happen. Pale alder trunks streaming with sere leaf blocked her view. Effortful sounds came up.

"You okay?" she hollered into the wind.

She caught sight of Domingo's parka, the orange lining of the hood, not where she expected it to be. He must be dismounted, trying to stomp a way for his horse up out of the hole she was in; Alice could hear the crunch of the crust breaking.

A few minutes later he appeared alone waist-deep in snow in the gap where they both should have come out. He swam uphill, paying out rope from the coil in his left hand. Below, the mare blew rattlingly, getting scared.

He called her, and she tried, leaping at the icy slope once, twice, the third time with the full strength of panic, but it was no good. Domingo slid down to her again, to stop her before she cast herself. Crooned into her flattened ear, hands on her neck and her chest.

Alice got down and tied Tom Fool's reins to a lashing branch; stepped off the path. At once she was in thigh-deep. She scrambled back up. Domingo climbed out where she could see him again, pale as clay with cold, shivering visibly.

"She's in a pozo," he yelled, shaping it with his hands, cup-like. "She need only two—saltos, pero after every time she—" a sliding-away motion.

Alice shouted, "If you go down in there with her, can you get back out again?"

"Yes, is only need—*I can grab the bushes and pull myself up. She has no fingers, and is heavy*." The gusts tore his breath away in white tatters, and like a strobe image through the screen of alder trunks Alice saw the red mare plunge at the wall of snow, rear and plunge, a terrified bursting whinny cut off short. This must not go on, she thought.

"We can pull her out," she shouted down. "Wait a minute," pulling off a glove with her teeth so she could free the quarter-cloth tied to the cantle of her saddle. She slipped halfway down to him, stopped with difficulty, let the blanket slide the rest of the way.

"Listen, brother, here's the plan. You have to put your loop around her, not her neck, but her whole body, understand? Todo el cuerpo, su cuerpo de ella, claro?"

"Okay."

"And see if you can wrap that blanket over the rope where it goes around her butt, so it won't cut. Then the line has to go from her chest, but not straight to me, okay? The line has to go across this gap and around that locust tree, that big tree over there, see it?"

"Okay."

"And then I'll take the rope and see if Tom Fool can pull her out. Claro?"

"Okay." His by far the hardest part, she thought, and she was already numb in brain and hand, and he was far more susceptible to cold.

"Look, do you want to change places?"

"No," starting down into the hollow where the chestnut horse reared and whinnied. Moving in dreamy slow motion; maybe already handless for the task. But the mare would hear no one else in her frenzy. Might not hear him.

As she fought her way back up to the path, Alice's heart sank under a premonition. The hag at the ford, the washer of bloody clouts came into her mind, the banshee of her race: death, white death, for someone. She knew it was only the cold and the exertion; she put no stock in second-sight, celto-romantic vision-courting, silly stuff. Just in case, though: my life between you and all harm, she thought toward Domingo.

By the time she made her way uphill along the ridge and down the slope again to the thick locust trunk, he had managed to circle the red mare with his rope and snug it up all around her. The fact that he did not for a second believe the rope would stand the strain he pushed away, having no better plan, concentrated on forcing his slow limbs onward. Paying out line, he crawled up out of the pit, saw Alice by the big tree, and plowed through deep snow toward her, the ice crust saw-ing at him; reached her, held up the coils of line like a prayer.

"Stay there," she panted, dragging him up onto the ridge with her and shoving him into the bushes on the other side. "This could get messy." Her one real fear, as she mounted and dallied down her line around the horn, was that the rope would break. What was the test-weight on it, she wondered? Hell's bells. It only needs to hold for three seconds, long enough for the mare to get a purchase with her hind feet and make a second jump. But a horse was heavier than a steer. Just hoped Tommy's cinch was tight, that was all. She turned her gelding down the trail.

It worked. As soon as the red mare felt the padded rope tighten around her hindquarters, she put her heart into a mad leap up the wall, Tom Fool skipping to keep the strain even, the singing-taut line holding her just long enough for a second wild bound up out of the pit and onto the churned-up snow of the gap. Loose powder flew up in a cloud. Alice turned back and shook slack into the rope as the mare lunged uphill toward the ridge, slipping to her knees at every step. At last she stood on the path, her plush winter coat flat with sweat, veins starting all over her chest and shoulders, panting like a locomotive and bleeding a little from one nostril, scarlet drops scattered like blossoms on the white.

They got the rope off her, the quarter-cloth over her neck. Alice made Domingo ride the gelding while she led his horse back down the trail. Lucky the beast hadn't burst a gut down in that hole. Still might suffer intestinal torsion from the strain, might colic or develop pneumonia, lathered up and smoking in this flaying wind. Respiration, heart rate still elevated, chuffing like a steam engine on a long grade. Alice talked to her, encouraged her. Very worried. Domingo kept turning in the saddle to look at them, finally got down and changed places with her.

At the gate, he caught at her jacket when she made to turn back uphill, "You don't go alone, you tell Jessie, tell me, *you* don't can . . ." he wasn't going to do much better in Spanish, stone-brained, abject with cold. Anyway, Alice yielded to sense.

"I'll get Jessie, then. You okay to deal with this horse?"

"I can walk, Aliz," wryly, "walk her and give little water, agua tibia."

"Okay, and put the cotton-mesh sheet under her blanket in case she breaks out, sweats again—"

"—clean the snow from the feet, bandage the legs," both nodding, standard remedies, "I know already." Pause. "I'm worry for her baby," peering for reassurance into Alice's face, not getting any.

High Idle, when found, had done just as expected, leaned over the pasture fence into the hayfield until he pushed a post down, caught a foot in the wire, and stood still, patiently awaiting rescue. How long had he stood there, four, five hours? Long enough to build up a hunger and a thirst. Freed, he hurtled away downhill, bugling for his buddies. Risking life and limb, dammit, thought Alice as she and Jessie Tillotson cobbled the fence back up, and she fretted about those refined and valuable legs all the way back down. But there he stood at the gate, sound and dry-coated, hobnobbing with the others, inquiring about lunch.

Domingo's horse did not colic, nor did she catch cold. She did however develop matching abcesses in her forefeet, awkward to treat in dead-cold weather. And she did, the following week, abort her sixth-month fetus.

"Aw, honey," said Alice, first down in the morning, finding the small, sad, dark-red package, shrink-wrapped in its crisping membrane. "Poor baby. Poor mare. She tried to keep it, didn't she?" petting Domingo and the red mare impartially, "She tried and tried, she really did."

He did not feel the loss as much as he expected to. Glad that no worse thing had occurred. But it was an omen, as he should have known. On Friday, when he went to the post office to mail money, there was a letter from Abuelita Fidencia. Which had never happened before.

The time had come, the old one wrote, for her to return to Mexico. She would go to her sister in Colima. So, this was to let him know, who had always acted as a true son-in-law to her, even though her crazy, crazy daughter refused to marry him. As for the man Graciela was with now: pithless, weak as a reed, as Domingo well knew. So, anyway, thanks, and farewell. They would meet in heaven. She would pray for him.

Nothing about the child.

And the fetal foal showed itself to him then, like a vision in broad daylight: expelled, abandoned. Stock-still among the heaps of plowed snow in the parking lot, wind whipped and snow blind, he knew he had to go.

"Aliz, listen," taking hold of her arms above the elbow. In the kitchen, finishing up the dishes, Jessie Tillotson still at Robey's making dinner, nothing more to do but a little data entry, which Alice was beginning to think could wait till tomorrow.

"What?" alarmed.

"I gotta leave here, tomorrow. I gotta go to my girl—"

Well, to be alarmed! Alice jerked back. "Let go. This hurts."

"No, stay here, please."

"Domingo, let go."

"I let go, you stayin' here?"

"It's you that's leaving!"

He let go, and she banged out the kitchen door before he could say a word, heedless of the arctic chill. "My girl"! The pain was real, physical. Heartbreak: the wrong word; not breaking but slow rending, like an orange pried open by horny thumbnails. Another fruit gone, she thought stupidly, first apples, now oranges. Then she got mad.

"I'm not giving you up!" she shouted, crashing back in. Domingo still standing there with his hands open, lightning struck. "By God, I am not!" And she grabbed him and held him so hard it hurt. He expected her to be cold, but no: dry-hot, fevered.

When he could, *"I'll be back so quick it'll be like I never went."*

"Every minute will be a potato peeler in my heart. Where are you going?"

"Yakima." Looking aside, "I got a girl over there."

That oblique look, and in English. Almost too ashamed to admit. But not too ashamed to go.

"Don't worry," he insisted. "Ten days, two weeks and I'm back here."

As if that made any difference. "Why—," Alice began miserably.

"There are some other people involved," dismissively, *"and some money."*

A woman, and other people, and money? He must have been, what, paying somebody off all this time? For what?

And then she got it, she got it! Somebody was blackmailing him about his immigration status. And now, with the 245i exemption on the books, he was going over there to confront them. That's it. Of course. So maybe he wasn't really leaving her, never mind "My girl." But, blackmail: this was dangerous. *"Will they hurt you over there, those sons of ducks? Shall I not convoy you?"*

"Sweetheart, what a mexicana you are! I'm unworthy to be so well loved. But don't worry. All will be well."

But "My girl"? "My girl"? "You'll miss Christmas."

"Yes," accepting her re-estimate of the time, *"but I'll be back long before the calves come."* Must be. He had but one card to play in Wapato, connive as he would. *"Truly, love,"* kissing her very tenderly, *"on my mother's eyes, I swear."*

Alice kissed back. Nothing else she could do.

"Come over here; I will tell you about my mother," he said, on inspiration. Holding her uncharacteristically pliant hand, he led her to the sofa, wrapped them up together in an afghan. *"You'll find this interesting. She was political, my mother."*

Alice relaxed a little. Maybe this was going to be all right. "She was a politician?"

"Oh no. I mean she had political opinions, ideals. By profession she was a teacher."

"This explains why you are so fond of Janet. What was her name?"

"María del Socorro Bicenta Menchú Ayala. Before she married my father. After that, she surrendered Ayala and added de Roque, to honor him."

Until then, Alice hadn't realized the importance of retaining the matronymic in so thoroughly patriarchal a system. Nor had she thought of taking one's husband's name as a mark of respect. Supposing she had taken Greer in that spirit, would Vincent have . . . ? But probably not.

"She came from Oaxaca," skating over this, not knowing what her feelings might be about his Zapotec connections. *"She was an orphan, she lived with the nuns, understand? Very good in school, so they educated her to be a teacher, the nuns. Which was a great gift. Because in México education is for the rich, and she was poor. But she became political at the teachers' college. Nationalist, activist. In favor of modernization, the rights of poor people, and against corruption in the government. And she turned against the Catholic Church. Poor nuns! Poor thanks for their charity."*

But why must you go? Why, why? Struggling to put it into perspective, to conquer her intuition that something very bad was happening. "Not unusual, though, is it?"

"To abandon religion? Not at the universities, no. But at a college run by the Church itself: my God. Did you ever hear about the uprising of uni-

versity students in the City? She took part in it, my mother; lucky for me the soldiers didn't shoot her. After that, she couldn't get employment in any church school. So the government sent her to the school at Lomas Chatas, very far from the capital, well, far from everything. Like Siberia, except hot. And there she met my father."

This was the family story about their meeting. The new teacher was painting the door of the schoolhouse her favorite color, Aztec red, her skirt hiked up and her hair braided up with a bufanda in the southern style, when the ranch foreman rode by with his vaqueros. He happened to be riding his best horse, a short-coupled golden dun with black points and big dapples. He glanced at her and she glanced at him; more would have been indecent. But he said to himself, I intend to have that woman. And she said to herself, I intend to have that horse.

Caught up in the story in spite of everything, Alice asked, "Were they happy?"

"No, sweetheart. Oh, they loved each other, always. But not happily." Sitting up out of the blanket and the hoop of her arm, he leaned on his knees and cracked his knuckles. This was difficult; how had he gotten to this place? It was territory he did not want to explore. But in some way he felt he owed it to Alice to press on. *"Maybe not loved in the same way. For example, she was twenty, I think, when they married. But even when young, she was never . . . submissive like a wife, not docile. People called her, aferrada, understand? 'Like iron.' Not complimentary, about a woman. Let me say, she was quiet, never shouted, seldom cried. She just . . . the word is 'formal.' Understand?"*

"Sí, entiendo bien," dignity, gravity, natural authority. A presence.

"And she refused to give up the school, almost until she died. And she made a lot of trouble with the patrón. She couldn't see injustice without speaking, and she never showed fear. One time she said to the patrón, 'You know and I know that what you are doing does not please God.' Imagine! Afterward I said to her, 'Mamá, do you even believe that God exists?' She told me, 'God is a stick that fits my hand.'"

Alice marveled. "No wonder you are so bullheaded, I mean, cabezón."

"*Yes,*" ducking his head, knowing it a compliment, from Alice, "*it comes from her, probably. And my father didn't want to love her so much. It was hard for him. He tried, I think he tried to kill the feeling, by drinking mezcal and doing crazy things. Going with other women. And when he knew she was going to die—*" He made the universal thumb-and-little-finger gesture of swigging from a bottle. "*And she never forgave him for that. She always loved him, but she never forgave him,*" gazing into the stove's refulgent eye. "*And that is not the Mexican way, Aliz. The woman is supposed to forgive everything. That is her strength; she has the power to make her man whole, all new.*"

"And shall I forgive you, love, for leaving me?" Not realizing she had spoken aloud.

Domingo turned around. "I hope so," prosaically, "when I come back. Time to look at the horses. When Jessie is coming back? She visits don Robey a lot, you notice?"

Alice had to drive him down to the Greyhound station in Walla Walla; there didn't seem to be any way around this. She got Jessie Tillotson to come too. That way, Alice thought, I'll behave myself. Even so, after the bus pulled away, they sat in the pickup for a long time, Alice staring over at the set-back terraces of the Corps of Engineers headquarters. It was like having a limb torn off, approximately; no anesthetic.

Jessie kept quiet. Then she said, "Well, look what the cat drug in." Alice looked over.

Brandon Galante, newly former-law-enforcement trainee, pulled up at the stop sign. Alice saw him register the Standfast brand on the door panel of the truck. Make rather a production of getting out a notebook and a pen. Oh, go away, she thought, too wretched to resent . . . Jessie slipped out of the pickup, sauntered over.

"Hi, there, Brandon."

Galante had watched her approach like he couldn't stand to believe his eyes.

"How you doin'?" Jessie said, easy, hands in back pockets. "That's good. Carrie's just fine, thanks for askin'; me too."

"Uh."

"Thing is, Brandon, you're kinda harassin' my friend there. Which is wrong. Idn it?"

"I wouldn't—" dropping the notebook into the footwell.

"Oh good. 'Cause I always kinda liked you, ya know. But if you keep on bothering my friends, I might have to give you a wedgie."

She watched him away up Second, strolled back to the truck. "Went to school with that guy," by way of explanation. "Always been a dork, can't help himself."

"You know him, Jessie? Ex-Deputy Galante? What did you say to him?"

"That he should back off," turning the rearview mirror so she could look at her teeth, see if the braces were working yet.

"Or what?"

"Or I'll give him a wedgie. Guys used to do that to him all the time. Prob'ly still kinda sensitive about it."

Alice struggled with herself, afraid to laugh in case she cried. Eventually, she said, "We better go and tell Janet. She oughtta be home by now."

At the Westons' she faced the back door, hands in pockets. A casseroled chicken began to scent the air. Jessie went into the living room to make a call on Janet's cell phone.

"That Jessie! I expect she's turned the trick. Nobody's going to take Brandon Galante seriously after this, even himself. What are you looking at?"

"Mimi; she's killed a bird."

"Ick. Is she eating it?"

"No, just viewing it. Domingo left this morning."

"Ooh, *darlin'*. What do you mean, left?"

"I brought him to town, and he got on the bus and left."

"Which bus?"

"Northbound."

"Not Concha Vélez, then. I wonder who"—swiftly—"what's up there. Did he say why he had to go?"

"No." She seldom lied to Janet, but she just didn't want to dig into this.

"You didn't press, I suppose."

Alice turned half-around. "Would you?"

"No, I hope not," Janet conceded. "Come away from there; don't court sorrow. When is he coming back?"

"Two weeks, it says here. Bit Ah hae ma doots. She might keep him, this time."

The teakettle shrieked. "She, who?"

"Whoever draws him over there, whoever he sends the money to. Chamomile, thanks."

"What a shame your cold's gone," setting the mugs down rather firmly. "You could have gone into a steep decline, made him feel really lousy when he comes back. All pale and phthisic, filmy, wafting garments."

"Hey."

"That'd put a little romance in the relationship." She opened the porch door. "Come in, but leave your victim outside, you assassin. I don't for one second believe that of the man, that he would play you false in that way. He's sound, right through, you said so yourself."

Alice sipped tea, heaved a sigh. "Yeah." Sipped again, burned her mouth, and got up to drink from the tap. "Here's my problem, peach. I just," sitting down, waiting for her voice to steady, "I've given myself away, no reserve. Like a kid."

"I know, Roan."

"And I can't see any way back, any place to retreat to." She wouldn't die, if he left her, because she wasn't daft. Nor would she take to drink, or any other kind of excess. But she would never want any other man, and she feared that for her the heat would go out of the sunshine.

"Let me tell you about *my* problems. So sure am I that yours are illusory." Janet crossed her fingers under the table.

Obscurely comforted, Alice said, "Nick, I assume."

"He threw up at school, they told me. I'll come get him, I said. Oh, he left school, they said. No idea where he was. I mean," with offering hands and a wondering shake of the head, "Fuckinunbelievable, as Nick himself would say. Luckily, Philip called. Nick vomited to make a point, apparently. Spent the rest of the morning at Phil's office, helping Sharon, lucky Sharon. Well, I'm thinking that's the end of high school for señorito Nicholas. I don't know what to do next. Can he go up to Standfast? He's very unhappy. What is that grating noise? *Is Mimi on your lap?*"

"Don't be jealous, Yannie; she's just mistaken me for a guy."

Collecting Jessie Tillotson, Alice moped on home, thinking to salve her heart with work. Poked through the detritus in the bottom of her satchel for her list, and found an antique fortune cookie, which she moodily ate, revealing the fortune: *Among the lucky, you are the chosen one.*

"I didn't know you could vomit at will," Alice said.

"A newly discovered talent," rather muffled. Nick was not quite proud of his feat.

Jessie Tillotson cooed, "Cool!" An exotic but uncommonly useful skill, in her opinion.

"But are you really sick, laddie?"

"Oh no. I eat my vittles fast enough, like the poem says," indicating his shiny plate. "It was just those sorority chicks, you know, having one of their soi-disant conversations, 'So he goes like, and I'm like, and he's all, and I'm going, As if!' on and on about who did what to whom via which goddam orifice over the weekend, and my gorge rose. And I said, to Earache actually, 'Life is too short to be spent in continuous vomiting,' and the bimbettes said, 'Yeah, right, like what would cause, like, continuous vomiting?' Expecting me to say, 'This lunch,' I suppose. Which is a slander, the one and only good thing about the place is the food. That and a couple of the teachers. But anyway, I said 'You.' And then I threw up, almost, and they all made those sounds they make, like fucking Chihuahuas barking, and ran away and reported me to Mr. Kipchak."

"Almost?"

"Kind of a long windup, you know. Like the cats do."

"Cool!" Jessie repeated, profoundly impressed.

Alice wanted to talk, to them or to someone, preferably to Domingo and Janet, about the future of Standfast. It was as if the tendrils of Robey's grapevines were tickling and coiling at the back of her mind. And the price of beef, dropping or at any rate never rising, the same effect, really, since the cost of bringing her steers to market—hay and grain, medicines, taxes, machines, and fuel—rose year by year, inexorably. For the first time it occurred to her that not having jumped her herd up to fifty head might resemble cleverness more than failure of nerve. God knew, they could never run enough stock at Standfast to qualify for farm subsidy or other federal largesse, and environmental strictures on livestock raising grew tighter and more bizarre all the time. "It's getting so you can't piss in your own crick," as Robey pungently observed. And already you could not let your animals do that; in fact, this year or next, they must fence the beasts off from Iwalu Creek, water them out of the wells and stock tanks alone.

But Nick wasn't interested, no stockman. As for Jessie Tillotson, though a summer on the racing circuit had certainly broadened her outlook, still she gazed at Nick as if a new planet had swum into her ken.

"Are you sad, Nick?" Alice asked, pushing toward Jessie the plate of iced blondies.

"Not very. It's just that I'm letting *them* down."

"I don't think so, really."

"They expect me to do great things, and all I"—clearing his throat—"I just seem to run off the rails."

"To hell with the rails, then. But anyway, J and P don't necessarily expect great things of you or Nan either. Just that you be good, and try your hardest."

Nick perked up a trifle. "What does it mean, to be good, though?"

"Not hurting anybody," said Jessie at once. "Or things."

"I'd jump on that train, I guess. Maybe add, try to help the ones that someone else is hurting, or circumstances are hurting."

"It seems like kind of a simple definition. I mean, simplistic," Nick said. "Are those the same?"

"Simplistic means simple to the point where you leave out important stuff. I think. So if so, what are we leaving out?"

"Hold the thought." Nick took their mugs into the kitchen for a refill.

"Like, what you did," Jessie said softly, "letting me stay here."

"No indeed, ma'am. That was self-interest. You are good help." Alice thought of the train tracks in Jessie's mouth. *What your sister is doing about your teeth, darlin'; that is being good.*

Nick came back. "Is being good the same as doing right, righteousness? If you say yes, I may well throw up, all the way." Alice and Jessie slid their chairs back. "Ha ha. But how about it?"

Alice pondered. Her nephew was fun to talk to these days, even if he wouldn't chew the cud of Standfast with her. "You're asking if being good means sticking to religious principles?"

"Well, ideologies. Not just religion."

"Yeah, but ideologies are just networks of principles." Jessie looked blank; were they talking about school again, or TV?

"Okay, granted. But, so, being good and doing right: same thing?"

"Not in my book. Though I reckon it doesn't make much difference till they get crosswise of each other, I mean till something you think is good to do conflicts with some principle you think is important. Too bad Domingo isn't here; he was telling me that his mother left the Catholic Church because of something like this."

"Where is he, anyway?"

"Over by Yakima, seems like." Alice scrubbed at her face, stretched and yawned, feigning unconcern.

"He coming back?" Tactful as a two-by-four.

Alice said the first thing that came to mind: "His horses are here."

"Oh," perfect certainty, "he's coming back."

Chapter Fourteen

First, he had to talk to them at the school, get them to make him copies of the records. This wasn't as difficult as he had expected; he had the birth certificate, all in order, and of course with the teacher his face was his passport. They were kind to him there; Spanish-speaking biculturals, several of them, who didn't require much explanation to understand the situation in its broad outlines perfectly well.

Then he had to hunt Graciela down. That was awkward, afoot as he was. But she wasn't expecting him, watching out for him. And so once he established where she was likely to be at certain hours, he was able to choose his occasions. It would not do to come face to face with her in a doorway. With her and whatever man she was out with. He wanted her to catch a glimpse of him now and then, that was the way. Catch a glimpse and not be sure. Just to rock her off the base of her extreme, her pathological self-absorption.

He had stopped loving her, was cured, his heart cauterized in that one instant long ago. But he hadn't stopped going to her family's house, in fact he'd gone there for dinner once a week, right through the pregnancy. Calm and cold, his father's true son. Old Mother Fidencia had counseled patience, patience. But Graciela never again said a civil word to him, though she'd said plenty of the other kind. Till the swell of her belly twisted her clothes out of shape, she'd gone out with any man who would take her, arranged to be going out as he came in. He always touched his hat to her: the mother of the child.

They hadn't understood it, the brothers. They gave up on her, blamed him. His only ally in the house was Señora Fidencia, who had stayed so to the end. Because of this, the old lady's connivance, it was Domingo who drove Graciela screeching to the hospital, he who filled in the birth certificate and paid the bills, he who named the baby. Graciela called her Yesica Yasmín. But that was not her name.

Then the family had broken up; Mauro got married to a Texas girl, Elías went to Alaska to the fish canneries. Graciela hooked up with one man or another, moved, taking her mother with her to look after the house and the child, then other children. Fidencia had let Domingo know; they kept in contact. Wherever the child was, he would go, find new work, continue to send money. He'd never failed with the money. And he always addressed the envelope to Fidencia but wrote the money order to Graciela—where had that piece of cold gabacho calculation come from?—and kept the receipt.

And Graciela, more than a decade later, had not a bean's worth more sense of decency; on that he was willing to bet. Though viewing her with perfect objectivity, as he could from the moment she'd covered him with shame in her mother's front garden, he thought her more lovely than ever. Blooming like rain-forest jasmine, extravagant, musky, and brilliant. Solis, poor fool, Domingo thought.

And that was the final step: to reach an understanding with the apple-tree trimmer, Manuel Solis.

"Death from complications of alcohol and drug abuse is the verdict. And they won't be pursuing you, Standfast. Self-defense in your case. Domingo's name doesn't seem to appear anywhere in the records at all; I'm sure we have Harley Carmichael's partiality to a fellow calf-roper to thank for that. Here you are, my little salade niçoise," setting a desert-dry martini down in front of Janet, who tossed a flurry of cocktail napkins into the air, relieved.

"Why," asked Josquin Levesque in his university-grade English, "does not Alice marry him, if you are nervous about his status immigration?" with the bold confidence of the newly naturalized. "Pourquoi pas? She likes him, does she not?"

Alice drank deep, said nothing.

"He would need to ask her," Janet said repressively, and aside to Alice, "Heard anything?" She shook her head.

"Now," Robey grunted, leaning forward to to smack Alice's trousered knee, "git them ears up, sister. You got that fella hog-tied."

"Why does not she ask him?" pursued Josquin. "Victoire invited me." Vicky spluttered wine onto her aptly Bordeaux-red sweater.

"Hell, Vera Jane asked me," Robey stuck in, to the nods of everybody who knew the old story.

"Now, tell about Nick," said Vicky, dabbing at her front. Not a disinterested request: Vicky and Josquin's babies were nearing school age.

"Oh, that *kid*!" Janet yelled. "The nerve of him, I can't believe he's ours; there must have been a mix-up at the hospital. The first thing he did, he·got Nan to drive him over to Richland High in a white-out blizzard and took the SATs. And did himself proud scorewise, by golly. Kudos to my boot camp–style reading program, I don't mind claiming. So that's high school taken care of," dusting her hands off. "That done, he goes to Philip, and he proposes that the old man take him on as a law reader, and Phil said yes."

"Like a paralegal, you mean? Don't you have to pass a state exam or something?"

"He said, apparently, 'I want you to make me a lawyer the Abraham Lincoln way.' And Philip, that wild romantic, agreed."

"Mais, qu'est-ce que c'est, Abraham Lincoln way? The old president, is that?"

"Lincoln worked in a law office for several years and studied on his own. He passed the bar without attending law school," Philip explained. "It was common in Lincoln's day, pretty unusual now. It's still a possible route to go, better than law school in some ways. A lot harder. Maybe better because harder." Alice found his tone hard to read. He might have sounded a little bit envious.

"All this unbeknownst to me," Janet went on. "And then because, he says, he doesn't want to be *just a lawyer*, sorry, Philip, he applied to Whetstone College as an extern student. History, two history classes. And then, of course, he had to let his puir auld mither in on the deal, because Whetstone is spendy."

Vicky asked, "Are you going to let him do it?"

Philip recovered first: "'Let'?" Janet went out to the kitchen to see to her fondue. "I'm hoping," he added quietly, "it will keep him occupied while we get Nan resettled. Whenever and wherever that may be."

Manuel Solis projected long-suffering patience like beer fumes, as if he had a permanent hangover. He'd had his fun, his long, slack, humorous face seemed to say, and now he had to pay for it. Domingo almost liked him. Of the three children in the Solis household, only one looked like the breadwinner. One looked like, exactly like, Domingo. The third, the three-year-old, resembled Graciela Gonzalez to a preternatural degree, putting in doubt the participation of any other parent at all. Solis was doing his casual best for them all, regardless.

He himself would not stand in Domingo's way. He was fond of Yesica, of course, but there was no denying she was a burden now, with the grandmother gone back to Mexico, her pension with her. And then here comes the child's own father, holding out a nice round sum of money as a bonus if he could induce Graciela to sign away custody and all claim to her. Smiles all around, you would think, because of course Graciela didn't give a rat's ass about any of the children. Except that the woman ran loca at the sight of the man, the father, went crazy with stored-up hate or something. She said Roque abused the child, but it couldn't be true; Yesica had never lived with him, not for one day. She said Roque abused her, but from what Solis knew of his woman, he imagined that abuse, if any, would have flowed in the other direction.

Luxuriating in the presence of Jessie Tillotson to take over the chores, Alice volunteered to drive to Pullman to bring Nan home. As prophesied by Philip, she was cutting loose from the university, needed the pickup's cargo capacity for her books and belongings. It was Alice's first time out of the Valley in a couple of years: no vacations for stock farmers. She drove up "the back way" toward Spokane, through Dayton and Dusty, turning eastward at Colfax. The Palouse country lay deep in snow, the roads dry and clear under a sky of Caribbean blue, twenty degrees Fahrenheit and dead-still air.

Dropping down into the big gulch where downtown Pullman nestled at eleven fifteen, she got lost on the university campus, asked directions twice, and pulled up finally in front of Nan's dormitory just before noon. The place looked deserted, but after a minute Nan came out of one of the stairwell doors, a duffel on each shoulder.

"Hey, Aunt Roan." She leaned into the cab and dealt her aunt a smacking kiss. "You can just sit here, if you want, and I'll load up."

"I'll come up," said Alice, needing the bathroom, and interested to see if modern-day undergraduate dorms resembled those of her own time. Little had changed. Same mess, same strident political posters and folk-dance club announcements, hard-used furniture, smell of socks and popcorn. Electronics everywhere, of course; that was new. Carrying Nan's books downstairs took five minutes; de-reticulating her music-CD collection from her roommate's required time and diplomacy. "It's like a damn divorce," Nan lamented, gazing mournfully around as, cover secured over the pickup's load-bed, they set off for Shari's for lunch.

How the kid could put it away! Steak and eggs, flapjacks, hash browns, quarts of coffee—impressive. "You're a credit to the clan, Nannie." Neither of the Weston children let stress come between them and their grub; well, it was a family trait. Alice herself had only drawn out so fine from brute overwork, never from nerves. Easy keepers, they were, every one.

"I missed breakfast," apologetically, pouring sugar into her coffee. Tilting the sugar caddy, watching the shift, flow, avalanche of crystals as she leaned it farther over. "And everything here is so good." She tilted the caddy the other way. "You know," nodding at the sugar, "I bet there's a formula that describes that, the rate of flow. Wonder if it's the same for salt."

They got on the road, Nan driving; Alice, up early, dozed, roused, and remembered her mission from Janet.

"We were talking about you, cookie, your ma and I. Home, or Standfast?"

"Well may you ask," unflurried. "Home, I guess. Yeah, that'll be best for now."

"What about later? In the—ahem—future?"

"Well," she fiddled with the radio, found a station playing what sounded to Alice like a car crash extended through time, turned the volume down. "I have about half a plan. I can work for you, can't I?" She was great with the animals, and understood engines well enough not to change the spark plugs on the diesel, a family joke that Philip never got, though oft explained. "My plan depends on whether the University of Chicago accepts me or not."

"Yikes! Now?"

"No, in the fall. They might; they just might."

"Wow, kid. Do your folks know you've applied there? To study what, anyway?"

"Math!" with a wild grin. "Combinatorics. They do, but I doubt they know the odds against." Yearningly, "Damn, I hope I get in."

"Combinatorics sounds like one of those Gaulish chieftains. You ever read Caesar? Vercingetorix, Orgetorix."

"Do you want me to explain combinatorics?"

"No, please."

"It's, like, God. What people in the past thought was God. Math is, I mean."

Alice leaned against the door and regarded her niece with alarm. "Mathematics is religion? Say it ain't so."

"No, not religion. God, the universe. Not peace and love, but—"

"Ease off the gas a little."

"Oh yeah, sorry, but stasis and change, risk versus security, what's necessary, what's impossible. See the difference? It's like, I dunno, learning the world, and all the possible worlds. Problem is, U of C's freaking expensive. The folks'll be pissed if I don't get in, but they'll be gutted if I do."

"Sounds like you've got 'em right where you want 'em, sis," chuckled her aunt. "Just remember this: we're not selling the farm for you, that's flat." But Alice felt kind of let down. Not that she had ever thought that Nan would take on Standfast. But she had assumed a . . . she didn't know what. A connection of some kind, at least. But no. Nan was outta here, clearly. Alice slouched in the shotgun seat, pulled her hat over her face. Might as well let her think she was catching a nap.

Domingo pulled open the screen door under the lighted plastic Santa Claus and knocked. Solis opened the door, and he looked past him through the house at Graciela at the kitchen table, cigarette and coffee cup, stiletto-heeled feet up on a chair, staring contempt. The two younger children faced the television amid the wreckage of Christmas.

"Here's the paper." Anxious to get the deal done, this *podador de manzanos*, lest the woman change her mind. Domingo examined the signatures, nodded, slid the paper into the manila envelope brought for the purpose. The document under his arm, he extracted bills from the inside pocket of his wallet, two thousand five hundred dollars.

"Count it!" she snarled, driving the butt into a saucer, making a clatter. Calling attention to herself.

"How did you persuade her to sign?' in an undertone. Solis made a fist. Domingo doubted it. That had been tried before, though not by him.

"Yesica!" Solis called, and the little girl came in from the bedroom. She had her jacket on, and her belongings in a pillowcase. Solemn eyes on Domingo.

"You know who this is?"

"My dad," the "a" quacking, nasal. American.

"You want to go with him?"

"Yes." In the kitchen Graciela snorted, her hands in fists on the table, and glared out the window.

"Okay," Solis said, not unkindly, "get your little buns out of here. Have a nice life."

Down the block and around the corner, her hand fast in his, sweat coursing the groove of his spine, Graciela's crazy malignity pursuing him. He stopped, leaned over the child from the back, and zipped up her grubby jacket. Socorro.

Jessie thought this was about the cutest thing ever. Alice was hand-walking Domingo's horse around in the covered arena, and Cath and Bee with lowered heads and toddling rushes were herding them. Einstein the cat in her arms, Jessie took up a station on the other side of the red mare.

"She's coming along, huh?"

"Yep," Alice said. "Full recovery, looks like."

"Good. This guy too," Einstein having cut the yearling Brave Wolfe too much slack and been stepped on. For two days the eloquent cat had gone mute. "He bawled me out just like old times today." Jessie cleared her throat. "I been thinking."

Alice, who had been and still was thinking, didn't answer. The girl glanced at her quickly around the mare's nose and said, "I been thinking about getting a job."

Nothing. Then Alice came to: Jessie too would be leaving. A bitter feeling of abandonment swept over her. Domingo, Nan, now Jessie; Nick too, eventually. Oh, hell. Would screaming and sobbing do any good? she wondered. No, and anyway she couldn't muster the strength. She stopped the horse and just stood, waiting for the damn details. Unnerved, Jessie rushed on: "I'm thinking of moving over to Robey Grade after lunch. Mr. Whyte, he asked me. 'N' I could still come up here and help out, sometimes. He suggested it."

Alice gaped. "Robey? You're going to live with Robey?" and Jessie shied like a whipped horse.

"It ain't what you think! It's like a housekeeper and general farm-hand, that's all it is! And he's gonna teach me all kinds of stuff, how to run the ranch and all. He's just lonesome, you know, and old. That's all it is!"

"Darlin', you don't have to tell me, it's between you and him. But it's an *excellent* plan, we couldn't have thought of a better."

"Rilly? You ain't mad or—?"

"Heck no, it's ideal for both, as far as I can see." It was, too, though what Vera Jane's daughters would make of the arrangement . . . but Robey would manage that, no doubt.

"Aw, great! 'Cause he's rill nice and everything. And, you know," confidingly, "I know a lot about old guys."

Before Alice could process this, much less devise a response, her phone peeped. "Standfast. Hey! Hey! Okay! Bus station, four fifteen, sí-sí-sí, 'mano, luego, besos, abrazos!" Clicked off, turned to Jessie Tillotson a face like the sun. "Hot diggity dawg! Oh, my dear sakes, Araminty! Here, walk this horse. I gotta bake a cake!"

The bus came in, and Alice was there to meet it. Four fifteen, full dark; the wind drove snow-snakes along the tarmac, but her veins ran whisky and honey. She saw only one face as the door hissed open. Only that one dear face. Not the small figure in front of him. Until he looked down, prodded the small person forward.

It was the same face.

Alice blinked. The same arched upper lip, a baby version of the long owl's-beak nose. The face of a short, chubby girl-child of ten or so. The shock of it took the starch right out of her knees; she squatted down, bringing her level with that second pair of heavy-lidded obsidian eyes. Stared wonderingly from one to the other, while the bus pulled out again in a flush of hydrocarbons.

At last she said, to the child, "We have a long way to drive home. Do you want to use the bathroom?" To Domingo, "The truck's around back."

She watched the little girl twist her hands under the hot-air dryer, not realizing she was staring, until the child turned to her and said clearly, "Are you Alice?"

"I'm Alice," by reflex, her hand to her heart.

"I'm Socorro," imitating the gesture. He's told you about me, Alice thought, but he hasn't told me about you. Walking out, Socorro held her hand trustingly and she fought down a roil of feeling as multi-colored as oil on a puddle. Domingo stood grim-faced by the pickup with Glen in his arms, said not a word. He stowed the collie behind the seats, helped Socorro in, and got in himself while Alice buckled up, all in electric silence. The child fell asleep at once, across his lap, the tension too much for her, Glen too. Still nothing said.

At home Alice held the storm door so that Domingo could carry his duffel and propel his daughter inside. Then she went down to feed her stock before they kicked the fences down. Thinking, Honey-baby, as she filled the chestnut mare's manger, Daddy's home, and hell's to pay.

After a while Domingo came to the hay-shed door. "Aliz."

She clattered the twine cutters into the barrow very hard, sparkling with wrath. Explain yourself! she thought furiously. And this better be good!

"She is my daughter."

"That's obvious!" So angry! She didn't understand herself. And too, a queer undercurrent of relief. For he might have brought home the child's mother, any number of other relations and connections for her to cope with. Because she already saw that coming: having to cope with Socorro.

"Why didn't you tell me?"

Swaying with exhaustion as he was, a cold pride upheld him. *"I tell you now. Socorro is my treasure, the best of me. Take us both, my soul, or neither."*

Alice felt again that rending sensation: first her heart, now her brain pried slowly open. And she thought she remembered half-apologizing for her barrenness, her inability to conceive—why? Were they talking of children?—even, on one occasion expressing thankfulness at not to have to deal with infant-rearing in addition to farming. If she had ever once managed to hold her chattering tongue, he might have found space to say, "I have a child, she is the seed and kernel of my life. If I am not her father, I am nothing." And then she would have known, and known him.

But *still*!

"Why didn't you tell me?"

"Because you, *don't you remember?*" This was tattooed on his heart: "*You told me it was impossible,* impossible. *And so I tried to think I could—but I have to have her with me now, I must. She has my name; I have to raise her to honor it. And, Aliz—I love her so much, you see.*"

He could barely stand upright, and Alice saw it. She went over there, and he put his arms around her inside her thermal coveralls; she hot with work and grievance, he shivering, sagging against her. She relented, murmured, "Amor, corazón! You're gey shuggly. Go on up, now, go inside. She'll be scared up there alone. Of course she's welcome; how could she not be?"

Welcome, he had assumed. Beyond that—probably he should wait, let them become acquainted. But in his extremity he rushed in where angels feared to tread, en un dos por tres: "*Love, listen to me. She needs a mother. From my knees I ask, I beg you: be a mother to her.*"

It took her a minute to translate this, the sense, and also the tone, plangent with hope. Her mind drew away, took refuge: why do our most serious communications keep on happening among hay and horse manure?

Came back to the point: it wasn't a proposal of marriage, nor an invitation to play godmother he was offering her. A connection both profounder and more quotidian; a contract on which she could never renege. To love his child and raise her, to suffer for her and with her. Every ounce of Alice, that's what he was asking. All of her, all she had to give, for life.

He was asleep on their bed when she came in. Outdoor clothes still on, boots on the bedspread, curled around the little girl. The child, though, was wide awake, sitting up. Alice got a blanket out of the closet and spread it over Domingo, tucking in, laid a hand to his bristly cheek.

"Come on, sister," helped her step over him, onto the floor, and led her into the kitchen, served up the stew. The table already set for two.

The youngster ate with good appetite. You'll fit right in here, Alice thought, buttering her another biscuit. "Where did you come from, Socorro? Where were you living, I mean, up till today? Over in Yakima?"

Pausing her spoon-hand just long enough: "Wapato." Her hair needed washing, so did her too-small pink jacket, in fact, the whole child—she'd taken off her shoes before getting under the covers, at least.

Probably not fair to quiz her without Domingo there, but since she was going to stay at Standfast, there were a few things Alice needed to know.

"Did you live with your mother?"

"Uh-huh," examining a section of green bean in the bowl of the spoon, deciding in favor, chewing with an inward expression.

"Just you and your ma?"

Socorro laid down spoon and biscuit and named them off on her fingers: "Graciela and Rafi and Raulillo and me, and Manuel Solis, and Abuela Chencha, and five little Yorkie-dogs. But Abuelita went back south a little while ago." Looked up as if to say, Is that enough?

Alice said, perplexed, "But what about your mom?"

"Graciela," she said. "And Rafi and Raulillo my brothers. But my dad is not their dad. And Manuel Solis is her, her novio. Esposo, I think, maybe."

"I see," Alice leaned her cheek on her fist. "Are you going to miss them if you stay here?"

She shook her head, mouth full. No hesitation. Swallowed, amplified, "I knew Papí would come for me."

Shaken, Alice went in to have a look at Domingo. She needed to think, and to touch him. What have you landed me with? "Domingo."

"Mm?"

"Eat or sleep?"

"Hm."

The coconut cake went down well. Just a sheet cake; Janet would have made layers, duded it up, but what the heck. Socorro downed two squares and a glass of milk, panting a bit at the end.

"Do you like horses?"

"Well," sitting back to give this some thought, "I don't know any. But I think I would. I like Chispa and Chamaca already. Papí said you got muchos."

"He told you I got muchos horses?"

"Uh-huh."

Alice stifled an incredulous giggle. The craft of the man! For most girls of ten or eleven, all you'd have to say about a person to make them think she was the cat's ass was that she got muchos horses.

They carried the dishes to the sink and washed them, and cleaned up the kitchen. Socorro had to pee again, and Alice showed her where the bathroom was. She led her up to the loft and set her to stowing the stuff in her pillowcase in a bureau drawer while she made up the bed in the room nearest the stairs.

"Now," she said, turning down the covers, "here's a little test. I'm going to stay here and wait, and see if you can go downstairs and find the room your dad is sleeping in, and find your way back up here by yourself. Think you can? Okay, go for it."

Socorro scampered off, peered over the loft railing, and trod carefully down the steep stairs. Taking the quest seriously. Alice, waiting, took up from the dresser the toy horse from Japan, given her for a birthday, that she'd intended to hand on to Lyon when he was old enough not to teethe on it. Exquisite little thing, with a black velvet coat, and a creamy mane and tail of real horsehair; she sat in the rocker and stroked it thoughtfully.

She woke in the dark and Domingo was gone. Alice felt the place beside her in the bed: still warm. Five fifteen, he'd let her sleep in.

She dressed, and ran her fingers through her hair, restored some sort of order. There he sat at the dinette table, forking up a slab of coconut cake. "She still sleepin'," pointing the tines toward the stairs. When Alice sat down, he got up and moved his chair around so that he could put his left arm around her while working on the cake with his right.

"Riquísimo," offering a forkful. She blinked at him, half-awake. Felt rode hard and put up wet. Like two days' work on no nights' sleep. Like hell under deferred maintenance. By kissing, Domingo induced her to open her mouth. Presented the fork again.

"Mm," she said, sitting up and taking over. He pushed the plate toward her.

"You make this pastel de coco for me?"

"Mm-hm."

"Why, Aliz?"

"'Cause I love ya, that's why. D'you want the rest?"

He wanted her to look at him, but she took the plate to the sink. He had in mind to point out the appropriateness of pastel de coco for a person named Socorro who was nicknamed Coco. But he went out to do the feeds instead.

Alice cracked eggs and sliced tomatillos. When she'd told him she wouldn't share him—he'd thought she meant, with anybody, probably. Not with anyone, even a child. She examined her feelings about this. Was it true? Could she not stand to share him even with Socorro?

Turning from the coffeemaker, she found the little girl standing by the table, scared. "Where's Papí?"

"Gone to feed the horses," Alice said, shocked all over again by her presence, and by how much she looked like her father.

"Can I go?" She'd put back on all the layers she'd taken off last night, including the pink jacket. Except for her sneakers.

"He'll be back in five minutes. Then we'll have breakfast, and then we'll all go feed the cows. Look, sugar," the kid not much reassured, "look out this window, you can see him. See? Down there by the pens."

Socorro clamped onto the window frame, nose to the cold glass.

Alice went back and got things frying. As she raised the skillet to shake it, the child darted past her, yanked open the carport door, and ran out into the snow in her socks. "Socorro, wait!"

But Domingo was right there, grabbing her in a spin-around hug. They came in, he backpacking her, wide identical grins.

"You two look like an echo," Alice said, grinning too.

"Yah, she looks like me a lot. Pobrecita."

Her question about sharing him was pointless, Alice realized. He and the kid were a matched set. Would she share him? Of course she would. She had to.

She took Socorro with her when they went to catch up the Clydesdales because she was after Maggie, who was sensible, and Domingo was after Mose, who wasn't. There was something awkward about the way the child traveled, Alice thought; a mincing gait, on the sides of her feet. Frozen, no doubt, those sneakers totally inadequate, probably too small. A trip to town for boots indicated, this afternoon if possible. Meanwhile, she boosted her up onto the big mare and gave her a hank of coarse mane to hang onto. Socorro gave a squeak at the first step, but then sat up and moved with the walk. A natural, Alice thought.

Domingo and Mose met them at the gate.

"How you doin', mija?"

"Okay, Papí!" A cold little crow.

"We gotta get her something warmer to wear," Alice said. "Listen, you know Vera Jane's old Solomon horse? He's about twenty-six, now. Let's see if we can borrow him, let him teach this kid to ride." Just naturally and unconsciously holding Socorro's ill-shod small foot against the Clyde's woolly side, that the child not fall off, that no harm come to her. Domingo got a cramp under his jaw. He pressed her up against Maggie's wall-like flank.

"If I wasn't crazy about you already," he said, *"I'd fall for you all over again. But tell me, sweetheart, tell me now why you were mad at me last night."*

"I wasn't really mad—"

"Yes, mad," he insisted. "I can notice. Tell me why."

Alice had to wait awhile, looking away up toward the swayback ridge, to get her voice under control. "Because all last week," she said at last, ashamed, "I was thinking you might be gone for good."

A bark, incredulous: "What? What?! You don't understand this too much already?" His fist in its ragged glove under her chin, making her meet his eye, their mingled breath white as smoke. Forcing his English to the sticking point: "Where do I go if not toward you?"

Janet was reconciled to Socorro.

Earlier, her attitude surprised Alice. "Do you have any idea what you're getting into here? Not that there's much you can do about it, looks like."

" 'Course not, who'd ever be a parent if they knew what they were getting into? Though it's not like I think it's all cupcakes and Christmas pageants, you know. But look, she's ten, so there's croup, and toilet training, and pre-school that I haven't even had to deal with."

Janet made a doubting sound, held up a pair of turquoise Osh-Kosh B'Gosh overalls; they were in Walla Walla, shopping upstairs at the Bon Marché. "Croup and diapers and pre-school are what get you up to speed for the hardball game, toots. S'pose she'd like these?"

"Color's right, for sure."

"Has she been abused, for instance? The long-term effects of that—"

"Domingo says not. He says they didn't hurt her; they just didn't give a rip about her, even the grandmother, apparently."

"So why didn't he just take her, long ago?"

"Well, of course, he had no home for her when she was small. He just had to follow them around, her mother and her grandmother, wherever they went, paying support money, maintaining his claim to her, to Socorro. He got to see her about twice a month, always on the sly with the grandmother's help. The mother wouldn't give her up, or him either. He says she hates him, but she . . . I don't know. It was the money, I suppose."

"Alice, this is very weird and worrisome," in a shaking voice. "What's to prevent this woman from giving him up to the Immigration Service?"

"She'd be ratting herself out, is why. She sold him Socorro, see. Selling a child is a crime, I'm pretty sure. He has a bill of sale with her signature on it; I've seen the paper."

"But," poking among the hangers for something to match, "is selling a child any more a crime than buying one? Domingo could wind up in jail."

"Or deported. Either way, the mother winds up in the hoosegow too. Anyway, the point is, Domingo refuses to be separated from Socorro anymore, end of story."

"And PS, you refuse to be separated from him."

"Right. And PPS, she's a very nice kid, as you know, and furthermore, she's nuts about horses and cows and she practices with the rope all the time in her room, there's a scuff mark all the way around the walls at loop height. She wants to know everything Domingo and I know between us about the vaquero business; now, can you say that about either Nan or Nick?"

Janet straightened up, her hands full of preteen apparel. "Well, no, I can't." Catching on, "Alice, what are you suggesting?"

"Well, I just wonder," she hadn't really framed this up for herself till now, but it seemed . . . "Maybe she's the next generation. It's a long way off yet, and she may change her mind, wind up taking up cosmetology or some damn thing, you never know. But right now . . ."

Alice watched her test the idea. A slow smile, mirroring her own.

"Reconquista," she murmured. Then, bustling, "Okay. Well, okay then. These turquoise ones, and the lavender ones. Give me a hug. I'll be her Tía Juanita. Shall I ask Domingo to be my brother-in-law?"

"No!" fiercely. "Janet Andison Weston: do you hear me? No. Just back right out of there. Do not go there."

"What an old-fashioned girl you are."

"Whatever. I'm warning you." Miming a terrific twisting pinch.

⌣

On March twenty-first, they saw the ground for the first time since Thanksgiving. All calved out, the hardest kind of calving, relentless cold, bludgeoning wind, snow and more snow. An exceptionally good result, however: cows, multipara, 35; live calves, 33 (15 bulls, 18 heifers); barren, 2; stillborn, 0; mortality, 0. Cows, primipara, 9; live calves, 9 (3 bulls, 6 heifers); barren, 0; stillborn, 0; mortality, 0. The second day of almost-fine weather, they turned the whole bunch out of the covered arena onto the Triangle field. Mooings and cavortings! As if it were really spring, instead of a tricksy interval between ice storms.

With great reluctance, Socorro had allowed herself to be enrolled in fifth grade. The school in Iwalu village was small and friendly, though; not too bad. She spent every free minute at Standfast on horseback. When she went to town with Domingo, she imitated his swaggering walk; stuck her hands in her back pockets like Alice did.

Alice gave her the Japanese horse. Socorro wanted no other toys.

Spring was long in coming, all the cultivation tasks set back a couple of weeks. They had fed hay on into April, a lot more than budgeted for. But now at last, here on the Dogleg, real forage. They rode around the herd to make sure the cow-calf pairs had found each other, that they'd settled to grazing. Domingo trotted ahead on his red mare. She was in season again, and temperish, warning the geldings away with backed ears and lashing tail, so Alice took Solomon's lead line, kept Socorro beside her.

The Dogleg was close enough to go home for lunch, but on a day like this Alice opted for a picnic. Plus, the opportunity to teach Socorro how to use hobbles.

They drew rein under the cottonwoods by the creek, dismounted, and stripped their tack off. Domingo held the mare's head while Alice helped Socorro buckle the hobbles on. "This way, she can go eat grass, but she can't go far, she won't run off home."

"What about Solomon and Tommy?"

"They'll stay with her," Alice said, wondering, Do I need to explain why? But Domingo said, *"It's the way of the world, daughter."*

Socorro wore Alice's old hat pulled down over her ears, a pheasant feather stuck in the band: the compleat wrangler. She looks like Domingo must have at this age, Alice thought, cupping that soft little chin. Such a surge of love came over her, she nearly toppled over.

"I'm gonna look for fish, okay?" Socorro said.

"Okay. Don't get in over your boots. Keep Bee and Cath out of the wa— never mind, too late."

Domingo found them a place on the bank, a dry bed of leaf-duff for sitting and a stump of columnar basalt to lean against. Alice brought the mochilas containing lunch.

"What says next the list, amor?" Hopefully, "Dairy Queen?"

"Fences, you optimist," said Alice firmly. Then, lightening up, "Though, I dunno, we can't do much but look at them till the ground dries, can we? And we need some stuff from the store. Not tortillas, though."

The night before, Alice finding her packaged torts gone blue and fuzzy, Socorro had stirred up some masa.

"You don't got a comal?"

"Got a griddle; that do you?" After a few minutes, "Domingo, come here, look at this."

Socorro flicked them a glance: what was so special about this, anyway? Done it all her life, Dios mío. And pat-pat-pat-pat-pat the pale circle bloomed out between her capable small hands. Domingo blinked rapidly. With emotion, "My daughter can tortillar!"

Now, he and Alice sat back shoulder to shoulder, the saved heat in the basalt working deliciously into their backs. Watched Socorro wading and poking, the young collies ploshing around, lapping creek water. Domingo took Alice's hand.

"She is happy," he said.

"Yup, seems to be." The sun-dazzle on the water made her drowsy.

"Aliz, do you know why I love you so much? I'm serious. Do you know? It's because you gave me a home."

That smile. It made him think of warm dulce de leche.

"You gave me a home to bring her to. Before I came here to Standfast, I could not imagine such kindness."

"Well, here's the way I look at it, boy. You brought me the dearest thing you had. Ain't that right?"

Domingo pulled off his Stetson so he could kiss her. Then he put it on again. Watching from across the creek, Socorro could hardly tell them apart.

READERS CLUB GUIDE

All Roads Lead Me Back to You

KENNEDY FOSTER

INTRODUCTION

Alice Andison never expected romance. She's a rancher who single-handedly runs the family outfit, Standfast, in the foothills of the Blue Mountains of Washington State. Horses and dogs are all the company she wants. Alice would do just about anything to protect Standfast from part-owner Jerry Graeme, who is threatening to sell the ranch to pay off his gambling debts.

Domingo Roque wasn't looking for love either. A Mexican ranch hand working illegally in the States, Domingo is on the run from the immigration police, fleeing with just his horse and the clothes on his back. A bad fall leaves Domingo half-frozen in the snow near Standfast, where Alice finds him. At first Domingo mistakes his rescuer for a man, and then he's even more puzzled to find himself working for a woman. Alice appreciates his help on the ranch, but she's breaking the law, risking Standfast for Domingo's expertise and companionship. To the amazement of both, through seasons of grueling workdays their tentative friendship slowly blossoms into love.

But Standfast is no refuge for the new couple. Jerry Graeme continues to menace its very existence. And though Domingo may have found a home, there's one last secret he hasn't told Alice—he has a daughter.

DISCUSSION QUESTIONS

1. What were your first impressions of Domingo Roque and Alice Andison? What do Domingo and Alice think of each other when they first meet? Are first impressions to be trusted in this novel? Why or why not?

2. Both Domingo and Alice share the stories of how their parents met. (104, 306) Although they take place worlds apart, what do the Andison and Roque family stories have in common? What do these histories reveal about Alice and Domingo's personalities?

3. What stereotypes does Domingo have about Americans and American families? What does Alice assume about Mexicans and Mexican families? How do they come to disprove these stereotypes?

4. How do you feel about Domingo's status as an illegal immigrant, and of Alice helping him to avoid the INS? Did you identify with him and his plight? Did this book change any of your prior perceptions of immigrants and immigration law?

5. Janet Weston says about illegal immigration status, "It's like

pregnant, darlin', either you is or you ain't." (38) What are Janet's views on immigration law? How do her opinions shift over the course of the novel?

6. A friend at the Westons' Fourth of July party asks Alice about Domingo, "'Is he a lover, a brother, a buddy?' Their ninth-grade formula for the perfect boyfriend." (264) Does Domingo fit the criteria for the perfect boyfriend? Is the formula relevant to Alice and Domingo's romance? Why or why not?

7. *All Roads Lead Me Back to You* has two antagonists: Jerry Graeme and Brandon Galante. Who do you find more sinister? Who brings the most trouble to Standfast?

8. Domingo defines "ranch romance" as "love for all seasons, getting on with whatever needed doing." (230) How is this ranch romance different from Alice and Domingo's previous romantic attachments? Why do you think this is?

9. Domingo says to Alice about Standfast, *"And so I'm bound to this place of yours. And may it always be yours."* (292) Why doesn't Domingo call Standfast "ours"? How does Alice's position as Domingo's boss impact their relationship? Can an equal romantic partnership exist on a ranch where Alice is owner and boss? Why or why not? By the end of the novel, whom does Standfast really belong to?

10. What challenges might lie ahead for Alice and Domingo? Imagine a sequel to *All Roads Lead Me Back to You*. What would happen in it?

ENHANCE YOUR BOOK CLUB

1. For your book club meeting, whip up a batch of quesadillas, the first meal that Domingo cooks for Alice. Use your favorite recipe, or try this one from *Gourmet*: http://www.epicurious. com/recipes/food/views/Chicken-Quesadillas-108378.

2. If there are stables in your area, take your book club for a horseback ride! Share the photos at your next book club meeting.

3. Teach your book club how to tie a lariat, or "lasso." Practice on some lengths of clothesline rope. You can find step-by-step instructions here: http://www.ehow.com/how_2105211_tie-lasso.html.

4. Research and discuss immigration law and its reform and enforcement.

A CHAT WITH THE AUTHOR

1. Have you ever lived or worked on a ranch? What were some of the challenges of conveying the rhythms and lingo of ranch work to your readers?

   I've never done ranch work, but it's all around us here. Our community college has a good agriculture department and a hot rodeo team, cowboys and cowgirls all over the place. Till a couple of years ago, the roping steers used to be trailed through town at Fair time. We townies may not have irons in the fire, but we know what's going on.

   That's a good question, about approximating the local working speech. Wranglers and farriers and such folks are not chatty. Also, a fair number of them are well-traveled and/or well-read, and some are bilingual. So expression is pretty diverse; it's not like a dialect you can learn. And you can't pack a notebook and a Bic around with you; people would wonder. You just have to keep your ears open. The hard part for me is distinguishing terms that readers will know or can guess at from words that will leave them stumped. For example, what do you guess this means: "He's pretty skookum with the julián"?

2. *All Roads Lead Me Back to You* provides information on a number of fascinating topics, including ranch work, immi-

gration law, property law, and Mexican and Scottish culture. How did you go about researching these topics for your novel?

To tell the truth, I haven't done much formal research, if you mean the library and the Internet. I'm my department's informal immigration advisor, so that stuff is ready to hand. And when we've lived in Scotland, I've usually found some kind of volunteer work to do to get into the community. (Scots are mostly welcoming and communicative; it's only the English who think they're dour.) As far as Mexico is concerned, two of my colleagues are true biculturals, absolutely fluent in both directions, and thoughtful about their situation. They've taken a lot of trouble to sort me out about certain things, and my Mexican students do their best for me when they aren't falling down laughing. And of course, as Philip Weston is wont to observe, property law is a mystery to everybody.

3. The dialogue between Alice and Domingo is truly unique, a blend of her comical Spanish and his tentative English. Which moment of miscommunication do you find especially funny or poignant?

The really awkward one was where he asked her whether she wanted another child. Wow. That could have gone real bad. But I still think it's funny when she yells, "Sonofaduck!"

4. The love story between Alice and Domingo progresses slowly but blooms quickly. How did you handle the pacing of their romance?

The first couple drafts of it were more gradual, but felt all wrong for the characters. They are adults after all, and pretty self-disciplined, self-controlled. And not looking for it. So I tried it out as more abrupt. That was better. But I thought, "Well, there must have been some *clues, for Pete's sake."* So I went back and tried to see where there might be signs that the reader would see, but those two wouldn't.

5. Immigration policy is a huge topic in the book. Was it difficult to portray the different sides of immigration law impartially? Which character's opinions come closest to your own views on immigration?

There's really only one aspect of the problem addressed in this story: the unfairness of the current laws to people who come here needing and wanting to work. To develop other sides of the question, such as the prospect of creating a virtual slave-class who can't appeal to our laws for redress of crimes against them, or the patent fact that illegals who work for less than minimum wage undermine the advances in pay and working conditions made by organized labor, would have made the novel a polemic. I suppose Janet Weston comes closest to my view.

6. Friends, neighbors, and work associates form a diverse extended family around Standfast. Which of these smaller characters is your personal favorite?

I'm pretty fond of Nick Weston. He's an irritating little toot, but kind of sweet.

7. Gender roles play a big part in the novel. Do you think that living on a ranch makes men's and women's roles more or less flexible? Why?

More. Because the work has to get done by somebody, that's all. If cows don't get fed in winter, they die, so they don't care who is cutting the baling twine.

8. Alice's nickname, Roan, refers to a roan mule, and Domingo's father used to call him an ox. How did you choose these two animals to describe your main characters?

The name Roan actually refers to Alice's freckles, but the mule business came from William Faulkner's oft-quoted line about a mule being willing to work for a man ten years for the privilege of kicking him once. She's such a model of unglamorous endurance—and such an easy keeper!—that she seems to have earned her kicking privileges. Also, she's childless, barren like a mule. About Domingo, "ox" is ironic: he's thoroughly masculine, also quick, clever, and good to look at.

9. Jerry Graeme is an unusual antagonist; Alice describes him as "her only enemy," (31) but she has mixed feelings after his death. Who inspired this sinister character? Do you have any sympathy for him, or did you cast him as a purely evil character?

I sweated over that guy. He's nastier than I meant him to be; I think that's why I got him out of the way so quickly after the attack. He was making me sick. The worst of it is, I know how scared and sad, how absolutely wretched such a person would feel practically all the time. People don't botch themselves; they get botched, and then they have to live like that. That's what Alice sees, once the threat is gone.

10. *All Roads Lead Me Back to You* is your first novel. What can readers look forward to in your next work?

Some of the same characters. I'm getting interested in JoNelle Jussum. And of course there's a lot more to be said about Socorro Roque. And my dad wants me to write something about the Army. Now, how's that going to work?